SHIELD AND FALTERED STEPS

THE ENERGY OF MAGIC
BOOK TWO

J.E. NEAL

For my children — Never doubt your own magic

CONTENTS

CHAPTER 1
ON THE ROAD
RAINER LAWSON

"She'll be fine," Logan assured Rainer as they fell back into the Mustang. They'd just dropped Emily off at the farmhouse on their way to the Pentagon for work.

Rainer rolled his eyes. He was growing weary of everyone's insistence that he was overreacting about Emily's safety when, just the day before, she'd almost been abducted by one of Wretchkinsides's top dogs.

"She has the ring of invincibility, remember?" Logan laughed.

Rainer forced a chuckle. He knew Logan, his best friend and Emily's older brother, was trying to get him to loosen up.

It was a humid July morning in McLean, Virginia. The fumes from Rainer's '65 Mustang convertible filled the muggy air around them as he revved the enhanced engine.

"So, you had no idea? About the ring, I mean?" Logan asked.

"No. All that stuff Vindico told us yesterday about the legend, or whatever, I'd never heard any of that. If I'd known my mother's ring was infused with enough promethium to let Em throw shields like that, I would've proposed in middle school. I can't believe my dad never told me." That was the thing that hurt Rainer the most.

Logan studied him for a minute. "I bet he either never knew or didn't believe it after your mom was killed."

Rainer had been in love with Emily for as long as he could remember. He let his mind reel backwards as he drove off of the Haydenshires' vast farm and took in the onslaught of pine trees and dogwoods along the route.

He remembered sitting in her bedroom with her when he was six years old, because she'd been afraid of a storm that had driven Emily, Rainer, and all seven of her big brothers in from playing in the back fields.

"You're my boyfriend," she'd informed him in her forthright redheaded sass that still drove him wild. She'd informed him of the same thing when he was four, but that day during the storm always stuck out in his mind.

"I am?" He was thrilled but didn't understand how that had come to pass. "How do you know?"

"Because I said so," she huffed as if Rainer was clearly not thinking straight.

"Okay..."

He smiled as he came back to the present. He would never love anything more than Emily. *I have to keep her safe.* The thought seared through his mind and tensed in his energy shield for what felt like the hundredth time just that morning.

"I'm still kinda hungry," Logan hinted.

Rainer hadn't consciously been aware of his own hunger until Logan had spoken up. He exited the interstate several miles before the Pentagon and pulled through a drive-thru.

"Do you care?" he asked the customary question that he and Logan shared whenever they went for takeout together ever since they'd both obtained their licenses.

"Nope."

Rainer pulled to the outdoor microphone. "Yeah, let me have four sausage burritos, four egg, cheese, and bacon biscuits, a pallet load of hash browns, and two large Dr Peppers."

A garbled voice told him to pull forward.

They were trying to ward off what the day was certain to hold. On top of everything that had happened to Emily the evening before, he and Logan had spent their first full day as Elite Iodex Officers training with their new boss, Dan Vindico.

After their first official round of training that morning, Rainer and Logan were being taken to Felsink Prison to learn how to drop off and retrieve prisoners who they would soon be responsible for taking in, subduing, and detaining.

Felsink was a Gifted prison in Culpeper. It was a solid hour away from the Pentagon, near the Non-Gifted limestone and granite quarries. It sat approximately three miles underground, the distance below the earth's surface where the Gifted people were unable to summon enough energy to escape.

Going to the prison was excruciatingly painful and could effectively leave a Gifted person drained for several hours to several days depending on the length of stay and the strength of their Predilect.

Rainer and Logan were strong Ioses Predilects and both were from powerful families. Their ability to summon the energies of the earth and harness them to their will reflected their hard work and their parentage, but Felsink could cripple the strongest of Predilects.

Logan offered him a ten for his half of their breakfast, but Rainer shook his head as he paid the uniformed employee at the window.

Rainer certainly didn't need the money. He'd just inherited his parents' vast estate.

The woman at the window didn't look any too thrilled to be at work that morning. She flung the large sack of food and dumped his change into his hand.

"Thanks." He drove away after he stowed the bag of food between them. As was their policy, they both reached in the bag, grabbed food, and began eating without any real concern as to who'd ordered what.

Food was one way to restore their Gifted energies that the prison would drain. Rainer wasn't certain if eating prior to visiting would help, but on the off chance that it might, he was willing to give it a try.

"Dad says the first trip to Felsink is the worst." Logan tore into another biscuit.

"Yeah, I know."

Logan and Emily's father was one of the five Realm governors who served the Gifted Realm of the United States under the Crown Governor. Governor Haydenshire was in charge of the governing boards of the individual states and had to occasionally visit the prisons if something was wrong or design changes were being made.

He typically only visited Felsink and Coriolis, the two Gifted reformatories in Virginia that serviced the DC area and let the state governors and the Senteon representatives check on the prisons in their own home states.

"Gonna suck, though."

"Mom's already cooking chili so that'll help."

Rainer grinned. He would never be able to thank the Haydenshires for all of their love and care over his relatively short lifetime.

Rainer's father had been assassinated when he was barely fourteen years old. His mother had been murdered nine years before.

The Haydenshires had gone to the governing board and demanded custody of Rainer after he'd spent several agonizing weeks with his asshole of an uncle. They'd added him to their brood of eight children —which later grew to ten--and raised him just like all the rest. There was more love and kindness on Haydenshire Farm than anywhere else on earth.

"You and Em gonna stay in New York for the whole weekend?" Logan seemed to decide that changing the subject was preferable to trying to discuss the prison system of the Gifted Realm.

"Just Saturday night. We'll be back for dinner Sunday."

It had been a long-standing tradition in the Haydenshire household, as their children had grown and moved out, that everyone came back to the farm for dinner Sunday evenings. It was rare that everyone was there all at once, but most of the kids made an effort to be there when they could.

Logan took long sips of his Dr Pepper and stared distractedly at the DC gridlock surrounding them.

"Why does he have to be so freaking helpful? He's making me crazy." Logan finally blurted out the thing that Rainer had known was brewing deep in his psyche. When you'd been best friends with a guy since birth, you knew when to ask questions and when to let things simmer a little longer. "'Come in early, *Adeline*. Let me give you a ride, *Adeline*. You're so talented, *Adeline*,'" Logan mocked.

Rainer tried not to chuckle. "Brad?" He didn't really have to guess.

"Yes!"

Adeline was a Valeduto Predilect and was training to be an obstetrics medio at Georgetown Hospital. Brad was the attending medio who was training her to be able to see patients on her own.

"First of all, Adeline is crazy about you. Second, it is his job to train her, and his training of her reflects on his own practice, so maybe he's not interested in Adeline. Maybe he's just doing his job. She's certainly not gonna go after some other guy just because he offered to take her to work."

Logan rolled his eyes in disdain. "Right. Let's think about it this way—the guy gets paid to stick his hands up women and feel all over them all day long, so I don't really see how that doesn't just automatically make him a perv."

Rainer cracked up as he shook his head. The scowl remained etched on Logan's face as Rainer pulled the Mustang into the Iodex parking garage. They flashed their badges to gain access to the Iodex wing of the Gifted Senate.

CHAPTER 2

SET THE TRAP

"What the hell's wrong with you?" Garrett quizzed as soon as Logan and Rainer joined him at their grouping of desks.

Garrett was one of Logan's older brothers and the only other Haydenshire who served as an Iodex officer. He'd joined the force right out of the academy, just like Logan and Rainer. He'd worked in almost every capacity of law enforcement and had just been reassigned to the Elite forces to help train and keep an eye on Logan and Rainer.

Garrett was an outstanding officer. He'd received numerous commendations for his service, including being named Officer of the Year twice for risking his life to save others.

He'd left his position as a liaison between the Gifted and Non-Gifted Realms at the Non-Gifted DC main police precinct where he'd worked for the last few years. He'd begun his career in Elite and had worked there until after his brother, Cal, had been killed. He'd taken a month off and then decided to step down to the liaison position. Only Elite Iodex Chief Officer, Dan Vindico, outranked him, but Garrett liked to play just as hard as he liked to work.

Vindico never played. As far as Rainer could tell, the only thing that Dan Vindico ever did was work. When he wasn't working on a case, he was working out. His massive size and chiseled strength made him particularly intimidating.

"He thinks Adeline's mentoring medio is making a play for her," Rainer explained.

Logan shot Rainer a look that said he wasn't supposed to have shared that.

Garrett shook his head at his little brother. He'd never seen the point of tying himself down to just one woman. He perpetually harassed both Rainer and Logan for their commitment to Emily and Adeline at what he considered to be a very young age.

Vindico's brow furrowed as he joined the conversation.

"I've seen the way she looks at you, Haydenshire. I don't think you have anything to worry about, but," he drawled with a wry smile, "you're on my team now, and that means we always have one another's back. So, if this guy decides to extend his hours, so to speak, he can take on all of Elite Iodex. Believe me, he doesn't want to do that. I don't care how well he can heal himself. Just go down there and flash your badge. The guy'll get the message, trust me."

A broad grin stretched across Logan's face. "Thanks. I might do that."

"Like I told you yesterday, I expect a hell of a lot from my guys, but there are a few perks as well." Vindico gestured into his office, and Rainer and Logan stood to follow him. Garrett, Portwood, Tuttle, Ramier, and Ericcson entered right behind them for the morning meeting.

"All right, there was a quake at Felsink last night. They've been expanding the chambers, so the energy is particularly unstable. It was pretty mild, but we're gonna delay our visit for a few hours. I'll take you two on the required tour of the Senate first, then we'll head to Culpeper to retrieve O'Ryan." He seemed more irritated with the change in his schedule than fearful that it might not be the best idea to visit the prison right after a quake.

Logan and Rainer shared a bewildered glance. Most often, the benign tremors felt around the earth that were associated with the use of dynamite were actually caused by Gifted prisons. Energy that far under the earth was unstable and often caused shifts that were blamed on fault lines that didn't exist. Earthquakes that caused major damage were on actual fault lines. The fault line lies were one of the many ways the Gifted hid their existence from the Non-Gifted.

"So obviously, after what happened last evening, Emily Haydenshire will now be given almost 24-7 security detail when she is not either on Haydenshire Farm or with our esteemed colleague here, whom I will teach to forcefully dismantle anything or anyone who might try to do her harm." Vindico gestured to Rainer.

Everyone nodded their understanding. Rainer appreciated the fact that no one was taking Emily's safety lightly.

"Garrett and I are gonna be tied up most of the day doing the tour here for Lawson and Haydenshire and then taking them out to Felsink. I'm bringing O'Ryan back with me. Tuttle!" Vindico barked.

Ryan Tuttle's eyebrows lifted from his cell phone.

"I want Mitchell and Scarlett O'Ryan here, but stick them in a questioning room until I finish with O'Ryan. I can't set the trap if I don't have the bait."

Rainer swallowed. His new boss clearly wasn't afraid of bending the rules if it helped him get his man. Right now, that man was Dominic Wretchkinsides, the head of the Interfeci. Vengeance etched every detail of Vindico's chiseled face.

Bloodthirsty and savage were the only ways Rainer could think to describe Vindico's determination when it came to ripping apart the entire Interfeci, piece by bloody piece. He certainly had his reasons, but his dogged determination was a little hard to swallow sometimes.

"Yes, sir." Tuttle gave a single nod.

"Next on the Wretchkinsides agenda is to come up with the evidence to prove that his new Summation team, The Sirens,"—he rolled his eyes—"is a front and then shut it down. We need to figure out where the money he used to fund the team and to refurb the stadium in Springfield came from. We'll start from there. I'd love to shut them down before the Northeastern Exhibition, which is a week from this Saturday. They've entered, and unless we do something to stop them, they'll be challenging.

"As Emily Haydenshire has just become the Angels' Junior Receiver, I'm certain you can understand my concern about having her on the field with Marlisa and multiple sources of energy that could be harnessed and used to harm someone," Vindico verbalized one of the many fears that were coiled deeply in Rainer's gut.

"Since you idiots haven't brought me anything useful lately, I plan to use whatever we learn from O'Ryan today to guide our investigation for a while. So, make me happy while I'm gone. Figure something out. The Interfeci has moved onto our turf, and we're not gonna stand for that. Now, go do something useful."

CHAPTER 3
IT'S A SMALL WORLD

"Let me check in with Sorenson, and then I'll find you," Garrett requested as Vindico directed Rainer and Logan to follow him.

Garrett was trying to smooth over his abrupt transfer back to Elite. Sorenson was the Non-Gifted chief and had grumbled about Garrett's leaving.

"That's fine. Do whatever you need to do. We'll leave for Felsink after lunch," Vindico agreed.

"Can't wait." Garrett chuckled with his own version of the signature Haydenshire smirk. It was one the governor often sported as did all of his sons.

Rainer and Logan followed Vindico through the heavy double doors that opened into the governors' branch of the Gifted Senate.

There were five governors of the American Gifted Realm, and one Crown Governor. Each of them had a rather plush office with a view of the Potomac.

"Stephen's working from the farm today. Worried about his baby girl, I'm sure." Arthur Vindico, Dan's father and another of the Realm governors, was standing outside of Crown Governor Carrington's office. They were deep in discussion.

Rainer's ears perked immediately. Stephen was Emily's father, and baby girl was his term of endearment for his one and only daughter.

Logan and Rainer shared a nervous glance. Neither of them had known that Governor Haydenshire had decided to work from his office at the farmhouse.

"Maybe I should take a page from his book," Governor Carrington replied gravely.

Governor Vindico shook his head. "Talk to Dan. They've got us all terrified over what happened to Emily last night. They're trying to scare you. They want us to back down. Serena will be fine. She's in capable hands, and Dan trained her security staff."

"Talk to Dan about what?" Vindico interrupted their conversation.

"I'm sorry. We didn't see you there." Governor Vindico cleared his throat and offered Rainer and Logan a kind smile.

"What's wrong with Serena?" Dan asked.

Regis Carrington had been one of Rainer's father's closest friends. When Governor Lawson was Crown, he'd asked Regis to run for the office if anything should ever happen to him. When Joseph was assassinated, Governor Carrington had run unopposed to succeed him.

"It's nothing new. She just got a little spooked this morning. The dogs were barking and growling, and she thought she saw someone out in the garden.

"One of the tires on her car is flat. She left it in the driveway last night, but you know we live in a gated community. I'm going to head home. I can't stand not knowing what's going on there, and she's scared." Governor Carrington seemed to have reached his decision as he explained what had happened.

Rainer's stomach churned. Serena was the Crown Governor's long-term girlfriend. They'd never married, so she wasn't the First Lady. Rainer knew Governor Carrington hoped the slight distance would protect Serena from suffering the same fate Rainer's mother had fallen victim to so many years ago.

Governor Carrington and Serena were closer than several married couples Rainer knew. He doubted he was the only one who noticed their devotion to one another, Wretchkinsides included.

Serena often worked with the Auxiliary department and with many of the civic organizations they sponsored. A native of Jamaica, she traveled back home to offer her assistance there as well.

She wasn't employed in any formal capacity and had been called many unsavory names in the press due to the fact that she and the governor shared a mansion out in Bethesda, Maryland. They also slammed the Crown Governor because of the age difference. Serena was twelve years younger.

But Governor Carrington never seemed to care what anyone thought. He adored Serena, and the Realm could say whatever they wanted. He had everything he'd ever need, and she was his queen.

It had been all over the Gifted press recently that he'd given her a brand-new, bright yellow Bentley Continental convertible for her fortieth birthday. The vanity plate even had his pet name for her—Inamorata—which might have been over the top. The sentiment, *woman that was deeply cherished*, was something shared in intimate moments between the Crown and Serena, Rainer assumed, as he'd never heard Governor Carrington call her that in public.

Vindico's demeanor somehow became even more intense. "Have you talked to Gallic?"

"Yeah, he changed the tire for her and assured me that he saw nothing out of the ordinary. I left early this morning for work, and her detail hadn't left their quarters yet when the dogs started barking. She'd gone out for an early morning swim."

Vindico tried to hide his disdain from the Crown, but Rainer caught the slight eye roll.

"Her security teams are happy to work in shifts. I've told you before. They would be much more effective if you didn't insist that they only work from seven in the morning until you get home in the evenings."

Governor Carrington's kind eyes turned resentful for a moment, though his calm, rhythmic intonation never changed.

"And I've told you every time we've had this conversation, I think Serena, and, quite frankly, I have given up quite enough of our privacy when it comes to running this Realm. If she wants to swim in the mornings, unaccompanied, or if I don't particularly appreciate having interruptions when we're alone in the evening, I don't believe I'm asking too much."

"Yes, sir," Vindico begrudged.

"Rainer, Logan, I trust Dan is giving you the grand tour," Governor Carrington turned his attention back to Rainer.

"Yes, sir."

"You boys were practically raised up here. I doubt you'll find that much has changed, but enjoy your day. I'll see you tomorrow." With a nod, he headed toward the exit doors.

"If his inamorata didn't insist on swimming in the nude every morning, I doubt she'd mind having one of the many officers I've assigned her keeping an eye out," Vindico sneered as soon as Governor Carrington was out of earshot.

"Daniel!" Governor Vindico scolded, "Regis and Serena are dear friends of our family. Not to mention the fact that he is the Crown Governor of this Realm and your boss, to whom you will show respect. Besides that, Regis is right, he and Serena have sacrificed quite enough for this Realm. Marriage and children would make the top of that lengthy list."

Rainer wasn't certain what was more shocking, Vindico's quip or watching him being reprimanded by his father.

This time, Vindico's eye roll was much more distinctive.

Governor Vindico turned to Rainer and forced another smile. "How's Emily?"

"She's all right, sir. She didn't sleep all that well, and she hates all of the attention and the extra security. She feels like she's causing everyone a lot of trouble."

Governor Vindico nodded his understanding. "It's like I was telling Regis. They've scared everyone half to death, and now we have to take a few extra precautions, but we can't keep letting fear rule our decisions. That's precisely what Nic Wretchkinsides wants."

"We need to get going, Dad. I want to show them everything this morning, and then we're going out to Felsink this afternoon. I need them up and working by week's end. We can't keep good officers tied up with required paperwork and protocol. I have actual work I need done."

"All right, son, fine. Enjoy the tour. I'm sure we'll be seeing you often." Governor Vindico gave a slight wave as he closed his office door.

"Now, since we were all raised by governors, we have a little more access than your average Iodex officer, but if you want to send someone else over here to the governors, they would need to talk to Frances."

He led them to a woman's desk that was situated directly across from Governor Carrington's office.

"Daniel, Rainer, Logan," she greeted them kindly.

"Hey Ms. Cogett," Logan offered.

Rainer grinned. They'd known Frances Cogett since she'd worked as his father's primary aide.

"I was just thinking about you, Rainer," she offered with her kind grin. "Do you remember when you were little and you used to come talk with me when your father was on the phone?" Frances appeared to have fond memories of Rainer that he couldn't recall.

"Kind of," he offered apologetically.

She shook her head. "You were too young to remember this I'm sure, but I was just thinking there was one day when you sat at my desk and told me all about Emily. It was so sweet." Rainer now knew why Ms. Cogett had been thinking about him. The entire Senate had been made aware of what had happened the night before.

Vindico chuckled. "If you let him, he'll probably still sit at your desk and tell you all about her." Everyone laughed. "As you know, Frances runs the court schedule, keeps our fathers on their toes, keeps Regis from losing his mind, and is in charge of everyone you see in this office." Vindico gestured to the dozens of people seated behind Frances, all working in some capacity for the governing board. "Without her, the entire Senate would fall apart."

"And I bake a mean sour cream pound cake."

Rainer and Logan both nodded. They'd been treated to the cake on numerous occasions.

Vindico grinned. "She does that as well."

"Don't work them too hard, Daniel. The chamber room is empty this morning if you want to show them in there."

"Will do. Thanks, Frances." Vindico guided Rainer and Logan out of the governing wing to the Senate Chamber and holding cells.

"I know you already know all of this, but I don't remember you being up here in the last few years, so here's the courtroom." He threw open two large oak doors and showed them the opulent courtroom with a place for each of the governors to sit. The Crown Governor's seat was slightly larger and in the center.

"Witness benches," Vindico pointed to several long, cushioned benches on the left side of the rectangular room. "The defendants are brought in through there." He gestured to two oak doors that matched the ones they'd entered through in the back of the courtroom.

"If you're testifying, you sit there. That's where you'll be when you start giving evidence on arrests you make." He pointed to several cushioned benches facing the governors' seats.

"And the Senteon sits there." He spread his hands, showing the rows and rows of blue cushioned seats taking up the entire right side of the room.

The Senteon heard trials and could vote on a person's guilt or innocence, though the final decision lay with the governors. At least four of the six governors had to be convinced of a person's innocence or guilt before a verdict was handed down, but the Crown Governor's vote counted twice.

Rainer was struck by how different the chamber room appeared to him. The last time he'd been in the courtroom, his father had been Crown Governor.

He was ten years old, had been running a fever, and had a terrible cough. His father needed to hear a trial before he took Rainer to the medio. He could still see his dad's deeply concerned eyes and hear his repeated apologies that he couldn't take him to the medio's office sooner.

"Your mom always knew how to make everything better," he'd choked out the deep regret. "I promise I'll get the trial over with as quickly as I can, and then we'll go get you healed up. We'll get some movies and ice cream and hang out 'til you're feeling better, okay?"

Rainer had nodded since he was having a hard time speaking. "Chocolate?" he'd managed in a strangled whisper.

His father had given his customary soothing chuckle as he scrubbed Rainer's hair. "Of course."

He'd spent the morning in his dad's office lying on the leather couch with his father setting healing casts to lower his temperature every opportunity he had.

They'd gone to the chamber to hear a trial. Rainer couldn't recall the details of the case, but he remembered thinking how important his dad looked, seated in the middle of the other governors, asking questions, and listening intently. It was one of the only times in his life that Rainer recalled being intimidated when he was with his dad.

In the middle of that trial, he'd begun shivering violently both from his fever and his awe, and Governor Lawson had immediately recused himself. He'd led Rainer from the room and taken him to the medio and then home, just like he'd promised.

They'd stayed on the sofa for the few days it took Rainer to fully recover from strep throat. His dad had never left his side. He'd even let Emily come over and play board games with them and attempt to nurse him back to health with all of her nine-year-old wisdom.

Rainer swallowed down a sudden onslaught of emotion and reminded himself that he was a grown man now and that his dad was gone. He had to stand on his own. He inventoried the courtroom once more and pushed away the memories of his father.

When he was a child, the room had seemed gargantuan, and the governors' voices had an odd, hollow, echoing effect. Somehow, it looked much smaller now.

With one last glance back to the chair once occupied by his dad, another memory assaulted his psyche. "You aren't all alone, and I won't let you ever be all alone. I'm going to take care of you and make you feel better, always. Always!" Emily's sobbed vow when Rainer had sat with her on a quilt in the yard the night of his father's murder ricocheted through his mind.

He let that feeling of her love, and her care, and her steadfast determination that she would always be there soothe his heart and his weary soul.

They moved on to the holding chambers. A dozen iron cells that were approximately seven square feet on each side, with bars on the doors, were lined along a darkened hallway just off of the courtroom.

"Run your hand over that, Haydenshire," Vindico's harsh voice shattered through Rainer's recollections.

With a hesitant grimace, Logan touched one of the bars, then jerked his hand away.

"They're made of a magnesium and iron ore blend. We run infrared light casts over them constantly, to keep anyone from getting any brilliant ideas about escaping while they're awaiting trial. The amount of light used can be adjusted here." He pointed to a slide bar on the opposite side of the room.

Logan shook out his hand and glanced at Rainer.

"Did it hurt?" Rainer whispered as they followed Vindico on to the next branch of the Senate.

"Not really. It just felt weird, like it messed my hand up. I don't think I could have summoned."

Rainer nodded and picked up the pace since Vindico was awaiting them. They moved quickly through the cafeteria and infirmary, and then into the entire branch devoted to service.

"This should make you proud, Lawson. This was all your mother's doing." Vindico gestured to the many offices full of men and women working toward making the Realm a better place. The Auxiliary Branch of the Senate was run by Receivers like Emily. Receivers' empathy often knew no bounds.

The Auxiliary department handled family counseling and education, therapy, adoptions, crisis management, disaster relief, prisoner counseling and reform, and they ran numerous Gifted addiction treatment facilities all over the country.

Rainer smiled and nodded. He didn't really want to think about his mother just then. The past day had held too many emotions already.

Between the Auxiliary Department and the event-planning portion of the Senate was the Gifted Hall of Records and library. Vindico smirked and gestured his head to the massive room with cold marble tile and floor-to-ceiling bookshelves. "If you ever get so bored that you decide to come dig through all of the old legends and texts, let me know. I'll find more for you to do."

They walked through the next set of heavy steel doors. "This is the event-planning part of the Senate," Vindico explained. "All of the balls, Senate events, or Summation challenges start here first." He showed them several offices at the end of the long hall.

They moved to the last portion of the Senate. Vindico smiled as they entered through a large set of oak doors.

"These would be the people you need to talk to about what to do with the massive amount of money we're paying you." He chuckled.

Rainer and Logan joined in. Although Iodex officers were well-paid for their work, they certainly weren't overpaid for what they did. *American Senate Banking and Financial Planning* was etched on a placard just inside the oak doors.

"That's Mr. Buffett's office," Vindico lowered his voice, as everyone in the area was either on the phone or in deep concentration as they stared at a computer screen.

Suddenly, the door opened, and a man stepped out. He smiled at Vindico. He appeared to be in his eighties and had a kind face. Rainer noted he was dressed very nicely and carried himself with a great deal of respect. "How's it going, Daniel?"

"Good, sir. Just showing my new team members around. How are you?"

"Good, good," Mr. Buffett smiled, "Rainer, I'm sure you don't remember me,"—he shook Rainer's hand—"but your father was a dear friend of mine. If I can ever do anything for you, help you with investing your inheritance, anything at all, I'd be only too pleased to be of service."

"Oh, uh, thank you," Rainer stammered.

Vindico smiled again. "You should take him up on that, trust me."

Rainer agreed to have lunch with Mr. Buffett the following week.

"You know, Rainer just proposed to Emily Haydenshire." Vindico smirked.

"I heard that, and Stephen allowed him to live, much to my shock." Mr. Buffett laughed.

After exchanging a few more pleasantries, they continued on through the financial planning area of the Senate. Duco Predilects, those gifted with the ability to calculate and plan with ease and who could read and summon the energy of the economy, made up most of the Senate Bank employees and financial planners.

Will Haydenshire grinned and stepped out of his office when he saw Logan and Rainer make their way past.

"You showboating your new team, Danny?" Will was the eldest Haydenshire child. He and Dan had been good friends since they were toddlers and their fathers had become Realm governors.

"You know it. How's Brooke doing?" Will's wife, Brooke, was pregnant with their first child.

Will grimaced. "Poor thing. She wakes up at five and pukes, then I try to get her back to sleep, then she goes to work, and when her assistant takes their class out to the playground, she pukes again. She's basically timed it so she's sick while her kids are out of her classroom and then comes home and collapses."

Brooke was a Scholera Predilect, and she taught kindergarten at McCarron Elementary. Since school was still out for the summer, she'd been working with one of the summer school programs for children whose parents had to work.

"Any idea when that'll stop?" Vindico looked genuinely sorry for Brooke's plight. "That seems like a load of pure bullshit just to bring one of your kids into the world."

"No idea. She's in her second trimester now so hopefully soon. Oh, and you can kiss my left ass cheek and lick the other," Will sneered as he and Vindico both laughed.

They worked their way back toward the Iodex offices and stopped just short of the designer gym used by both Elite Iodex and the Non-Elite officers. Vindico gestured his head to two heavy metal doors that led to an adjoining corridor.

"This is the Legal department. Stariff's team is in these offices." He continued to walk and talk as they passed by another door, this one a deep, cherry wood with "Jackson W. Stariff ~ Attorney at Law" engraved on a black marble placard.

Rainer needed to talk with Jack Stariff regarding his will and his vast inheritance. He knew Emily wouldn't want to think about his reasoning for naming Logan his beneficiary, so he decided to make the appointment and not mention it to her.

He tried to hide his slight shiver as he considered the thought that his uncle would harm him just to get his hands on the Lawson family fortune.

Logan was going to be highly trained in defensive maneuvers just like Rainer. If his Uncle Stan should try something and succeed, Logan would make certain Emily got all of the money and that Stan never saw a penny.

With that morose thought plaguing his psyche, they ended their tour back at their desks in Iodex.

"All right, I've given you both copies of information on every current member of the Interfeci. They're in the files on your laptops. Look them over. Memorize everything you can. You should know those mug shots and raps like the back of your own hands. We're running seven miles, then lifting, then a two-mile cooldown, then we'll shower and grab lunch before heading out to Felsink," Vindico barked his brusk orders.

"Yes, sir," Rainer and Logan agreed as Vindico returned to his office and shut the door.

"We're running nine miles, and lifting, and then we're going to Felsink?" Logan panicked.

"Apparently so." Rainer sank into his chair to question his life choices.

CHAPTER 4
WHAT'S GIVEN...
CROWN GOVERNOR REGIS CARRINGTON

"You didn't have to come home, *puttus*." Serena wound her arms around Regis's waist after she caressed his face. He clung to her fiercely.

"I had to check on you, angel. I was going crazy at work. I missed you, and I was worried." Regis let his hands glide up the soft, silky skin of her back. She was wearing a backless fuchsia shirt that tied at her neck and wound its way low along her waist. The enticing top was paired with one of her long, flowing, floral skirts.

He fought the desire to untie it altogether. She looked like the Caribbean sunset over the shadowy waters. Her lush, dark skin, set against every color of the rainbow in the fabric, and lit the ethereal fire in her eyes.

"I shouldn't have called," she sighed. "Gallic told me not to. You're a busy man."

Fury flooded through Regis's rhythms. "You call me whenever you want to. I don't care how busy I am. I am never, ever too busy for you."

Her sweet rhythmic waves swam with elation. They matched the coursing waters of her island home. Regis let his eyes close as he began drinking in the heavenly tranquility of her.

"Do you want to come with me to The Garden? I would love for you to."

Regis considered her offer. It was Tuesday, and Serena always went to volunteer at The Garden Food Pantry downtown. She'd gained them a great deal of attention from the press, which brought donations from her admirers and consideration for their cause. Underfed children generally left Serena in tears, but she cared for each and every one of them as they came through the doors each Tuesday.

She adored the little ones, and it pained Regis that she'd given them up because of his position and the constant scrutiny and danger it would put their children in.

Her sisters all had children. Serena would insist that being an aunt was enough, but he knew it wasn't. Pained regret filled his rhythms, and she picked up on the shift immediately.

"If I go with you, all of the security and press will prevent you from working and might prevent people who need you from getting inside. What if I just drive you down there, and then I'll pick you up this evening? I'll go back to the office once I know you're safe inside."

Serena smiled and nodded, but disappointment echoed in the rhythms through her satin skin and her tender soul.

"I love you, my precious inamorata." He allowed the longing and the deep penetrating love he felt to perforate his tone in an effort to soothe all that he'd taken away. She stepped back and gave him the sexy grin that only he was privileged enough to receive.

"I know," she assured him with that intoxicating glint in her eyes. "And you are my everything, so stop worrying."

CHAPTER 5

GET IT OVER WITH

RAINER LAWSON

Garrett was laughing at Rainer and Logan outright as he followed them into a booth at Frye's, the restaurant that catered to most of the upper-level Senate employees. It offered everything from steak and cheeseburgers, to salads, baked potatoes, and pasta dishes.

"Eat," Garrett commanded. "This isn't the academy anymore. You made it to Elite, so now you're gonna have to suck it up and take it like you two actually have four nads between you."

Logan rolled his eyes and glared at his big brother. As he and Rainer had grown up being harassed by the elder Haydenshire brothers, neither was particularly offended. They would have thrown out something equally as insulting if they hadn't still been gasping for breath.

Vindico hadn't mentioned that their seven-mile run, which they were expected to complete in sixty minutes, would include wearing weight vests and completing an obstacle course where they would need to throw their shields and dodge mock shots being taken at them.

Rainer was ravenous and quickly decided that he didn't care what Garrett or the waiter thought. He went on with his order of two cheeseburgers, two loaded baked potatoes, and a side of macaroni and cheese. If he was going to have to work out like that and then withstand Felsink, he was going to need calories to burn.

"Do we do that obstacle course thing every day?" Logan asked after he'd consumed his first cheesesteak.

"No." Garrett shook his head. "He's trying to make certain you're equipped to deal with whatever is headed our way. After what happened to Em last night, Dan's not gonna take any chances. He wants you both trained yesterday. Wretchkinsides is getting richer and more powerful every freaking day, and we've got to figure out how to stop him." He downed a sip of tea. "The first time we get called out, you'll understand why we have to do shit like that."

That thought had Rainer's stomach churning as he reconsidered his pasta choice.

"Nic stands to make millions with this trumped-up Summation team he's loaded his fortunes into."

"What's Felsink like, really?" Rainer decided he didn't want to hear any more about Dominic Wretchkinsides. He had to be ended because Rainer would not allow the only person who ever really understood him, the only girl who ever meant anything to him, to have to go on living in terror. It didn't matter what needed to be done. He was going to see that it was taken care of, because he would never allow anything to hurt Emily.

Garrett shrugged as he considered the question. He did seem to be taking his part of training Logan and Rainer very seriously.

"This will be the worst trip you make by far. You're both strong Ioses Preds, so your Shields will restore your energy once you're out of the ore fields for a couple of hours. But you'll be exhausted and starving no matter how much you eat here. You'll probably run a fever. You might puke, and you won't be able to get it up for a day or two, so I hope Em and Adeline are okay with that."

Logan rolled his eyes. "You're so full of shit."

"I'm not joking."

He seemed sincere, but Rainer joined in Logan's acrimony. He chose not to recall all of the times growing up that Garrett had answered any question either of them had about most any topic as honestly as he'd been able.

He would always harass them about it, but Logan and Rainer had been going to Garrett for years because he would always give them a straight answer.

"It'll get better each time you go out there. The first time is really rough. I stayed at the farmhouse the first night I went out there. I already had my apartment, but I was too sick to stay by myself," he added humbly. "Your body gets used to it, as long as you don't stay out there too long each time you go."

They finished up their lunch and begrudgingly walked back to the Pentagon. Rainer called Emily as they waited at a crosswalk.

"Hey," she soothed.

"Hey baby, are you okay?"

"I'm fine, how are you? You sound good. I expected you to sound exhausted or something."

"We haven't gone out to Culpeper yet. We're just coming back from lunch, and I wanted to check on you."

"Oh," Emily paused and then asked, "Are you nervous?"

"A little." He never would have shared that with anyone but her.

"I'll take care of you when you get home. Mom and I have been making chili all day, and Dad said to double the meat. Mom was a little tired, so she's lying down. I brought the twins outside to play."

"Is your mom all right?" It was unlike Mrs. Haydenshire to ever rest for any reason. Rainer had personally seen the woman, who'd raised him through his adolescence, cook a full dinner for all ten of her children when she had a horrible cold. The governor was always trying to get her to rest and let him do whatever needed to be done.

"I kind of think it might've been what happened yesterday that sort of got to her," Emily admitted with a slight choke.

"Yeah, I'm sure."

"I'm okay. I promise. The Iodex security people have checked on me and the twins constantly since we came out to the swing set."

"Good, that's what they're supposed to do."

Suddenly, Garrett grabbed Rainer's phone with a wry grin. "Em, it's me. Pretend Rainer said all the shit he tells you before you actually let him get off of the phone 'cause he's gotta stop calling you so much, or Dan's gonna chew his ass. I'll bring him home in a few hours. He'll feel like hell so don't expect much tonight. Bye, baby sis." With that, Garrett ended the call as Rainer glared at him. "Let's just get this over with." He shoved Rainer and Logan forward by the scruff of their necks.

CHAPTER 6

FELSINK REFORMATORY

Rainer drew deep breaths and tried to steady himself as he followed Vindico to a line of black Expeditions. They were all equipped with enhanced engines, shield casts, and tinted windows. The government tags matched those of the Non-Gifted Realm, save the lower right corner that held the abbreviated Realm crest.

All Gifted police and Iodex cars were unmarked. Marked police and sheriff's cars meant the cop was not Gifted. An unmarked squad car or SUV with the Realm crest indicated a Realm Iodex officer who was serving in some capacity.

"Hop in." Vindico gestured to the Expedition nearest them. He climbed into the driver's seat and backed the car out. "I always feel like I'm driving a freaking school bus in these," he lamented to Garrett who'd joined him in the front.

"Doesn't handle quite like your Brutale, I'm assuming?" Rainer chided as he tried to relax a little.

Dan laughed and shook his head. "No, not quite. Pay attention to where we're going. You'll be bringing prisoners here by yourselves soon."

Logan and Rainer glanced out the windows. They both knew how to get to Culpeper. Garrett and Vindico began discussing the upcoming football season and the Northeast Summation Exhibition.

"Too bad Emily can't play in that ring. The Angels would kick some serious ass this season." Garrett laughed.

"I just hope Cascavel didn't figure out how she threw that shield," Vindico sighed as they barreled down the interstate.

Rainer swallowed down the bile that flooded his throat every time the memories broke through the dams he'd erected in his mind. Emily lying on the parking lot cement sobbing with the shrapnel of her cell phone littered around her.

Cascavel—the name dripped from Vindico's lips like poison. Rainer had hated him from the moment he and Emily had seen him at the beach weeks before. Emily's receptors had picked up on his black energy instantly, but Vindico's wrath-fueled venom whenever he said the man's name had abject hatred and fear coiling in Rainer's veins.

If Wretchkinsides realized Emily's engagement ring gave her supplies of energy via the promethium infused within the large diamond, she would remain at the top of the list of people who had something Dominic Wretchkinsides wanted.

People on that list very rarely escaped with their lives. Rainer shuddered and stared out the windows as the city faded into the blurred haze of fields.

Vindico summoned once they were out of DC gridlock, and the Expedition shot forward. They would make the hour plus trip in less than forty-five minutes if he kept his current speed.

Signs for the tiny town of Culpeper looked welcoming, and the square was well-known for being friendly. Almost all of the residents were Non-Gifted. No one with Gifted energies wanted to be anywhere near the prison. Rainer's heart raced, and his mouth felt oddly dry as the parking brake gave its rapid rhythmic clicks.

Vindico's boots hit the sandy gravel that made up the parking area. It was roped off with barely visible polyester twine. After drawing a deep breath, Rainer and Logan exited onto the sandy ground that seemed to vibrate disconcertingly under their feet.

Garrett slapped Logan on the back. "There's really no way to prepare you for this. It hurts like hell, so my policy has always just been to get in and get out."

Vindico nodded and offered Rainer and Logan an almost-concerned half smile. "Your shield will adapt to the iron ore after you've been out here a few times. It'll still hurt like hell, but this time will be the worst."

"Sort of like getting your own cherry popped only no fun at all. Just sucks." Garrett chuckled

Logan managed an eye roll, but Rainer was far more concerned with the faint screeching hum that was developing against his skull as he followed Garrett and Dan down a shallow embankment. His boots slid on the loose rocks, and Logan reached to steady him.

"Thanks." Rainer hoped his boss hadn't noticed his misstep.

They passed several mine entrances, each marked with a different company's logo. A few men leaned against shovels and offered them nods as they passed. The air swam before Rainer's eyes. It seemed stagnated with impending doom.

As they came to another entrance, Vindico halted abruptly. He wiped the sweat from his brow and leaned down to lift a fallen piece of plastic caution tape that appeared to have given up the will to live. He reattached it to the thin metal stake in the ground.

Caution signs marked the cloaked entrance. They all declared it to be impassable.

With a quick wave of his badge over a screened keypad in a rock, a low metallic groan echoed from a vast metal door that slid to the side in front of the men. It was the same sandy color as the ground, and Rainer had almost missed it. The staked caution tape warning signs and a few ragged bushes were the only markers for the entrance.

"Let's get this done." Vindico entered the number on his badge into the keypad.

"It's hard to summon here, so there's no other way to get in these locks. You have to have a badge and ID. Magnetic pulses won't work," Garrett explained. He was beginning to pale, and beads of sweat dripped from his forehead.

Rainer took solace in the fact that Garrett was struggling as well. The screeching drone in his ears grew louder with each passing moment. It was the only discernible sound he could identify as they entered the door. Another solid steel door was to the west, revealing a jagged metal staircase.

Rainer's lungs seized, and he became aware of the blood pulsing through his veins. His heart seemed to be fighting to keep it moving through his body. It was heavy and sluggish as he followed Vindico onto the stairs.

"The elevator is this way." Garrett guided them toward the set of stairs.

Logan shuddered as he followed. He squeezed his eyes shut and swallowed harshly.

Nausea washed over Rainer. His skin was cold and clammy as his temperature fluctuated from blazing hot to freezing cold in a matter of seconds. His body was unable to regulate it.

Vindico gave a nod to the two guards stationed at the elevator doors.

"Sir," they offered succinctly. All Gifted-prison guards were Non-Gifted men and women who were selected from mineworkers living in the prison area. They were well-paid for their work and for their silence. The energy fluctuations were not discernible to them in any way.

Rainer forced his feet to move him onto the shaft's elevator. It was nothing more than a metal encasement that would take them miles below the earth's surface.

Rainer's stomach lifted warily toward his throat as the elevator dropped them toward the prison cells. With each foot they descended, he willed the contents of his lunch to stay inside.

He shuddered and clung to the wall as the metals in his body begin to react with the surrounding iron ore as they sped downward into darkness.

"Are you okay?" Garrett managed in a choked whisper. Rainer tried to nod, but the weakly casted light in the elevator didn't illuminate him enough for Garrett to see him.

He wondered momentarily who had set the permanent cast on the light. Who would've been able to summon and cast when the drain began to rob him of breath and any access to his Gifted energies at all?

The elevator finally halted, and the doors opened. He blinked several times as his eyes tried to take in the lighted area.

Certain his head was full of water, he tried to catch Logan as he stumbled forward, but his timing was off and his hand moved through the air and landed on nothing. Vindico caught Logan.

"You're all right. Just try to relax. Your body's fighting. It's trying to regulate your energy streams, but you can't. Try not to fight it." His voice reached Rainer through the infuriating screech echoing in his ears.

They walked down a dirt-walled corridor and reached a stone-covered desk.

"Get me Mitch O'Ryan," Vindico coughed out the order.

Time seemed to tick out of rhythm along with Rainer's disjointed heartbeats.

After what felt like a decade, the armed guards returned with a man that Rainer assumed was Mitchell O'Ryan Jr.'s father. There wasn't enough light to see any resemblance, and O'Ryan Senior's face was sunken and appeared to be graying under his haphazardly shaven beard.

Vindico and Garrett both pulled their Glocks from their hip holsters. They shoved O'Ryan back toward the elevators.

They made it back topside, and Vindico pushed O'Ryan into the very back of the SUV. He tossed Rainer the keys so he could keep an eye on the prisoner.

Rainer miraculously caught the keys and managed to crank the engine while he prayed he'd make it back to Arlington without vomiting or passing out.

"Rainer, are you okay to drive?" Garrett watched over him. He popped the tab on four Dr Peppers, and handed one each to Logan, Rainer, and Dan. They knew that the enhanced soft drink would help their bodies begin to restore their energies.

Vindico kept the pistol trained on O'Ryan.

"I'm fine," Rainer lied through his teeth.

He drove back to the Pentagon on instinct alone. He was immensely thankful that driving had always come easily for him.

After pulling the Expedition onto the parking deck, he tried to get his eyes to focus through a series of blinks.

They stumbled out of the SUV and watched as Dan led O'Ryan through the security checkpoints and then into an interrogation room.

"Are you okay?" Rainer attempted to wipe the sweat from his brow.

"I'm not really sure," Logan admitted.

CHAPTER 7

INTERROGATIONS

Tuttle timed it perfectly. While Vindico was pushing O'Ryan into the interrogation room, his wife and son were paraded by him just out of reach.

The room and the move were distinctly cold. A slight shiver quaked through Rainer as he took in the barren gray room with a painted steel table and a few chairs. The paint on the table was chipping badly, and it was beginning to rust. The room looked nothing like the plush offices of Iodex and the rest of the Senate.

"Sit down!" Vindico shoved O'Ryan into a chair.

Rainer and Logan seated themselves quickly beside Garrett.

"Why is my wife here?" O'Ryan managed to speak as he collapsed onto the hard chair. The longing in his eyes pricked at Rainer's heart.

His head was beginning to pound, and Vindico handed out another round of drinks. This time, it was electrolyte-infused water, which would help their Gifted energies settle. He slapped a bottle down in front of O'Ryan as well.

"I thought you might like to see her. Does that sound appealing to you, Mitch?"

"Depends," O'Ryan choked as he tried to down the water. "What will it cost me?"

Vindico chuckled ominously. "We've got you for three years on tax evasion and another year and a half on forgery. I got a call from a Felsink guard last night who said you aren't doing too well out there. Seems your health might be suffering."

"What do you want? I don't know where he is. Knowing you, I'd have to slice his throat myself to buy my way out of that hellhole you've sent me to."

"Nah." Vindico shook his head. "I'll take care of the throat-slashing. You just tell me everything I need to know to take his organization apart piece by piece, and I'll see if we can't ease that sentence up a little. The more you talk the longer you stay out."

"How long are you gonna let him do this to you?" O'Ryan challenged as he threw his grimy hands out to Vindico. "How long are you gonna let him win? He's got you by a string, and he knows it."

Vindico's eyes narrowed in hatred. "I'll let this go when he's no longer polluting this earth by drawing breath, or when you and I are riding a ski lift in hell. Now, do you want to help me, or shall I have some of my officers escort you back to your home away from home?"

"Amelia's gone. Move on. You'll never catch Nic."

Fury lit through Rainer though he was certain it was nothing compared to what Vindico must've felt.

"Amelia is gone, Mitch," he spat, "because Wretchkinsides took her. Now, are you going to help me, or shall I send your wife and kid home and you back to the rock you've been living under?" he growled as he leaned across the table.

O'Ryan edged away instinctively. He swallowed down another sip of water like it was full of nails. "So my choices are dying in Felsink or dying by Nic's Magnum when he finds out I'm helping you." His tone was plain. The statement didn't seem to hold much doubt. It sounded as if O'Ryan already knew his fate and had accepted that there was no way to alter his outcome.

"You give Nic too damn much credit," Vindico argued. "You help me end him, you walk free. You and Scarlett can use one of your many offshore bank accounts to retire somewhere out of my sight, and we're done."

O'Ryan gave a half-hearted eye roll and a nod. "Right." Silence drowned the room as Vindico kept his eyes locked on O'Ryan's. After what seemed an endless moment in time, he shrugged.

"Scarlett knows more than I do. I've heard a few things, and Scarlett lets me know some things when she sends letters. I'll help you, but I want out Thursday and then all weekend. We'll talk Monday. I'll tell you everything I know including what I learn when I'm at home. Then we're gonna talk about how long I can stay out as long as I keep you in the know."

Garrett's crude warning about not being able to get it up for a day or two flashed through Rainer's mind.

"I'm gonna need a little more than that if you think you're getting out for a long weekend."

O'Ryan didn't look surprised by Vindico's counter offer. He gave a soft nod and seemed to turn introspective.

"Nicky just bought himself a few pieces of property, and the boys have a few new hangouts, but no more intel 'til I get a weekend with my wife."

Vindico studied him before turning to Rainer. "You and Haydenshire go down to the Auxiliary Department. Tell Mrs. Eleanor I need a favor, now."

Rainer attempted to stand and hold his head upright. It felt like he'd been half-drowned and was still full of water. Garrett helped Logan up and guided him toward the door.

Logan's brow furrowed. "Why does he want her?"

"I think he wants to see if O'Ryan really knows what he says he knows. If he's lying, Mrs. Eleanor will pick up on the deceptive energy." Rainer rubbed his forehead. His skin was oddly clammy, almost spongelike.

Anna Eleanor was the highly esteemed head of the Senate Auxiliary Department. She ran everything from the International Adoptions within the Realm program to the task force to help feed the hungry in the Non-Gifted Realm.

Most any Receiver with any strength at all could pick up on the emotions that occurred when someone was telling a lie. According to Emily, it was a specific distortion that always included relief. Receivers could read any emotion at all. It wouldn't be difficult to discern if O'Ryan really knew where Wretchkinsides's men were hanging out and where he was buying up land.

Since Receivers' emotional reads were not admissible in court trials, Rainer was surprised Vindico would ask for Mrs. Eleanor's help. This wasn't a trial though.

They entered the Auxiliary wing and explained Vindico's request to Saxby Higgins, Mrs. Eleanor's administrative assistant. He nodded and then knocked delicately on her office door.

After a brief whispered conversation, Mrs. Eleanor offered Rainer and Logan a kind smile and followed them back to Iodex.

"If more people understood how Receivers can help law enforcement, we'd get a lot further in catching criminals and then reforming them," she stated as they walked.

In 1917, a man named Theodore Dinkerton had set out to disprove Receivers' abilities. He'd performed rudimentary tests and had proven that Receivers' own emotional rhythm strains could affect their reads from other Gifted people.

Rainer knew that if Emily was upset about something or even feeling sick, her own tremendous reading abilities were slightly diminished. However, she was never completely without any ability at all, and her reads were almost always spot-on.

Dinkerton's report was the documentation that prevented Receivers from reading emotional strains during testimony and therefore many criminals walked free. There were a great number of Gifted people who doubted Receivers' abilities completely. They were deemed overly emotional, overly sympathetic saps with no real use.

Logan held the door for Mrs. Eleanor, and they fell back in their chairs, thankful not to have to walk any farther.

"Yes, Chief Vindico, what can I do for you?" Mrs. Eleanor checked her watch. Vindico looked mildly amused.

"I just thought you could tell me if Mr. O'Ryan is shooting straight with me. I'm sorry to interrupt your day. I'm certain you're very busy. I know you have a great deal on your plate, but this is extremely important."

To Dan Vindico, whatever had been going on in the Auxiliary

department was not as important as catching Dominic Wretchkinsides. That was obvious.

Mrs. Eleanor's eyes narrowed. Rainer was certain she'd picked up on Vindico's ego and arrogance immediately. He wondered if she would agree to help.

"Fine." Mrs. Eleanor took the seat Vindico politely offered to her.

"Tell her what you just told me. If you're shitting me, O'Ryan, I'll think about letting you blow Scarlett a kiss through the window of one of my squad cars."

O'Ryan bristled.

"May I?" Mrs. Eleanor lightly touched O'Ryan's hand. She grimaced over the soot and ash that had gathered under his fingernails from his time in Felsink.

"I know where Nic's been buying up land, and I know where a few of his dogs have been hanging out. I'll tell Dan everything I know and everything I find out from Scarlett after this weekend. Lucinda's coming in soon. Scarlett will see her. She does love her sister despite who she married and the shit she runs for Nic."

Mrs. Eleanor eased her hand away and nodded.

"He's telling you the truth, Chief Vindico." She stood and showed herself out.

"Thanks." Vindico leaned across the table and glared down at O'Ryan. "All right, Mitch, be my guest." He gestured toward the door. "Go spend a few minutes with your wife and kid. I'll send officers to pick you up Thursday morning, and you can have your long weekend with your family. Stay inside your house, and if you decide you'd like to get smart and make a run for it, just remember that nothing would make me happier than catching you again and extending your stay in Felsink.

"I'll be by your lovely home Sunday night at eight. We'll see what you come up with, and I'm feeling generous today, so I'll let that determine when you make your return to the Felsink Boys. I'm sure the choir won't be the same without you." Vindico rolled his eyes. "Get him out of my face."

With that, Garrett hoisted O'Ryan out of his chair. He stumbled slightly as he rushed to the door.

Rainer swallowed as Scarlett O'Ryan fell into her husband's arms with tears streaming down her face.

"You two go on home. Be ready to work tomorrow. Sleep, then eat, then sleep more. Drink lots of water." Vindico guided Logan and Rainer toward the doors.

"Thanks," Rainer managed as he focused on the exit sign that swam before his eyes.

CHAPTER 8
COMFORTS

"Do you want me to drive?" Logan offered.

"Do you mind?" Rainer prayed he wasn't just being nice. He wasn't certain how he'd be able to drive his beloved Mustang back to the farm.

"Nah, I'm okay I think. I don't know how you made it back from Culpeper. I kept thinking I was gonna puke."

"Yeah, believe me, I understand."

Rainer let his eyes close as he tried to steady his heartbeat, and the next thing he knew he was bounced awake as Logan turned onto the gravel drive that led up to his parents' home.

Emily raced out of the farmhouse. "Are you okay?" She attempted to help Rainer out of the car and then to help Logan.

"I'm all right, baby." Rainer was better because she was there.

"Get in the Hummer. I'll take you both home, and you can sleep."

Logan managed a nod and fell into the middle seat of Emily's new Hummer.

"I should have driven there. I wasn't really thinking," he confessed through a deep yawn as he rubbed his eyes.

Emily offered her big brother a sympathetic smile and drove them across the vast fields of her family's farm.

Rainer had to grin. Emily began mothering them as soon as they made it through the garage door.

"Lie down on the couches. I'll cover you up and then go back up and get some of the chili. Mom's still napping." She directed them to the couch and love seat in their living room. They were hand-me-downs from the Haydenshires. They weren't really long enough for them to lay on, but neither Rainer nor Logan had enough fight in them to argue. They collapsed and let Emily tend to them for the moment.

Rainer's mind drifted back to her at nine years old caring for him when he had strep throat. He fell into a deep sleep with dreams of her hands on her hips, her brow furrowed, and her lips drawn in a deep purse. "I think you're supposed to be lying on the couch. How are you going to get well if you keep playing?" she'd ordered with all of her sass and determination. "Let me take care of you. I know how to make you all better."

"Rainer," her whisper broke through his bizarre dreams. "Daddy said to wake you up. You need to eat." She dragged her fingers through his hair. It was wet. He attempted to sit up.

"You had a fever, but I think it broke."

That explained his damp hair and why he was shivering slightly.

"Here." She helped him up and propped pillows behind him before placing a tray in his lap.

They must've been out for hours. Adeline was already home from the hospital. He glanced at the sliding glass doors that led to the back deck. The sky was settling somewhere between the bright orange of the humid day and the inky black of night.

"Thanks." Rainer stared down at the huge bowl of chili that was topped with loads of sour cream and cheese. She'd sliced up a jalapeno and put that on top just like he liked it.

Mrs. Haydenshire had prepared her cheesy, onion, and jalapeno cornbread, and there were two slices on a plate near the chili.

"This looks great." He brushed a kiss on Emily's cheek before she stood. She gave him his grin, and he began to feel human again.

Logan and Rainer consumed three bowls of chili and an entire round of the cornbread between them. Adeline casted both of them, and after a few minutes of that, Rainer shook himself and stood.

Adeline was a very Gifted healer. She, just like all healers, had copious amounts of extra energy to be used for the purpose of healing others.

Valeduto Predilects like Adeline had energies they used for healings, and then their own personal energy streams. Logan never minded Adeline healing Rainer or any of his brothers since he was the only one who benefitted from her personal rhythms when they were in contact and, most certainly, when they were in bed together.

Rainer did note that Adeline had added in her own soothing love when she casted Logan. He'd recovered much faster.

"I'm gonna get a shower." Rainer leaned his head to either side until he popped the crick out of his neck and tried to unkink his spine.

The hot water beat against his back as he tried to let it wash away his exhausting day. When he stepped out of the shower, Emily handed him a towel she'd heat-casted.

"Thanks." He dried off and then pulled her close. Rainer inhaled her sweet, spicy scent. Citrus cloves mixed with vanilla and her personal brand of musk filled his nostrils and his heart. Everything about her soothed him, and holding her against his bare chest eased his weary soul.

"Let's go to bed."

With a nod, Rainer ran the towel haphazardly through his hair and pulled on a pair of boxers before falling into bed with her.

"I'm sorry. I'm just beat tonight." They'd hoped that moving into their own place would allow them to engage in the physical side of their relationship a little more often.

The last two nights hadn't gone that way. Rainer hated to admit that Garrett had been right. He wouldn't have made for much of a lover right then.

Emily giggled. "It's okay. I wasn't really expecting that. I'm just glad you seem to feel better." She brushed sweet kisses on his chest and then on his cheek.

He rubbed his hands up and down her back as he cradled her in his arms.

Emily's soothing Receiver's cast spun out of her pores and wound around his body. His breath panted from being inside the very essence of her. The only time he was ever closer to her was when he was physically a part of her, when he made their bodies one as he thrust deeply inside the heavenly confection between her legs.

"Go to sleep," she whispered.

He let his eyes close and drank in her adoring love with every draw of breath.

CHAPTER 9

FOLLIES

"I've got to go talk to Stariff," Rainer whispered to Logan. He was careful not to take his eyes off of the work he was studying at his desk. He glanced back discreetly. Vindico's office door was open, and he was on the phone dictating the terms of O'Ryan's house arrest for the officers on duty that weekend.

Logan nodded his understanding. "Even Adeline complained about us staying late." As Adeline rarely complained about anything at all, Rainer understood the depth of the sentiment.

"I know. Em's been asking me to come pick her up from practice instead of one of the Non-Elite guys. She was nearly asleep Wednesday when I finally got home. Playing for the Angels is wearing her out. If I ever want to see her awake, I'm gonna have to be home before ten o'clock." He checked his watch again. "I don't want her to know about the whole will thing with Stariff. It'll just freak her out. I was supposed to be in his office a half hour ago. I need to go sign whatever it is I'm signing and then go home before she suspects something."

"Just go," Logan urged, "You told him Wednesday you had to, and he said it was fine."

"Yeah, after I got a lecture about my work being my top priority."

"Stariff's not gonna stick around forever on a Friday night. He doesn't have a boss. He's the head of the Senate Legal Department."

With a nod, Rainer swallowed down his nervousness, called himself a coward, and then leaned into Vindico's office.

"Sir, I need to head on to my meeting with Stariff, and then I need to get home. Emily and I are leaving early for New York tomorrow."

"Fine, Lawson, have a nice trip. Be careful and call me if anyone shows up there when you're getting the ring duplicated. No one needs to know why you're there. You took Emily to spend the weekend in the city and to visit her uncles, nothing more."

"Yes, sir. I know." Rainer noted that Vindico seemed better about his guys leaving at five, instead of ten, when he felt that he'd given the order to do so.

"Good man. Keep her safe, Lawson."

"Yes, sir." Rainer rushed back to his desk to grab his badge, pistol, and the file folder Stariff had given him with the documentation making all of the Lawson family fortune Logan's if anything should ever happen to him.

After apologizing repeatedly for being late, Rainer rushed through the documents of his last will and testament.

"Tell Dan not to burn you out yet. Some people still have a life to live." Stariff pointed to three additional lines on the lengthy document that required Rainer's signature.

Though he would never have quoted that to his boss, he did find the statement both true and almost heartless. Vindico would stop at nothing to avenge Amelia, his fiancée, who had been kidnapped from their home and brutally murdered by Wretchkinsides.

Rainer never questioned Vindico's obsession with revenge. It was a banner he would gladly carry alongside his boss. The unspeakable emptiness Vindico must be living with haunted Rainer. He would carry those unending moments of sheer terror after Emily had been attacked with him forever.

"All right, Lawson, sign here and here, and you can go home to your sweet redhead. I think this is a brilliant decision. Stephen was right. You are one hell of a guy, and Emily Anne is a lucky girl." Mr. Stariff had been a friend of the Haydenshires since long before either

Rainer or Emily had been born. He tended to still view Emily as a little girl with freckles and pigtails, but Rainer appreciated his assessment.

"Thanks. I'm just trying to keep her safe. If my uncle ever tried anything, or someone else," Rainer choked as he discussed his own demise, "Logan would make sure Em had access to everything without her being in danger."

"I know, son. That's why I said it was a brilliant decision." Stariff gathered the documents and formed them into a solid block. The paper representation of Rainer's lifelong goal, to take care of Emily, tapped succinctly against the cherry wood desk.

"You're home!" Emily raced to the garage when the Mustang pulled in. Rainer flashed his badge to the officers standing in the driveway. They nodded and quickly fell into their squad cars, thankful to be off for the evening as well.

He and Logan had worked up a story to cover why Logan might be home before him in case they had to use it.

"Hey there, baby." Rainer drew her into his arms. She'd already showered and changed into a pair of tight sweatpants with Arlington written down her right leg and Angel scrolled across her backside.

Her beautiful face was scrubbed free of makeup. Her faint freckles, the ones that Rainer adored but she hated, were showing. Emily had donned one of Rainer's old Ioses T-shirts on top of her sweats.

As she folded into Rainer's arms, he was immediately aware that she was no longer wearing a bra. Her ample cleavage slid against his chest as she squeezed him and sighed contentedly. His mouth watered as he inhaled the sweet spicy scent of her.

Emily raised her head and gave him her deliciously mischievous grin as she felt the effect she'd had stiffen against her stomach.

She blushed slightly, and Rainer chuckled. She tried so hard to be more wanton than she was really capable. She wanted to be qualified as extremely experienced, but Rainer found her sweet innocence absolutely intoxicating.

"We ordered Chinese." She took his hand and led him inside their home. It was small and occupied by Logan and Adeline as well, but Emily was there and the cozy familiarity eased his endless week.

"Good. I'm starved." Rainer grabbed a box of shrimp fried rice and fell onto the sofa.

Emily snuggled in beside him, and the exhaustion washed from his soul. It was replaced by hunger. A hunger that was fed not by the rice he was devouring but by watching her run her fingers through her long auburn hair, watching her emerald eyes glimmer as she smiled up at him, and her soft curves melding into his muscled frame.

"Did you see the papers this morning?" Emily rolled her eyes.

Rainer shook his head. "Vindico pretty much buried me in work and told me to dig my way out."

"They're saying that you've been seeing Samantha Peterson on the side for a few years and that you were hiding it from me because you lived at our house."

Rainer rolled his eyes. "Where do they come up with this crap? Why Samantha or anyone else they've said I cheated on you with for the last five years? How do they pick them? Why can't they just say Rainer's crazy over Emily Haydenshire, and she will always be it for him, and let that be it?"

Emily brushed a kiss over his cheek. "It's okay. I know that, so that's all I need," she assured him, though he knew the constant insistence that he was cheating occasionally shook her confidence.

"What did Vindico make you do tonight?"

Rainer appreciated the subject change, though he remembered to phrase his response carefully. "Mostly we've been going over old evidence. He's trying to get us caught up on the past few years that they've been after key members of the Interfeci."

"Vindico is about to bust wanting to find out everything Mitch's dad knows," Logan jumped in as he stood to get another egg roll.

"How'd you get out?" Rainer quizzed stupidly.

"Wait, you didn't leave together?" Emily's brow furrowed.

Logan came to his rescue just as he always did. "No. Vindico sent Rainer down to legal to get a few things. Dad came in and told him to let us go home—that we'd worked enough this week. He sounded kind of pissed. He told Vindico that working constantly and not having a life outside of the office meant that Wretchkinsides was already winning."

Emily nodded. "Good for Dad. I haven't seen you all week."

"Aww Em, I never knew you cared like that," Logan harassed as he walked by and tousled Emily's hair.

She rolled her eyes. "I don't."

Rainer laughed as Logan feigned heartbreak. "We have all weekend in New York. It'll be nice to get away for a while."

He set his empty box on the coffee table and grinned as Emily laid her head in his lap. Her eyes held a spark of the fire he loved to ignite. They darkened slightly. Her lips were swollen. They needed to be kissed.

"Yeah, I can't wait." She bit her lip and then with a sassy smirk, she pulled the quilt up higher until his lap was covered, and she traced her index finger along his zipper line with her eyes locked on his.

Rainer's entire body tensed in need. It had been too long. The week with its terror and exhaustion had taken too much, and he'd done nothing to restore their physical relationship.

"Let's go to bed," Rainer all but commanded. His voice was low and eager. He hadn't meant to let his need show so readily.

Logan rolled his eyes. "It's barely seven thirty. Keep your pants on, geez."

"We have to get up early, and I'm tired," Emily lied.

"Right." Logan shook his head.

"Night." Rainer led Emily toward their bedroom.

He didn't particularly care what Logan thought. He wanted her underneath him, with her eyes closed and that tight, silk channel enveloping him completely.

He needed to hear her moan and gasp her approval as he took her. He wanted to worship her, to feel her in his hands as he caressed and pulled the erotic energy from her. He wanted to explode inside of her, and everything and everyone else could just wait outside the door.

CHAPTER 10
NEW YORK, NEW YORK

Rainer's phone sounded at five. He groaned and slapped his hand across it. The sun had yet to make an appearance in their bedroom, but he was thrilled to wake up with Emily in his arms and her hair cascaded across his chest.

He allowed himself a long, drawn-out minute to recall her begging him for more the night before as he'd made her all his own.

A long groaned, "No," was her morning greeting.

Rainer chuckled. "Hey there, baby. We'd better get going."

She whimpered and slid farther down under the covers. "Come on. You get to see Tad and Nathan, and I feel very certain that I'll be spending a great deal of time in Bloomingdale's. I was thinking I'd see if I could score us a room at the Gansevoort."

Her eyes blinked open as a broad grin spread across her face.

"Really?" She wiggled her way back up the bed to seat herself beside him.

"Yeah, I think we could use a little getaway from everything, and you always say you want to stay there whenever we visit."

"You are the most fantastic fiancé ever."

"Have you had many others?"

She giggled. "No, but as fiancés go, I still say you're the best."

"Good. You deserve the best."

Emily brushed kisses along his bare chest. With a sigh, she crawled out of bed. Her hair was in a tangled mass on her shoulders, and she had sheet marks across her cheeks, but he was quite certain he'd never seen anything more beautiful.

"What?"

He sat up. "I was just thinking how beautiful you are and how lucky I am." He watched her give her customary eye roll at what she considered hyperbole, but he was serious.

She tugged on his hand. "Get up and take me to New York, and then take me *in* New York."

After giving her the ravenous growl she was looking for, Rainer pulled her to him. "So…" He slipped his hand to her backside and massaged it heatedly. "Would you like to be taken in the steam shower or in the whirlpool tub?" He let that imagery play out in his mind.

She shivered and seemed thrilled with what was becoming the focus of their weekend.

"Maybe in the rooftop pool." She waggled her eyebrows at him.

Rainer laughed. He could only imagine what the relentless press, endlessly fascinated with him because of his father, would make of that story.

"Although I'm fairly certain Uncle Tad would come bail us out, I don't think your parents would be too impressed if that came up, say…at Christmas dinner this year."

Emily wrinkled her nose. "Yeah, probably should skip the rooftop pool."

"Don't worry. We can make use of many of the surfaces at the Gansevoort without getting arrested."

She stretched up on her tiptoes and brushed a kiss across his jaw.

A little while later, Emily was still hemming over what to pack. Rainer shot her a knowing grin and tried to hurry her along.

"We need to go, baby. We're coming home tomorrow. You don't need much."

"I'm almost done. I was just trying to decide what to wear for you tonight."

He raised his left eyebrow in intrigue. "How about nothing at all?"

"But I need something to sleep in."

He wrapped his hands around her waist and pulled her to him. "I'll keep you warm." He lavished her mouth with a long drawn kiss. "Inside and out."

"I can't wait."

"If you hurry, we can get out of here."

She whisked away from him and threw something that was skimpy, hunter-green, and all satin and lace in her bag as he pretended to sneak a peek.

She donned the stacked ring set her uncle had given her a few years before and, checked her makeup, and declared them ready to go.

Rainer loaded the bags into the Hummer. While Emily ran back inside to grab a few Dr Peppers, he projected a detection cast over the car like Vindico had instructed him to do before she rode anywhere. There was no detectable energy anywhere except inside the battery, so once Emily returned, they were off.

"This is the first road trip we've taken since we got engaged."

Rainer grinned at her and made his way toward the interstate. "Am I supposed to do anything differently now that we're engaged than I would have when we were dating?" He pulled into the gas station he always stopped at just before getting on the interstate.

As he put the Hummer in park and turned off the engine, she cocked her jaw to the side and raised her left eyebrow. "Well, you always said we couldn't have sex in your car, but this is my car."

He brushed a quick kiss across her lips. "That's not true, Miss Haydenshire. I said our first time wasn't going to be in my car."

He filled the Hummer and then went inside to purchase her favorite cinnamon candies and a few other snacks, along with additional Dr Peppers. He thought it might be nice to have some in the hotel room.

When he returned, Emily was on her phone. "We'll be careful, Mom," she sighed. "I promise."

. . .

They'd been on the turnpike for a little while, talking and laughing. Since she had him locked in a car, Emily decided to corner him about wedding plans.

Rainer tried to answer her questions, but truthfully, anything that got them married was all he really wanted. He didn't care much about the details.

He was good with Governor Carrington performing it in his office, but as he recalled all the times Emily had begged him to play wedding with her when they were growing up, he knew the dress and the details meant a great deal to her.

Her cell phone rang again, and Rainer hit the brakes as he entered New York gridlock.

"Hey, Uncle Tad." She grinned. "Yeah, well, if you want a turn, I think you'll have to get in line behind Rainer and Dad."

Rainer furrowed his brow and studied her.

"To severely injure the guys who tried to take me," Emily whispered. Rainer nodded his adamant agreement.

"Really?" Emily exclaimed excitedly. "Oh, thank you. You are the best uncle ever!" The sudden turn of Emily's mood had Rainer smiling again. "Okay, well, we've been on the turnpike for about fifteen minutes, so we'll be there in about an hour, I guess."

She fell silent for a moment before continuing, "No, Rainer's going to try to get us a room at the Gansevoort."

"I know, but we don't want to put you and Nathan out." Her eyes twinkled as her mouth fell open. She laughed as her cheeks colored again. "Uncle Tad," she gasped.

Rainer could hear Tad talking.

"Okay, well, that isn't the only reason we're not staying with you."

A few minutes later, Emily ended the call and began bouncing in her seat. "Uncle Tad is getting us the room, and Nathan knows Vera Wang."

"Who is Vera Wang?"

She rolled her eyes. "She's like the most amazing wedding dress designer ever."

"Ah, and I take it you would like to have a Vera Wang gown?"

"I don't know, maybe, but I kind of don't want one that's been in every bridal magazine. Mom said I could wear hers if I want."

"And have we decided when I might get to see you in the dress at the end of an aisle?" Rainer winked at her as he edged the Hummer forward in New York traffic.

"I don't know. I'm thinking spring when the cherry trees bloom, but I just can't decide," she hemmed. "Our last challenge will be at the big Summation Exhibition the day after Christmas, so definitely after that. I want to have a long honeymoon."

"Why's that?"

She giggled deliciously as she slid her hand to his crotch. "Because there's so much I want to do with you."

A shuddered moan escaped Rainer's lungs as he tried to remember to concentrate on the traffic surrounding their car. The flirtatious challenge in her eyes had him reeling.

He began to ponder what might happen if he tapped into her rebellious side this weekend. They had a night to play in one of her favorite cities, and he decided to make the most of their reprieve.

CHAPTER 11

THE GANSEVOORT HOTEL

After fighting through the horrendous traffic for well over an hour, Rainer pulled up to the Gansevoort. He was forced into the valet lane, but he certainly wasn't allowing anyone that kind of access to Emily's car or luggage. He rolled down the window as the attendant approached. The heat from the city and the bright sunlight hit him in a suffocating blast.

"Tad Anderson phoned a little while ago and booked our room."

"Ah yes, Mr. Anderson did call. I spoke with him myself. He booked one of our suites for the evening for a Mr. and Mrs. Rainer Lawson?"

Emily glowed and bit her lip in delight.

With a slight chuckle, Rainer nodded. "Yeah, that's us." He winked at her as she tried not to giggle.

"I'd be happy to park the car for you, Mr. Lawson, and we'll bring your luggage up immediately."

"Thank you, but I'll take care of the car and the luggage."

He'd been lectured repeatedly by Vindico on all the many things Wretchkinsides did or had done in the past to get what he wanted. Having employees at banks, hotels, restaurants, media venues, everything from cleaning service companies to sanitation workers all fell into the complicated Interfeci structure, and all were paid very well to get Wretchkinsides information he wanted.

Rainer parked and helped Emily out. She grabbed her purse and makeup bag. He grabbed the suitcase and then casted the Hummer in a fierce shield cast.

They entered the sleek check-in area of the Gansevoort hotel. The bar glowed from their left, lit with purple, green, and blue neon lights. Emily took it all in with a beaming grin as Rainer secured the keycards and guided her to the elevators.

After checking the corridor to make certain no one was watching them, Rainer summoned and passed his magnetized hand over the keycard reader. He held the door open to let Emily enter ahead of him.

She took in the opulent contemporary décor of their suite. He thought it was a little over the top, but he knew she loved the hot-pink and purple accents on the cushioned headboard of the king-sized bed. Sexy imagery of couples photographed around the city hung on large canvases in the suite. There was a rounded, hot-pink couch near the window that offered them a view of Chelsea. A wet bar, a glass-topped desk, and a sleek black dresser ran along one wall.

"Wow!" She moved into the large, tiled bathroom. Rainer followed after her. The bathroom was decorated in shades of steely grays and onyx black. There was a large steam shower along with a stand-alone bathtub, plenty big enough for two.

Rainer chuckled at her exuberance as he glanced at his watch. They needed to get to the jewelry shop so Tad could start copying the ring.

He pulled Emily against his chest and smiled as she wrapped her arms around him.

"I think,"—he squeezed a handful of her luscious backside—"we should go see your uncles so Tad can get started on the ring and then I think we should come back and you should let me give you a bath," he rasped in her ear.

She trembled in his arms, and Rainer's heart gave its customary longing beats that occurred every time he thought of her naked and in his arms.

"And what shall I give you?" Her sassy flirting always made him ache.

"Don't worry. I'll show you, baby."

Her breaths quickened. She slipped her hand to his zipper and began massaging and groping him as he stiffened all for her.

"Well, I think,"—she led him out of the bathroom—"that Uncle Tad can wait just a few more minutes." She pushed him down on the pink couch.

"Do you?" Rainer began unbuttoning her shirt. All thoughts of racing to the jewelry shop flitted quickly from his mind. She gave a heavy nod as she loosened his belt and popped the snap on his jeans.

He watched the fervent storm begin to swirl in her eyes. Need surged through her as her energy began to spike.

He moved to kiss her, but she stopped him with a naughty grin and fell to her knees in front of him. She'd revealed his cock, strained tight and needy for her.

A hungry growl echoed from deep within him as she dragged her tongue up his length. She licked him, then ran her fingers down his thickened veins. She reached lower and cupped him as he panted.

She swirled her tongue around his head and then drew him in deep and drowned him in her mouth.

She moaned as she continued her work. He'd never felt anything so exquisite as the vibrations of her voice rocked through him. She bathed and sucked him as she spun her tongue along his ridge. As she sucked, she pulled his erotic energy into her rhythm strains straight from the source.

He was going to lose it. He started to panic. Every move she made drove him wild. Her long hair swept across his thighs softly, and he pulsed in her mouth. She moaned again. He had to stop her.

"Em, baby, stop," he pled. She swirled her tongue again before releasing him.

"Why?" Her hot breaths lashed his throbbing cock before she drowned him in that heavenly fire again.

He groaned from the sensation. "Baby, please," he begged, but the last thing he wanted her to do was stop. His mind filled with the erotic thoughts of her drinking him. He shook himself.

"Stop, Em, I'm gonna…" he tried to explain. His body was at an all-out war with his mind.

"That's the whole idea," she purred and huffed hot breath around his length. She went back for more. She pulled him deep and he bucked, unable to stop himself.

Everywhere she touched or licked set him on fire. He throbbed in her mouth once more. "God, baby, drink me," he begged.

A low, guttural groan tore from his lungs as he watched her drink him dry.

"Damn," he panted as she slid back onto the couch. She appeared rather proud of herself. "Are you laughing at me?" He was still unable to move and could barely catch his breath.

"You're cute," she teased.

"That's not how that's supposed to work." He was still unable to believe what she'd just done. He tried to rectify the situation, but she shook her head.

"You can make it up to me later."

"Gladly."

"We need to go see Uncle Tad."

"Yeah, just give me a minute to try to wipe this stupid grin off my face."

She smirked. "Get it together, Lawson. You don't want Uncle Tad to know I just gave you a blow job."

"Ah, more Christmas dinner conversation."

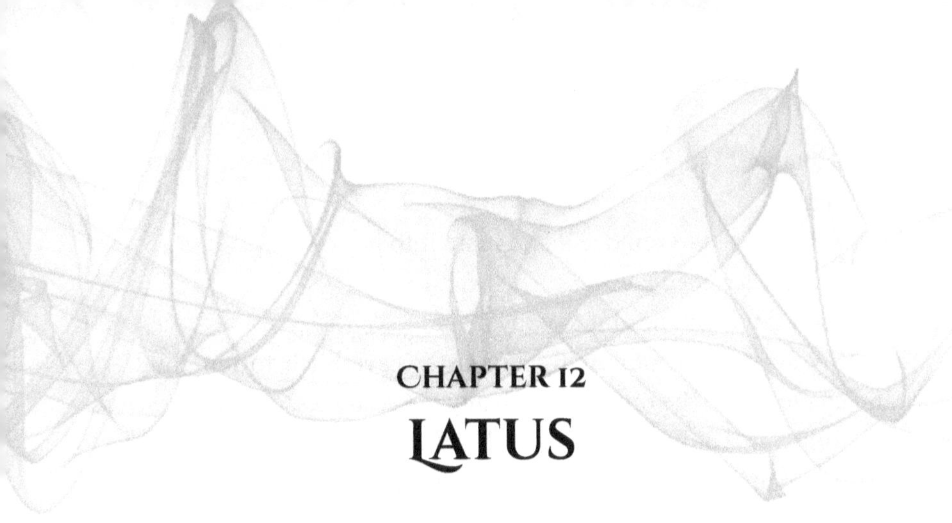

CHAPTER 12

LATUS

Rainer hailed a cab and directed the driver to Latus Jewels, Tad and Nathan's shop deep in the heart of Chelsea.

Emily glowed as she entered the small shop full of unique pieces of jewelry and high-end gifts.

"There they are. I was wondering where you'd gotten to. Nathan was all, 'You got them a room at the Gansevoort. They're making use of that, of course.'" Tad rolled his eyes, and Rainer tried very hard not to blush. "How is my favorite niece?" He hugged Emily tight.

She laughed. "I'm your only niece."

"Okay, fine, you're my favorite niece or nephew. Just don't tell your brothers."

"Emily, Rainer." Nathan smiled as he came around the glass counters to give them both hugs. "Look at his face. I told you they were having fun in the room."

Rainer glowed bright red, and Emily laughed hysterically. There was no one else in the store, so Tad lifted Emily's left hand and began studying the ring.

"Very nice." He pulled out a jeweler's loupe. "So, you had no idea?"

"No idea," Rainer confirmed.

"And the transference goes through the band, so it's virtually undetectable." Tad grabbed a few sheets of paper and began sketching the ring.

Emily started to remove it and hand it to her uncle.

"No." He stopped her.

"But…don't you need it to copy it?"

"My sweet, precious Emily, my sister gave birth to ten children, and so far you're the only one with any taste, so please, child, leave the ring on so it will keep you safe. I'll make a few sketches, write a few notes, bada bing, bada boom, Uncle Tad is a hero, you have two rings, and you become the most fantastic Arlington Angel ever known without cheating."

With that, he gave a deep bow as Rainer and Emily laughed. "Here, you come over here, and look at some of my ideas for the wedding, while I sketch."

Since Tad was holding Emily's hand, he guided her toward one of the back glass display cases.

Rainer followed but gestured to Nathan. "So, I need a wedding ring that will match her engagement ring. Do I let her pick that out?"

Nathan smiled. "Let Tad design it for her. You know she'll love that."

"All right." Tad wrote one more note on his sketch and then smiled. "Now, I know you're all engaged lovebirds, but I don't get to see either of you very often, so when Lill called last night, I took the liberty of making reservations for you two at Nightingales."

Emily's mouth fell open. "Uncle Tad, oh my gosh." She threw her arms around his neck.

"But after dinner, you have to come over and have drinks at our place before you go off to enjoy the Gansevoort," he insisted.

Emily was jumping up and down.

Rainer tried hard not to laugh at her outright. "Thank you. I could never have gotten us in there."

Tad scoffed, "I'm pretty sure you could have, Mr. Lawson, but as you don't care for using your name to get you places, then it does help to have uncles who have people who owe them favors."

"Oh my gosh, Nightingales," Emily buzzed. "I don't have anything to wear."

"Hmm, now where on earth in New York City could a girl find a dress for dinner? I mean, the city just has nothing to offer," Nathan joked.

"You are the best uncles ever in the history of uncledom," she vowed again and hugged him tightly.

"And don't you ever forget that," Tad drawled. "All right, now go shop. I'll have the ring ready tomorrow. Your reservations are at seven. Be at our apartment by ten, or I'm calling the governor."

CHAPTER 13
QUITE A NIGHT

Several hours and many department stores later, Emily had located a dress she deemed worthy of New York's most romantic restaurant and had picked out a new coat and tie for Rainer.

Once he was ready, he settled himself on the couch to watch television while Emily finished.

He let his mind recall in great detail everything they'd done on the couch earlier in the day. He glanced at the watch that had been his father's to note how many hours it would be before he could get her back to the room and make up for what she'd done for him.

He was lost in dizzying fantasies when Emily emerged from the bathroom.

"Wow, you look gorgeous, baby."

She spun for him, and he let a low whistle slide between his teeth. She was wearing a strapless hunter-green dress with a very short skirt and stiletto heels with straps around her ankles.

Her ample cleavage was on stunning display in the low-cut dress. Her hair was pulled up in a loose twist with just a few tendrils cascading softly around her face. Her neck was exposed, and Rainer longed to kiss it and drag his teeth along her tender skin.

"Absolutely gorgeous."

"Thank you." She bit her lip sweetly. His eyes tracked downward. He deeply admired the way her backside looked in the figure-hugging dress.

"Are you certain you want to go out tonight?" he flirted shamelessly. "We could stay here, and I could help you out of that dress."

Emily giggled and shook her head. "First dinner, then you can play, Mr. Lawson."

"Oh, I intend to do more than play, sweetheart." He watched her skin flush. The rosy-pink heat crept seductively up her bare neck and pooled in her cheeks. It drove him wild.

To prove his point, he brushed a kiss across the spot where her neck met her shoulder. He kept kissing across her collarbone until he spun his tongue in the hollow of her neck, making her whimper slightly. Her eyes closed as she reveled in the sensation.

"We are going to Nightingales," she insisted in a breathless pant.

Rainer decided perhaps he would simply draw out their evening rather than trying to get her to shorten it.

"Just a preview, baby."

A slight moan escaped her as he took her hand and led her toward the door.

The maître d' held the door for them as they entered the beautiful restaurant. Lit only by candles and fireplaces, the red walls gave the restaurant an extravagant feel.

In true Tad style, he'd booked Rainer and Emily one of the best tables in the house. It was a rounded booth, complete with red velvet-cushioned seating and a long, pristine, white tablecloth, that sat in the back corner of the large restaurant. The table was nestled behind a grand staircase and near one of the fireplaces, which blocked it from the view of other patrons.

Rainer gestured for Emily to enter the booth before he slid in beside her. The table was lit with two long candles. Red roses stood gracefully in a thin vase in the center.

"This is so beautiful," Emily whispered as she studied the romantic surroundings.

Rainer wasn't quite able to admire the décor. She just looked too devastatingly delicious, and he wanted to let her know dinner was only to be the beginning of their evening.

"Not as beautiful as what I'm looking at." He gazed deeply into her eyes. She scooted closer to him and brushed a kiss across his cheek.

He drew measured breaths and tried to leash his lust.

"I'm starving." Focusing on the menu didn't seem to help. Desperate desire coursed through his blood as he took in Emily, lit by the fireplace and the candles. He caught the scent of her perfume in the wafting heat from the flames. She reached to hold his hand in her lap, and his heart thundered against his rib cage.

A waiter appeared with a water pitcher, took their drink order, and then recommended the oysters or the scallops for an appetizer.

Rainer gestured for Emily to pick. She shrugged slightly and bit her lip. She and Rainer had eaten oysters at the beach the summer before. Neither were huge fans, but Rainer ventured to guess the oysters they were serving at Nightingales that evening were vastly better than those being steamed on the beach.

"Let's go with the scallops," Rainer guessed.

Emily looked relieved. The waiter gave a polite smile and disappeared.

"Baby, why didn't you just say you wanted the scallops?" Rainer tried to get her to relax a little. She blushed, only furthering his desire as he studied her.

"I don't know. Oysters are supposed to be a romantic thing to eat. And this is such a romantic restaurant." Her blush became more pronounced. "I've been with you since I was four. Why am I nervous?" She seemed to ask this of the air around their table, and she sounded thoroughly baffled.

He put his arm around her and drew her closer. "First of all, I think you're nervous because I haven't really had the means to bring you places like this until very recently, and dating as adults out of the academy is different. I'm a little nervous too. Not to mention everything that's happened since we started working."

He didn't want her to spend too much time thinking about their harrowing week. He wanted her mind on what he had planned for her that evening.

She gave a slight nod and laced her fingers through his. She drew from him deeply and allowed his protective energy to soothe her.

Rainer tried to be discreet, but the feeling of their energy swirling together was heavenly. He fought the desire to take her anywhere more private and then fill her full of his energy, his love, and his release. He swallowed down his need. "Besides, I don't need oysters as an aphrodisiac, baby." He reached over and let his thumb caress her neck and shoulder. "Just looking at you in that dress is about to drive me right over the edge. Oysters might have been more than I could handle."

She shivered and then allowed his energy to calm her. She relaxed against him.

"You are so beautiful, and it's just us, okay? I want you to enjoy this. Get whatever you want. Let's just try to forget the rest of the world for tonight."

"That sounds perfect."

Rainer kissed the side of her head and let himself enjoy the feeling of her beside him as the heat from the fireplace enveloped them.

The waiter returned with their scallops and sparkling water. Since they were having drinks with Tad and Nathan later, Rainer and Emily had decided to forgo wine with dinner. She had informed Rainer that she wanted the red snapper for her entrée, so when the waiter asked, he ordered for her and added his New York strip steak at the end.

This had always been Emily's preference. It made her feel taken care of. He'd figured this out when he'd taken her to dinner before one of the many academy formals they'd attended in the past six years.

Since taking care of Emily was always his top priority, he'd taken the responsibility seriously, but he'd been chastised in the papers over it on several occasions.

After the waiter wrote down Rainer's preferences for his steak, he smiled. "Now, we want you to have an intimate dining experience here at Nightingales, so I won't bother you after your meal orders are placed unless you need something else. When you're ready for dessert, or if you should need anything at all, simply flip this tab upward." He pointed to a small, hinged tab on the wall near their table. "And I'll be by to take care of you."

"Thank you." Rainer began to understand why this was New York's most romantic restaurant. He settled back in the booth and kept his arm wrapped around Emily. Several intriguing thoughts swirled in his mind, but he didn't want to do anything that would make her uncomfortable.

"So, are we thinking 'gosh, we're paying a lot of money to not be waited on constantly,' or are we thinking 'hmm, I wonder how far she'll let me get in a restaurant?'" Emily sassed.

Rainer laughed. She knew him far too well. "Definitely the second. I don't give a damn how much it costs to get to sit here looking at you and spend the evening listening to you laugh, getting to really talk to you uninterrupted. Even if all I get to do is hold your hand, it's worth every penny."

The darkened restaurant and the quiet, secluded booth began to take on the feeling of the sanctuary he'd been seeking. No press, no Wretchkinsides, no interruptions. No one, other than her family, even knew they were in town.

Peace washed through him as she settled beside him and laid her head on his shoulder.

She seemed to have come to the same conclusion. "I take it you like the dress?"

Rainer thought she must've somehow missed the dozens of mirrors in the restaurant and apparently also the ones in their room.

"Baby, you look phenomenal. Absolutely stunning. We're not staying at your uncles' long, because all I can think about is getting you out of it."

A mischievous light danced in her emerald eyes. She scooted closer and gave him a naughty grin. "Good." Her blinks were heavy. Her lips were already swollen, full, and ripe, eager for his kiss. "And that shouldn't take too long," she drawled seductively, "because there's nothing underneath it."

Every muscle in Rainer's body seized in anticipation. "Em,"—his hot breath caressed over her neck and shoulders—"you're driving me wild, baby. I may take you right here."

She shivered deliciously. He let his eyes close and drew from her until he could feel her energy around him. Need, desire, pent-up emotion, and fear—they were all there. The looks she gave him said she wanted him to soothe each and every strained rhythm.

Before he could address any of the things he felt from her, the waiter returned with a large platter of food.

Rainer reminded himself that they were, in fact, in a restaurant full of people. The waiter left a pitcher of water for them. After supplying them with their meals, he reminded them of the tab if they should need anything else.

Rainer thanked him again and waited on Emily to take a bite of her snapper. "This is delicious."

He cut into his steak. He agreed with her assessment, but he couldn't seem to get his mind off of her.

He chastised himself for acting like he hadn't quite finished puberty. His eyes couldn't seem to remain anywhere but on her cleavage displayed in plump perfection in the low-cut dress.

Stop staring at her. You get to go back to the room with her. Get it together.

But I know how beautiful they are, what they feel like in my hands, what they feel like when they swell against me when I'm inside of her, his body argued with his mind.

A slight giggle escaped Emily. "Uh Rainer, baby, my eyes are up here."

"Uh-huh, but I really want my hands to be right there." He watched her neck and chest flush from his desires. She seemed thrilled that she was so thoroughly distracting him. Her pleasure over his need did nothing to quell his overactive libido.

The release she'd given him earlier had driven him mad all day. It had been amazing, but it felt unfair. He wanted to give her everything she'd taken from him and more. He wanted desperately to taste her, to touch her, to feel her pulse around him, and to revel in the way she swelled tight just before she came all for him.

She leaned over and breathed a sweet kiss across his cheek. "Don't worry, I'll take care of you when we get back to the hotel."

But that wasn't what he wanted. He knew as soon as the words exited her lips. He swallowed down another bite of steak and took a long sip of his water. He leaned back and wrapped his arm around her. He drew her closer until his mouth was right beside her ear.

"No, baby," he corrected, "tonight is all about you." He ran his thumb up and down her arm. As most rational thought left the head above his beltline, he began explaining his desires.

"I want to taste you. I want to touch you and suck you. I want to feel you come around me. I want to hear those sweet sounds you make only for me." Her body tensed in sweet anticipation. "I want to make love to you all night." His voice was rough and reverent from need. "And quite honestly,"—he studied her and watched her eyes as they darkened and her cheeks as they flushed deliciously—"I want to start right now." He kissed her neck just below her earlobe.

Deep desire mixed in with her heady need as her energy began swirling in jagged peaks all around him. She shuddered in lust-filled anticipation. She studied him. He saw the fear and bewilderment behind the raging storm of temptation in her eyes.

He slid his hand to her thigh as her breath caught. Her eyes flashed hot with desire. He kneaded her thigh in his hand, edging higher, but then he pulled it away and cut another bite of steak.

He wanted the desire to build, and he wanted to make certain he wasn't doing anything she didn't want him to do.

The look she shot him said that the very last thing she wanted was for him to stop. So, with a smirk, he took another sip of water and glanced around to make absolutely certain no one could see the two of them or what he was about to do.

He leaned back to her. "No one can see us, baby. No one knows what I'm about to do to you."

She nodded heavily. He slipped his hand back to her thigh and began massaging again. She let her legs fall open for him. He stifled a groan.

To watch her offer herself up to his touch drove him wild. He edged his hand higher, and he continued to grope.

"You have to be quiet, baby," he soothed. "Can you do that for me?" But then with a grin he winked at her, as she spread her legs farther.

Her eyes were desperate, and need quaked in her rhythms. "Let's see if I can help with that, actually."

He quickly summoned with the hand that wasn't on her leg. He used just one of the many moves Vindico had taught him and summoned the sound waves around their table, then pushed them out, creating a sound barrier.

"Touch me, Rainer," she begged in a pleading whisper just as she had that night on the beach. He pulsed and then willed himself to calm and give this to her. He wanted to give her everything she wanted.

He used the long tablecloth and the high table as a cover. He slipped his hand under the short skirt of her dress.

She shuddered. Her body seized as he traced his fingers up her inner thighs and slowly drew patterns on her legs.

He edged closer and closer to where she wanted to be touched with each pass. With the next reach, he felt the heat her body emanated for him.

Rainer glanced around again and made certain he was not only giving her what she wanted but that he was protecting her as well. The few patrons he could see from his vantage point were eating and talking or laughing. He saw several long sultry kisses in a few booths, but no one even seemed aware they were there.

He slid his hand higher and watched her eyes beg him for release. He leaned closer, granting himself a better angle.

"Are you already wet for me, baby?"

A slight moan escaped her, but she quelled it quickly. He glanced around again to make certain his sound barrier cast held. It had. No one had heard her. "I know you are. Let me feel it." His declaration drove her wild.

With a smooth languid movement, he sipped his water, checked the area again, and slipped his fingers between her lips.

She was dripping wet and fevered. She leaned back slightly. She wanted him in deeper. The realization caused a slight groan to escape him. She shuddered against him. He held her eyes with his own and watched the fear play in them for a moment, but then she gave in to the need.

"No one can see you. They have no idea I'm touching you. Let me take care of you." He continued to massage her. He spun his fingers over her clit, then moved back and made her tense and pant as she tried to quell the all-consuming feeling. Her breaths became frantic as she clenched her jaw and shook her head slightly.

"Just feel it. It feels good, doesn't it, sweetheart?" He slipped his fingers deeper into the hot, slick space.

Her muscles clenched around his hand. She laid her head on his shoulder. He shielded her and let her writhe against him. He held her in what would appear to be a hug as he continued to whisper.

"Come on, baby. Give it to me. I want to feel you come in my hand. Let me make it feel better."

Her eyes flashed wildly as she buried her face in his shoulder. She couldn't quite give it up. Her energy would spike, but she would push it away. He felt her pulse and swell, and he decided to do whatever it took to finish the job.

"When I get you back to the room, I'm gonna lay you out." She moaned, and he kissed her before continuing. "I'm gonna hold you down and make you take it until you scream all for me. I'm gonna fill you so full you ache. Make you take it all."

With that, she came undone. She writhed in his arms and buried her moans deep in his collar. She tensed in waves around his hand.

"That's it," Rainer soothed as she clung to him. He pulled his hand away and drew it across the napkin in his lap as he watched to make certain she was all right. Her breath was still frantic, but she calmed a moment later.

"Dessert, sweetheart?" He waggled his eyebrows with a slight smirk as he gestured to the dessert menu. She kept her urgent eyes locked on his.

"Take me back to the room. I need you inside me."

Rainer kissed her cheek and kept her cradled in his arms. He released the barrier he'd been holding.

"Not yet, baby. You haven't even eaten your fish, and then we'll have dessert. It's not time to leave for Tad's yet, but I promise you, I'll make it worth your wait."

She gave him a look that said for him to come and take whatever he wanted. He closed his eyes lest he drag her from the restaurant and back to the room. He drew a steadying breath and reminded himself to eat the steak.

A few minutes later, he reached and flipped the tab up to alert the waiter that they'd like dessert.

"Are we ready for dessert then?" the waiter quizzed. Rainer noted his smirk and prayed he hadn't noticed where his hands had just come from.

"Could we split a bowl of your sorbet?" He grew more uncomfortable with the look on the guy's face the longer he stood before them.

"Certainly, sir." The waiter nodded. Emily engaged him in several sweet kisses while they waited. He kept his arm draped around her as he whispered how beautiful she was and how much he loved her.

A moment later, Rainer's head lifted as did Emily's. A different waiter was approaching their table. He was coming from the pastry chef's kitchen, and he was Gifted. Waves of Occamist energy swirled around him. He looked thrilled with who was seated at the table. Rainer cursed under his breath.

The waiter beamed at them with a great deal of show as he set the bowl of mixed sorbet balls between Rainer and Emily. He completed the picture with two spoons.

"Thanks." Rainer prayed he'd leave quickly.

"I'm really not allowed to do this," the guy began to gush.

"Then why don't you stop?" Rainer hadn't meant to be rude, but he didn't want a media circus. He needed as few people as possible to know they were in New York.

Emily elbowed him. "What did you need?" She smoothed over his terse reply.

"I was just wondering if I could get your picture and maybe your autographs? You're the it couple now, right? And you're the newest Angel."

With a slight sigh, Emily hemmed. "We'll be happy to sign something for you, but could we skip the photo? It seems hard for people to resist putting them all over the Internet."

Rainer narrowed his eyes, daring the guy to argue. He looked deeply disappointed.

Photo or not, this was it. Their whereabouts would be known all over the Realm within a matter of moments.

"Sure." The waiter shrugged dejectedly. He grabbed an empty notepad, used for taking orders, and handed it to Emily.

"Your name?"

"Roger."

With a grin, Emily picked up one of the spoons and tasted one of the raspberry sorbet balls. She wrote, "Roger, thanks for the great sorbet," then shooting a vexing gaze to Rainer, she continued, "Nightingales gave us an amazing night to remember. Thanks, Emily Haydenshire AA #3."

Roger slid the pad to Rainer, who signed his name under Emily's. Of all the things that being Joseph Lawson's son brought him, being asked to give his autograph seemed the most ridiculous.

His father had been a great man. People should certainly have wanted his autograph when he was alive. Rainer had done nothing, by his own estimations, and couldn't fathom why anyone would want his signature.

"Great! Thanks!" Roger gazed down at the paper.

"No problem." Emily elbowed Rainer again in an effort to remove the scowl from his face.

Roger left the table, and Emily shook her head at him as she scooped up more sorbet.

"What? I can't have one night with you and no cameras?" He plunged his own spoon into the dessert with more force than was necessary.

"Does that mean you don't want to make a sex tape?" She giggled. Rainer couldn't help but join in her infectious laughter.

"Can you imagine if that got out?" He shuddered at the thought.

"No tapes for us, ever."

"Ever," Rainer reaffirmed.

Emily glanced around the restaurant again. Rainer noted the nervous pulses in her energy streams. She'd picked up on something.

His stomach churned uncomfortably.

With a slight headshake, Emily set her spoon down and wrapped her hands around Rainer's arm. She tried to soothe him, but the nervous twists in her own streams only made him more concerned.

He squeezed her thigh again. This time he kept his hand over her dress. He scooped up more of the raspberry sorbet, her favorite, and fed it to her. Her rhythms began to calm. She seemed to have decided that nothing was wrong after all, or perhaps to pretend that everything was fine. Rainer couldn't quite tell.

He kissed her forehead and stole a few bites of sorbet for himself, which made her giggle. Over half of the large bowl was left, but he was stuffed.

"Do you want some more, baby?" He scooped her up another bite.

She shook her head. "Let's go to Uncle Tad's early."

"Yeah, because then we can leave early, and I can have the rest of my dessert."

Her eyes lit. "What's that?"

With a cocky grin, Rainer chuckled. "You."

He flipped the tab back up, and their original waiter appeared. "Could we get our check, and would you mind calling us a cab?"

"Certainly, sir. Where might you be headed after dinner this evening?"

He knew better than to answer that question, so he smiled and shook his head. "Haven't decided yet."

The disappointment in the guy's eyes had Rainer grinding his teeth.

The check took longer to arrive than any of the food had taken. Rainer tried not to panic. He kept his hands on Emily as he brushed his lips over her cheeks and neck and inhaled the scent of her mixed with the sensuous perfume she was wearing. It was one he'd given her on her last birthday, and she'd worn it with every intention of driving him wild.

Finally, the waiter returned, and Rainer paid the bill quickly, before leaving a tip on the table and standing to help Emily out.

He cursed as they approached the door. He'd known all along. He just hadn't known how to stop it.

"What?" Emily studied the restaurant again.

He gestured his head to the sidewalk, and she understood why the check had been held so long. With a sigh, she let Rainer drape his sport coat over her bare shoulders. She'd been slammed in the press lately for dressing too provocatively for a governor's daughter, and Rainer had been called out for not insisting that she dress more conservatively.

"No one is supposed to know we're here," he huffed.

"Too late for that."

He shoved the door open into a cameraman. A whispered expletive left his lips on the wind. The cab that had been ordered for them was almost a block away. Nightingales wanted shots of them in front of the restaurant. It was good advertisement.

"Why are you in New York, Rainer?" the question came from several reporters. "Have you broken it off with Samantha Peterson?"

Rainer positioned Emily between the brick wall of the restaurant and his body. They started to run.

"Is this a reconciliation?" Reporters raced to keep up.

With a dramatic eye roll, Rainer reminded himself that answering any of the questions only made things worse, so he kept Emily shielded, and they moved as quickly as they were able.

An overzealous photographer leapt in front of them and snapped a picture right in Emily's face.

"Get the hell away from her, now." Rainer shoved the photographer out of her way.

"Are you here for the Angels, Emily?" sang a female reporter, who was keeping up with them.

"Is this for the wedding?" called another.

"Where are you staying?" every reporter surrounding them asked.

Mercifully, the cabbie was holding the door for them.

"Thank you." Rainer allowed himself to breathe as the door shut.

"Are you famous or something, kid?" the cabbie huffed as he fell back in the driver's seat.

"Or something," Rainer lamented. "Call your uncle, baby. He doesn't want all of this at his apartment, and I don't want anyone to know why we're here."

Emily pulled her phone from her purse. "Are you ready to play dodge-the-reporter?"

Rainer chuckled at her eagerness to play the game they'd invented years before right after his father's death.

"Where to, Sinatra?" the driver, in his early sixties, inquired. With a quick glance at Emily, Rainer grinned.

"The Waldorf Astoria and take it nice and slow."

Rainer pulled his cell as well. He scheduled a car to meet them behind the Waldorf.

"I'm sorry," Emily apologized to her uncle. "No, that sounds great. Okay, we'll see you in the morning."

Rainer took a cursory glance at the cars surrounding their cab. It was difficult to tell which of them contained reporters and cameras, but he assumed most of them did.

"I can speed it up. Might lose some of 'em," the cabbie offered kindly.

Rainer smiled and shook his head. "Not trying to lose them. I want them all there."

The cabbie shrugged and slowed down.

"The Waldorf," he called as he opened the door for Emily.

"Thanks a lot." Rainer handed the man the fare with a generous tip.

Emily stepped out of the cab with Rainer right behind her.

This time, though, they moved slowly. Rainer wrapped his arm over her and led her toward the vast entrance of the Waldorf Astoria.

He pulled the door open for her and paused as she engaged him in a long, drawn kiss. The cameras clicked constantly. Rainer swore the noise had been the backdrop of his existence since his father death. The sickening sound of his life being dissected click by click.

They joined other tourists in the grand lobby. The cameras were pressed to the glass doors and continued to snap away.

Rainer guided Emily onto one of the elevators. They exited on the tenth floor and then switched to another. They rode elevators for several long minutes until they finally took another one down to the lobby, laughing the entire time.

They rode the elevator until it had acquired numerous other guests, then they exited with the group of people and discreetly headed to the service entrance door of the hotel.

Rainer glanced around constantly to make certain no one saw

them. He pushed the door to the loading exit open and led Emily to the waiting car, camera-free.

She beamed. "We're getting pretty good at that."

Rainer nodded his begrudged agreement. It would be nice to just take a cab to their actual hotel without having to play games, but that didn't seem like a possibility in the near future.

He held the door for her and instructed the driver to take them to the Gansevoort.

They switched off their phones as soon as they entered the cab. An overzealous reporter might go so far as to try and ping their phone and get their location when they figured out that Rainer and Emily weren't staying at the Waldorf.

The chase may have annoyed him, but it certainly had their blood pumping. The thrill had Emily ready for more.

She leaned into Rainer in the back of the cab, and with one sultry, anticipatory gaze, he devoured her mouth. He let his hand slide down her neck and used the cover his jacket provided to caress her breast as she panted slightly.

"I want you bad, baby." His whispered desires were barely audible even to her. She let her eyes close as she felt his energy swirl rapidly around her.

He tenderly caressed her face with his hand and kissed her exposed neck. Her eyes darkened and her lips swelled. The rebellious desire to be with her alone, despite the Realm's insistence that their whereabouts were always to be known, drove his voracious hunger.

"I want to touch you and taste you. I want to feel you around me. You're always so tight for me, baby. I need to feel it," he demanded in a reverent growl.

His urgency nearly drove her over the edge without him even touching her. Her energy spiked and made him ache to give her what she so clearly wanted.

"The Gansevoort," the driver called. He rolled his eyes at what was going on in his back seat.

"Thanks." Rainer pulled Emily out of the car. They raced through the lobby. They didn't want to be seen, and the need to go somewhere, anywhere more private quaked in their rhythms.

CHAPTER 14

DESSERT

They entered the elevator and waited for an older couple to exit. With every gained floor, they gave each other looks that could ignite the entire building.

The couple smiled at them as they mercifully left Rainer and Emily on the sixth floor. The sliding doors took far too long to shut, but Rainer let the elevator climb a little more before he summoned and halted it in its tracks.

Emily moaned as he pressed her to the wall with his body. He caressed her face and guided her mouth to his as he traced his fingers down her neck and over her cleavage. With his other hand, he hoisted her skirt up as she reached and pressed her hands against his straining length. She began massaging him heatedly.

"Spread your legs for me, baby," he growled as a loud aching moan cried from her, and she did as he'd commanded.

He sucked her bottom lip, pulling his teeth over it, as he plunged her depths with his fingers. She throbbed around his hand, and he dropped to his knees in front of her. He lifted the skirt to reveal her, and separated her slightly. He began circling his tongue slowly along her clit until the liquid form of her energy drowned his lips.

A delicious gasp of approval panted from her body. "Take me to bed now," she demanded.

Rainer forced himself to stop after he'd dipped his tongue inside of her. He allowed the taste of her nectar to satisfy him momentarily.

Releasing the cast on the elevator, he ordered himself to wait as she righted her dress.

After he locked on to the energy of the lift motor, he forced it to climb as fast as it would safely go. He engaged Emily in deep, heated kisses as they rocketed skyward.

"I don't give a damn about the press or anything else. Right now, I just want you. I'm gonna lay you out and have my way with you. Take you hard, make you feel it." Desperation took over his entire body.

"That's all I've wanted all day."

Mercifully, the elevator opened on their floor, and Rainer pulled her toward their room.

He summoned magnetic energy from the air around him and touched the card reader on the door lock. It opened instantly.

He spun Emily into the suite and kicked the door shut as he backed her up to the wall. With a yearning like he'd never felt before, he turned her and had her chest against the wall as he pulled down the zipper of her dress and watched as it fell away from her. Her ass jiggled, and he growled his approval.

"So damn gorgeous." He slid his hands down her rib cage then to her waist. He moved quickly to massage her backside on full display, with her in nothing but heels.

She spun suddenly. Her eyes were dark and needy as she unbuttoned his shirt. He pulled his tie off, unbuttoned his pants, and dropped trou quickly.

She dragged her hands down his chest and traced her fingers over his nipples as his breath caught.

A low, guttural groan echoed from him.

Simply unable to wait any longer, he lifted her into his arms. He laid her out on the large bed that had been turned down for them.

He traced his hands down her stomach and watched her muscles shiver in anticipation as he let his thumbs trace both of her lips. He barely touched her. He throbbed as her needy hips writhed wildly.

"Did you set the cast, baby?" Rainer squeezed his eyes shut as he forced himself to halt long enough to ask. She shook her head. He summoned from the erotic energy that was thrumming all around them. He casted her and closed off her womb.

He added in his own soothing rhythms so she felt no pain and then continued to let his hands track down her inner thighs, past her knees, and over her calves, until he caught her left ankle.

He unbuckled the high heel and pulled it off. After deciding that he planned to set her free of more than just the deliciously high heels, he moved to the other foot.

She bucked and pushed what he wanted to taste into his face as he stood over her. He caught her hips as she let her legs fall open for him.

"Please," she whimpered.

He blew cold breath across the fevered space as he opened her slightly. She cried out for him. He leaned in and began to suck and lick her swollen lips. He consumed everything her body gave up for him. She tasted like heaven. Her breath stuttered as he delved between her folds.

Her moans grew frantic. She couldn't keep from bucking under him. Her energy was too potent. It filled the air around him. He wanted to drown in it. She grasped his hair and pushed him deeper. He growled from her need.

"I'm gonna…" her warning was cut off by her needy moan, but that was exactly what he wanted.

"That's it, baby. Come in my mouth." He lapped his tongue in rhythmic patterns and gave her the force and friction she begged for.

She broke hard, screamed out his name, and gripped the bed sheets underneath her as hips undulated.

He drank her, then moved his hungry kisses to her thigh, replaced his tongue with his fingers, and built her again. He massaged inside of her and slowly edged to where she wanted to be touched. He traced his fingers up over her clit with his other hand as he sucked her inner thigh with frantic urgency until he knew he'd marked her. "You're all mine. All for me."

She went wild as he stroked his fingers over that magic spot once more, and she spiraled into ecstasy.

Their energy danced and rolled in red, heated need. It was so desperate to be joined, the air seemed to vibrate with their longing rhythms.

"Take me now. I want it." Her voice was rough and raspy in her hunger. With a wild look in her eye, she flipped over on all fours and shook her ass in his face. "I want it now."

"Oh, fuck yeah." Rainer had never seen anything so intoxicatingly sexy. An ardent growl spilled from his lungs. He almost lost it all just from watching her like that as she begged to be taken.

He clenched his jaw and ordered himself to remain in control. He grasped her hips and jerked her back over him, piercing through her hard and fast. He'd never felt anything so exquisite. He'd never been so deeply wrapped in the hot, wet perfection of her, and the view was utter bliss. He watched himself enter her repeatedly.

She broke again. They were coming faster now. She pressed back against him with a plea for him not to stop. A moment later, she made another demand that threatened to end it all as she turned back to stare into his eyes, letting him see the fiery storm swirling in their emerald depths. Her back dipped low and her sexy ass tensed against his sac with every pounding thrust.

"Harder," she demanded, and he hammered into her. He forced her open past his hilt and pounded into her. She shuddered and pulsed around him. She swelled, and he couldn't hold out any longer.

"Take it all, baby. I'm gonna fill you full." His demands sent her over the edge again, and he exploded inside her. He collapsed on top of her and tried desperately to catch his breath and to remember to move so he wasn't lying directly on top of her. He rolled to his back and panted in utter ecstasy.

"Okay, wow," she gushed when she'd caught her breath. As everything they'd just done filtered back through his hazy bliss-filled recollections, Rainer grimaced.

He sat up and caressed over her backside. She still hadn't turned over.

"Let me see your leg, baby."

Her brow knitted as she eased over on her back. "Why?"

He spread her legs again and revealed a rather large, purple mark on her upper thigh. It was the approximate shape of his open mouth.

"I'm sorry."

She sat up with her brow still furrowed. "What are you sorry for? That was the most amazing sex we've ever had. Seriously, I will think about that forever."

Caught between being ecstatic she was so satisfied and somewhat concerned over what he'd done to her, he traced his finger tenderly over the mark. "For this." He ran his finger gently over it again.

"Oh." She studied the marking. "I didn't even know. You made me feel amazing."

Her promises eased his guilt-ridden conscience, but he couldn't shake the feeling that he'd let his control slip, that he'd taken things too far.

Governor Haydenshire's face flitted through his mind.

"I think it's sexy," Emily declared. Rainer couldn't halt his broad grin.

He agreed and decided he didn't care what anyone else thought. She was his, and whatever he'd done that had her up on all fours, begging to be taken harder, he was all for.

"Since you are currently employed by the Arlington Angels, and you dress out and shower with eleven other women every day, I think I should probably heal it up."

Rainer summoned from his own energy that was spinning around the room and still joined to hers. He touched his hand to the hickey, cooled the energy in his hand to remove the swelling, then he sped up the blood flow around the area and added in heavy doses of his own energy to force her body to heal. The mark began to slowly disappear under his casting.

"Do you remember the one before? At least you know how to heal them now." She laughed as they watched the purple mark fade away.

Rainer chuckled as he recalled that night before he'd begun at the academy. Emily still had a year left in Non-Gifted high school. They'd been up in her loft drowning their devastation over not going to school together in each other.

He'd known then, just like he knew that night, he'd been marking his territory. Since Rainer hadn't begun his Gifted education yet, he had no idea how to heal her. She'd worn turtlenecks for several days, despite the hot weather.

Garrett had been over for dinner a few nights that week just as he always had. He'd waited until Governor and Mrs. Haydenshire weren't around and then he'd grabbed Emily's hand. He jerked the turtleneck away from her neck. After laughing hysterically and harassing both of them, he'd quickly healed the mark for her and never said a word to their parents.

When the mark was gone from her thigh, Emily slid off of the bed. "Let's go take a bath in that pool-sized tub."

"Why? You're not hurting, are you?" He had to make certain. He had to take care of her. It was who he was. He was her Shield. Every rhythm strain of his Gifted energy rang with the need to keep her safe and let her know how much he adored her.

"No, I want to take a bath with you, and we only get to stay here tonight."

Her eye roll let Rainer know he was overreacting.

CHAPTER 15

IN THE DAYLIGHT

They made use of the bed once more before falling asleep and used the steam shower the next morning before meeting Tad and Nathan for brunch.

"I'm gonna miss this room," Emily sighed longingly.

Rainer brushed a kiss on her cheek before he hoisted her bags into his hands. "I'll bring you back, baby."

"And we can do all of that again?"

"Oh, hell yeah." He opened the door and carried their bags onto the elevator. He'd called an hour earlier to check out of the room. That turned out to be a huge mistake.

As the bellman held the door open to the parking deck, they stepped out into a sea of photographers and reporters.

"Did you elope?" they began screeching as soon as Emily was fully out of the hotel.

"Why was the governor not aware you were getting married, Rainer?" A male reporter ran alongside them.

"We're not married!" Emily gasped.

"Will you be taking his name and crest, Emily?" a female reporter called.

"Why did you come to New York for the wedding?"

"Where did you elope?"

"Are you running away from your parents, Emily?"

The questions were relentless and made no sense to either of them.

They finally made it to the Hummer, dodging reporters and cameras the entire way. Rainer pulled his shield cast from the car and opened the door for. He tried to block her from view as he helped her inside.

"Did you stay here or at the Waldorf last night, Rainer?" called a newspaper reporter from the *Times*.

Suddenly, he remembered Tad had assigned the room to Mr. and Mrs. Rainer Lawson as a joke. Someone had gotten wise to the trick they'd pulled the evening before and had called hotels asking for a reservation in their names. They had inevitably stumbled upon the joke.

His stomach turned as he thought about the phone calls her parents must've gotten that morning.

"Baby, check your phone." Rainer drove away from the Gansevoort.

"Oh, I forgot to turn my ringer back on." She grimaced. "Oh no," her tone turned panicked. "I have nine missed calls from Mom and eleven from Daddy."

"Yeah, we need to call them. Now." Rainer explained what he believed had happened.

"Mom," she hesitated. Rainer could hear Mrs. Haydenshire yelling. "We didn't…Mom, stop shouting…Mother! You know why we're here. Uncle Tad made the reservations for us, and he put them under Mr. and Mrs. Lawson as a joke. The press found out and went wild.

"Wait, what's in the paper?" Emily demanded. She snapped her fingers at Rainer and pointed to a newsstand.

He parked in the next available spot, which was a block away. Quickly glancing around to make certain they weren't being followed, he hopped out of the Hummer. He immediately casted the car before sprinting down the sidewalk to purchase a plethora of papers and tabloids. He leapt back in a few minutes later.

"I'm sorry, Mom. We did not get married. I would never get married without you and Daddy and neither would Rainer," she assured while Rainer nodded his adamant agreement. "Okay, he just got the papers. Let me go see. I love you." With a quick "Bye," she ended the call.

As she pulled one of the tabloids from the stack, Emily's jaw clenched. Rainer panicked over whatever had been printed this time that had the Haydenshires so upset.

She summoned and waved her hand over the newsprint. *"Quite a Night,"* was the headline.

After reports earlier in the week that Rainer Lawson, son of beloved Crown Governor Joseph Lawson, had cut ties with his uncle, Stan Lawson, after his uncle's arrest by Iodex the day after Rainer's twenty-first birthday, it seems that Rainer is back on with his on-again off-again girlfriend, Emily Haydenshire. There had been speculation over the summer that Rainer had taken up with Samantha Peterson. The entire Haydenshire family was unavailable for comment but The Inquisitor caught up with Rainer's estranged uncle, Joseph's brother, Stan.

"Oh, great," Rainer groaned as his eyes fell to that line.

Stan didn't have much to say about the love triangle, but Lawson feels his nephew is being recalcitrant and is only trying to keep the Lawson fortune out of Stan's hands instead of sharing it.

Although Stan did mention that Rainer seemed much closer to Logan than to Emily, and he wonders if there might be more to the story. He stated that when Rainer visited his uncle while he was growing up it was usually Logan who visited with Rainer instead of Emily. Sources closest to Miss Haydenshire have assured us that she was shocked and devastated to learn that perhaps Rainer and Logan had more than a platonic friendship. The Inquisitor wonders if the couple will survive. Just a few weeks ago, Rainer was linked with Samantha Peterson.

Rainer cracked up as Emily shook her head and rolled her eyes.

"First of all, my uncle doesn't even know what recalcitrant means, so I'm doubting that was a direct quote."

"Sources closest to me..." Emily spat. "So, that would mean *you* told them that I was shocked and devastated that you and Logan were more than friends?"

Rainer grinned at her. Of all of the things the papers had fabricated in the past years, this was a first. "I'd sure as hell rather marry Logan than Samantha Peterson."

"Wait, there's more." She turned to the next page.

In an effort to mend the crumbling relationship, it seems Rainer decided a weekend getaway was just the thing. The couple was seen here last night at New York's premier restaurant, Nightingales, where Rainer and Miss Haydenshire couldn't seem to keep their hands off of one another.

His heart raced. Nausea washed over him in waves as he took in very grainy photographs of him and Emily at their table at the restaurant from the night before.

"Oh, no!" Emily panicked. There was a shot of her leaning her head into his shoulder in an effort to bury the moans from her orgasm.

"No one knew what I was doing." He was lightheaded suddenly. It was accompanied by pictures of the two of them kissing in the booth and a few of him running his hands all over her and feeding her ice cream.

The reporter went on to inform the readers of the dishes they'd eaten the night before. Rainer's head fell with a defeated whimper, as he was yet again called abusive and controlling. The paper stated that he'd chosen Emily's dinner for her and then only allowed her to eat half of their shared dessert.

After a dramatic eye roll, Emily tossed that paper down and picked up another. This paper didn't have shots from the restaurant, to Rainer's great relief, but it did have the two of them rushing from Nightingales and then exiting into the Waldorf.

"Ah, here we go." Emily pointed to the paragraph halfway down the page.

This reporter doesn't lose a story once he's on the chase. After being denied an interview with the power couple, I checked with a source at the Waldorf and found that the newly-minted Lawsons did not have a suite there. A suite registered to the new Mr. and Mrs. Lawson was found at the posh Gansevoort Hotel.

I spoke to Samantha Peterson, who we still suspect Lawson had a brief fling with just before academy graduation. She tells Gravity *that she broke things off with Rainer because of his overly controlling ways, which is what drove him back into the arms of Emily Haydenshire.*

Samantha commented that she wasn't surprised Rainer and Emily spent the evening at the Gansevoort. She explained that when she was with Rainer, she was shocked by his kinky preferences and stated that Rainer would prefer a more posh and overtly sexual locale like the Gansevoort to something as classy as the Waldorf. The Gansevoort is known for features like large whirlpool tubs in their suites and a rooftop pool.

All of the blood in his body slithered quickly to his feet. "What the hell?"

Emily nodded but was too stunned to speak. The article went on to say that the only way Emily would take Rainer back after his tryst with Samantha was if he agreed to marry her instantly, so they'd eloped in New York.

"This is unbelievable," Rainer huffed.

"It's also libel. If I find out Samantha Peterson actually gave that interview, I'll kill her," Emily fumed. "Surely it can't get worse than *Gravity.*" She picked up *The Realm Times.* The business section discussed ways Rainer could go about keeping Emily from ever getting her hands on the Lawson estate and then invited Rainer to invest in journalism.

"Right. That'll happen."

After locating the Entertainment section, Emily sighed and took in the photos of them leaving the restaurant the evening before and then making their entrance into the Waldorf.

As she began to read, she gasped.

"What does it say?" Rainer had noticed that they were late for brunch so he had pulled back into traffic. He was still reeling from a paper reporting that Samantha Peterson had called him kinky.

Emily read—"Times *reporter, Arnold Sherraton, interviewed the couple's waiter from Nightingales, and he confirmed that the couple got very cozy at the restaurant last evening. He commented that Lawson couldn't seem to keep his hands off of Miss Haydenshire/Lawson. The Times is still trying to confirm that the couple eloped while visiting the city.*

'There was a while there where we couldn't even see his hands,' the couple's waiter commented with a knowing chuckle."

Rainer nearly drove into the car in front of him.

The couple denied an ardent fan a photograph but did agree to sign something for him. The pastry waiter commented that Lawson was rude and had upset Emily.

Rainer sighed. He should've expected that. Emily continued.

"The couple headed to the Waldorf after their dinner but didn't have a room booked at the Astoria. It seems the supposed newlyweds spent the evening at the Gansevoort Hotel. There was no one available for comment from the Gansevoort, but Rainer and Emily did not make another appearance anywhere else in the city last evening."

"There's the coffee shop." Emily pointed to a small, out-of-the-way shop in the theatre district, where Tad had instructed them to meet.

Rainer began searching for a parking place. He located one a few blocks away and exited the Hummer. Pale dejection etched Emily's beautiful face as Rainer wrapped her up tightly in an embrace.

"Are you okay?" He knew perfectly well she wasn't, but he hoped to get her talking.

She shrugged and blinked back tears.

"Em, baby, you know none of that is true."

"I know, but it's hard to read sometimes, and I know Daddy always reads *The Times* so…" her protest drowned in her sorrow. She started again with renewed vigor. "I hate that people think you're…" she searched for an appropriate description.

With a furious huff, Rainer supplied, "A kinky control freak."

Emily nodded and then, to his delight, she began to giggle. "Why can't they just tell the truth? You and Logan have been best friends since you were born, and you've said less than five words to Samantha

Peterson in your entire life. And that you're obsessive with taking care of me and that you're the greatest fiancé ever."

"Thank you." He kissed her cheek as they walked. He noted a photographer who had followed them from the Gansevoort and was setting up to snap a photo of the two of them. "They don't say that because that doesn't sell papers."

He was infuriated at the way that the press had no issue selling out his name and associating him with out-and-out lies. The Realm seemed to eat them up without thought. It was as if he and Emily weren't real people with real feelings and real emotions.

The two of them were simply a commodity to be sold. It didn't seem to matter if the lies told about them might take away so much more than the few dollars people paid to read them.

CHAPTER 16

BLOOD IS THICKER...

They made their way into the coffee shop and smiled as Tad and Nathan waved them over.

"My word, it's like having brunch with the king and queen of the Realm." Tad shooed away several photographers from the front of the shop. "Tell us what happened last night," he demanded while they glanced over the menu.

Emily began the story but left out several key pieces. Rainer nodded several times as he waited for Emily to stop the long, drawn-out tale before asking what she wanted to eat. She picked up again with what was in the papers after he'd ordered.

"I saw the *Times*." Nathan clicked his tongue. "It's the most romantic restaurant in the city. What did they expect you two to be doing—shaking hands?"

Rainer and Emily laughed and began to loosen up.

"I just don't understand when kissing became news." Tad shook his head and thanked the waiter when he returned with their coffee and pastries. "I'm sorry over the whole business with the Gansevoort. I just never thought."

"No, it's fine," Rainer reassured him. "You shouldn't have to think about things like that. They must've been up all night calling every hotel in the freaking city. It's ridiculous." He pulled off a piece of his pastry and threw it in his mouth. Nathan and Tad both nodded.

"And controlling? How ridiculous! Why don't they interview me? I'll tell them no one takes care of Emily the way Rainer does, even the governor. As if I would let my one and only niece be with a guy who wouldn't let her finish her sorbet. She has seven older brothers. Do people ever think about that? If you were a horse's ass, they would've beaten you into the ground years ago," Tad scoffed as if that much should have been painfully obvious.

"Thank you." Rainer laughed. "I appreciate that...I think." He was shocked at how much better Tad's declarations made him feel.

"And who does this Samantha think she is anyway?" he continued. "Have they looked at her and then looked at you?" He held his hands up in exaltation to Emily.

"You might be a little prejudiced. Samantha is very pretty," she sighed.

Tad shook his head with a knowing grin. "Honey, bitches are never pretty once they're in the sunlight."

Emily gazed up at her uncle adoringly. She swallowed back the emotional energy that seemed to pulse very close to the surface that morning. "Thank you."

Rainer kissed her cheek. Tad and Nathan beamed just before they all heard cameras clicking outside the small restaurant. Photographers were positioned at the large plate-glass windows.

"This is why we stay on the farm all the time." Emily rolled her eyes.

"And kinky? Please!" Nathan threw his hand toward the reporters outside. "Trust me, you should be so lucky, but money and kinky only fit in one set of trousers in romance novels."

Rainer promptly choked on his coffee. He began coughing as Tad, Nathan, and Emily all cracked up.

They finished their delicious brunch. Rainer hadn't felt much like eating after everything he'd read that morning, but the food did ease his nervous stomach. "We'll just walk you to your car," Tad insisted, and Rainer understood that he was trying to give him the ring away from the cameras' ever-probing lenses.

They chatted, all well aware that several photographers were following them as they walked.

"Now, once you get your dress, we'll come to Arlington for a weekend, and I'll get started on the jewelry," Tad explained.

"And if you want to do a lunch with Vera, you'll let me know?" Nathan quizzed.

"Oh my gosh, yes," Emily vowed. "I can't believe you know Vera Wang."

Nathan tsked. "All for business, but you'll love her."

Suddenly the hair on the back of Rainer's neck stood. He began studying the area around them as they came into view of a man sprinting away from the Hummer.

His stomach clenched of its own accord as he reached and halted Emily's progress. In all of the chaos, he'd forgotten to cast the car when they arrived for brunch. Her brow furrowed as she picked up on the panic in his energy streams.

"What's wrong?" She hadn't seen the man.

"Em, I want you to cast a shield again, okay?"

"I don't think it works like that." She clung to him. "I think I have to feel like I'm in danger to draw on it like I did."

Rainer nodded. He threw his shield over her instead.

Thanks to his extensive training with Vindico, he was able to summon with his second hand and hold it outward. He began his radar scan at the front bumper and moved it back.

Cursing, he sprinted to the car and reached under the driver's side wheel well.

Emily, Tad, and Nathan followed after him as he pulled a small device from the car.

"What is that?" Tad demanded as Emily clung to her uncle.

"It's not a bomb, is it?" she begged.

Rainer shook his head. His heart raced as he tried to think of what to do next. "It's a GPS tracker."

"Did the press put it there or…?" Tad paused, "Or someone else?" Worry etched his features.

"I don't know."

"It must've been the press. I didn't feel any dark energy," Emily insisted. She sounded absolutely terrified. "I would've felt it." Her vow held far more pleading terror than assurance.

"Yeah, I'm sure it was, baby." He lifted his cell from his pocket. "I'm gonna call Vindico just in case."

CHAPTER 17

YOU'RE SURROUNDED

After he'd explained to his boss what he'd found on Emily's car, Dan was quiet for several minutes.

"Okay, Lawson, listen up." The command came a minute after Vindico had used his laptop to check something. The fact that his boss was working on an early Sunday afternoon didn't surprise him. "Carrington and Serena are in New York. They attended some charity gala last night."

Rainer wondered how that hadn't made the papers. How were his and Emily's evening plans more important than the Crown Governor supporting charity?

"Put the tracker back on the Hummer," Vindico ordered.

"What?"

"Put the tracker...back...on...the...Hum-mer." He sounded annoyed he'd had to repeat himself.

"Okay, how about why?"

"I'm calling out five undercover cars from the New York Iodex precinct. I'm leaving with two elite teams as soon as we get off the phone. You're going to have Emily's uncles take her to the airport. Tell her to be discreet. Glasses, hat, one of those head-scarf things, I don't care, just so long as she isn't identified.

"Carrington is waiting. She's going to fly home with the Crown and Serena while you drive the car back. We're going to see who shows up for a chase." Vindico's bloodthirsty delight rang in his tone.

"I want Emily to leave with Carrington in an hour, but I don't want you to leave for two or so. Give me time to get close enough to intercept you en route. They want to play cat and mouse, then I'll be happy to clean out the traps."

"Uh." Rainer glanced back at Emily. "Okay, I guess." There didn't seem to be anything to do but agree.

"You strapped, Lawson?"

"Yeah, my pistol is in the glove box."

"What?" Emily gasped. She looked astonished that Rainer had come to New York with a gun she was unaware of.

"Good. Tell Emily to head to JFK. One of Governor Carrington's guards will meet her at the entrance. They'll escort her to his plane. I'll see you soon," was Vindico's parting line.

Emily was rapidly approaching panic as Rainer tried to determine if where they were standing was a safe place to give her the instructions.

"Let's get in the car." He urged after another cursory glance up and down the surrounding street. They all piled in, and he explained the plan.

"I am not leaving you," Emily huffed. "What if it's Wretchkinsides? What if you get hurt? I need to be there. I can cast the car. I can keep you safe."

"Em, no." Rainer had been prepared for this battle. "I'll be fine. I'll have Iodex officers with me the whole time, and in case you forgot, I am an Iodex officer." He said this more for himself than for her.

"Rainer," Emily's stubborn will set in.

"Emily Anne." Tad patted her back from the seat behind her. "I have the duplicate ring right here. You wear this one, and let Rainer wear yours. The transference will work as long as it's anywhere on his skin. I can get him a simple chain to wear it around his neck. As long as it's touching his chest, he'll be able to throw the same kind of shield you threw on Monday."

"No." Rainer shook his head. That would not be happening.

"Yes," Emily argued.

"Oh, good grief." Nathan sighed. "If she's supposed to be at JFK in an hour, we need to get her there. One of you is going to have to agree to something."

In the end, Rainer won out, and Emily climbed into a cab with her uncles to be driven to the airport.

Nathan had hurried to purchase her a wide-brimmed hat, and she'd twisted her hair up in a quick bun. She'd pouted as she stomped toward the cab her uncle had hailed, while Rainer blocked any view of the exchange with the Hummer.

"I'll be fine." Rainer hugged her tight and kissed her goodbye. "You'll be back on the farm in under an hour. The Crown Governor's jet is the fastest enhanced plane in the whole Realm. I'll be on my way, and the officers who are following me are already waiting."

Her chin had trembled as Tad whisked her away.

He drew a deep breath and watched the cab ease back into traffic. She disappeared in a sea of yellow taxis and large buses.

The emptiness in his gut had him shifting uncomfortably. He tried to determine who might've tagged Emily's car. Wretchkinsides certainly had men in New York. If the press hadn't outed them, no one would have known they were in town. He'd been instructed not to move the car until Iodex was in position.

Rainer's cell shook him from his vengeful reverie. He rubbed his eyes and answered on the third ring. It was Vindico.

"Lawson," he barked. "Emily is on the farm. New York guys are set, and I'm almost to the turnpike. There are several law enforcement cut-throughs where we can intercept you. Highway patrol is on the lookout as well. You just drive. Get out of the city as fast as you can. If anyone wants to play, make sure you have a clear shot before you pull the trigger. We'll ask questions later."

Rainer swallowed down his fear as he tried to envision himself aiming and shooting at someone while driving a car on a crowded interstate. "Yes, sir."

"Cast your phone to the radio frequency of 173.1 MHz, encrypted, and set it near you. That's Iodex's frequency. Everyone will hear you. If you need help, just speak up. We're tracking your cell, so we'll know where you are the entire time."

"Okay, I'm heading out."

Emily is safe on the farm. She's safe. The thought gave him the willpower to make the drive, though ominous terror still tensed constantly in his shield.

"You'll be fine, Lawson. This is precisely what I've been trying to train you to handle. I wouldn't have hired you if I didn't think you had the balls to pull this off. Now, get it done."

The call ended, and Rainer casted his phone to the frequency Vindico had provided.

He laid the phone on the console beside him and drew a deep steadying breath. He cranked the car and willed his heart to stop shaking his rib cage as he eased into the gridlocked, New York City traffic.

He received slight nods from the officers who were riding with him. They never stayed close enough to be identified as his backup, but he appreciated the fact that they were there. They'd been on the turnpike for almost a half hour when Rainer's phone crackled.

"Sir, I've got a white, late-model, Ford Econoline Cargo. Back windows are modified and covered. No tag. Been with us a little longer than I like," one of the New York Iodex officers alerted Vindico.

"I hear ya, Coggins. Stay with it. See if there's anyone that seems to be running with him. Lawson, you still okay?"

"I'm fine," Rainer lied as he kept watch in his rearview mirror. He'd noticed the van earlier, but it had slowed in the last few miles. He could no longer see it.

"There's a cut-through to your left in another twenty-five miles. We'll join you there." Vindico sounded almost sympathetic, but the excitement was still ripe in his tone.

"Yes, sir," Rainer agreed, as did every officer in a vehicle near his.

He pushed the pedal harder. Something about having Vindico and Elite officers nearby made him anxious. He tried to remember to watch the road ahead of him, but watching his rearview was just as important.

There it was again. Rainer swallowed as the black Mazda Protegé came up fast on his left. He'd seen it several times.

"You see that, Lawson?" one of the New York officer's voices rang in his phone.

"Yeah, Vindico, that's the fourth time a black Mazda Protegé has come up fast and then stopped just behind me," he informed his boss and hoped that he sounded both competent and unbothered.

"Anybody see who's in the car?" Vindico asked.

"Yes, sir. I've got two men, Caucasian, medium height and build. They look a little nervous if you ask me," the unmarked black Expedition that had moved into position on Rainer's left, just beside the Protegé, informed Vindico. "One sec, I'll get you a tag."

"All right. Stay on him," Vindico demanded.

"Yes, sir, it's a Jersey tag number Zulu Oscar Kilo Nine Seven Papa. And the van's still with us."

"Hold that," Vindico ordered. Another mile passed and the van drew closer. The Protegé backed off slightly. The driver had answered his cell.

"All right, listen up, boys. Milepost seventy-three is a mile away from you. We'll meet you in an abandoned parking lot a mile off the pike to your right. Seems The Rabbit Ears Adult Shop is no longer in business," Vindico explained. "Got an owner on the Protegé. Not who I was hoping for, but I'll take this moron over one of Nic's boys for today anyway.

"Coggins, you and Snyder stay with Lawson. The rest of you take the next exit and head on home. Thanks for your help. This should be fun. Just drive, Lawson. You're fine. Pull in the parking lot and let's play."

"Yes, sir." Confusion swam in Rainer's rhythms as he tried to determine who was following him. It was obviously not one of Wretchkinsides's thugs, but who else would have tagged Emily's car?

Rainer made the exit to the sound of squealing tires as the van swerved frantically to make the exit with him. He searched for the empty parking lot as he made the right-hand turn.

"I see you, Lawson. Turn in and park near the building. We'll make our appearance in a moment," Vindico guided.

Rainer eased the Hummer into the parking lot. The Protegé turned, but the van's driver seemed to think better of it.

"Gotta runner, Tuttle," Vindico alerted over the radio.

"Got it." Tuttle laughed as his squad car appeared behind the van a moment later with sirens blaring.

Suddenly Vindico, Portwood, Ericcson, and three Non-Elite officers raced in from the street. Blue lights and sirens filled the air as they blocked the exit.

Vindico sprinted to the Protegé and flung the door open. Rainer leapt out of the Hummer, gun drawn and eager to see who'd caused all of this.

"You're surrounded, Fenton." Vindico laughed. "And you're under arrest." He spun the driver into his own car and slapped cuffs on his wrists.

Rainer recognized the passenger but wasn't certain from where. His mind reeled through the dozens of mug shots he'd memorized in the past week.

"Fenton?"

"This is Theodore Fenton. He's the new hotshot reporter for *Kinetix*. Aren't you, Teddy? Seems *Kinetix* planned on following you and Ms. Haydenshire back from your weekend getaway in hopes of getting a jump on a story about the two of you. That went well, didn't it?"

"You can't arrest me. I have freedom of the press," Fenton cried pompously.

"You have the right to free speech, you fucking moron. Let me tell you what you don't have. You don't have the right to place a tracking device on a car you do not own. You don't have the right to follow an Iodex officer while he's working. And you've broken so many privacy laws and acts that I'm not going to waste any more of my day listing them off for you, but I feel certain that the national governing board will be very interested in this case. I think I'll bring the trial to Arlington instead of letting Jersey handle the proceedings, seeing as how it was one of the governors' daughters whose car you tagged. I bet Governor Haydenshire won't think this is particularly funny.

"Put them in a car and have theirs towed. Take them to McCullough and let me know when you get their papers filed. I'll have

Governor Haydenshire petition to have the trial transferred," Vindico informed the Non-Elite officers from New Jersey Iodex. McCullough was the Gifted Prison near an abandoned mine in Franklin.

"Yes, sir," they answered succinctly. They shoved the two men into a squad car and pulled away.

"Sorry about that, Lawson. I'm sure that wasn't what you had in mind for today, but you're probably used to that by now. By the way," —Vindico moved until he was standing alone with Rainer by the Hummer—"let me offer you a little advice." He rolled his eyes. "Grow the fuck up. Now. The next time you decide you'd like to finger your fiancée, take that on back to your room."

He threw his leg over his Agusta and led the crowd of cars back to Arlington.

Rainer tried to tell himself Vindico had assumed that's what he and Emily had been doing the night before in the restaurant, and that he hadn't known anything for certain. He phoned Emily to tell her who'd been following him and just to hear her voice.

"Yeah. Chief Vindico called a few minutes ago to tell Dad it was the press." Emily sighed.

"I'll be home in just a few hours." He wasn't certain which of them was more eager for his arrival.

Emily swallowed audibly. "Uh, remember it's Sunday night. So just come to Mom and Dad's."

"Oh, right." Panic rocketed through Rainer again. Vindico's comment reverberated against his skull. "Did your dad see the papers?" He hoped against hope.

"Yeah," Emily lamented.

"What did he say?"

"I got the 'you need to remember who you are to this Realm, Emily' speech, but I kind of get the impression he's waiting for you."

"Great." Rainer fought the urge to whimper.

They talked for the next few hours, and Rainer let her voice lull him
into hopeful serenity until he pulled the Hummer into the barn where
all of the Haydenshire cars were parked.

Emily raced out to meet him. She threw her arms around him, and
Rainer squeezed her to him. The governor could wait. He kissed her
and took her hand, and they walked very slowly back toward the
farmhouse.

CHAPTER 18

TALK THE TALK

Emily's grandparents, Nana and Paps Anderson, drove up as Emily and Rainer were making their way up the walk. Rainer and Emily stopped to help them out of the car.

"I take it Taddy came through for us?" Nana quizzed.

Emily nodded and glanced down at her hand instinctively. "Yes, ma'am. I tried on the other ring while I was on Governor Carrington's plane. It looks identical, but it does feel different. I can't believe I never noticed there was anything weird with this one."

"And you're not married?" Nana gave a dismissive chuckle.

"I would never get married without my family there." Emily gave a slight eye roll. They entered the warm kitchen together. Mrs. Haydenshire smiled at Rainer and Emily as she directed Adeline to keep stirring the sauce.

"Tread very carefully," she whispered to Rainer as she came to give them hugs. Rainer grimaced as he mentally instructed his heart to stop hammering out of rhythm.

Emily's father entered the kitchen. He narrowed his eyes at Rainer. Logan followed his dad and shot Rainer a grimace that made it clear he was going to hear about everything that had been in the papers.

But with a smirk, he goaded, "Hey, Dad, I think I might take this old bread out and feed the guppies. You wanna come?"

Rainer glared at Logan. Given the chance, he'd strangle him.

"Yeah, that's a good idea." Governor Haydenshire nodded. "It's still a few minutes before dinner right?"

After giving Rainer a sympathetic gaze, Mrs. Haydenshire sighed. "Yes, but don't be too long."

"Rainer, why don't you join us." The governor gestured to the back door.

Nana gave Rainer a reassuring pat on his arm as Emily's head fell.

"Sure, Governor Haydenshire." Rainer followed his future father-in-law out the back door with Logan right behind them.

Rainer's slid his eyes to the side. "I will kill you for this."

This only furthered Logan's delight.

They traipsed to the lake and began the customary path around.

Logan tried to hide his laughter while he threw pieces of bread into the water.

"Why don't we start with why the suite was reserved for Mr. and Mrs. Lawson?" Governor Haydenshire demanded without even giving a pretense for the walk.

"Tad made the reservations. Not me. He did it as a joke, and I just didn't correct them. It didn't seem like a big deal at the time."

"You're not married yet."

"Yes, sir." He sighed as the governor launched into his lecture.

When he landed on the "And where exactly were your hands when the waiter couldn't see them?" portion of the inquisition, Rainer panicked.

Logan grimaced and appeared to feel some slight remorse for the stunt he'd pulled.

Rainer drew a steadying breath and met Governor Haydenshire's pointed gaze. He held his eyes steady as he promised, "Nowhere they shouldn't have been." He wasn't certain if he was lying or not, but he never dropped the governor's glare.

"Good. However, half of those photos looked like they should have taken place inside of your hotel suite not in a public restaurant. Perhaps if you and Emily cooled it a little, the cameras would back off."

"Doubt it," Rainer mumbled under his breath.

"What was that?" the governor demanded.

Rainer cleared his throat. "I don't think so, sir. They tried to trace Emily's car. It's never seemed to matter what we were doing."

"Well, for my sake, why don't we try it, and see if it might work?"

"Yes, sir."

"Now, I would like to commend you on your decision to name Logan as your beneficiary. That not only took a great deal of thought and maturity, but it shows me that my baby girl's safety is your top priority. I want you to know how much I appreciate that. I'm not so certain you should be keeping that from Emily though. I know you're trying not to frighten her, but you'll find in marriage that sharing too much is always preferable to not sharing enough."

Rainer's breath came easier now. "I know, sir. I'm not trying to hide anything from her. I just wanted to wait to tell her. She's still freaked out about what happened and then with the car today. I'll tell her when things settle down."

"I'd tell her soon. We had ten children. If I'd waited to tell Lillian things until everything was calm, we wouldn't have spoken for nearly thirty years. That isn't how marriage works."

After that piece of advice, Governor Haydenshire slapped Rainer on the shoulder and headed back into the house.

Rainer and Logan meandered to the end of the dock. A goading smirk etched Logan's face, but he was quiet for a few minutes as Rainer contemplated everything Governor Haydenshire had told him. It wasn't the first time he was immensely thankful that the Haydenshires didn't read the tabloids like *The Gravity*.

"So," Logan quipped, "where *were* your hands, Rainer?" He mimicked his father's voice.

Rainer rolled his eyes as he skipped a rock out over the lake. Logan studied him, then cocked his jaw to the side and shook his head. "In a restaurant? That's sick, man."

"I don't know what you're talking about."

"Uh-huh, I don't think so. We've been best friends since we were born. I might even say I know you better than the girl you had your fingers up in a restaurant in New York last night. I knew you were lying when you told Dad that."

He refused to either confirm or deny Logan's suspicions. He tried hard not to laugh. Logan leaned and knocked him to the side with a great deal of force. "You eat with those hands?"

Rainer raised his eyebrow with a goading grin and waited on Logan to catch on to the unspoken insinuation. Logan shuddered and pretended to gag. "I do not want to think about that!"

"You said it. Not me."

They sauntered back in the house with Logan still harassing Rainer about what he'd done to Emily in the restaurant.

CHAPTER 19

APPROPRIATE DINNER CONVERSATIONS

Mrs. Haydenshire served dinner after Rainer and Logan set the table.

"Geez, did you wash your hands, Rainer? We're about to eat," Logan teased with a goading smirk as Rainer narrowed his eyes. He didn't like where this was going.

"Yes, Logan, I did." He shot his *former* best friend a warning glare.

Emily and Adeline studied Logan confusedly. Conversation picked up as Connor casually mentioned that he was thinking of asking Katie, the Angels' Junior Shield, out on a date when his father inquired about his love life.

Rainer picked up the napkin in his lap and wiped his hands before cutting another bite of his chicken.

"Oh, what's wrong? Get something on your *fingers?*" Logan goaded with heavy emphasis on the last word.

Rainer glared at him hatefully. Emily rolled her eyes. She still didn't understand what Logan was up to and went back to encouraging Connor to ask Katie out for the after-party after the first challenge.

"This is delicious, Mrs. Haydenshire." Rainer gestured to the roasted chicken on his plate.

"Yep…nice and juicy," Logan quipped.

Rainer shot another warning glare and mouthed, "Shut the fuck up."

After laughing silently, Logan shook his head and waggled his eyebrows at Rainer.

"Hey, Mom, you know what we should have soon?" Logan was on the brink of cracking up.

His mother studied him speculatively. "What's that, dear?"

"Chicken fingers."

Rainer took a well-aimed kick into Logan's shin. Logan stifled a groan. "Yeah, I think chicken fingers would be very pleasurable. I think they'd really hit *the* spot."

"If you want chicken fingers so badly, I can make them for you," Adeline offered. She studied Logan like he might've lost his mind.

Rainer laughed, unable to help himself, as Logan turned bright red. Governor and Mrs. Haydenshire shared a quizzical glance.

Irritated that Rainer had gotten the last laugh, Logan decided to up the ante by discussing human hands.

"Think about everything we can do with them." He held out his right hand and gazed at it in mocked awe. "We summon with them, eat with them, make things, fix things, *feel* things." He stared directly at Rainer.

Rainer rolled his eyes and shook his head. Suddenly, Emily figured out what Logan had been discussing and what Rainer must've confessed. She glared at him.

He shook his head slightly and willed her to understand, but she threw her napkin down, declared herself done, and stomped away from the table.

"I'm, uh, finished as well," Rainer stammered quickly. He cleared his and Emily's places and then raced out the back door to find her.

He started toward her loft but then spotted her out on the dock. He took off in a heated sprint and made it to her in under a minute.

"Em, your dad asked me about the paper, and Logan knew I was lying. I didn't mean to tell him," poured from his mouth in a heated plea.

"How could you?"

"I didn't."

She began pacing up and down the dock.

"Baby," Rainer tried, but her eyes flashed dangerously, and he knew he was in for it.

"Don't 'baby' me! How dare you tell him something like that? That was private and special and…" She narrowed her eyes. "Why do you all have to be such stupid macho pigs?"

"Please, I'm sorry. I swear I would never have told him about that. He was standing right here when your dad asked me where my hands were, and he knew I was lying. He's known me since I was two days old. He kind of has my number."

"What did you say to my dad?" she demanded.

Rainer drew a deep breath and hemmed. "He asked me where my hands were when the waiter couldn't see them, and I said they weren't anywhere they shouldn't have been. Which, if you think about it, is true."

She shot him a look that said he should consider himself very, very lucky if his hands got anywhere near her crotch at any point in the near future.

"I didn't know what to do or say. I'm sorry. You know what that means to me, and you know I would never brag about something like that to Logan."

"It really wasn't his fault," Logan explained as he made his way to them in several long strides. Since neither he nor Emily had noticed his approach, Rainer was thankful it wasn't Governor Haydenshire.

"Don't beat him up. He didn't tell me. I guessed, and it was in the paper. I knew he was lying to Dad when he asked him, and I called him on it. I'm sorry. Be mad at me not Rainer."

Emily spun and shoved Logan hard in the chest.

"Why did you keep doing that at dinner? You're not twelve."

"Hey." Logan caught her hands before she could push him again.

"Let go of me." She wriggled, and Rainer grasped Logan's wrists.

"Let her go."

"Not if she's gonna shove me in the freaking lake."

"She's not." Rainer turned his warning glare on Emily. Logan released her arms, and she crossed them over her chest with her temper at full tilt.

"Neither of you will ever say another word about any of this," she shrieked in Logan's face.

Logan and Rainer nodded their agreement.

With that, she stomped back toward the house. Rainer reached for her, but she shifted quickly to the side and away from his grasp.

"She's a hot mess, man. Are you sure you know what you're getting yourself into?" Logan glared at his sister as she marched away.

"Just shut up." He took off to catch Emily before she made her way back into the house.

"Emily, please," he called as she neared the back porch.

She halted and spun to sit on one of the lower steps. Hot tears were flowing down her face.

"I'm so sorry. I should never have done that in a restaurant. I really didn't think anyone would ever know. I just wanted to share something private with you, something only we would know about. I guess that's more than I should ever hope for."

"No." She shook her head and let him brush away her tears. "I really loved that. I felt like that too. Like it was something just for us." She shuddered as her tears began spilling from her eyes faster. Her chin trembled as she laid her head on him. The motion soothed his soul, and he wrapped her up in his arms.

"I don't think it would've bothered me so much for Logan to know if the whole stupid Realm didn't know."

"Nobody knows anything. No one saw what I was doing, sweetheart. For some ridiculous reason people want to pretend they know everything about you and me, or me and whoever they've decided I'm cheating with this week." His anger grew with every word.

"Samantha, or hell…Logan. No one seems to give a damn if there's any truth to any of it or not." He held her tenderly, but the fury free-flowed through his veins. "What we shared last night, that was just you and me. We are the only people who really know what went on in that booth. And even if Logan did figure it out, he doesn't have a clue what that meant to me. He doesn't know how much I loved giving you that, or what I feel when you let me in, when you're with me like that. No one will ever know how much that means to me. No one but you."

He squeezed her tight and willed her to feel the love that flowed so readily out of him and into her.

"You always say stuff like that, and then I can't be mad at you anymore," she whispered.

"It's the truth." He held her chin between his thumb and index finger. "I love you so much, and I will do everything in my power to make certain that our dates don't end up in the papers anymore."

"Last night was perfect. I'm just going to pretend the press never showed up because I loved last night, and I love you."

He let her words heal his fractured heart and mend his weary soul. He squeezed her tighter. "I love you too. More than life itself."

"But I kind of feel like you're keeping something from me, and then you told Logan that." She shrugged. "I don't know. I just feel something weird from you."

His boss having figured out what they'd done and his assigning his inheritance to Logan seared through Rainer's mind. It was extremely difficult to keep anything from a Receiver, especially one you were sleeping with.

He worked hard to keep his emotions regulated whenever he was around her. As long as he didn't think about his will, it was fine.

He considered telling her everything. He didn't like keeping things from her, but now didn't really seem to be the best time. After deciding that he would tell her everything soon, Rainer squeezed her tighter.

"I've just been really stressed with work, and I'm so worried about you all the time." He wasn't going to lie to her outright. Those were both true statements.

Emily nuzzled her head under his chin. "Don't worry about me. I'm fine as long as I know you're fine and that you're not keeping anything from me."

"Okay," Rainer carefully agreed as he kissed the top of her head.

CHAPTER 20

BE CAREFUL WHAT YOU WISH FOR...

"Is Em still asleep?" Logan asked as Rainer poured himself a bowl of cereal the next morning.

"Yeah, she doesn't have to be at the arena until nine." He began flipping through the paper. He wanted to see if there had been anything else about his and Emily's New York trip that might've made it to the presses.

His heart sank rapidly into his stomach as he dropped his spoon. Rainer let his eyes close and willed the headline to say anything different than what he'd just read.

"What?" Logan and Adeline shared a concerned glance as Logan jerked the paper out of Rainer's hand. "Are you freakin' kidding me?"

Rainer opened his eyes to see that the headline still read:

Stan Lawson, brother of beloved Crown Governor Joseph Lawson, to sue nephew for half of the Lawson estate.

Logan shook his head, and determination broadcasted from his jawline. "Man, you know no one's going to give him a dime."

"I know," Rainer sighed as his eyes fell to the line:

Stanley Lawson is claiming that his nephew, Rainer, has proven himself irresponsible and unfit to manage the estate, due to his engagement to newest Arlington Angel Receiver, Emily Haydenshire, without first making her sign a prenuptial agreement.

"Rainer, I'm so sorry." Adeline gave him a sweet smile.

He reminded himself that no one in the Realm would award his good-for-nothing uncle a penny, but he didn't want to go through a trial and drag Emily into it.

"It'll be another field day for the press." He plunged his spoon into the bowl viciously. "Hey, I don't want Em to see that yet. I'll tell her later. It'll just upset her, and they're trying to get ready for the exhibition this weekend."

Logan shared another quick glance with Adeline. "It's none of my business, and I want to keep Em safe too, but have you thought about how many times you've said that lately?" The concern wasn't well-concealed in the warning.

"I'll tell her everything. Just not right now. I'm not gonna go wake her up before she has to go practice just to tell her that our estate is threatened by my moronic uncle, and that his premise for the suit is me not making her sign a prenup."

Logan shrugged. He folded the paper and then handed it back to Rainer. "That sucks, man. I'm really sorry."

"I figured he'd do something. I was just waiting to see what. I guess now I know."

"Are you gonna hire Jack?"

"He's the best, right?"

"Yeah," Logan agreed then glanced at his watch. "Hey, we better go. Vindico's probably already buried our desks."

Low black clouds hung on the horizon and heat swam in the air that surrounded Arlington.

Rainer drove to the Pentagon and tried to come up with a way to tell Emily that he'd named Logan his beneficiary and that his uncle was suing them.

She wasn't likely to handle the lawsuit well. She'd decide it was her fault, but delaying telling her things didn't actually seem to make them any easier.

"I wish we would just do something at work. I'm sick of looking at evidence," Logan grumbled.

"I know." Rainer quickly joined in his acrimony. "If all of Wretchkinsides's guys are out there or whatever, then why the hell can't we go get them? I'm sick of sitting at our desks. That's what we did at the academy, and I was in the lamest car chase in history yesterday."

He would never have admitted, even to Logan, that before it was over he'd been quite terrified.

Logan laughed. "Maybe we'll get to do something cool today. Mitch's dad was supposed to tell Vindico stuff over the weekend."

"Hopefully." Rainer had almost forgotten the deal struck between Mitchell O'Ryan Sr. and Vindico.

He followed Logan in through the Iodex checkpoints. Defeat settled on him as he took in a new stack of evidence folders sitting on his desk.

"Hey, Lawson, I saw the paper this morning. I'm sorry" Vindico offered kindly.

"Yeah, I'm going to need to talk to Stariff again."

Vindico glanced at his watch. "Why don't you head down there? Jack's in early today. There's a trial this morning, and we still have a little while before everyone will be in. I'm gonna go over everything I got off of O'Ryan yesterday, but your assignments won't start until around lunch, so you have a little while."

Rainer stood. He tried not to sound shocked. "Thanks." He gave Vindico a genuine smile.

Thunder bellowed outside the Senate as he made his way through the governors' wing. He lifted his phone from his pocket.

Emily was terrified of storms. A driving rain had blackened the sky when her family had gotten the call that Cal had been killed, and it had rained even harder when her car had been run off of a bridge as she'd searched for Rainer that evening.

Rainer passed the Auxiliary Wing of the Senate. Most Receivers hated storms. He saw a few of the Receivers on staff slinking away from the windows and gathering near the coffee makers closer to the door.

They could all feel the sheer amount of violent energy inside a storm. It affected their reads on the emotions around them. Their Receiving energies spiked and dipped erratically and generally made them weak and nervous.

"Hey," Emily answered on the first ring.

"Are you okay, baby?" He could see her in his mind's eye. Her hair would be a mess after sleeping. Her bottom lip would be in her mouth from worry, and she would pace as she tried to stay away from the windows.

His heart sank as thunder rent the sky again. She would tremble whenever the windowpanes shook from the force.

"I'm okay." He knew she hadn't meant to lie. It was what she thought she was supposed to be. Her terror over storms embarrassed her.

"Are you sure you're all right to drive to the arena? I can try to come home and get you." He tried to come up with some way to make Vindico understand that Emily's fear of storms was more than even most Auxiliary Predilects.

"No, you have to work. I'll be fine. I'm gonna leave in a minute, so I can drive really slow." She seemed to decide this as they talked.

"Okay. Call me if you need me."

"Will you call and check on me at lunch?"

"Of course. I love you so much. You're gonna be fine, okay? I can try to come pick you up tonight if I get out of here at a decent hour."

"That would be great. I've wanted you to come out and meet everyone. I mean, you know, just like you and not like all of Iodex because you've been called out." She fumbled over her explanation.

"I'll do my best. Maybe your dad will make Vindico let us go again."

"I'll call Daddy." Her tone had regulated. She sounded excited. The lilt in her voice made him determined to be at Angels Arena at six when they finished practice. "I'm gonna go get dressed."

"Bye, baby. Love you." Rainer spoke quickly as he was standing outside of Stariff's office now.

"Love you too."

~

Rainer returned to Iodex an hour later much more relaxed. Stariff had talked him through what would likely happen at the trial and had assured him that his father's will was ironclad.

His inheritance would forever be his and Emily's until it was handed down to their children. The thought made Rainer smile as he reheated the coffee he'd left on his desk and followed everyone into Vindico's office to hear the report on O'Ryan.

"Okay." A genuine smile was actually affixed to Vindico's face. "O'Ryan was very forthcoming with information, and we struck a deal. The more information he supplies us on Wretchkinsides, the longer I'll keep him out of Felsink. If he helps us bring him down, I'll get him out for good."

Everyone inside Vindico's office leaned forward in eager anticipation. It seemed everyone was ready for a little action.

"First thing." Vindico spread out a map of the greater DC area. "Three safehouses I hadn't yet found. Here, here, and here." Vindico drew red dots on the map all around Clarendon. Crime had certainly picked up in that area.

"So, we will most definitely be keeping an eye on these. But," Vindico's smile widened, "he also informed me that the Interfeci members who have been moved to the States have been hanging out at a strip club called The Tantra near the airport.

"So, today, I want five men inside and two out. Get as close as you can to these men, but don't get yourselves recognized." He plastered his desk with mug shots of men who were known associates of Wretchkinsides but hadn't been seen outside Europe until recently.

"I want to know everything they say. Only observe. Do nothing else. I don't want them to know we're on to them just yet. Throw on some ball caps and keep your heads down.

"They open for an early lunch. You can fight over who gets to go in. I don't give a damn, but you better have me a shit load of evidence when you show up back here tomorrow morning. Stay through several shifts, or at least until Nicky's little league team leaves."

Rainer broke out in a cold sweat, and Logan looked like he might be sick.

"Oh, I'm definitely in," Tuttle chortled.

Rainer's heart pounded out an SOS. Not only did he have no desire to go to some strip club, but the thought of what Emily would say had him reeling.

"Get out of here. Try to work through more of that evidence before you leave," Vindico ordered. Everyone filed out of the office and back toward their desks.

"I am not going to a strip club." Logan shocked everyone by the adamancy of his vow. Rainer understood immediately.

For all of the heartbreak and discord him going might cause Emily, if Logan went to The Tantra, it would devastate Adeline. She wasn't particularly self-secure, given that the woman who'd given birth to her and raised her did not deserve to be called mother.

She was strung tight, and her entire self-worth was tied up in Logan. She didn't believe she was pretty or that she had anything at all worth loving, and Logan going to a place where other women were pulling their clothes off for money may very well drive her right over the edge.

"He can fire me, suspend me, do whatever the hell he wants, but I will not go in a strip club," Logan demanded again.

"All right, all right," Garrett soothed. "You can stay outside, geez, chill."

Rainer opened his mouth to state the very same plea but was cut off by John Ramier. "My wife is eight months pregnant." He looked like he might actually break down in tears. "She can't even see her feet, and that's entirely my fault. I cannot go to a strip club. She spends most of the time in tears already. I'm terrified to even imagine trying to tell her that I have to spend all of my workday at The Tantra."

"All right." Garrett took over. "You and Logan can stay outside, and we'll call if we need any backup."

As Portwood and Ericcson sauntered back to their desks, Tuttle discussed how great this assignment was.

Rainer and Logan cornered Garrett.

"He can't just send guys who are, like, happily married and shit into strip clubs," Logan defied.

"I'm not going."

"Yes, you are, Rainer. You're an adult. This is a job, and I'm sure my baby sister will pitch one hell of a fit. I'll even help you deal with her when we're done. But this is what your boss told you to do. You're going to do it," Garrett stated firmly. "Do you really think you're going to see something today that'll make you want to take that ring back off her finger?"

"No," Rainer retorted in horrified disgust.

"Then chill and get the job done. Emily will be fine. Don't tell her yet. What she doesn't know will keep you from getting shouted at. Tell her later." Garrett shrugged.

Rainer swallowed down the bile that rose in his throat as he gave a slight nod.

CHAPTER 21

THE TANTRA

After what seemed like only a few short minutes, Garrett pulled the Highlander into a seedy parking lot complete with a light-up neon sign advertising the strippers' names and the lunch special.

Rainer's stomach spun in violent, jarring twists as his palms began to sweat.

"Here." Garrett handed him a couple of fives and then twenty one-dollar bills.

"Oh, fuck no." He thrust the money back against Garret's stomach. "I will leave this club tonight, and go home, and swear to your sister that I did not look at or touch one single woman here today. So, you can keep that all for yourself."

"Fine." Garrett rolled his eyes. "But you're going to need to order food and drinks." He handed Rainer back two tens and a twenty.

"Whatever," Rainer fumed.

Logan and Ramier made their way across the litter-lined street to a drug store with most of the light-up letters in its name darkened.

Logan shot Rainer an apologetic glance as he pulled his cell phone out. He was trying to let Rainer know if he needed him, he'd be there.

Rainer plodded toward the door to the club. He willed away

thoughts of not only what Emily was going to say and do but also of what his father would say if he knew where he was.

Garrett opened the door and stepped inside. Rainer followed. An extremely scantily clad woman appeared to welcome them.

As he stared steadfastly at the black carpet complete with swirls of neon greens, pinks, and purples that shimmered slightly when the lights hit them, Rainer bristled.

"Well, hey, good lookin'," the blonde drawled as she linked her arm through Garrett's. He smiled and gave her an appraising look.

"We're meeting them." He let his finger run just over the waistband of the nonexistent outfit the woman was wearing. Portwood, Ericcson, and Tuttle were already seated inside.

The blonde smiled and nodded. "Just follow me." She grasped Garrett's hand in both of hers to lead him to a table. Rainer returned his gaze to the floor.

"Anywhere, baby," Garrett drawled. Rainer allowed himself a split-second eye roll. The waitress giggled with a bit too much show.

He pulled out a metal chair with a red leather cushion and fell onto it with a huff. He tried desperately not to think about what had gone on in the chair he was currently occupying as he seated himself at the table.

"Enjoy, gentlemen," the blonde called before she waved to Garrett and moved back to the door.

"Okay, obviously that's them." Portwood threw a glance to the round booth very near their table that was full of Wretchkinsides's men. "They just told Jennifer"—he gestured his head back to the blonde who had seated them—"that they were expecting a few more friends."

Garrett pretended to glance around the club. Before any further comments could be made, a tall brunette, who was falling out of the waitress uniform she was wearing, made her way to their table. She leaned over to show off all of her assets. Rainer kept his gaze on the scrolling pattern on the laminate table that was supposed to look like wood.

"And what can I bring for you to sip while you enjoy the show?" she flirted. Garrett chuckled and stepped up again. "We'll all have a beer." He slapped Rainer on the back. "Loosen up," he spoke through his teeth.

"You paying, stud?" the waitress drawled, but then to Rainer's horror she draped herself across his back. "Or is this heartbroken sweetheart picking up the tab?" she fussed in a pitying whine. Rainer slid forward and away from the woman.

"I got it," Garrett supplied. He threw Rainer a warning look. The waitress nodded. She slid her hand along Rainer's cheek, and he jerked away from her garish, red fingernails.

"Poor baby, don't you worry. A few hours here, you'll forget all about her." He cocked his jaw to the side and glared hatefully at Garrett.

"He's fine. We're just here hanging out. Haven't seen each other in a while."

Portwood and Tuttle nodded their agreement.

With a slight shrug, the waitress nodded and went to pour the beer.

"Get it together," Garrett demanded. "You're gonna blow our cover and that could get real serious real quick."

A minute later, two more men joined the round booth and were greeted heartily by two mid-level thugs who worked for the Interfeci.

Rainer glanced toward them as they slid into the booth. He shared an ominous glance with Ericcson. The tension around the table was palpable. The waitress moved to take their order. They began pretending to carry on a conversation though they were listening in on the Interfeci discussion.

Several of them had Eastern European accents, and Rainer struggled to understand their muddled English.

"Now that we're all here, we want to see the show, doll," a large man, seated in the back corner of the booth, demanded with a sneer. They all stood and followed the waitress up a set of stairs.

"Okay, we need to be moved to the club level," Garrett explained as soon as Wretchkinsides's men were out of earshot.

"When the waitress brings back the beer, I'll ask if we can be seated upstairs," Portwood agreed.

"All right, boys." The brunette had returned. "Here are your drinks.

Can I do anything else for you?" The double entendre rang loudly in her offer.

"Uh, actually, we'd like a club-level table, with a good view," Portwood urged.

Rainer knew Portwood was very happily married. He'd even complained about the assignment, but he seemed determined to get the job done.

Maybe I am overreacting. Maybe Emily will understand that I had no choice. Rainer tried to console himself with what he knew was pure bullshit. He was sure another decade of maturity would've been very helpful. Unfortunately, neither of them had that.

The brunette giggled obnoxiously. "I'm sure you would, honey, but that'll cost you." She dragged her fingernails lightly across Portwood's chin.

Rainer saw Portwood grind his teeth at the unwelcome advance. "I'm sure that won't be a problem…honey," he added with a slight grimace. His act was slipping the closer the woman got.

"Whatever." The brunette furrowed her brow. She didn't appear accustomed to her flirtations being thwarted. "I'll get Bridgette to take you up."

With a nod, they all began sipping the beers they'd been provided.

"I will never understand you straight guys." Ericcson scowled at another of the waitresses thrusting her cleavage in a patron's face.

"As you know, I'm both very straight and very happily married. I don't get any of this either, trust me," Portwood vowed.

"Do I even want to know what happens on the club level?" Rainer grumbled.

"I don't know," Portwood admitted. He slapped Rainer on the back. "I can assure you I don't look forward to finding out, either. The only woman I want to see naked is my wife, and trust me, I'm not gonna be seeing that for a long while after I tell her about this."

Tuttle rolled his eyes. "What is wrong with you? Who decided that just because you get married you can't appreciate the scenery?"

Rainer saw Portwood's jaw clench.

"I enjoy the scenery at home," he spat. "So, why don't you pipe down."

A few seconds later, a woman appeared dressed in a barely there frock similar to the ones on the rest of the waitresses, but Rainer noted that she seemed younger and a little less sure of herself. She was overly eager to please.

Garrett's brow furrowed.

"Uh, hi, my name is Bridgette. Carol said you'd like a table upstairs?"

"Thanks." Garrett grabbed his beer and stood to follow Bridgette. Everyone else followed him.

"This good?" Bridgette led them to another table. This one was even closer to the Interfeci, so with a smile, Garrett nodded.

"Perfect." He winked at her, and she preened slightly. After taking the seat beside Ericcson, Rainer prayed this wouldn't be as bad as he was envisioning.

He finally allowed himself to look around. He took in a long catwalk with several poles placed along it. Several cages were located around the room. These all contained women dancing inside.

He began to sweat as he pushed his beer away. Wretchkinsides's men were talking and catcalling to the girls in the cages.

Once she'd seated them, Bridgette turned with an eager smile. "Is there anything I can do for you or that you'd like to see?" With that, she spun around, making her extremely short skirt flare to accentuate the point of the offer.

Garrett chuckled as Rainer quickly returned his gaze to the table. He was determined to keep it there for the entire afternoon. He was supposed to be listening. So, that's all he would do.

He began memorizing the lines in the wood on the tabletop and tried not to look at the girls in cages. It reminded him of the way he always felt when he and Logan went camping with the rest of the Haydenshire brothers when they were teenagers. Porn was always passed around. Rainer had certainly seen the best of what *Playboy*, *Jugs*, and *Spank* had to offer.

Emily never knew about that either, he reminded himself as he allowed the debate in his mind of just never telling her where he'd been all day to continue.

The guilt layered itself in his soul. His chest tightened as he tried to draw steadying breaths. How had things gotten so out of hand in one week? Besides the porn on their camping trips, Rainer couldn't think of a time in the last twenty years he hadn't wanted to tell Emily everything.

Music with a heavy lurid beat began blaring as red and purple lights flashed around the room. Bridgette made her way back to their table and refilled their beers.

As she left, Garrett elbowed Rainer. "Do you think she's old enough to work here?"

Rainer glanced Bridgette's way and shrugged. She did look young. She was probably his age, maybe a year or two older.

He was determined to tell Emily truthfully that he hadn't looked at any woman while he was here. So, he wouldn't allow himself to study her in any detail.

"The show will start in about five minutes," Bridgette drawled, "unless I can do something for you now."

Garrett smiled but shook his head. "We're fine for now, but don't go too far." He winked at her again and made quite a show of easing a one into her G-string.

Bridgette seemed thrilled as she spun and pointed to the back of the panties that came up over the top of the sheer skirt she was wearing. "How about another, stud?"

"You got it, baby," Garrett agreed as he slid another bill in the banding at the top of her backside.

The stage lights lit as women in elastic bras with no cups and G-strings took to the poles on the stage.

CHAPTER 22

THE UNDOING

LOGAN HAYDENSHIRE

Logan's phone rang again in his pocket. Sheer panic flooded through his rhythms. He didn't know what to say. Why did she keep calling him?

"Uh, man. Is that your mom or something?" Ramier finally asked. He'd been listening to Logan's pocket buzz for the past forty-five minutes.

"No, it's my sister."

Ramier nodded confusedly.

"Emily. You know, like, Rainer's fiancée, my sister."

"Oh, and he doesn't want her to know he's in there?"

Logan nodded as he glanced back across the street at the neon signs shaped like legs that flashed intermittently.

"That's a bad plan Lawson's got going. Always better just to fess up. Trust me."

"He'll tell her. He tells Em everything, but he didn't want to tell her over the phone," Logan defended Rainer. It's what they'd done since they were old enough to talk. He may have teased him about the whole crazy thing in the restaurant, but this was entirely different.

His phone began its annoying buzz again. It sounded more and more agitated with every hum.

"You better talk to her," Ramier urged.

"Yeah, maybe I can take some of the heat off of Rainer."

Emily began shouting before Logan could even get his phone to his ear.

"Em," he tried, but she wasn't going to stop. He decided to listen instead. He needed to try and figure out what she already knew.

"Two Iodex officers showed up here in the middle of practice and brought me this thing that said we're being sued by Stan. I've been calling Rainer for over an hour, and he isn't answering his phone. I called Dad, and he went down to Iodex. Vindico said he was on assignment or something. Where are you? Is he hurt? He's hurt, isn't he? That's why I have such a horrible feeling. Is that why you haven't been answering? Tell me where you are right now."

"Em, chill. Rainer is fine."

"Then why isn't he answering his phone?"

"Uh," Logan froze.

"Logan…"

"Vindico sent us out. Rainer didn't know they'd send the court summons to you."

"What? Wait. Rainer knew we were being sued for half of his inheritance because of me?" The haunting disbelief in her tone crushed Logan.

"Well, kind of. He was gonna tell you. He just didn't want to upset you. He's already talked it over with Stariff. He said not to worry. I'm sure no one's gonna give Stan anything." He continued to spin the web that would ultimately ensnare his very best friend. He just didn't know how to stop.

"He knew, and he talked to a lawyer without me?" Emily's voice trembled.

"He was gonna tell you tonight. I swear." Logan's rhythms tensed and then sank rapidly.

"Logan," she drew a shuddered breath. She was crying. Why did she always have to cry? "I need you to tell me the truth. I can tell you're lying. Where is Rainer right now? I need to know. I know something is wrong."

Logan swallowed. "He never meant to hurt you. He was going to tell you everything. I swear. He didn't want to go. He had to."

"Where is he?" she asked again in a pained, harrowed whisper.

"Vindico sent everyone out here to The Tantra to spy on some of Wretchkinsides's guys." Logan glanced around to make certain no one but Ramier could hear him. The only other person in the derelict store was the shopkeeper, who was looking at a magazine behind the counter.

"What's The Tantra?" She demanded.

"Uh...it's...kind of...like..." He tried to stall Rainer's inevitable undoing.

"Logan..."

"Like, a strip club. But, Em, I swear he didn't—"

The call ended suddenly.

CHAPTER 23

SO EASY TO BREAK, SO HARD TO REBUILD

RAINER LAWSON

Rainer's resolve not to look up eased slightly as one of Wretchkinsides's men began to chortle lewd remarks at Bridgette. Suddenly, he unzipped his pants and made an extremely vulgar request.

She rolled her eyes. "They are such jerks. Go to hell, Vasquez." With that, she spun and stomped back to the bar.

Rainer and Ericcson shared a nervous glance as the lights dimmed again. The room was bathed in blackness. The only light came from the now-lit catwalk and the spinning, colored lights in the ceiling.

Wretchkinsides's men let out more catcalls and wolf whistles as two girls climbed on poles in the center of the stage. Rainer put his head in his hands and willed this to be over quickly. He began formulating what he wanted to say to Emily as soon as he got home.

He studied Wretchkinsides's men. They'd had a fair amount to drink. They were all watching the pole dancers with avid interest, all except Vasquez, who was still eyeing Bridgette viciously.

As another song started playing, dancers began exiting the stage to walk around among the patrons. One of the pole dancers made her way to the table and offered a dance to any of the gentlemen surrounding Rainer.

"Sure, baby," Tuttle drawled. He flashed a stack of bills as she gave him a naughty grin. He scooted his chair back.

Certain he was going to be sick, Rainer ground his teeth. It was difficult to keep his eyes down when the guy across from him was getting a rather lurid lap dance.

Other dancers moved to the Interfeci table, and several of them took the girls up on their offer. Bridgette returned to see if they needed their drinks refilled.

With an uneasy glance, Rainer saw Bridgette had noticed Wretchkinsides's men's drinks were empty. She gave a dramatic eye roll and when the dancers left their table, she went to see if they'd like refills. As she leaned to pick up Vasquez's empty glass, he grabbed her hands and yanked her toward him.

Rainer and Garrett both started to stand as Portwood and Ericcson did the same. She struggled against Vasquez, and Rainer took quick inventory of the room.

"Where are the bouncers?" he hissed to Garrett.

"I haven't seen any. That's why they're hanging out here."

No one was going to help her. No one else was even able to see her.

Rainer whipped his head back around to Vasquez. He watched in horror as the man seated next to Vasquez flipped Bridgette's skirt up and reached to grab her. A large, brutish man seated in the back of the booth cupped his hand and summoned.

"Shit." Garrett leapt and sank his fist into Vasquez. He jerked Bridgette out of reach. Rainer and Ericcson summoned and halted two other men, who'd started to release furious heat from their hands toward Garrett. The glasses on the table shattered as the air filled with deflected casts.

Rainer saw Vasquez cup his hand until a pinkish-grey light formed. Rainer's heart raced. That was a mind-altering cast. He was going to try to get Bridgette to submit to his will by taking over her thoughts. The electricity housed in Non-Gifted people's minds made the mind-cast one they were susceptible to. If Vasquez could harness that electricity, she'd likely do as he wished.

Rainer let his training with Vindico work for him instinctively. He cupped his hand and threw a powerful shield cast over Bridgette, then he spun back. She stumbled back from the force. He concentrated hard and locked on to one of the other men's energy and subdued him. Portwood had another one down and had pulled his handcuffs from his belt. He was summoning until the cuffs glowed a brilliant green. Ericcson took out the huge guy in the back corner.

Rainer reached for his phone to call for backup. Seventeen missed calls. Absolute panic seized him as he forced himself to phone Logan.

"We need your help. We just arrested five guys."

Several minutes later, he helped load Wretchkinsides's men into one of the black SUVs that had driven up. Vindico slid out of the driver's seat. He was furious.

"So, you arrested the fuckers, yet we have virtually nothing on them, and you blew our cover, all in one afternoon?"

Rainer reeled as stunned fury washed over him.

"He summoned a mind-cast. That's illegal."

"Yes, but he didn't cast her. He'll be out in a few weeks. He won't roll over on Wretchkinsides for that!"

Suddenly the events of the past week and all that Rainer had endured, and the seventeen missed calls from Emily, were all more than he could take. He narrowed his eyes dangerously at Vindico.

"I'm so sorry, but I thought that protecting the Non-Gifted from assholes like that was part of being in Iodex," he seethed in Vindico's face. Vindico looked momentarily stunned. "Maybe I was mistaken, but I'm not going to sit by and watch someone be assaulted so that you can get your guy!"

Logan and Garrett stared wide-eyed at the hateful glares being exchanged between Vindico and Rainer.

Rainer spun, seated himself in the passenger side of Garrett's Highlander, and slammed the door.

As soon as the prisoners were loaded, Garrett and Logan climbed into the car with Rainer. It was a quarter to six when Garrett cranked the car. No one spoke.

Garrett's cell rang as they drove back to Iodex. "Hey there." He sounded genuinely thrilled to be talking to whoever was calling. "Is she okay?" His tone turned concerned a moment later. "All right, I'll tell him, but Fi, he really didn't have a choice." He paused again for a long drawn minute.

"Okay, call me if you want me to come out there." He ended the call and turned to Rainer.

"Emily's going over to Fionna's for a little while. Apparently Vindico had the officers who were delivering the summons for the lawsuit sent over to the arena, so she got that and then couldn't get you on the phone. Then she called Logan."

Garrett glanced at Logan in the rearview mirror. He looked extremely annoyed.

"I tried to tell her that it wasn't your fault. I swear. I told her you were gonna talk to her, and she made me tell her where you were. She cried."

Rainer's eyes closed in infuriated defeat.

"Fi lives over in Alexandria, but I wouldn't go over right now. She and Em are getting really close. They're both powerful Receivers, so let Fi try to talk to her. She said she'd either call me or text you when Em's ready to go home."

CHAPTER 24
TALK LOUD, RAINER

"Do you want me to catch a ride with Garrett?" Logan mumbled.

Rainer knew he felt bad about what he'd told Emily, but he just couldn't quite bring himself to forgive him yet.

"Do you mind?"

"No, and I'm really sorry. I was only trying to get her to calm down."

"I know." Rainer flung open the door to the Mustang. He wanted everyone to stop speaking to him altogether. He didn't want to hear anything. He just wanted to go back in time and not screw up everything the way he had.

He wanted to go to the arena and pick up Emily. He wanted to call her at lunch just like he'd promised. He wanted desperately to be able to go back and keep his word. How could he have kept so much from her?

On instinct alone, Rainer cranked the car and made a rapid exit from the parking deck. He let his Mustang soothe him. The metallic thrum of the motor, the feel of the leather seats that Emily had picked out, the gearshift in his hand all offered to carry him to an easier time. He did nothing but drive.

After an hour of clocking miles that led him nowhere, Rainer pulled into the parking lot and turned off the Mustang.

He tried to determine what exactly had led him here, but it didn't really matter. He knew he was there to talk to the wisest man he'd ever met. The one who'd been happily married for well over fifty years until his wife had died suddenly a few years back.

Rainer shoved open the door to the Mustang and stepped out. He drew a deep breath and inhaled the gasoline, motor oil, car fumes, and the scent of Old Spice aftershave. The combination soothed his frantic rhythms.

"Well, look at what the cat drug in," Sam drawled. He studied Rainer closely.

"Hey, Sam." He offered a forced smile.

Sam wiped his hands off on a dirty rag that he took from his coveralls.

"Your clutch sticking again, Rain Man?"

He shook his head and came to stand beside Sam. He stared under the hood of Sam's GTO. The inner workings of the car made sense. Nothing else did.

"No, the Mustang's great."

"Uh-huh." Sam moved to the Coke machine in the shop. It was from the sixties and only dispensed glass bottles. He'd refused to replace it with a newer model, although associates from Atlanta constantly pled with him to upgrade.

"*It's a classic,*" he'd always inform them, "*and I like Coke in glass bottles,*" he would add defiantly.

Sam inserted two dimes and picked up two cold bottles of Coke. He handed one to Rainer.

"Something's sticking." He raised his eyebrows and waited on Rainer to supply the real reason for his visit.

"Just thought I'd come by and see how you were doing. Is that all right?"

Sam gave a slight chuckle. "You know I love to see you, but that isn't why you're here."

By the end of the bottle of Coke, the whole sordid affair had been retold, including the court summons from his uncle and not telling Emily that he'd made Logan his beneficiary.

"She's over at one of her friend's houses. I've called, like, five times. She won't answer. She won't even speak to me to let me try to explain." He kicked a loosened stone in the gravel under his feet.

"Uh-hmm," Sam nodded, "That's because she thinks you had your hands on another car's bumper, and she knows you saw headlights that weren't hers. And I'd bet she doesn't really want to hear you tell her that you didn't because you already haven't been telling her the truth about a whole lot of things."

Rainer nodded.

"And did you?" He looked Rainer in the eye.

"Which part?" He wasn't offended by the question. There was no judgment in Sam's tone.

"Did you have your hands somewhere other than on your fiancée?"

"No. I would never do that. No lap dances, no nothing. She's it for me. Like I said, it was for work. I had to go."

Sam moved back to the hood of the GTO. "See, that's the crazy thing about love and fear, and the whole world revolving around one of those two emotions. It's like that, you know? The whole damn world is playin' for one team or the other."

Rainer watched Sam work, and he listened intently.

"She's scared, Rain Man."

"I know, but I don't know how to make her not afraid. I didn't mean to hurt her. I was trying to protect her."

"That's not what she's needing from you right now."

Rainer furrowed his brow and waited.

"I don't think Emily is afraid of you hurting her. I think she's afraid she won't be enough for you. That you might've seen something at that club she doesn't have, and you might decide you can't live without. You and I know it's crazy, but she's worried.

"Then you went and did stuff she should've known about, and now you swearing you didn't touch anything means no more than that rock you keep kicking. Your word isn't any good right now." Sam pulled the dipstick from the GTO and wiped it down with a rag.

"That's insane." Rainer began to pace from the GTO to the large tool chests on the wall. He wanted to combat The Tantra much more than he wanted to admit that he'd lied to Emily even if it was by omission.

"To you but not to her. Listen to me." Sam stopped working and leaned against the car. He stared at Rainer as he halted. "Nothing kills love like fear, and the other way around too. Now, I know there's a whole crowd of women that would holler at me for telling you this, but let 'em scream, because you need to hear me.

"In all of your trying not to worry her with things, and then you going off to places that bring nothing but trouble, I don't care who sent you or why, she doesn't feel safe anymore. She don't feel secure. That's a big problem, and it's your job to make her feel it again.

"Seems people nowadays wanna throw out the whole car 'cause the clutch sticks, but I taught you better than that. You know you keep all the great stuff in that car, and you just fix the clutch. You've got to make Emily understand that it isn't her body that makes your eyes pop out of your head. It's her heart and her mind and her soul.

"It's about way more than buying her a Hummer and decking it out to keep her safe. Keeping things from her isn't keeping her safe. It's right the opposite. She's gotta know you're gonna keep her heart safe."

Rainer managed a haggard nod.

"Seems to me that going to see other women take their clothes off might not be the best way to go about that, but you already figured that much out. You need to get Miss Haydenshire out of the fear side of things and back to the love side. Make her believe you, no matter how many times you gotta say it. Don't let her fear get a hold of her, or she might convince herself she don't have enough to hold you, and decide to trade you in. Listen to what she's saying even when she isn't talking, and then you gotta talk over the fear."

"Thanks, Sam." Unable to stop himself, Rainer threw his arms around Sam's neck. He chuckled and patted Rainer on the back in his embrace.

"Talk loud, Rain Man. You gotta make her hear you. Then you gotta build back that trust, and that isn't gonna be easy."

"I will. I promise." Rainer rushed back to the Mustang. To his delight, his phone chirped as his hand landed on the door handle.

> Hey Rainer, it's Fionna Styler. I kind of stole Emily's phone from her purse and took your number while she was in the bathroom. I'll tell her I did that. She's kind of big on people not lying to her right now. I think she's probably willing to talk to you if you want to come over. Maybe take her somewhere she feels safe. Her rhythms are really frightened. They're almost fractured. I'm worried about her. Receivers need to feel safe in order to connect to our powers. You've thrown everything off. Nothing makes sense to her right now.

She dropped a pin to her location.

Harrowed guilt took up residence once again in his gut. He swallowed down the terror. He'd fight. He'd plead. He would do anything in his power to undo everything he'd done in the past week.

This was never how it was supposed to be. He was supposed to be her Shield, and all he'd done was hurt her. He didn't want to keep things from her, and he never would again.

> I'm on my way

Rainer responded before he cranked the Mustang and backed out.

He let Sam's words of wisdom and Fionna's knowledge of Receivers reverberate through his soul as he drove.

He forced himself to consider the past week. He'd moved her out of her home, and then spent that week vowing to hunt down and destroy a monster who'd had a hand in her brother's murder.

She'd nearly been kidnapped on her first day of an extremely high-profile, high-pressure job that he'd largely ignored. He'd gone to a Gifted prison just following an earthquake and then needed her to take care of him. He'd been exhausted and inattentive, and when it came right down to it, he'd taken her for granted.

Then he'd taken her to New York where he'd acted like an idiotic teenager and had gotten them in the paper, sharing something that should only have been between the two of them.

To ice the bitter cake he'd baked, he hadn't informed her about a lawsuit that threatened half of their financial stability, hadn't told her that he'd had a will drawn up that did not include her, and then he'd gone to a strip club and not told her.

"Good job, Lawson," he stated out loud. He'd never been so thoroughly disgusted with himself.

CHAPTER 25
HELL HATH NO FURY...

Rainer raced out of his car and up the steps that led to Fionna Styler's '40s bungalow. It was only a few miles from the arena and from Sam's, so he'd arrived in less than ten minutes.

He drew a deep breath, not certain what he was going to find, but he knocked on the door anyway.

Fionna answered a moment later. She offered Rainer a kind smile, but she appeared to have been crying as well. Receivers who were particularly close often felt the emotion of their friends so intensely that they physically shared the emotion with them. Fionna Styler was said to be the strongest Receiver of their generation. At that moment, Rainer was certain that was true.

"Come on in." She stepped back and gestured into the house.

"Uh, thanks." He searched the cozy living room for Emily.

She appeared from the kitchen. Her eyes were almost swollen shut, and her face was red from her sobbing.

"I'm so sorry," Rainer pled.

She rolled her eyes and shook her head. Tears welled again.

"Why don't you go on home? I'll come over in the morning. We'll go get coffee," Fionna soothed. Emily nodded and hugged Fionna fiercely.

"He really does love you, so much. I can feel it," Fionna whispered.

Emily shot Rainer a vicious glare that physically wounded him as if she'd just backhanded him. He wished she'd just hit him. He'd gladly trade physical pain for emotional at that moment.

She walked as quickly as she could to the Mustang. Rainer tried to reach for her once, but she jerked out of his grasp.

"Do not touch me."

"What do you want me to say? I'm sorry. Please believe me. It was awful. I hated every second of today, and I never meant to lie to you. I was trying not to worry you."

She raised her head with baleful fury burning through her disbelieving eyes.

"How can I make this better? I'll do anything. I swear to you. I didn't want to go. I hated every second I was there. Ask Garrett. The whole thing was sick and disturbing, and I was going to tell you about the lawsuit."

As he begged, he realized how utterly ridiculous it was to even ask someone to forgive you when you had spent the last week keeping things from them.

"And when exactly did you plan on telling me that you'd changed your will that I didn't even know you had, and that you named Logan the person who gets the money or whatever?"

"Yeah, the two Iodex officers who showed up at practice told me that was probably what prompted the lawsuit. What was I supposed to say when I didn't know about that or the stupid lawsuit? You made me look and feel like a fool. I hate you. I hate you for making me feel like this. I hate you for saying you'd tell me everything and then not. You lied to me so many times. How can I ever trust you again?"

Her fury echoed off of the car windows and quaked in Rainer's blood. It pounded against his skull. She'd always had a fiery temper. They'd had their fair share of fights, but she'd never said she hated him.

"I know you don't believe anything I say to you right now." Rainer fought back the emotion that had his throat in its fierce grip. "And I don't deserve for you to believe me, but just please, please know how sorry I am. I swear to you. Everything I did, I did to protect you. I hated every moment of today. I was going to tell you everything tonight. I hate not telling you things. I'm just so sorry."

She crossed her arms over her chest and stared up at the darkening clouds. Hot, angry tears leaked down her face the entire drive back to the farm. Rainer pulled into the garage and turned off the car. He eased toward her.

"Please look at me, just please." He hesitantly pushed her hair behind her shoulder but was mindful not to touch her skin.

She cut her eyes to his with a hateful glower. "Do not touch me!"

"I am so sorry for how awful this must've been for you. I take full responsibility for how I made you feel. I could not be more sorry." He swallowed hard but refused to blink and break eye contact. "Please believe this—it was awful for me too."

Thunder cracked ominously around them, and she was momentarily terrified. Rainer reached for her, but she backed away. It shattered his heart.

Suddenly, she bolted into the house. Rainer raced after her but was greeted with their bedroom door being slammed in his face.

Logan and Adeline were seated on the couch. "I…made some soup and sandwiches." Adeline gave Rainer a truly sorrowful look.

"Thanks." He tried to determine what to do next.

"Hey, maybe you should just give her a little while. I think this all really shook her. You know?" Logan tried.

Rainer stared at their bedroom door. He turned the knob. She hadn't locked it. He momentarily debated Logan's advice but shook his head and pushed the door open.

She was lying facedown on her pillow. The movement of her shoulders betrayed the shudder of her tears. He moved into the room and closed the door quietly behind him. He sat down beside her.

"Em," he whispered, "I'm so sorry."

She turned her head slightly and nodded. "I know."

"Am I allowed to hold you?" He was afraid of her answer.

"I don't know." She drew a shuddering breath and then with vengeance scorned, "Did you hold anyone else today?"

The terror in her eyes was all that kept him from shouting, but he stood and walked away from her. He willed himself not to lose his temper.

"Do you really think I would do something like that?" He was unable to keep his anger at bay. She sat up and watched him pace. Finally, he moved to stand over her.

"Emily, I love you and only you. I don't have to go somewhere else to see attractive women. I have the most beautiful woman in the world lying in bed beside me each night, and I would never ever do anything to jeopardize what we have."

She stared up at him, trying to blink away the tears that flowed from her eyes. He sank down in front of her and wiped away the tears with his thumbs.

"Do you want me to tell you everything that happened? I will tell you every single thing, not leave anything out. I'll even go get Garrett, so you'll know that I'm not lying or covering anything up."

"No, you don't have to do that. I believe you. I can feel it, remember? The thing is, I don't know what to believe about the lawsuit or the will or anything else. I really, really hated today. I never thought you would lie to me, especially about things I should have been the first person you told."

Rainer joined her on the bed and started to put his arm around her but thought he should ask first.

"May I please hold you?" The hurt was clear in his tone. She shook her head vehemently but looked anguished.

"So, you didn't enjoy anything you did today?" The question rang with disbelief.

"No." He held her eyes with his own and willed her to read the truth in them. Rainer knew there were several reasons she refused to let him touch her. She was telling herself that he might've had his hands on another woman, but deep down she knew that wasn't true. She didn't want to feel his energy, and she didn't want him to feel hers.

Emily's internal Receiver's shield was set firmly. She'd been hurt and was protecting herself, but Rainer had shared her energy so often, he might be able to penetrate her shield if he tried. She didn't trust him enough in that moment to allow him access. She believed he might actually force his way in. It killed him.

A while later, he emerged from the bathroom. He was still racking his brain as to how to reassure her. She was lying in bed staring at the ceiling like it had greatly offended her. He went to lie beside her but made certain he didn't touch her. He didn't think he could watch her jerk away from him yet again and not come unglued.

"I love you," he whispered.

"I know." She drew a deep audible breath, and suddenly she moved to lie on his chest. He embraced her immediately. The motion made him feel whole. Hope sprang in his heart. He wanted desperately to vow to her that he would never keep anything from her again. He clung to her.

"I love you too." She moved away from him a moment later. She turned her back on him. She couldn't do it. She didn't believe him, and she couldn't let him hold her. It was far too intimate. She refused him her fear and her tears. She refused him her emotions, and those were the most important things in the world to a Receiver. They were how she existed. She refused to let him have any piece of who she was.

A dozen horrifying emotions swirled violently in the pit of his stomach. Hurt, anger, and heartbreak made a volatile cocktail as it coursed through his veins.

CHAPTER 26

COLD AND ALONE

Rainer awoke in the middle of the night cold and alone. He sat up and reached across the bed only to find it empty. Concern flooded through him. He glanced at the clock on his phone. It was almost three in the morning. He clambered out of bed while trying not to panic.

He crept out of their bedroom and into the kitchen. He stopped just before he stepped around the corner. He could hear Logan whispering.

"I swear he did all of that because he loves you so much. He just wasn't thinking. He knew you were freaked about everything that happened at the arena last week. He was trying not to scare you more. He didn't want to go to that stupid club. Garrett said he didn't do or see anything. He stared at a table the entire time. He's crazy about you."

He sounded like he had been saying these same things for quite a while. Rainer heard her ragged breath and peeked around the corner.

She was huddled on the sofa, covered in a quilt, with her head on Logan's shoulder. His T-shirt was wet under her face.

"Go back to bed. Wake him up. Talk to him. I can't fix this for you, as much as I wish I could."

She shook her head combatively. Logan glanced up and saw

Rainer standing in the corner. With a sorrowful shrug, he got off of the sofa. Emily's chin trembled. She appeared confused as to why he was leaving her. Rainer stopped him as he passed.

"Did she wake you up?" He was devastated that she was so upset she'd gotten Logan out of bed when he was right beside her.

He shook his head. "I couldn't sleep. I heard her crying in here."

Rainer slipped into the living room as Logan returned to bed. He knelt in front of her. With a harrowed breath, he touched her face.

"Em," he whispered. He tried not to sound as defeated as he felt. "Is there anything I can say or do to make this better? I will do anything."

She shook her head. "I'm fine," she lied.

"You're not fine. And it's my fault, and I'm going to fix this. Go on back to bed." He moved so she could stand. "I'll sleep here." He draped the quilt around her shoulders and watched her pad back to bed.

A gnawing sense of loss settled on him as he sank onto the couch.

CHAPTER 27

A NEW DAY

Rainer was silent for the entire car ride to work. Logan apologized repeatedly on Emily's behalf and thanked Rainer time and time again for going to the club so he didn't have to. But that wasn't the most egregious offense by a long shot.

"Hey," Logan gave up on Rainer and answered his phone a few miles before the exit for the Pentagon.

Rainer found himself listening but not really caring who Logan was talking to. "No, Rainer slept on the couch last night. She moped around until we left."

Rainer assumed it was Garrett who had called. He listened with slightly more interest.

"I don't care how young she is. She's being a bitch."

"Stop it now. Do not ever call her that!" Rainer spat furiously.

Logan's mouth dropped as he nodded his understanding. "Okay, sorry," he offered hesitantly. "Hey, Garrett, we're almost there. I'll see you in a sec, okay?"

After flashing his badge, Rainer moved behind Logan, not really seeing anything in front of him. Emily had walked past him that morning from their bed to the couch once he'd gotten up. She hadn't spoken. She hadn't even acknowledged his existence in any way. Her eyes were swollen, hollow, and heartbroken.

The only person she'd ever trusted with her heart, with her awe-inspiring empathic energies, had let them slip through his hands without thought. Her Shield had forsaken her, and there wasn't anything he could do to fix what he'd done.

He slunk to his desk and yawned. He hadn't slept at all. His muscles ached with the pain of raw desolation.

Garrett and Logan shared a concerned glance, but Rainer did nothing to try and look like he wasn't miserable.

Vindico emerged from his office and ordered the members of the Wretchkinsides task force to his desk.

With a dejected huff, Rainer followed Garrett inside. He leaned back against the wall, too tired to do much besides glare at his boss.

"I owe you all an apology," Vindico began. "And, Lawson, you were absolutely right—maybe I let the big picture cloud my judgment a little too often. I'm sorry."

Rainer was shocked at the fervency of the apology. Vindico studied Rainer closely for a minute before going on.

"Three of the five men you arrested had pending warrants in Mexico. The others are singing like songbirds. They're hoping to stay out of Felsink." Vindico grinned.

Far too exhausted to feel vindicated, Rainer continued to listen.

"So, as a peace offering," Vindico chuckled, "I want you three,"—he gestured to Garrett, Logan, and Rainer—"to stake out a safehouse I got out of Flores. He's new to the game and wasn't feeling too loyal to Nic last night. It's in the Highlands. Portwood and Ericcson will replace you at noon, and you can have the rest of the day off."

"Thanks, man." Garrett grinned.

"No problem. You earned it. Teach them the rules of staking out a house while you're there though."

"You got it."

With that, Rainer followed Logan and Garrett back to their desks. Before he could begin strapping on his shoulder holster and grabbing his badge, Governor Haydenshire came through the Iodex doors.

"Daniel, can I borrow Rainer for just a few minutes before you send him off to wherever it is you've got them going?" he requested, but everyone in the office was well aware that Vindico had no choice in the matter.

Rainer's weary heart tried to hammer nervously but only managed a few stuttered beats before it returned to its sluggish cadence.

"Oh, yeah, I guess," Vindico huffed. "Just leave whenever you're finished."

"Yes, sir."

The governor gave him a kind, soothing smile. He slapped Rainer on the back and caught his shoulder with a reassuring shake.

"We won't be long."

"We'll wait in the parking deck," Garrett eased as he and his father shared an unspoken conversation.

CHAPTER 28

WISE COUNSEL

"Sit down, son. I'd offer you coffee, but truthfully, right now you look like something much stronger might be in order." The governor tried for a joke, but Rainer didn't feel like laughing.

"I'm all right, sir."

"That might be the biggest lie I've heard in my lengthy years as a dad, and believe me, I've heard some doozies." The governor joined Rainer on the couch instead of sitting behind his desk. "So, you're not all right, and my baby girl is not all right, and I was kind of hoping that just because you turned twenty-one and moved out of my house it didn't mean you were going to stop asking me for my help occasionally."

"I'm not really sure you can help me this time, sir." His heart lightened just a little as he stared into the kind, concerned eyes of the man who'd raised him.

"I appreciate your confidence." Governor Haydenshire chuckled.

"I didn't mean it like that," Rainer redacted. "It's just I screwed up pretty bad this time."

"I heard," the governor soothed. "Baby girl came up to the house after you left for work. She wanted Lillian. They always want Mama when something goes wrong, but I did get to listen in on the conversation."

Rainer tried not to let his heartbreak that Emily had sought out her mother show on his face. He couldn't recall the last time Emily had been so upset she'd gone to her parents instead of talking to him.

"Being an adult, honestly, sometimes it doesn't seem to matter what you do, it just ends badly. I know how much you adore her, and I know that the very essence of your energy is to protect her. I just think you might've gotten a little off track as to how to go about that."

Rainer nodded, and hope began to make a timid return to his heart.

"You already know this, and I'm certain you'll correct it in the future, but I'd say you probably should've told Emily before you went to talk to Jack about naming Logan your beneficiary. As much as she seems like she doesn't want to talk about some things, believe me, she doesn't want to hear that from Iodex officers who show up at Angels Arena and announce something like that in front of a bunch of people she'd really like to impress. And, if I may, I'd say finding out that you're going to be involved in a lawsuit that threatens half of your inheritance would've been worthy of waking my baby girl up."

"I know," Rainer agreed.

"And I know where Daniel sent you yesterday and that you don't want me to know that. I know you saw things you didn't want to see. I also know that you're terrified of the pain you caused Emily and that I might be disappointed in you. And I'd dare say the thought of your old man seeing you in there yesterday, God rest his soul, has you just about sick."

"My father fought and died for women's rights within the Realm, for them to get equal pay and be able to be Senteon Representatives and on the governing board, not for them to be put in cages to dance for assholes."

Governor Haydenshire gave him an understanding nod. "I know it's mighty hard to see the thousand shades of gray in something you're sure is black and white, but women's rights means that they can dance in those cages if that's what they want to do and there shouldn't be any shame in that."

Rainer added that to his lengthy list of mistakes.

The governor cleared his throat. "If I tell you a story, do you think we could keep it between us? You can tell Emily if you want. I know you well enough to know you've promised yourself never to keep things from her again, but I'd prefer the boys not know this."

"Yes, sir."

The governor shook his head, as the memory seemed to form in his eyes. "A few weeks before Lillian and I were set to walk down the aisle, she showed up at my studio apartment, the one I'd somehow gotten her to agree to move into after the wedding."

Rainer smiled. The motion eased his soul and felt odd at the same moment.

"She, uh...she was sobbing," Governor Haydenshire choked. His voice turned haggard from just the thought of Mrs. Haydenshire crying.

"Why?" Rainer didn't care that he sounded like a child being told some kind of fantastic tale. He knew in that moment the man who sat before him, who had raised him, and who'd been married for thirty-two years, was the only one who could help him.

"Well," Governor Haydenshire sighed. He glanced out the window that overlooked the mighty Potomac. "I remember thinking she'd finally realized what a huge mistake she'd made when she said she'd marry me, that she'd finally come to her senses and was giving the ring back. I thought she was crying because she didn't want to hurt me."

The truthfulness of his statement spoke volumes. Rainer was sitting in the office of one of the most powerful men in the world, an American Governor of the Gifted Realm. Mrs. Haydenshire hadn't ever worked outside of their home, to Rainer's knowledge. She'd birthed the governor's ten children and raised them up solid and strong and moral along with Rainer. She'd cared for them, nourished them physically and emotionally. She'd endured the Realm's obsessive chatter about how many kids they had. She'd undergone scrutiny time and time again about her weight.

All the while, she'd stood solidly by the governor's side with a smile as she gazed up at him with a look that told the entire world she could never love anyone more or be more proud of her husband.

As Rainer listened to Governor Haydenshire's story, he

understood. Everything the man had accomplished and done would never have happened—it would all have been null and void—had it not been for his wife. She held all of his cards, and he'd walk away from the plush office, and the power, and the position in a heartbeat if she wasn't happy.

"She didn't give the ring back," Rainer stated knowingly.

"No." Governor Haydenshire drew a deep breath. "She didn't. She was carrying this paper bag, and I didn't know what to do. But she'd showed up on my doorstep with tears running down her beautiful face, so I wrapped my arms around her and eased her inside. I begged her to tell me what was wrong, what I could do to fix it." He drew another steadying breath.

"I had a futon that I got at a secondhand shop. So, I sat down and she sort of fell beside me. When she sat down, the bag opened, and I saw it. That bag held the sum total of all I'd taken from her and all that I couldn't give back. I won't call it a mistake, because it wasn't, but if I had it to do over I'd probably change the order of things just a little."

Rainer was thoroughly confused. He hoped the governor would explain what had been in the bag without him having to ask.

"See, son, I wasn't a governor back then. Your dad and I were trying desperately to get the Realm to overturn the current governing board because they were all corrupt. We tried to get the Realm to see how we could do it so much better, but then I was nothing more than a lowly Senteon aide.

"I hardly made enough to feed myself much less Lillian. And there I sat and stared at a positive pregnancy test lying on my secondhand futon. That might've been why I was a little hard on you after your beach trip a few weeks ago," he allowed. "But back then, it was a much bigger deal than it would be now. The Realm had been stripping women's rights away from them for years. They'd taken away her choices. They'd removed all of her options. And what they hadn't taken from her, I had."

Rainer's mouth hung open. He'd known Will had been born almost nine months after the Haydenshires' wedding, but he'd always assumed they'd conceived on their honeymoon.

"I think I'll leave that very long conversation between my wife and me between us, but two weeks later it was the night before the wedding and I was a disaster. I tried to be there for Lill and assure her that I would take care of both of them, but I had no real idea how I was going to do that. I'm sure my reassurances ran rather dry.

"Our wedding was to take place at eleven the next morning. The night before, your old man, and Regis, and Arthur Vindico, and a few other guys who'd been working with us to get us all elected, showed up to take me out. I'd told Joe and Regis about Lillian, and they'd decided I needed a break from beating myself up, I suppose.

"So, your dad thought maybe we should have a proper bachelor party and suggested we hit a few clubs down near where you were yesterday. Trust me, if you'd spilled the god-awful mixed drinks they were serving on one of the tables, it would've covered vastly more than any of the women dancing that night were wearing."

"My dad took you to a strip club?" Rainer gasped.

This made the governor laugh. "He did, and Joe would be telling you this story if he were here right now instead of me. I spent the evening drowning my sorrows in liquor-infused paint thinner and watching women take their clothes off in my lap. I remember thinking that I was supposed to enjoy what we were doing, but I didn't. It just wasn't what I wanted to see. I think so often men go to places like that hoping to find something fulfilling, but they actually end up with less of themselves.

"I kept drinking, and kept getting lap dances because I thought I was supposed to, and I just kept feeling more and more disgusted with myself. The well tends to run very dry, very quickly in places like that.

"So, back to this debacle with my little girl. Think about what I just told you. I'd left my pregnant fiancée at her parents' home, after our rehearsal dinner, the night before our wedding, to go out and see other women get undressed. I didn't even have the my-boss-made-me-go excuse. I went of my own accord." He shook his head.

"I feel certain you remember Lillian being pregnant with the twins a few years ago, but let me reiterate that sometimes when women are pregnant, they are extremely emotional. Not that I had any business doing what I was doing, but the fact that she could hardly zip up that skin-tight wedding gown was entirely my fault. And I was out looking at other women, ones who weren't carrying my baby and who weren't wearing my ring on their swollen fingers. It didn't matter how many times I swore that none of them were as beautiful as she was, or how many times I told her that I hadn't even enjoyed the evening. She wasn't going to believe a word I said. I did convince her to go on with the ceremony, but I slept on the floor, without even a blanket, of our honeymoon suite that her parents had paid for on our wedding night."

Rainer's mind raced. "How did you get her to forgive you?"

"First, let me tell you that Emily is the one who told me Daniel sent you and that you went so Logan didn't have to. So, she's still coming to your defense, which is a lot more than Lillian was doing back then. Emily Anne was curled up on my kitchen window bench, staring out at the barn like it was going to collapse along with the rest of her world this morning because she let that red hair fly and told you she hated you. It wasn't because you went to a strip club, or didn't tell her about the lawsuit, or had a will arranged without her knowledge."

Rainer was stunned. He let that wash over him for a full minute before he could respond. "She has every right to hate me."

The governor smiled kindly before he went back to his story. "On my wedding night, I lay there on the floor, which in my opinion was generous on her part. I would've slept in the hallway or the truck if she'd asked. I just lay there and racked my brain trying to figure out how I'd done what I'd done. How I'd hurt her so badly in one night's time. I got up off the floor and sat in this chair in the corner. I watched her sleep. I remember sitting there and thinking that she was so strong, and I was so incredibly weak. I understood so much, in that moment, just watching over her. She was the strongest person I'd ever met, and I knew that I was the only person who could really hurt her, because I was the one she'd allowed to hold her heart."

Rainer nodded but didn't want to speak. He was afraid Governor Haydenshire would stop his story, and he desperately wanted him to keep going.

"All of the moments from the time I'd asked her to go to that formal with me right up until she walked down the aisle, no one else knew about those or felt those with her. I held every memory and everything she'd ever given me in my hands, and I'd been so incredibly careless. I'm certain you've heard more of my father's expressions over the years than you'd ever cared to. But, if you'll allow me one, my dad used to say, 'Stephen, either make hay or get the hell out of the way and let the army get it done.'"

Rainer was shocked to find himself laughing with the governor.

"I didn't want the Gifted Army anywhere near my wife and my baby, so I decided I'd better figure out how to be the husband Lillian Anderson deserved, because I wanted her to be proud to be Lillian Haydenshire. God knows I'll never deserve that phenomenal woman, but I will never stop trying to be everything she needs. I watched over her while she slept all night long in that gigantic bed that she did her best to take up most of, because she was damned and determined I wasn't getting anywhere near her."

The governor laughed heartily over the memory. "Emily Anne gets her temper from her mother, but I'll deny ever saying that."

Rainer was still chuckling as he nodded his understanding.

"Sometimes, our spouses need something to hold on to. Some symbol that we know we screwed up and that we swear we'll never screw up like that ever again. They need to know that when the going gets tough, we're not going to keep things from them or end up at a strip club. It doesn't have to be a physical thing, but something that reminds them that you're in this with them and that, come hell or high water, you want to be wherever they are, fighting the tides right beside them.

"A gesture if you will. Rebuilding Emily's trust will take you making the right choices over and over and over again until she believes you, but something that makes her see that you plan on making those right choices from now on might go a long way. A marking in time that shows her that from this moment on, you're going to do better, and be better, and that you'll never stop trying to be what she needs you to be."

"Okay, I can do that." Rainer wasn't certain what he was going to do, but having some kind of plan was much better than the hollow emptiness he'd walked into the office with a few minutes before.

The governor nodded and gave Rainer a wry smile. "Nobody

makes my baby girl smile like you do, so I feel certain you can come up with some way to prove yourself. As for Lillian, I sat up all night long and just thought about what our life was going to be and how I might be able to provide for her and show her that I was in this with her. I made a late-night phone call to your old man and borrowed several thousand dollars that he never would let me pay back. I figured out that if we checked out of that swanky chalet in the Poconos the next morning, that they would refund the rest of the week to us. I had her coffee ready and waiting for her when she woke up the next morning, and I made my plea. I told her that I didn't need a honeymoon or anything else, that I had everything I would ever need glaring at me in the ugliest flannel nightgown I'd ever seen. She'd taken it from her grandmother's home when she found out where I'd been the night before our wedding."

Rainer doubled over laughing, and the governor joined in.

"I took her home and got rid of the futon and everything else in that apartment she hated. I took her shopping. We got a crib, a couch, and a real bed, with sheets and blankets that barely fit in that one room. We bought her that old pot and pan set that she has out in the storage barn now. She won't ever let me give it away. It was the best we could do then, and she certainly has much nicer now, but that meant so much to her then. I bought her a teapot she admired and all of the tea she wanted. I picked up a few quilts and a set of mixing bowls, the yellow ones on the counter at the house that she uses when she makes you kids those chocolate chip cookies you love, and the other things she wanted that let her make a home. Because the home was what she most wanted. She's an Occamist and creating is her power.

"I made certain that she knew that I would be in that home with her every night and every day right beside her, and that was the only place I ever wanted to be. Then I bought a set of 50th anniversary champagne glasses. As I recall, the 50 is painted in hunter green and burgundy, and they have a horrible gold rim, but I do intend to make a toast to her, here in about eighteen more years, and to drink out of those glasses. That's why I bought them. I wanted her to know that I wasn't going anywhere, and that in fifty years I was still going to be right there, right beside her, no matter what happens."

"Those are the ones in the china cabinet," Rainer realized.

Governor Haydenshire nodded. "On the top shelf right in the center. They're in front of our wedding china."

Rainer had always assumed those glasses had belonged to some distant relative, but he understood they were just as much a part of the present as they were the past and the future.

"Did, uh...she let you use the bed you bought?" He wasn't certain he should ask.

Governor Haydenshire laughed. "Yeah, I was allowed in the bed that night in our home with my wife and our little boy between us."

Rainer was eager to leave. He wanted to get started right away. A million ideas swam in his head. He just needed to figure out which ones were perfect.

"Before you go off and spend a fortune on my daughter, a few more things. Remember it doesn't have to be a physical thing. Try to think about what she feels is missing in your relationship currently, and how you can show her that you won't let things be missing anymore. Emily's power is in emotions so you likely need to make an emotional appeal. And I'd like to talk to you about Iodex and Dan Vindico, if I can have a few more minutes of your time."

"Oh, yes, sir." He settled back on the couch.

"I know Dan told you and Logan about Amelia. That was certainly a horrible thing that happened to her and him alike. But Daniel has let that one horrible moment in time drive every decision he's made since then.

"As much as he's vowed never to let you or anyone else live the hell he's been through, he is perfectly willing to use you to get what he wants. It will take a very, very special person to get Dan to see there's more to his life than the vengeance he seeks. And that would require Daniel actually allowing someone to get close to him again. I don't hold out much hope for that, but Amelia isn't here with us anymore. Emily is here, and you have a life outside of that office." He threw his thumb back in the general direction of Iodex.

"I know it makes a great deal of sense to you to end the danger that you see threatening Emily and to make that your top priority. But let me ask you, son, if you hunt down Dominic Wretchkinsides but lose her to your inattention somewhere in between, what will you have gained?"

Rainer gave a slight nod. "I wanted to tell Vindico all last week that I needed to be the one to pick her up from the stadium, and that I can't work endlessly every night like he does. I need to be home with her. We need to be in our home together. She has to be the most important thing always."

The realization brushed the confusing webbing from his mind. He hadn't known when to stand up to his boss because he hadn't been able to decide what was more important.

"Smart man." The governor nodded. "Why don't you let Governor Willow and me speak with Dan, but if what you're working on at five o'clock can wait until tomorrow, then I suggest you go and pick Emily up from the arena and be her fiancé instead of just her Shield."

"Thank you, sir, for everything. Really!"

Governor Haydenshire stood. The pride in his eyes had Rainer desperate to prove himself worthy once again to the governor and Emily.

"Don't get so caught up in making up with Emily that you forget you're supposed to be going somewhere with Garrett and Logan. I told Dan I really thought he'd worked his task force quite enough lately and that I thought you could use a little time off. I suspect he took 'a little time' to mean that he would allow you to leave after lunch."

Rainer grinned. "Yes, sir."

"Go on and get whatever it is he has you chasing after today caught. Then the next time I see you and my baby girl, I wouldn't mind a few more smiles."

"I'm working on it. I promise."

CHAPTER 29

TO RIGHT A WRONG

He barely stopped moving as he flew by his desk to grab his badge. A moment later, he was on the parking deck. Garrett and Logan were leaned against the Highlander engrossed in a tight-lipped conversation.

"Are you ready?" Garrett ended their talk abruptly.

"Yeah. Logan, would you mind riding with Garrett? I want to leave as soon as Portwood and Ericcson show up." He wasn't playing anymore. He wasn't going to try to pacify Vindico, and Logan, and everyone else. All of his desperation to keep everyone thinking that he could handle it all had done nothing but hurt the only person who mattered.

"Uh, sure." Logan shrugged. He looked mildly annoyed, but he covered it well.

"The 'Stang is a little recognizable, Rainer." Garrett shook his head. "Bring it, but we'll have to park it several miles away."

Rainer leapt into the driver's seat. He cranked the car and touched Fionna's name on his contact list at the same moment. He found it mildly odd that he was calling one of the most famous Arlington Angels in the history of Summation, but that it didn't seem strange at all.

"Hey, Fionna, it's Rainer Lawson." He started as soon as she answered.

"Uh, hey, Rainer. Is Emily okay?"

"No, not really, but I'm working on that. Would you mind telling me if you're still planning on taking her out for coffee?"

"Yeah, I'm headed out to the farm in just a few minutes. I thought I'd see if some retail therapy might help too."

"Thank you, that's perfect. Could you help me with a surprise for her?"

Fionna agreed to do anything she could to help.

Rainer ended the call and followed Garrett to Aurora Highlands. Garrett pulled the Highlander into a busy grocery store parking lot.

Rainer emerged from the Mustang and set one of the shield casts Vindico had taught him. It was a specialized cast that used less of his energy to maintain but was stronger because it continually pulled energy from the air around the car.

"The house is a few miles that way." Garrett pointed down an adjacent street. "The main thing about a stakeout is not to be noticed. You need to blend in with the surroundings."

Rainer climbed into the back of the Highlander as Garrett continued.

"The next rule of a stakeout is to buy really good snacks, because the Senate is reimbursing you," he joked as he pulled into a gas station parking lot. "But liquids are not always your friend so keep that in mind. I recommend avoiding water unless the stakeout is set to last more than eight hours." They each purchased Dr Peppers along with peanuts, Twizzlers, and Doritos.

They climbed back into the car, and Garrett eased across the litter-lined street. He pulled next to the curb several houses down from Wretchkinsides's safehouse and hid the Highlander between two other cars.

It was a two-story house in ill repair. The shrubs had taken over the sagging front porch. The paint was peeling, and it appeared to have been abandoned. They sat there in silence for a long while, occasionally checking the interior of the home with a pair of binoculars but not seeing anything.

Rainer barely paid attention to the home or the stakeout. He replayed Governor Haydenshire's story along with the advice he'd gotten the night before from Sam in his mind.

He could buy her most anything in the world, but that wasn't going to solve the problems he'd created. She needed time, and a commitment, and a fiancé instead of just a Shield.

Rainer sighed. He'd had sex with her repeatedly over the weekend and then promised he wasn't keeping anything from her. Getting her to have sex with him was not his goal, not that he would turn her down.

They needed to talk for hours about everything that had happened. They hadn't really even discussed Cascavel and her attempted abduction. Rainer had served only to try and quiet her fears, not listen to them and hear her out. He didn't want her to be afraid. His Predilect had taken over his brain. He'd been treating her like an infant.

"Hey, Logan," Rainer broke the silence in the car. "I will pay for you and Adeline to stay wherever you want tonight as long as it's not at our house."

"Is she really that bad?" Logan quizzed, and Rainer was pleased to see that Logan's irritation with Emily seemed to have dissolved into concern.

He nodded and glanced toward the house, so he didn't have to look at either Logan or Garrett.

"Yeah." Logan nodded. "But I'll take care of it. I owe you anyway."

Garrett nodded his approval.

"Thanks," Rainer breathed his appreciation.

"Look at what we have here." Garrett pulled out his phone and began snapping pictures of none other than Dominic Wretchkinsides.

"Why can't we arrest him? He tried to take Emily," Logan demanded.

"Whoa there." Garrett's massive arm slung across Logan's chest to keep him from getting out of the car. "He was inside Les's pub when she was almost taken. Don't you get it? That's how he works. He always has an alibi, and he never gets his hands dirty. He's the mastermind with more blood on his hands than anyone in the entire

Realm, but we don't have enough evidence on him to keep him in Felsink for a month. We also don't have a warrant for his arrest, and we have no evidence that would get us a warrant."

"What about Amelia?" Rainer wondered out loud. "Vindico watched him kill her, right? Why can't we arrest him for murder?"

Garrett was visibly impressed. "Unfortunately, Dan went to complete shit that night. He never called me. He never called Caddick. He just went all alone. Then he got himself mind-casted. Medios and most Gifted people can see the residuals of that kind of cast for days after the casting. A person who's been mind-casted can't testify because they may not have actually seen what they thought they saw. If Dan had just taken someone with him, someone who could have seen Nic set the cast, even if we hadn't gotten Amelia out, we could still have arrested Wretchkinsides. But he was a pompous dumbass."

Wretchkinsides had returned into the house for a moment but then walked back out toward the side yard.

"What's he doing?" Garrett continued to snap pictures.

Suddenly, Wretchkinsides lifted what appeared to be a well-hidden wooden door into the ground. He descended into some kind of bomb shelter or maybe an old still hideaway.

"Dan'll be thrilled with that little bit of info." Garrett seemed stunned that they'd gotten something to take back.

Nothing happened for several long minutes, and Rainer's mind went back to Emily. Everything from romantic clichés he knew she loved, to places he might convince her to talk to him, to her favorite kinds of flowers flitted rapidly through his mind.

Her loft and their tryst from a few weeks before intrigued him but, truthfully, making out in the loft was in their past, and as important as that was, what Emily needed was a piece of their future.

"I'm hungry," Logan whined.

"You're not hungry. You're bored," Garrett scoffed.

Food suddenly became a part of Rainer's plan. He didn't want to take her out though. He wanted her alone. They needed to talk about everything and nothing.

He'd order anything she wanted. He didn't care where he had to go to acquire it, but he wanted them to stay home where she could scream at him or cry—whatever needed to happen so that they could heal.

He needed to be able to talk until she really listened, and that wasn't going to happen in a restaurant full of other people and the intrusive press.

"No, I'm hungry," Logan argued.

"Fine, let's go get some sandwiches." Garrett rolled his eyes as he eased the car forward. "We need to park somewhere else anyway. We've been here too long."

Debate filled Rainer's mind. He needed to prove to her that he would always take care of her. He also needed to prove to her that he wanted to work with her to fight the tides together just like the governor said.

Rainer's rapid thoughts left him startled when he heard the Highlander's emergency brake engage. He followed Garrett and Logan inside a small sandwich shop that didn't seem to fit in with the run-down storefronts.

Rainer breathed in the peace it afforded him. The smell of freshly baked bread in the warm glow of the restaurant soothed him.

A woman with wind-pricked cheeks greeted them. They smiled and exchanged pleasantries and ordered several sandwiches, chips, and Dr Peppers, before heading back out into the drizzling rain.

They returned to the safe house. This time Garrett parked on the street behind. Rainer unwrapped his sandwich and took a bite.

Logan all but moaned. "This is the best sandwich I've ever had."

Garrett chuckled and nodded his agreement. "Yeah, well, I wouldn't be telling our mother that."

The sandwich was delicious, Rainer agreed, and a sudden thought occurred to him. He considered more evening plans while keeping an eye on the safehouse, but nothing interesting was going on near it.

"Hey, you know, I once got a girl to sleep with me by packing her an indoor picnic," Garrett began to brag as he lifted the sandwich in exultation.

Logan rolled his eyes, and a genuine chuckle escaped Rainer's mouth.

They both seemed thrilled they'd gotten some kind of reaction out of him, so Garrett continued, "You know, candlelight, fireplace, wine. You can feed her. She can suck you."

"Thanks, I got the picture," Rainer quipped.

As Garrett continued on with the lewd story, Rainer's mind became resolute. He had no intention of letting Emily do anything for him, not that she was offering. He'd taken her to one of the nicest restaurants in New York, and he'd acted like a prepubescent moron. Taking things back to simpler times was definitely the way to go.

A picnic sounded perfect. Life had been much easier before they'd graduated and gotten jobs, before he'd inherited the vast Lawson estate that he now stood to lose half of, and before they'd started sleeping together.

Life just keeps going, Rainer, even when you want so badly for it to stop for a little while, or even just slow down. It keeps right on going, and we have to go with it. So, son, just hold on tight because it won't wait on you to catch up. His father's words of wisdom rang in his ears and reverberated against the recesses of his mind.

He'd never been closer to losing the thing that meant the most.

At a quarter til twelve, Garrett drove back to the grocery store parking lot. Portwood and Ericcson were waiting for them.

Rainer gave them a half wave as he sprinted to his Mustang. He pulled the cast back into his body as he neared.

"Are you going to get more sandwiches?" Logan called. Rainer nodded as he flung the door open. "We'll meet you there."

"Well, hello again, boys. I hope you haven't come back because you didn't care for your sandwiches?" the woman fretted momentarily.

"Oh no, ma'am," both Logan and Rainer assured her that their lunch was delicious.

"Actually," Rainer cleared his throat and gave her what he hoped was a dazzling grin, "I was hoping you might be willing to help me with something."

She looked eager to help, so he continued.

"I'd really love to take my fiancée on a picnic, and I was wondering if you might be able to pack up some sandwiches and maybe a few desserts in a basket or something for us this evening?"

"Aren't you just so sweet. I hope your fiancée knows how lucky she is." The woman began glancing around the chilled counter area, considering.

"I'm not thinking lucky would be Emily's take right now," Rainer said under his breath.

Logan slapped him on the back. "It's Em, so if by tonight she just no longer wants to suffocate you in your sleep, you've made really good progress."

"Thanks." Rainer rolled his eyes.

The woman stopped suddenly and gazed out the windows. Rainer glanced at his watch. Fionna had agreed to keep Emily out of the house for a couple of hours, but he needed to hurry. He still had several other stops to make.

She offered Rainer a condoling smile. "I'm worried it's been too rainy for a picnic. Maybe come back tomorrow, and I'll pack you something extra special. She won't want to be out of doors now. It's just too wet." She seemed to believe Rainer was too in love to make rational decisions.

He tried to discern the best way to persuade this woman to pack the picnic without telling her that he intended to eat it in their bed.

Garrett chuckled but then came to Rainer's rescue. "Girls like indoor picnics. Right, Rainer?"

"Oh, my husband proposed at a picnic in front of a roaring fire." The woman clasped her hands as she reminisced with a glint in her eye that made Rainer hopeful.

She came back to the here and now and eyed Rainer for a moment. "I know you're young and obviously just getting started, so how much did you want to spend?"

He smiled and tried not to laugh. "The sky's the limit."

She looked slightly taken aback but gave him an impressed smile as she began pulling things out of the chilled cases. She glided into a back room and returned with a large basket.

After questioning Rainer as to Emily's favorite kinds of sandwiches, salads, and pastries, she began to put together a beautiful spread.

After adding small bags of gourmet chips, she smiled. "Now, do you have a blanket? You'll need a blanket even if you eat this on a rug in front of a fire."

"Oh, yes, ma'am." It was way too hot for a fire, but he didn't comment. "I'll take care of it."

"How about some chocolate candies?"

"Yeah, that'd be great."

With a thoughtful nod, she began adding tiny, heart-shaped chocolates wrapped in pink foil around the sandwiches and containers of salads.

"Oh, I know." She went to a refrigerated counter near the drinks and pulled out some strawberries. "These will be a bit more money," she said tentatively.

"It's fine, really," Rainer reassured her again.

As she was adding up the contents of the basket on the cash register, Logan and Garrett placed an order for two more sandwiches each, which Rainer suspected was the reason they'd accompanied him in the first place.

As the woman prepared Logan's sandwiches, Rainer swiped one of his cards. He thanked the woman profusely before he turned to leave. Logan took the paper bag that contained his and Garrett's snack and followed Rainer out the door.

"Come back and let me know how she likes everything," the woman called sweetly.

Logan laughed outright, while Rainer thanked her again and promised to return to let her know how Emily had liked the picnic.

"So, when exactly are we allowed to come home?"

"We have to work tomorrow, so I assumed you'd be home after that, honey," Rainer sneered. It felt good to be able to joke with Logan again. "Oh and I'll be late to work from now on, so would you mind taking Adeline to work or her taking you? I'm going to be taking Emily to the arena the mornings she has to work."

"Uh, that's assuming she thinks this picnic thing is sweet and not stupid and actually agrees to get in the car with you."

CHAPTER 30

A FOUNDATION

As Rainer turned toward the interstate, doubt took up residence where his momentary hopefulness had just vacated. *It's a picnic. I lied to her, hid things from her, and to top it all off, she's telling herself I essentially cheated on her with strippers.*

He knew the kinds of things going on in Emily's mind. He just didn't know how to combat them.

He shook his head and tried to forcefully remove the doubt. *This has to work. I have to make her believe me.*

A sudden thought occurred to Rainer. He needed to link their past and their present while proving he would always be there for their future, just like Governor Haydenshire's champagne flutes. He did need to make an emotional appeal. He needed to communicate in her preferred language.

Rainer exited the interstate in McLean and made the first of several stops.

He checked his watch again as he raced up the farmhouse steps.

I need another half hour.

He sent the text to Fionna and then flung open the door.

Mrs. Haydenshire's head shot up as she clutched her chest. "Rainer, what's wrong?"

"Oh, I'm sorry. I should've knocked. I'm just in a hurry," he apologized.

"Sweetheart, when have you or any of my other children ever knocked? Can I help you do something?"

Rainer found it odd that she was seated on the couch with her feet up in the middle of the day. He tried to think of another time he'd come home and not found her doing something in the kitchen either with the twins or cooking.

"No, ma'am. Would it be all right if I went back to my old room?"

"As long as you're not going up there because Emily has locked you out of the guesthouse, you can go up anytime. Yours and Logan's room will always be yours."

"Thanks." Rainer tore up the stairs. He raced to the end of the long hallway.

Their room looked basically the same as it had when they'd moved out a few weeks before. He opened the right-hand set of closet doors.

Rainer tapped the loosened floorboard in the back of his old closet with the toe of his boot until it sprang upward.

Out of habit, he looked back down the hallway to make certain no one was coming. With a quick prayer that this might work, he leaned in and eased the wedged shoebox out from the hiding spot he'd completely forgotten about when they moved out.

He'd stuck it in there to make certain Logan, or any of the Haydenshire brothers, never knew he was keeping so many of his and Emily's notes from the past thirteen years. That would've gotten him harassed mercilessly. He remembered to restore the floorboard before he tucked the crumpled shoebox under his arm and raced back down the stairs.

"Thanks, Mrs. Haydenshire," he called as he flew past her and headed back out the door.

He sped across the pastures and leapt out of the Mustang as soon as he'd jerked the key from the ignition.

He grabbed the four dozen roses from the front seat and quickly began unloading the car.

His brain moved rapidly through all of the things he wanted to do for her if she'd just give him a chance. He started the bath water. He lit and heat-casted the candles he'd purchased, remembered to add the bubble bath, and then tried to figure out how to make the roses look right in a vase.

That seemed hopeless, so he laid one of the pink dozen on the dresser and began ripping the petals off of the others to scatter on the bed. It didn't look quite the way he'd seen it done in movies, but it wasn't bad.

Racing back to the kitchen, he grabbed the picnic basket, along with several Dr Peppers from their fridge that he balanced under his chin.

After kicking the door closed, he arranged the basket on the bed and chill-casted the drinks.

He considered and then sped back to the kitchen. He couldn't find any wine in the house, and he didn't have time to go purchase any. *Dr Pepper it is, then.*

He grabbed the shoebox of notes and a few sheets of paper and wrote a lengthy letter to his fiancée. This one was so much more important than any of the others, so he poured out his heart in the letter. He tried to explain why he'd done the things he'd done. If she refused to listen to him, maybe she would read.

He smoothed out a crumpled envelope that he located and stuck the new note on top of the box that he laid on their bed.

He checked his watch and began to pace.

CHAPTER 31

THE CALM BEFORE...

He heard the chugging motor of Fionna's canary-yellow MR2 convertible shut down, and hoping against hope, he flung open the door.

Fionna gave him a hopeful grin as she waved and backed out as soon as Emily had exited the car.

"Why are you here?" Emily managed in a fretful whisper.

"I got off early, and I'm not gonna be working so much anymore. I need to fix everything I've done somehow," the words spilled from his mouth without much finesse.

"Where's Logan?"

She didn't want to be alone with him. His heart sank as he drew a deep breath.

"Uh," he stammered, "he and Adeline are spending the night in DC, I think."

"At the Senate?"

"No, I think they got a hotel room."

"Oh." She nodded. "Why?"

Rainer wasn't sure what the correct way to answer that would be, but he'd already decided never to lie to her or keep anything from her again, so he went on with the truth. "I asked them to."

Her brow knitted. "Why?"

Rainer let his eyes close for a moment and took her hands.

"Because I need to make this better. I need to know that you believe me, and that you know for every idiotic thing I did, I'm so sorry. I did it all trying to protect you and take care of you. I was an asshole and an idiot, but somewhere in my head it made sense to my shield. I need to know that you know how much I love you, and that I never ever meant to do anything that would make you doubt that, ever."

With that, she let him pull her toward their room.

Emily eased inside the room, taking in the display. Her hands glided over the quilt on the bed. She stared up at Rainer in shock. "When did you do all of this?"

"Uh, this afternoon, mostly."

"This is amazing." Her bottom lip slid between her teeth. Rainer knew she was still worrying about something. "You didn't have to do this."

He couldn't help himself. He went to stand near her but stopped short of pulling her to him. "I think I did."

Tears rimmed her eyes. He took her hands again. "Em, baby, what? Why are you crying?"

She shook her head. "I feel terrible. I don't know what's wrong with me. I can't seem to shake all of these images out of my head, and you went to all of this trouble, and it's so sweet, but I'm still so angry at you. I told you I hated you. How could I have said that? I don't deserve this. I've been acting crazy since yesterday. I was just so mad at you, and so scared, and you wouldn't answer your phone.

"People put that thing on my car, and I had to leave you. The men who killed Cal tried to take me. And those officers came to the arena. When they walked in, I thought they were coming to tell me you were hurt. You haven't been talking to me. I don't know what's going on with anything. Our coaches keep talking to me about staying safe while I'm on the field with Marlisa. Every time I try to tell you that I'm scared, you brush me off. But I *am* scared." Her body convulsed, and her breath shuddered as tears began to pour, once she'd gotten all of that out. "You lied to me."

She seemed to find relief in saying it out loud. Without thinking, he pulled her against his chest and hugged her even though she bristled.

"I'm so sorry, baby. Please, please, let's talk now, or after your bath, or whenever. I don't ever want to keep anything from you ever again. I didn't mean to do that. I swear I never meant to brush off your fears. I'm scared too. I don't know what happened to me."

"You made me a bath?" she whispered in shock. Rainer couldn't help the chuckle that exited his lungs.

"Yeah, I miss taking care of my baby. That's what I always want to do. I know I screwed up really bad, but please, let me try to fix this." He knew water could help wash away some of the emotional energy Receivers took on. He wanted her to understand that he'd been listening and learning all of the ways she needed to be cared for. He just hadn't done a very good job of showing her the past few weeks.

She seemed torn in confusion as she stared down at the floor. Frightened regret and doubt pulsed in her rhythms.

"Emily," he soothed again, "nothing happened at that stupid club yesterday. I would never have let anything happen. It was work. I stared at a table when I wasn't casting one of Wretchkinsides's men. That was all. I swear to you."

"I know. I let my imagination run away with me yesterday, and the lawsuit, and you wouldn't answer your phone, and..." She stopped as he lifted her chin with his thumb and index finger until she was staring into his eyes.

"I know you don't believe me because I lied to you, but if you've ever believed in me or trusted me at all, please know that I would never cheat on you. I would never ever have let anything happen at that strip club."

He wanted desperately to kiss her. He wanted to take away the pain he'd caused or alleviate it in some small way, but he stopped himself.

She was still wary, and he wasn't going to push anything on her. She needed to think about where they were going from here, and he had to give her time, as impossible as that felt.

"Do you want to take a bath?" He gestured his hand toward the bathroom and studied her.

"Are you going to join me?" she asked cautiously, and Rainer knew it wasn't an invitation. After taking a moment to steel himself, he looked away and clenched his jaw. "No." He sounded angrier than he'd meant to.

"Why?" She let her gaze fall back to the floor. He looked back at her until she raised her head again.

He let his thumb graze her cheek tenderly. "You don't even want me to kiss you. I don't think you want me in the tub with you." His voice was haggard as the truthfulness of his statement settled harshly in his throat.

He glanced away and tried to figure out what to say next.

"You go get in. I'll…bring you some tea." He stepped away from her and then concluded, "And then I'll come back in here until you're finished."

He slipped out of the bedroom without waiting for her response. He fixed her a cup of tea and returned to the bedroom, determined to do whatever it took to make her believe how much he loved her and that he'd never meant to lie or keep anything from her.

The room was empty, and the bathroom door was closed so he knocked softly. Rainer clenched his jaw. Walking back out of the bathroom after seeing her would probably be one of the hardest things he'd ever do, but he resolved to do just that as he heard her voice call softly, "Come in."

He stepped into the bathroom and let his eyes graze over her. She'd pulled her hair up into a sloppy bun. Her face was flushed from the warm water. The bubbles covered some of her, but it was enough to make him ache to see more. Hot tears cascaded down her face and fell into the bathwater. She was reading the letter. Her chin trembled as she began to sob.

"I'm so sorry," she cried.

"Baby." Rainer fell to his knees beside the tub and haphazardly set the mug on the floor. "I'm the one who screwed up."

She was mouthwatering. He wanted desperately to touch her flesh, but he clenched his fists beside his legs.

"Rainer," she whispered.

His eyes closed as he let the sound of her calling him make everything in his world begin to spin again.

"Hmmm?" was all he was able to get out of his mouth as he stared at her. She let her eyes fall on a stack of washcloths. She handed him the letter.

"Will you help me? You know, wash my back?" She attempted his favorite mischievous smile as she wiped away her tears, but it didn't reach her eyes.

He considered for several long moments. He weighed everything that had happened in the past two weeks.

"Are you sure you want me to?" He was unable to take his eyes off of her.

She nodded and handed him one of the washcloths, but he didn't take it. "I don't think I can just wash your back." He'd gladly show her that she was always his weakness. He wanted her to have a chance to back away if she needed to. "So, if that's really all you want, then I'm gonna wait on you in there, okay?" He gestured his head toward their bedroom and awaited her answer.

"That's not all I want," her voice was strained. He didn't believe her.

"You're sure?" He studied her reaction and tried to determine if she was saying this because she thought he wanted her to. She could feel his every feeling, and he refused to let her powers make her weak to his wishes. He would not allow her to make him happy at her own expense. Receivers often did that. That's why they needed a Shield.

"Please." Her emerald eyes locked on his.

He knew how much this had to be costing her after what had been going through her mind for the past two days. He took the washcloth from her and laid it beside the tub. He rolled up his sleeves and lathered his hands instead of the washrag. He wasn't willing to even have a piece of cloth between his hands and her body. He began to wash her.

He forced himself to work slowly. He took his time as he massaged her neck, shoulders, and back. He tried to will calmness into her as he eased the strained muscles he'd caused. He longed to touch other things as he let his hands graze her collarbone.

"You're sure this is okay?" he asked again. He let his eyes drift slowly back to her face and was elated to see the fire he loved just beginning to swirl in her eyes again.

He groaned from relief as she arched her back and slipped her breasts into his hands. He began groping her greedily. He let his hands dip below the water line to trace her stomach.

Desperation took strong hold of him as he half moaned, half begged, "Can I please touch you, Em, please?"

He didn't want to take anything for granted. He had to know that she wanted him to before he was going to do anything. It didn't matter how much he longed to be with her. If she wanted him to stop, he would, even if it killed him.

His hand seemed to move of its own accord. He edged closer to what he wanted, but he forced himself to stop until she answered.

Her eyes drifted closed as she moaned and let her legs fall open for him.

His hand slid lower and pushed against the water. He stroked her gently and then let the water enter her. She shuddered and with her eyes beseeching him, she whispered his name. He leaned down to kiss her softly.

Suddenly, she moved to get out of the tub. He helped her up and let his eyes rake over her naked body, dripping and covered in bubbles. He wrapped her in one of the warmed towels.

She stepped out of the tub and into his arms. She braided her fingers in his hair as she pulled him to her and devoured his mouth.

A low, wounded groan escaped him as he wrapped his arms around her. He dragged her body closer to his and let her soak his clothes as he consumed her mouth.

His hands grazed her body. He couldn't seem to touch enough of her silky alabaster skin. He forced all of the love he felt to flow into her. She stepped back and took his hands. She led him out of the bathroom.

"I'm sorry," she began, but he crushed her lips back to his and slipped his tongue into her mouth. She pulled away. "I didn't mean to be so..." she started again, but Rainer let his mouth drift to her breasts. He flicked and prodded her nipples with his tongue as he sucked, and she began to moan.

She quickly unbuttoned his shirt and slid her hands across his chest, then slipped them into his jeans. He regained a moment of clarity and pulled away from her as he gasped for breath and strained under the effort of his offer.

"Are you sure?" he drew a steadying breath. "We don't have to do this. I just wanted you to know how much I love you, and how sorry I am about everything that happened. We have to talk. I have so much to apologize for."

She covered his apology with her lips this time as she popped the snap on his jeans and lowered the zipper.

"I know," she murmured and traced him softly with her fingertips. A forceful moan echoed from his chest.

"You're certain you want to do this? That you want to be with me right now? After everything I put you through..."

He wanted her to know he would take everything from then on at her pace. He'd never take her for granted again.

"You didn't touch anyone else? No one danced for you or anything? No one... felt you? I don't have any idea what goes on at strip clubs. I'm stupid and naïve and..."

"You are not stupid," he vowed. "You're scared. I am too. But baby, I would never ever put my hands on another woman, and I sure as hell don't want anyone dancing for me, except maybe you, and then only if that's what you want to do. You are everything to me, and I would never do anything to make you feel like you weren't enough or do anything that would jeopardize what we have. This,"—he moved his hand in the small space between their bodies—"this is all that matters to me."

A sigh of overwhelming relief issued from her, and he felt her finally relax against him. He removed the picnic basket from the bed, then turned back and lifted her in his arms. He laid her down gently.

"I want to take care of you, baby. I want to do everything that lets you know how precious you are to me, and how beautiful you are, and that getting to be with you like this is the most important thing in the world to me."

She moaned as his vow restored her.

He forced himself to move slowly, to show her he would take care of every concern that lay hidden in the recesses of her mind.

"Do you need me to set the cast, sweetheart?"

She nodded. With an adoring smile, he cupped his hand and reveled in her energy as she let him in. He soothed her body as he closed her womb. As soon as he was finished, he lavished her lips with deep, fervent kisses as she wound her body around his.

He pulled off everything he was still wearing. He wanted her to be able to feel his energies as they rolled in hungry waves that came from every piece of him.

"I want to touch you again, okay?"

She shivered in anticipation. He kissed his way down her neck, and as he caught her breast in his mouth, he slipped his fingers inside her. She writhed from need and the expectation pent up deeply inside of her. He kept his other arm wrapped around her and cradled her to him as he worked her over. "Does that feel good, baby?"

She panted, unable to catch her breath. A loud, needy moan answered his question.

He kept up the deep, fervent strokes and then kissed his way across her stomach and licked up her slit. He laved her clit with his tongue, taunting the swollen bundle of nerve endings, as he kept his fingers massaging deep inside her.

She broke hard. She convulsed and cried out for him. All of the stress and emotion had her bound. Her body seized as he lessened the intensity of his strokes and soothed her.

Her pleading moans overwhelmed him. He needed her to know that she was his. Nothing else would ever come before her again. He needed to possess her.

She was throbbing and fevered. Her body was primed all for him. Her needy hips rose and fell with hunger. He moved back up her and spread her legs with his hands as she called out his name.

"What, baby? Tell me." He angled his knee to keep her thighs spread.

"Take me." She bucked underneath him.

He caught her hips as they rose, and he entered her fully as she cried out for him.

"My god, you feel incredible," he groaned in ecstasy.

She began to beg him for release, and he pounded into her harder. Her legs wrapped up over his back.

She wanted him deeper. It was a physical request he was only too happy to grant as he lifted her body and drove himself in.

He buried himself in the heavenly perfection of her. He forced her open past his hilt. Her eyes flashed as she took all of him with a gasp of approval.

He drove her further. He felt her pulse around him as she trembled, and her breath washed from her lungs. He pushed his shield out around them, keeping her safe in the sanctuary of his energy.

Suddenly, she cried out his name. Her body contorted under his as he pushed her over the edge.

Their energy spun in tantric accord as she pulled his from his body and supplied him with the intoxicating waves of her own. They remained locked tight inside his shield.

He watched her writhe. Her hair splayed wildly across the bed as her face displayed her ecstasy, and he lost it all.

He spilled everything he was inside of her.

Her body seized and tightened around him as he collapsed on top of her.

Rainer held her tenderly to him for a long while as they allowed the serenity to envelop them after the tempest. He eased her onto his chest and kissed her head.

"Do you want to eat, sweetheart?" he asked sheepishly. "I really meant for us to eat first. I got a little carried away."

She laughed but then pulled on a shirt. Rainer pretended to pout just to hear her laugh again. Then they laughed together as they removed rose petals that had gotten stuck to their bodies. "This might be one of those better-in-the-movies things." He smirked. She pulled another petal out of the crevice where her thigh met her ass.

"Yeah, but it was really, really sweet."

He picked up the picnic basket and helped her unpack it as he began telling her about the sandwich shop and his day.

He was pleased she seemed to enjoy the sandwiches as much as he had. They chatted a little about the Summation Exhibition on Saturday.

Emily seemed more herself, but he wasn't fool enough to believe the images she'd conjured and the doubt he'd created weren't still lurking beneath the surface.

"I still feel terrible you went to all of this trouble," she explained.

He collected their sandwich wrappers and wrapped his hand around a can of Dr Pepper. After chill-casting it until slight ice crystals formed, just the way she preferred, he handed it to her.

"Baby, I know how awful yesterday must have been for you, and I also know I haven't done a great job of showing you that I will always be there for you and only you, that I will always take care of you and keep you safe. I was keeping things from you so you didn't have to worry, and I just ended up scaring you more. So, if all of this,"—he gestured around the room—"even makes up for a tiny bit of the damage I've done, it was more than worth it."

"You are an amazing fiancé, and I know I completely overreacted yesterday. It just…" She stared down at her ring and shook her head. "I don't think this ring just makes me able to throw shields when I'm in danger," she whispered.

Rainer's brow furrowed. "What else does it do?"

"I asked Fionna about it, and she said I'm probably right. She's taught me so much about what being a Receiver really means and what I need to become comfortable with my powers. She's amazing."

"Right about what, baby?"

She gave him a tender grin. "I'm a Receiver, so emotions are my power, right?" Rainer offered a quick nod. "I think…the ring makes me feel everything stronger than I would without it. So, all of the deceit and fear and anger and shame that I felt yesterday was so powerful it overwhelmed me."

Rainer set their drinks down and pulled her on his chest as he considered that. "That's why you said you hated me."

She nodded against him. "It was just all really hard things to have to think about, and I was so angry I had to think about them at all. I went crazy. I didn't know what else you hadn't told me." Her voice caught as she shuddered and waged battle against emotions that threatened to overtake her.

He slid his hands under the T-shirt she'd put on as he began to rub her back and cradle her closely.

"I swear to you there isn't anything else."

She drew several steadying breaths. She leaned away from him, and her jaw clenched as she willed calm from the air around her.

"I think"—she let her eyes close for a moment before forcing herself to go on—"I'm the luckiest girl in the world. I've been in love with you since I was born and,"—she shook her head in utter disbelief—"and somehow you loved me back.

"I never had to go through having a crush on you and then watching you go after or date other girls. I don't think I ever realized how amazing that is until I sat on Fionna's couch yesterday knowing that women were parading themselves around in front of you, taking their clothes off. And that they're able to do things I don't know how to begin to do, with way more experience than I have, and you're a guy. And you'd been keeping so many things from me."

Her tears returned, but she tried to go on. He couldn't watch her sit there and cry. He was simply unable. He pulled her back to him and held her as she sobbed.

He waited to assure her once again, to combat the images in her head that had her shackled and bound.

She pulled back and wiped her face before forcing herself to finish. After drawing a deep breath, she clenched her fists. She dammed back the flow of tears with sheer strength of will. "Why didn't you tell me about the will and about the lawsuit?"

She seemed to will repose that continued to elude her. She shook her head combatively. "Yesterday, I just sat there praying I had something that would make you come back to me. That would make you tell me everything again, that would make you love me like you used to again. I sat there knowing I can't compete with strippers."

Stunned disbelief rocked through Rainer as he held her tightly. "I don't even know where to begin, so I'm just going to say everything in my head. I really need you to listen to me."

His temper spiked, but he did his best to quell the fury. "First of all, yeah, I saw them, and they flirted, and threw themselves at all of us because that's what they get paid to do. So, I watched Tuttle get lap dances and your brother flirt with every woman who walked by, and I was sick."

He held her chin in his hand, not allowing her to look away from him. "All I could think about was how cheap and unfulfilling that must be, and how badly I wanted to come home to you." He used his thumb to wipe away more tears as he cupped her face.

"Don't you get it, sweetheart?" His voice rose in accordance with his fervor. "You don't ever have to compete with anyone or anything because you are the fantasy. I don't ever want or need to see any other woman. I have the most beautiful and amazing woman in the world right here in bed with me. Why would I ever want anything else?" He shook his head and willed her to hear what he was saying.

"So, if that's what some guys want, for some woman they don't know to shake it in their lap, and then to go home alone, they can have it. But I have every single thing I have ever wanted or ever could've dreamed about having, sitting right here in my bed, looking up at me crying because I really screwed up. I didn't make you understand all of that before I got sent to a strip club for work. And if I'd told you everything when I should've, I bet you would still have been a little ticked that Vindico sent us there, but you wouldn't have told me you hated me.

"And I know we're pretty rare as couples go, but that's just one more reason why I would never do anything to jeopardize what we've been building since that day you dared me to kiss you when I was eight years old." He shook his head as he recalled the memory. "I was terrified. I knew Logan and Connor would never let me live it down, but I didn't care. I wanted to kiss you, and as soon as I let my lips touch your cheek, that was it for me. I knew, right then and there, you were all I ever wanted. Somehow, I must've done something right along the way because I got you." He let his eyes close for the length of one heartbeat. He drew a steadying breath before continuing.

"See, baby, those women do that because that's their job, and guys are flashing cash in their face, so as soon as one guy's out of ones then they move on to the next. And I guess it's a cheap momentary thrill for the guy, some kind of a distraction, I assume. It sure as hell didn't do a damn thing for me. But this,"—he gestured from his heart to hers —"this is a life. This is love. This is a kiss, and then watching each other grow up, and then a little more than kissing, and then a whole lot more than kissing." He chuckled as she grinned.

"This is sitting in your room holding your hand because even at six years old, I knew that's where I always wanted to be. This is teaching you to ride a bike and you holding me when my entire world fell apart. This is lying over you in a hospital bed sobbing and praying that you'd wake up. This is refusing to leave your hospital room for days. This is holding you out on a deck in the middle of the night at your parents' beach house and getting to explore you. And this is holding you close to me, so terrified to hurt you but completely overwhelmed that I somehow got to be the guy lucky enough to get to take you to bed. This is a ring, and a wedding, and a house, and kids, and a porch swing when we're old. You are my other half. Nothing else matters unless you're with me.

"The girl who brings me chili made just like I like it when I felt like I might die, and the girl who tells me to meet her in the shower and makes me feel like I've never been more alive. That's all I have ever wanted, and all I will ever want. And all I can do is pray that's what you'll always want too." He finished his diatribe and brushed a stray strand of auburn hair behind her ear.

He gazed at her with all of the love in his heart, which at that moment felt like it might be more than his body could contain.

"Rainer." She began to sob again. She fell on his chest and let him hold her. She let him cradle her to him, to shield her from the corrosive world as he prayed a silent prayer of overwhelming gratitude for all he had when he held her in his arms.

He heard Sam's voice echo for him to talk out loud, and he decided to keep going. "The only guy who's ever kissed you. The only guy who's ever felt you up, and yes, I remember the first time. They weren't quite as big then." He chuckled as she blushed crimson.

"The only guy who's ever touched you, or seen all of you, or laid you down and been with you. That makes me the luckiest man in the world, and I sure as hell will do anything in my power to make sure I'm always the only guy who gets all of that. What we have, what we do, I don't do because it feels so damn good, baby. I do it because I love you. When I feel you like that, when we're close enough that all of this energy that makes us the way we are joins, and I can't tell where I stop and where you begin, that's unbelievable. I can't begin to describe to you what that means to me."

"Thank you," she whispered as relief drove the tears from her eyes. "You're just incredible."

"That's you, baby." They lay there in the soothing silence of the love they'd created, as he cosseted her tenderly in his arms. "Let's talk about the lawsuit, okay?"

Another round of relief washed through her rhythms.

"I'm sorry I didn't tell you when I saw it in the paper yesterday. You were asleep, and I didn't want to burden you with it, but that was wrong and it affects you just as much as it does me. I know I did nothing to help you feel like the money is both of ours by keeping that from you."

She sighed but did finally give him a nod of hesitant agreement.

"I talked to Jack Stariff at work. I know I should have waited until you were with me, but I didn't."

"It's okay. Just tell me what he said."

He held her hand in his, thankful to be able to do that again. He'd never realized how important it was to him. It seemed like such a small thing until it had been taken away.

"He says Dad's will is ironclad, and that we have nothing to worry about." He gazed deeply into her eyes. His whole world swirled right there in the emerald depths. "But we will have to go to trial and hash this all out. Stariff thinks my uncle knows he won't get much from the estate but that he's hoping I'll pay him off to keep it out of court, or that he'll get awarded something from the Senteon if he can get enough of the governors to agree that I've been irresponsible with the money so far."

Emily shook her head. "I can't believe the things money makes people do. It makes me so angry how much he's hurt you, and I have this ring so now my anger is tenfold."

Rainer grinned at her. "I'm hoping you're okay with the ring even if it makes things a little intense."

"Fionna said she thinks I'll probably get used to it, and it won't feel so overwhelming all of the time."

"Fionna's really smart." Rainer winked at her. "In terms of the lawsuit, the fact that we stayed on your parents' farm and restored an old house instead of buying something big and new and pimped out," he teased, "plays well for us."

He didn't really want to tell her what else Mr. Stariff had pointed out, but he was going to.

"But buying me a Hummer doesn't." She knew exactly what he was about to say. He nodded begrudgingly.

"So," he continued as he reminded himself that when he kept things from her it only landed her on the fear side of things. "I'm going to have to get on the stand and tell them that I was scared for your safety. I'm going to talk about the wreck."

She hated to talk about it or even think about it.

"On the flip side,"—he smiled at her in an effort to erase her frown —"it's apparently a good thing that I gave you my mom's ring instead of buying you something from your uncle. And Stariff thinks that since the engagement is the reference point for the lawsuit, the ring will be a big deal."

"When will all of this happen?" she asked.

"I have no idea. I guess whenever we can get it on the docket for the board. And I knew you didn't want to think about the will, so I just did it. I don't want to think about it either, but I had to take care of you. I don't really know what my uncle is capable of. That's why I didn't tell you. I was just trying to literally put a shield between you and the money, but also to make sure you are always, always taken care of. I never want you to be scared," he concluded as he let the last of the tension that had been pent up inside of him go with a huff.

She gazed at him and then leaned and brushed a sweet kiss across his jaw. "You know when we were little, and I used to make you and Logan play wedding with me?"

Rainer laughed. "Yeah, I'm glad I always got to play the groom, and you didn't want to pretend to marry Logan."

She giggled and wrinkled her nose. "Eww," she shuddered.

They laughed together and the sound soothed Rainer's weary soul.

"But do you remember, I used to make you put a grape-flavored ring pop on me in the ceremony?"

He nodded as he allowed the memory to form in his mind. He could see Logan rolling his eyes and holding a copy of an old dictionary they'd found in the barn. Emily, beaming with her freckles on display from the summer sun, one of her mother's long white dish towels pinned in her hair as a makeshift veil, and clinging to Rainer's hands.

He couldn't help himself. Before she continued, he leaned and kissed her lips. "I love you, and I can't wait to marry you for real."

She nodded as tears formed on her lashes again. "Well, I would've taken a ring pop and still said yes. Just give him the money. I can't stand it that he might try to hurt you. I don't want the money. I just want you."

He wrapped her up in his arms as emotion flooded through his entire body.

"You are the most incredible woman in the world." He held her tightly. He didn't want to let her go. "But I'm not giving him anything. My dad and my grandparents and great-grandparents all worked hard for that money. It's for you and for our kids to have when we're gone. My grandfather wrote him out of the will for a reason. I'm not going to turn around and undo his wishes.

"I want you to come to work with me next week, on one of the days you don't have practice. I want both of us to talk to Mr. Buffett. We need to make sure all of the money is invested wisely because it will look good for the trial and because I don't want you to ever have to worry about money. After that, as long as we don't do anything too crazy that makes us look irresponsible or ends up in the papers, the trial should be open and shut. Okay?"

"Okay, so probably no more fingering me in restaurants." She blushed, and Rainer mentally lambasted himself once again.

"I should never have done that in the first place."

Relief eased her flushed face as she nodded. "Yeah, I think that emotion is stronger too. I wasn't thinking."

"We'll both adjust," Rainer assured her.

"I love you."

"Then that's all in the world I need."

Emily let him cradle her against his chest as they continued to talk. They recalled things from their childhood and things they'd done at the academy.

He recounted the story for her of when she was twelve and her father had forbidden her from going camping with Rainer and all of her brothers. She'd run away to the loft and refused to come in the house until three in the morning when she was freezing.

She teased him about how long it had taken him to work up the courage to ask if he could feel her up, and how he'd choked over the words. She'd finally just grabbed his hands and gone ahead with it.

They settled back onto the bed, entangled in each other, still talking and laughing. Rainer's world had righted itself once again.

Eventually, they were kissing more than they were talking. As lust spiked his blood again, he pulled off the T-shirt she'd put on before they'd eaten and told her just how stunningly gorgeous she was.

He grabbed her hand and wrapped it around his cock. He was throbbing and hard as steel for her.

He'd proven his point, and her excited moan had him aching to feel her again.

He had everything he would ever need wrapped up in his arms, and he let her moans drown out the restless murmurs in his mind.

He didn't want anything else. He only wanted her all to himself. He wanted the rest of the world to slip away.

Pulling her body underneath his, he consumed her mouth with deep, drawing kisses. With a heady, lust-filled groan, he moved to claim her again.

CHAPTER 32

INVITATION FROM THE PAST

Friday evening, Rainer scrubbed his hair with a towel, after he stepped out of the showers off of the Iodex gym.

"That was a good workout, Lawson. Let's go over everything O'Ryan just pulled out of his ass when I threatened to take him back to Felsink for the weekend," Vindico commanded.

"Sorry, sir. I'm picking up Emily in just a few minutes. I'll get it done Monday morning," Rainer stated firmly.

He knew Governor Willow and Governor Haydenshire would back him up. Vindico knew that as well. His jaw set as he gave an irritated huff, but he didn't say anything else as all of the Wretchkinsides task force headed back to their desks.

Logan and Rainer found Benji Williams standing by their desks. They shared a quizzical glance.

"What's up, Benj? Did you get lost on your way up to see your dad?" Logan quizzed.

Benji had been in Ioses with Logan and Rainer in school. They'd all graduated together and had been good friends right up until the point Rainer had moved to London to try to protect Emily from the press.

Benji had waited approximately two hours before he'd texted Emily to tell her how much he'd always liked her, what a jerk Rainer was, and how he was so glad she'd wised up and dumped him. Then he'd asked Emily out.

Benji had begun dating Sydney Shelton their junior year at Venton. His father worked for Governor Peterson, Samantha's father, and handled most of the governor's public relations campaigns. He also was known to fudge service records for Governor Peterson on a regular basis.

Sydney was Samantha Peterson's best friend, Rainer recalled as he narrowed his eyes. He'd forgiven Benji, for the most part, but he most certainly hadn't forgotten.

Benji smiled as he greeted Logan and Vindico. He turned to Rainer and extended his hand. "Hey, man, congrats! I heard you and Em were engaged." He sounded genuinely happy for Rainer.

"Uh yeah, I asked Em-i-ly,"—he emphasized her full name. Benji wasn't calling Emily by Rainer's nickname for her—"at the beach at the beginning of summer."

Logan and Vindico chuckled at Rainer's scolding. It had always irked Rainer that Benji had taken it upon himself to decide that he was close enough to Emily to call her Em.

"Yeah, I saw the papers. It's always been you, so I guess I'm not surprised." He may not have been surprised, but he was definitely disappointed.

Rainer ground his teeth as Vindico slapped him on the shoulder. "Whoa there, stud." He chuckled under his breath. "She's wearing your ring."

"I'm actually headed out to pick her up." Rainer gestured his thumb toward the door to speed along whatever Benji wanted.

"Oh, yeah, I heard she made the Angels. Do you get to go inside the arena and stuff?"

A smirk formed rapidly on Rainer's face. "Yep, I get to go pretty much wherever I want."

Logan tried to turn his laughter into a cough.

"That's...cool," Benji fumbled slightly. "I...uh, I just came by to drop off the wedding invitations. Sydney said I had to give them out to my friends if I wanted them there. But tell Em-i-ly," he repeated her name back just the way Rainer had instructed, "that I said hi."

"Uh-huh." Rainer forced himself not to roll his eyes.

"I didn't know you were engaged." Logan's brow knitted.

"Yeah," Benji shifted uncomfortably. "Well, I mean, you knew Sydney and I were dating, right?"

"Okay," Logan agreed as Rainer choked back a chuckle. Logan clearly hadn't known that Benji and Sydney had been dating for a while.

"When's the wedding?" Rainer asked. He rather liked the idea of Benji being married.

"Next Sunday." Benji looked terrified.

Vindico and Garrett both began laughing.

Logan's brow knitted. "When did you ask her?"

He hadn't figured out what was going on. Benji's father was a bigwig in Peterson's branch of the Senate. Sydney's mother worked under Ms. Ellington in the Auxiliary. They weren't going to let Sydney have a baby out of wedlock and be born without a crest and a name, as stupidly patriarchal as it all still was.

"Oh, uh...yesterday," Benji admitted. Suddenly, Logan's eyes lit as he nodded.

"Oh, well sure, we'll be there as long as Adeline doesn't have to work. I guess." He tried to smooth over his gaffe.

"Are you still with Adeline?" Benji scoffed.

Palpable fury rolled in Logan's shield. Garrett grimaced.

"Yes, I am. I plan to be with her forever."

"Oh, yeah, yeah," Benji realized his mistake. "I kind of thought you'd move on after school. I mean with your dad being a governor and all." Though he hadn't said it, the implication was in all of the unspoken lines. *I kind of thought you'd find somebody better after graduation.*

Logan ground his teeth. Fury set in his eyes as Rainer stepped in.

"You know how it is. Once you've found the one you're meant to be with forever, you don't let her walk away." The threat was implicit in his tone.

"Oh, yeah, I know," Benji lied. "Well, I need to get down to Dad's office. Here are the invitations. I really want you to come."

"We'll be there," Rainer huffed.

. . .

"So, Benji Williams knocked up Sydney Shelton, and now we have to go to their wedding?" Emily fell into the booth at Lesco's, across from Logan and Adeline.

"Ding, ding, ding, ding, ding, you win a prize for being so smart Rainer will buy you a milkshake and then let you lick his straw," Logan goaded.

"She figured it out before you did, smart-ass."

Emily laughed as she leaned and kissed Rainer's cheek.

"Be nice." Adeline shook her head at Logan.

"You know Samantha is going to be her stupid maid of honor," Emily began glancing over the menu they all knew by heart.

"And...?" Rainer wrapped his arm around her. He still didn't understand why Samantha Peterson irked her so badly. He couldn't stand Samantha. As far as he was concerned, she was a conceited bitch with something to prove.

"She never even talked to you in school, and now she's telling the press that you two had something going on," Emily reminded him. "Did you see that interview she did in *Gravity* yesterday? She's all over the papers and tabloids screaming that you cheated on me with her."

"Em." Logan softened. He couldn't stand for her to be upset either, and it was very apparent that Samantha Peterson's antics had shaken Emily. Rainer reminded himself that she felt everything bigger with the ring on. "Think about it. It seems pretty obvious why Samantha Peterson is trying to get Rainer's attention now."

Emily's brow furrowed. "Why?"

"It has a whole lot to do with my twenty-first birthday," Rainer explained.

Les approached with his kind, beaming grin. "If it isn't the Haydenshire foursome. Are you still letting him hang around, Miss Emily Anne?"

Emily planted another kiss on Rainer's jawline. "Yeah, I kinda like him."

"Kiss from a redhead's something else, ain't it, Lawson?"

"You know it," Rainer agreed with a wry grin.

. . .

They arrived home an hour later. Rainer handed Emily the mail he'd retrieved from the box. She was always so disappointed that most of their mail still came to her parents' house, so if anything arrived addressed to both her and Rainer, it delighted her. The letter on top was addressed to Mr. and the future Mrs. Rainer Lawson.

Her eyes lit when she read the envelope. "It's from the academy."

Rainer wondered why Venton Academy was sending the two of them mail. He shared a concerned glance with Logan.

It seemed far-fetched that someone might've finally figured out that he and Logan had frequently summoned and sped up the clocks in classes they hated. Or that they would often use the school stationery that Patrick lifted from the Admin building to inform a few mentors that their classes had been cancelled for the day.

Emily's face fell, and Rainer began to panic.

"They want money." She rolled her eyes.

"Of course." Relief flooded through him. He certainly wasn't surprised. His wealth was known throughout the Realm, and Emily had just signed a very lucrative contract with the Angels. They'd obviously be at the top of the alumni donor hopeful list.

"Why is money the only thing anyone cares about anymore?" Emily laid the letter on the coffee table and curled herself up into a ball in Rainer's lap.

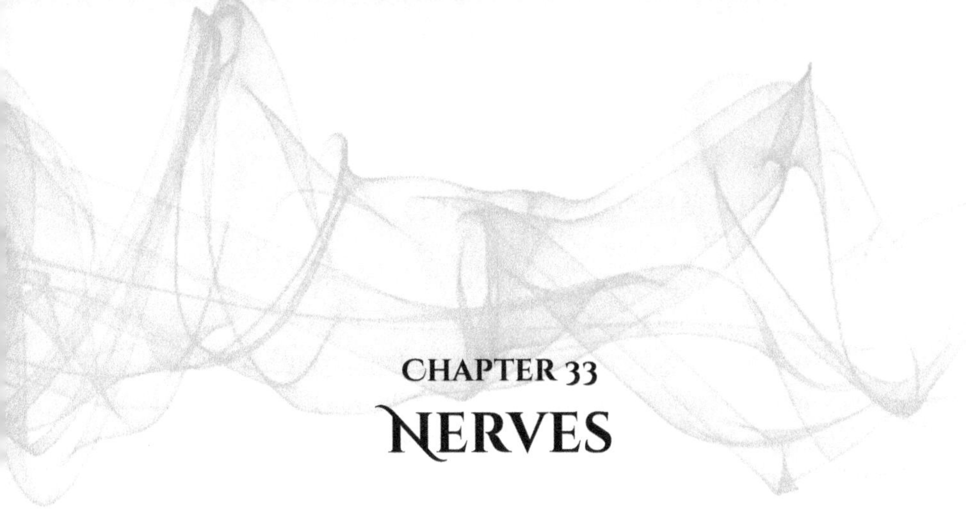

CHAPTER 33

NERVES

The bed was empty as Rainer's cheek warmed from the rising sun. He blinked and tried to determine why he'd awoken two hours before he had to get up.

He sat up and scrubbed his hands over his face. With a slight headshake, he smiled and went to find his baby. She was pacing in the living room. Emily was gnawing on her lip and staring at a mug of tea on the coffee table.

"Hey there," Rainer went ahead with his customary morning greeting.

"I didn't mean to wake you."

"Nervous?" He wrapped her up in his protective embrace. She nodded against him. Rainer cradled her head in his hand as he tucked her tightly to him. "You're gonna be great."

Nervous tension and fretful disbelief pulsed in her rhythms. "What if they made a mistake? What if I'm not good enough to be an Angel, and somehow I just got really lucky at the tryouts, but now I'm just gonna screw everything up?"

Rainer chuckled. "So, we've blown right through first day of school nervous, gone on past what if I hurt someone's feelings level of worry, and landed squarely on completely irrational then?"

She held up her left hand and pointed to the ring with her right.

Rainer drew her back into his embrace. "You're going to be amazing. You always are. No one made a mistake. You're an incredibly talented Summation challenger."

"But what if the ring made me better at my tryouts, and I didn't know that's how I did it so now I'm cheating."

"Baby," Rainer sighed. "Listen to me. The tryouts weren't about the amount of energy you could summon. It was a timed tryout. If it had been an amount of energy thing, they would've made you wear joule meters. The ring has nothing to do with your talents. You challenged all through the academy without the ring, and you've been an Angel for several weeks now. They all told me how great you are."

"No one said that. All everyone talks about is the Sirens, and how they're gonna suck, and how Marlisa will try to hurt me. What if they cheat or something?"

Rainer had been trying to put his fears about Emily being on a Summation field with Marlisa Wretchkinsides out of his mind. He didn't want her to pick up on his terror.

"They did tell me how great you're doing. We're all worried about the Sirens, sweetheart, but I'll be there. Logan and Garrett will be there. Even Vindico is coming to make certain nothing happens. Your dad will be there, along with most of the governors. I don't think Marlisa or her idiotic friends would try anything in front of so many witnesses. They could lose their license to play." He allowed his own words to soothe his worries as well as hers.

"That's what Chloe said." Rainer kissed the top of her head. "Are you gonna wear my shirt?" Her head shot up as she asked the question.

Rainer had no idea what she was talking about. "What shirt?"

"You know the Angels shirt for our significant others with my number on it?"

As Rainer had never been seated in the Angels box before, he assumed that's why he hadn't seen the shirts at the challenges they'd attended growing up.

"Of course," he scoffed. "I want everyone to know you're my Angel."

She giggled, but her nose wrinkled a second later. "Chloe designs them every season, and they're a little...dirty, kind of."

"Dirty how?"

Emily took his hand and led him back into their bedroom. He decided to go ahead and climb back into bed. He planned to see if he could coax her into sleeping a little more.

Emily hoisted her huge Angels duffle bag up onto the bed beside him. She pulled out three T-shirts, all much too big for her, and laid them on the bed.

Rainer laughed as he studied them. "Very nice. Your dad's gonna love that." He pointed to a dark gray T-shirt with the Angels logo—a tilted halo that hung off of large double letter As with wings and a lightning bolt through it—along with Emily's number 3 on the pocket. Written on the back was: "I keep my Angel's tank full." Another number 3 was under the phrasing.

Emily handed him the next option.

"I told you they were dirty, but it's kind of cool because only we can get these. So, only our significant others can wear them."

Rainer winked at her. "There sure as hell better not be another guy there with one of these on."

The shirt in Rainer's hand was white with black lettering. It had the same Angels logo on it, only it declared, "My Angel gets it done on the field and off." The printing formed the number three.

As he tried to envision Governor Haydenshire's reaction to seeing his future son-in-law in one of the shirts, Rainer flipped over the last option.

This one was blue, but the lettering was red and a flame had been added under the traditional Angel logo. "My Angel makes my energy run red hot."

Erotic energy that spilled from Gifted people's bodies when they were in the process of having sex, or even aroused, could come in many colors. The heat that flowed through them when they were in the act of making love, and usually just before orgasm, tended to make their rhythms a deep crimson.

Rainer was certain the "red hot" T-shirt would send the governor right over the edge, so he chose the "My Angel gets it done" T-shirt.

"Okay now, my little red-hot Angel, why don't you come back under these covers with me, and let's get a little more sleep."

Emily cleared the bag off of the bed before she crawled back into Rainer's arms.

"When we get back from the exhibition, I will fill your tank for you though," he teased just before he was overtaken by a yawn.

"If you're good," she sassed.

"I'm always good, baby. Trust me." He kissed her cheek and cuddled her back to sleep.

CHAPTER 34

NORTHEAST SUMMATION EXHIBITION

Rainer walked Emily to the Angels' locker room. "You're gonna be great," he assured her for what had to be the hundredth time.

They slipped into a small room off of the long hallway that held the Angels' showers, gym, and the very well-appointed locker and workout rooms.

"Here's your ring." He handed her the duplicated engagement ring. This only seemed to make her more nervous as she switched the rings and handed Rainer the original. He quickly slipped it onto a delicate gold chain that he'd borrowed from Emily that morning. He attached the necklace around his neck and dropped the ring under the shirt he was wearing.

"And I got you a present," he smirked.

"I love presents!"

"I was aware."

He reached into his pocket and pulled out a grape-flavored Ring Pop. Emily gasped as her hands flew to her mouth.

"That's so sweet. Thank you."

As he still felt he had quite a bit to make up for, he was thrilled she was so taken with his present. Emily did love gifts, but they didn't have to be expensive. Just a small token that reminded her that he cared would always light her eyes and make her smile his smile. Receivers could feel the emotional energy that went into a gift.

"I'm going to go get my seat, baby. I can't wait to see you out there."

"I love you so much." She threw her arms around his neck and hugged him fiercely.

"Is she okay? I thought she was gonna chew a freakin' hole in her lip," Logan asked as he followed Rainer up to the Angels box.

The Angels were hosting this year's opening exhibition. Currently, the field was full of tables displaying all of the participating teams' memorabilia that could be purchased by their fans.

"It is kind of a big deal." Rainer gestured to the people clamoring for their memorabilia and the excited buzz all around them.

"Yeah, I know. And by the way, Dad's gonna shit a brick house when he sees that shirt," Logan informed him as they flashed their specialized tickets and were admitted into the box.

Garrett and Will had already arrived. Rainer was relieved to see that Garrett was wearing the tank full T-shirt with Chloe's number one scrawled across it.

He knew Garrett and Chloe Sawyer, the Angels' team captain, had been dating off and on for over a decade. He also knew it was never going anywhere. Garrett would never settle down. He just hoped the governor might not come completely unglued since Garrett was wearing a shirt as well.

The Haydenshires entered the Angels box. Someone stopped the governor to shake his hand. Rainer slid farther down in his seat. Mrs. Haydenshire leaned to hug Logan, Rainer, and Adeline before they took the seats directly behind them.

"Grandpa is coming over after the game, so I thought we'd have our family meal tonight instead of tomorrow," Mrs. Haydenshire broached.

"No problem, Mom," Logan agreed.

Rainer turned to offer his acceptance, and the governor scowled.

"We'll be there, Mrs. Haydenshire." He smiled hopefully.

She elbowed her husband as she winked at Rainer. "They're all wearing them."

"That is our daughter he's talking about," Governor Haydenshire grumped.

"I believe the phrasing you're looking for, is that is my baby girl he's talking about. The one I just cannot let grow up. The one who is not only now an Arlington Angel but the one who got him that shirt and asked him to wear it."

The governor didn't seem to have a comeback, but Rainer did hear an audible huff.

The United States was divided into six Summation leagues. Arlington was in the Northeastern league, and each league hosted its own exhibition the week before any actual challenges began. At the end of the season, right after Christmas, there would be an all-star match in Vegas, where every team in the country would compete.

Rainer watched as the New York Neutrons stalked into the arena. They looked fierce as they headed into one of the locker rooms.

Vindico flashed his Iodex badge and was waved into the box seats.

The Sirens had just entered the arena with Marlisa in the lead. They were all wearing matching, smug glowers to go with their crimson uniforms.

"Wonder if Daddy's gonna show up to see her challenge?" Vindico growled.

"Man, it's an exhibition game. You're supposed to smile and shit," Garrett harassed as Dan came to sit beside him.

"I'll smile when I make damn sure that those wenches from hell aren't going to make trouble." Vindico gestured his head toward the Sirens.

The crowd quieted as Governor Sapman's voice was magnified and projected throughout the arena.

"Thank you everyone for coming out to our Northeastern Summation Exhibition. This year, we have seven teams participating in five rounds of challenges, so you'll get to see all of their skills today."

The crowds roared. The stands vibrated with the excitement and anticipation rolling in rhythmic accord from the Gifted fans.

"Let's meet this year's participating teams…" Governor Sapman drawled. "First, give a round of applause to last year's American Cup winners, The New York Neutrons!"

Neutron fans lit up the stadium with raucous cheers and waved banners with the American Cup symbols over the Neutrons insignia.

"Next, give it up for the Bombers of Boston!" Boston fans joined in with the New York fans who hadn't yet quieted.

"How about those Phenoms from Providence, Rhode Island?"

As each team was called, they raced onto the field and waved to their fans.

"Let's welcome the newest team to our conference." Governor Sapman's enthusiasm waned slightly, "The Springfield Sirens!" The new team was well-represented and did receive polite applause from the crowds.

Rainer wondered if Wretchkinsides had paid people to come out and support Marlisa's team.

"All right, let's welcome the Annapolis Amps to the exhibition today," Governor Sapman continued.

"And the Pittsburgh Salks will be showing us their skill today. Let's give them a round of applause!"

Rainer saw Emily and Fionna line up behind Chloe just off of the field. A grin formed automatically on his face.

"The team bringing us this opening season exhibition today," Governor Sapman roared. "The lovely ladies of Summation! Please give a hearty welcome to our very own Arlington Angels!"

The crowd went wild. As the Angels were the hosting team and most of their fans were local, the arena exploded in thundering applause and cheers.

"The Angels are captained for the eighth season by Ms. Chloe Sawyer." Chloe stepped forward to wave and blow kisses to her fans. Garrett joined in the wolf whistles Chloe was receiving.

"Joining the team this year, we have two new players. Ms. Katie Bellows has stepped in as the Angels' Junior Shield. She'll be coached by Senior Shield, Sasha Cohen, for her rookie year.

"And the American Realm's own sweetheart, the Angels welcome a brand-new Junior Receiver, Ms. Emily Haydenshire!" Rainer's wolf whistle echoed over all of the applause.

"Yes, folks, that is Rainer Lawson's ring there on Ms. Haydenshire's hand." Governor Sapman continued to pump the crowds.

Emily laughed and waved her left hand. She searched the box until she located Rainer. He blew her a kiss which she returned. Then to Rainer's delight, she stuck out her tongue and revealed the purple coating of the sucker he'd given her.

"Emily will be led by Angels Senior Receiver, none other than Ms. Fionna Styler. She's a beauty, isn't she, folks?"

Rainer and Logan shared a quizzical glance as Vindico gave a genuine chuckle. He appeared to heartily agree with Governor Sapman's assessment of Fionna. She was drop-dead gorgeous, but Rainer so rarely saw his boss smile it struck him as odd.

Fionna was waving and blowing kisses. Her sweet, humble demeanor was evident in the way the crowd's enthusiasm seemed to surprise her.

"All right, let's get to the exhibition. We'll begin today with the Duco Visium Obstacle Challenge. Captains along with the Visium and Duco position players, please approach the puzzle tables on the field."

"This is always the boring one." Logan dragged Rainer up to the concession area of the box.

As Visium and Duco Predilects were puzzle solvers by nature, Rainer disagreed with Logan's assessment, but he went along. He wanted to see Emily compete. That was all that really mattered to him.

At the end of the Obstacle, the Neutrons and the Salks were on top, with the Angels falling into third place. The Sirens, however, had come in dead last. Marlisa looked ready to maim as she stepped up for the captains' challenge.

Rainer smiled as he noted the fierce fire in Chloe's eyes. She stared Marlisa down.

The captains' challenge was an intricate maze of energy diodes, which would either add to the energy streams or remove it through energy drains. Each captain had to draw from a large battery and then convert the energy to electricity. The electrical current had to be moved through three drains and three additional sources, then pushed through a magnetic field. An iode sat at the end of the obstacle. It would only release when it was hit with exactly 12 volts of electricity.

"Captains, prepare to summon." Another announcer had taken over for Governor Sapman. He'd joined his wife and his two sons in the Angels box. "Summon!"

Chloe had the battery drained first and shot the stream through a drain. The other captains hit a source first. It was a risky move. Rainer leaned forward in his chair to watch the energy fly around the field.

Marlisa chose to balance her draws and drains in order. She hit a battery draw, and then immediately hit a drain.

Chloe, who'd been challenging since she was the captain of the Venton Vixens at the academy, had an entirely different approach. She hit her three drains in a row. She had barely any left by the time she completed the last drain.

With a smile on her face, she pushed what little electricity she had left into the three sources in succession. She had more than 12 volts easily. She passed it through the magnetic field until she felt she had the correct amount, and then shot a violent stream of electricity at the iode. It exploded on impact and the Angels raced onto the field to embrace her.

"Chloe Sawyer of the Arlington Angels takes first place in the Captains' Challenge!" The announcer sounded disappointed.

Rainer leaned forward to see the press box. The current announcer was dressed entirely in Neutron blue.

"So much for a nonbiased announcer," Logan joked.

Rainer turned back to the field. Marlisa was carefully moving her current through the magnetic field. She was ahead of the Bombers' captain and the captain of the Amps.

She leapt and shot the current at the iode, but nothing happened. She passed it through a drain again briefly, and then shot again. Her iode exploded at the same moment as the captain of the Amps. They'd tied for fourth.

Marlisa's fury visibly grew with every step she took back toward her teammates. Chloe and the Angels were still celebrating on the sidelines.

"Ok, Em's in the next challenge," Logan urged. Every Haydenshire in attendance eased forward to watch the Kinetic Competition.

Each captain would use one of their team's Receivers and one of their Shields to try to convert as much potential energy as they could draw out of the available diodes and into their team's iode.

The iodes for this kind of challenge had energy reflectors surrounding them. It would be Emily's job to convert the energy that Chloe passed to her, then get it around the reflectors and into their iode.

The iodes were almost touching and were completely surrounded by deflectors. It would be easy to accidently drop the stream in the wrong team's iode. It took a great deal of finesse.

The Shield would try to prevent other players from drawing on Emily's stream when she threw it toward the iode. Since the point of the exhibition was to showcase all of the players' skills, Chloe had chosen Emily and Katie for the Kinetic.

Emily and Fionna would also be competing at the end of the exhibition in the Receivers' Relay, with all of the Receivers from the other teams.

Rainer stood with the Angels' fans and cheered as Emily, Katie, and Chloe raced back onto the field. For this challenge, the players' joule meters would be monitored just like they are in challenges between two teams. Emily would need to get the energy stream into the iode before her joule meter was depleted.

The buzzer sounded, and Chloe summoned from one of the five diodes near her. She shot the kinetic energy to Emily. Katie immediately summoned and casted a shield around the stream.

The Receiver from the Neutrons had been just slightly faster than Katie, and he was pulling from Emily's stream. Katie raced closer and amped her shield. Her joule meter dipped to four bars.

The Neutrons Receiver's draw was bounced back, and Chloe drew from another diode. This time, she waited on Katie's shield before she added to the one Emily was already holding.

Rainer studied the field. Marlisa was drawing from her third diode, but their shield wasn't holding. The Bombers receiver was pulling half of their draw.

"Looks like our newest little fillies of Summation are having a tough day," the announcer tried to sound sympathetic but missed the mark. "Looks like there may only be room for one all-ladies team. The Angels of Arlington have always been Summation's sweethearts. Haven't they?"

The fans went wild. Emily beamed as the Angels' iode began filling rapidly. She edged closer to it.

The Angels were going to come in first. Katie's shield held, and Chloe fed Emily the kinetic energy in rhythmic pulses. She was losing very little in her conversion. Rainer's heart raced as he saw Marlisa's face contort in ire.

She drew from her fourth diode and shot the stream. Her Receiver could barely hold the amount of energy she'd already been given to try and convert, but winning was no longer Marlisa's goal.

Rainer leapt from his seat. His heart pounded in his ears. He couldn't draw breath. The stream hit the reflector that was less than two feet away from Emily.

Marlisa had calculated it perfectly. It appeared that she'd missed her Receiver, but the stream bounced off of the reflector, and with a horrifying scream, Emily's body doubled over. She clutched her right side and collapsed on the ground.

"Shit!" Vindico gasped.

"She's okay. She's getting up." Logan tried to reassure Rainer, but deep concern was evident in his tone. Emily took a few steps but then she cringed and clutched her right side again. She went down hard. Chloe, Fionna, and Katie raced toward her as the referees halted the challenge.

Rainer couldn't stand it. He tore out of the box with Garrett, Logan, and Vindico right behind him. He shoved people out of his way and did his best to dodge the vast number of cameras that appeared to be coming out of nowhere to capture his sprint.

Rainer made it to the medios' tent on the side of the field just as Chloe and Fionna helped Emily limp inside.

"Baby!" He rushed to her. She laid against his chest and finally gave in to the tears she'd been fighting. A cameraman shoved through the tent flaps. Vindico ordered him out.

Rainer's shield spilled from his pores. He filled it with soothing energy as he held her tenderly. The medios stood back from the powerful shield but were ready to aid at a moment's notice.

He kissed her forehead and edged her shirt up slightly. She was still clutching her right side. A medio stepped closer.

"Just give me a minute," Rainer demanded.

He grimaced. Huge purple bruises were forming over the side of her rib cage.

"Hold on to me, sweetheart." She managed a slight nod. Her entire body trembled with every breath as he slid his fingers over the bruising as tenderly as he was able. The medio who stood nearby awaited Rainer's assessment. "They're broken."

The medio moved in, but Emily clung to Rainer.

"No." She shook her head. Pain etched her face. Her rhythms faltered. She shuddered with every breath she attempted to draw. "I want Rainer to do it."

His shield kept some of the pain away and kept her from having to feel all of the emotions around her. Everything from her brothers' worry, to the medio's tension, to the reporter's dogged drive to get in. Without his shield, she could feel it all.

Rainer's heart fractured. He glanced at Garrett.

"Em," he soothed. Fionna nodded and urged Garrett on. "The medio can do it so much faster. Rainer's a Shield, not a healer."

The medio, who appeared well-equipped to handle broken ribs, stepped in and gave Emily a kind smile.

"How about I mend them, and you hang on to him. Ribs can be tricky, because I have to move around your lungs, okay?"

Rainer prayed Emily would agree. To be Gifted with a healing Predilect usually meant you had a very pure heart, just like Adeline. They had to be able to take over a person's energy and guide the body to heal itself. It required a very empathetic person, who was able to put patients at ease enough for them to relax and allow the medio's extraneous energy to join with their own.

Ioses Predilects were the most difficult to heal because of their body's drive to protect itself. After a few more tears, Emily begrudgingly agreed.

"Hold on to her tight," the medio instructed. "This is going to hurt."

Emily began to shake as Rainer embraced her. He watched the medio summon, but Emily was too distressed. She blocked him instantly. Rainer could feel it as he held her.

"Come on, baby," he whispered. "I've got you. Just let him heal them, okay?"

Garrett looked distraught as he watched Emily cry. He rubbed her leg consolingly. "He's got you, Em. You're all right," he soothed.

Logan's eyes closed in anger and angst.

"Fionna, you're going to have to step in for this challenge." Medio Sawyer, the Angels' majority team owner and Chloe's father, stepped into the medical tent.

"No problem." Fionna patted Emily's leg and returned to the field.

"Shhh…come on, Em," Rainer continued to soothe.

"Keep talking, Mr. Lawson," the medio whispered. "I believe you hold the key."

Her rhythms soothed to the sound of Rainer's voice.

As the medio summoned again, Rainer began whispering in Emily's ear how much he loved her, and that he'd take her home right after the challenge and take care of her.

She relaxed enough to let the medio in. The bruising morphed from purple to yellow. After several long minutes, she was able to draw a full breath without wincing.

"There." The medio smiled as he released Emily. "That's about all I can do for you right now. If you still want to play in the relay, you can."

"No," Rainer commanded.

"I have to," Emily argued.

"This is actually a good thing, Lawson. Think about it," Vindico whispered.

"How is this a good thing?" Rainer was on the verge of shouting.

"If Cascavel went back and told Nic how she threw that cast when he tried to take her, then her getting hurt would make him doubt that she has any kind of special powers," Vindico spoke through his clenched teeth.

"Thank you," the governor huffed as he threw back the tent flaps. Rainer hadn't heard him coming but assumed by his demeanor that the press had mobbed him on his way.

"Are you all right, baby girl?"

"Yeah, they healed me. It was three broken ribs," Emily explained dejectedly. She sipped from a can of seltzer water that one of the nurses had handed her.

"I spoke with the referees. They felt it was a mistake and that there was no foul play," the governor informed them quietly.

"Right." Vindico rolled his eyes.

"But you want me to send her back out there with that bitch who tried to kill her?" Rainer vaulted.

"I don't want you to do anything," Vindico spat. "All I said was that this wasn't all bad."

"She is not going back out there. Let me see your side, Emily." The governor lifted her uniform shirt.

"No, Daddy, I'm fine." She jerked the uniform shirt out of her father's hand. "And I am going back out there. This isn't like at Venton where it's no big deal. I get paid to do this. I have to work that relay. Then I can leave." Her determination seemed to gain intensity the longer she spoke.

"She's right. Marlisa won't even be out for the Receivers' Relay. She'll be fine," Garrett vowed. "Nic's little bitch princess will have to be on her best behavior now anyway. If she tries anything else, they'll end her career."

Vindico continued to infuriate Rainer. "Just let her go compete, then I can use this to get Sapman to allow Iodex to be on the field for next week's challenge. I told you, all in all, a few ribs isn't so bad."

Medio Sawyer returned to the tent. "Is she okay for the relay? It's about to start."

"She's fine. Probably won't win much for the Angels right now, but she'll make it to the end. Just try to get some rest this afternoon, Ms. Haydenshire. Try to lie on your left side. Mr. Lawson can run a cooling wave through his hand and place it gently over the area for about twenty minutes, once an hour, for a few hours today. By tomorrow, you'll be back to normal," the medio gave his instructions.

"Yes, sir. Thank you." Emily slid off of the table. "Just pick me up at the locker rooms."

The fear in her eyes crushed him, but before he could stop her, she was back on the field.

CHAPTER 35

CONFLICT

When they all arrived home, Rainer set Emily's bag in their room and pulled her close.

"Let me see the bruising again." He wanted to make certain it was still healing.

"I cannot believe I came in last place because of that bitch!" Emily screeched.

"They couldn't even get your joule meter to read five. Of course you came in last. You should never have competed. Your energies were trying to heal you, not transfer electricity to heat."

"As soon as I put my ring back on, it stopped hurting," she explained as Rainer lifted her shirt. She dispensed with all of her uniform.

"Good." He turned to admire the view of her in a sports bra and boy-short panties. He ran his hands over the approximate location of the broken ribs. The bruising had been yellow just before they'd left the arena. She'd put her engagement ring back on in the car, and she appeared to be healed completely.

She yawned as he traced over the area with slightly more pressure to make certain the ribs were all in one piece.

"Why don't you take a nap?" He patted the bed beside him.

"Will you hold me?"

"Of course." He knew her confidence was shaken, and she was scared, though she never would've admitted that.

He waited on her to crawl into bed beside him, covered them in the sheets and blankets, and then pulled off his shirt.

He wanted to be able to feel her energy with more than his hands while she slept. He wanted to know if she was in any pain. She sighed contentedly and wiggled down into his embrace. Rainer said yet another prayer of overwhelming gratitude that she was all right as he watched her fall asleep.

This had to end. Wretchkinsides and his daughter needed to be stopped once and for all.

Rainer guided Emily into the farmhouse kitchen. He inhaled the familiar scents of home.

"EE!" Keaton squealed as he raced into Emily's arms. Rainer chuckled as Keaton's head shook back and forth when he scrubbed his hair.

Henry toddled behind his brother and extended his arms up to Rainer. With a delighted grin, Rainer tossed him in the air before he landed him back in his arms and fed him a cracker from the jar on the counter.

The governor carried in a large platter of burgers from the grill. He kissed Mrs. Haydenshire's cheek and then Emily's.

"Are you okay, baby girl?"

"As soon as I put my ring back on, it healed completely." Emily lifted the side of her shirt.

"Good." Her father glanced nervously at his wife. "Garrett just called. He's on his way."

"Good. As soon as your dad gets here, we'll eat." Mrs. Haydenshire gave a weary smile.

"Are Nana and Paps coming?" Logan asked.

"They'll be here too," Mrs. Haydenshire assured him.

Emily and Rainer began buttering the hamburger buns so they could be toasted.

Adeline carried Henry on her hip while she set the table. Garrett arrived, followed by Will and Brooke. Patrick was unusually quiet as he slunk into his seat at the vast dining room table.

"Is Lucy coming over tonight, son?"

"No, Dad, she's busy," Patrick said.

"Did you break up or something?" Logan asked.

"No, we didn't break up. Mind your own business."

"Patrick." Mrs. Haydenshire raised her eyebrow in irritation. "Could we please eat in peace?"

"Sure, 'til Grandpa gets here."

As if on cue, a knock sounded at the door. Grandpa Haydenshire marched to his seat at the table. He scowled down the line of Haydenshire men seated at the table until he landed on Emily.

Grandpa appeared to be in a more vicious mood than usual. Rainer braced as everyone began passing around platters of burgers and baked potatoes.

"So, I hear you decided to move in with Mr. Lawson there and give up the milk before he buys the cow." Emily's eyes goggled as Rainer's mouth fell open. He tried to think of how to defend her.

"Dad, could we make it through the blessing before you start saying offensive things to my children?" Governor Haydenshire spat.

Grandpa Haydenshire did manage to keep his mouth shut through the blessing, and he helped himself to a burger and slaw.

"And I hear you're planning on adding more to this litter?" He gestured to everyone seated around the table as he asked Will the question.

"Uh, yeah." Will didn't seem certain if he should take offense. "Brooke's due around Thanksgiving." Brooke beamed as Will rubbed his hand across her abdomen.

Will and Brooke had waited until Brooke was well into her pregnancy before they'd informed their families, and her bump had grown quite a bit since they'd made the announcement.

"That's what got you in trouble in the first place." Grandpa Haydenshire pointed to Will's hand on Brooke's stomach.

"We aren't in trouble," Will seethed. "We've been married for several years. I just got promoted. I'm one of the Senior VPs of the

Senate Bank now. Brooke's been teaching since before we got married. This is exactly how we wanted it."

"Boy, you call me when that kid comes out of her, and she's crying and the kid's crying, and you don't know what the hell to do, and then we'll talk about who's in trouble."

Mrs. Haydenshire gave a distinct eye roll. "We'll certainly be there to help Will and Brooke after the baby arrives, and I'm certain the Bethencourts will be available to help when they're in town." She smiled kindly at Brooke who nodded her agreement.

"Humph," was Grandpa Haydenshire's reply.

"These burgers are delicious, Governor," Adeline tried to sweetly soothe the table. Logan stared at her with rapt adoration.

"I take it the butter churning's still sweet then, Logan?" Grandpa Haydenshire plunged his fork into his potato.

Logan's eyes goggled as blood pooled in his cheeks.

"Gonna sour, trust me. Just like Korea, boy, mark my words."

Governor Haydenshire shook his head. "Dad, Adeline is Logan's girlfriend. She's not a war. Would you please pipe down?!"

Rainer and Logan shared a knowing grimace.

"Wasn't a war…a conflict. That's what they told me down in my foxhole in Busan."

The governor rolled his eyes. "You are Gifted. You were not in a foxhole anywhere. You were in a cushy office in Seoul trying to save our soldiers."

"You think just because you're a governor now, son, you know where I was before you were even born?" Grandpa Haydenshire fired back.

"No, Dad, I don't. I would just like for you to stop insulting my children and their dates."

"Insulting?" Grandpa Haydenshire huffed. "Someone in this sea of shit that we call the world needs to tell these kids what life is really like. It ain't a freaking daisy festival, as much as you two would have them believe. That one's gonna turn." He stabbed his fork toward Adeline. "I can see it in her eyes, and you better all get your waders on and stop shoveling the shit around. You need to get yourselves out of it."

222

Adeline looked utterly astonished as tears welled in her eyes.

"What does that mean?" she whispered to Logan.

"Nothing." He glared hatefully at his grandfather. "It means absolutely nothing."

Everyone's heads shot upward as another fierce knock sounded at the oak front door.

The governor tossed his napkin on his plate and stomped to answer the door.

"Governor, I'm really sorry about this, but we need to speak to Adeline Parker and to your sons," Rainer heard as the governor stepped back, and three Iodex officers stepped inside the farmhouse.

Vindico's Agusta roared up a moment later. He entered the house as well.

"What's going on, Daniel?" the governor demanded.

"I'm sorry, Governor Haydenshire. I went down to the McLean precinct, or I would have beaten them here." He gestured to the officers Rainer had never seen before. He assumed they worked for McLean instead of for the Senate.

"They're here to do one of the tests," he sighed uncomfortably. "And uh, Candy Parker has alleged to her lawyer that you and your sons were supplying Adeline with money for drugs in exchange for…" he choked.

Rainer had never seen his boss so uncomfortable. It was almost as shocking as what Adeline's own mother had told the police.

"That is insane and you know that!" Governor Haydenshire appeared ready to throttle someone.

"Of course I know that, but we have to investigate this. If I don't do everything by the book, when she goes to trial, it could look bad for her, and it could jeopardize Logan's job. This is a Non-Gifted court trial. I don't have the pull I normally would and neither do you. They haven't even figured out how they're going to go about handling this between the two Realms, but we don't have any room for missteps."

Governor Haydenshire's fingers located his temples, and he began to rub. "What do we need to do?" he sighed.

Garrett stood with a fierce scowl. "Are you kidding me, man? No one here is sleeping with Adeline, save Logan, and trust me, he isn't doing that for drugs."

"No sleeping!" Keaton announced from his highchair as he popped a tiny bite of cheeseburger in his mouth.

Adeline began to sob as Logan glared at his brother.

"What? That's totally true," Garrett scoffed.

"It was a little crude, Garrett," the governor pointed out.

"Adeline, sweetheart, why don't you and Logan go on into the living room and see what they need, and we'll finish up then we can do whatever needs to be done," Mrs. Haydenshire soothed.

"Come on." Logan guided Adeline away from the table as uncomfortable silence drowned the room.

"See, son, I told you. She's not just gonna sink Logan, she's gonna capsize the whole ship," Grandpa Haydenshire sneered.

"Dad,"—the governor drew a deep breath—"for the love of everything good in this world, please just shut up."

Vindico instructed the officers who had come to collect a urine sample from Adeline to try and be discreet. Adeline was mortified.

He and two of the other officers worked their way through the governor, Rainer, and all of the Haydenshire men. They all vowed adamantly that they'd never slept with Adeline, nor had they ever given her money for drugs or ever accepted anything from her.

Adeline continued to cry throughout the entire process.

The officers apologized repeatedly for their inquiries. They insisted that being thorough now would save Adeline when it came time for her trial.

When her mother's apartment had been raided at the beginning of June, Candy had vowed that all of the drugs in the apartment belonged to Adeline. Candy had been taken in for prostitution and drug possession and was high at the time of her arrest.

Vindico had fixed it with the Non-Gifted courts to make it appear that Adeline had been arrested on suspicion and then released.

Adeline had agreed to random drug testing to prove her innocence. Rainer knew she never expected someone to show up for a sample at the farmhouse in front of Logan's entire family.

Almost two hours later, Vindico made yet another apology and did finally accept Mrs. Haydenshire's insistence that he eat.

"You see there, Logan? That's precisely what happens when you try to put your leash on a stray cat," Grandpa Haydenshire spat.

That did it. That was the proverbial straw. Adeline burst into heaving sobs and raced out the front door.

"Adeline!" Logan sprinted after her.

"Logan, wait." Rainer rushed out the door with everyone staring after them for a long, drawn moment before every other Haydenshire child, save Keaton and Henry, followed in his wake. They caught up to Logan and Adeline a second later.

"Come on, you know what an asshole he is," Will tried.

Adeline was sobbing inconsolably. "I'm…so…sorry," she managed in a convulsive shudder. Logan pulled her into his chest.

Emily shook her head. "You didn't do anything wrong. You have nothing to apologize for. We're so sorry you're having to go through all of this and that Grandpa is so awful."

The pause in conversation afforded everyone the opportunity to hear shouting from inside the house.

Garrett summoned and caught the fluxing waves of sound spilling from the house. Will amplified for him.

"You see that, Dad? Those are the kinds of kids we raised, whether we gave birth to them or not," Governor Haydenshire bellowed. "The kinds of kids who are there for one another, no matter what! You hurt one of them, then you'd better hope you have your beloved Gifted Army, because they're all out for revenge."

Connor and Patrick smiled and nodded. Levi winked at Adeline. "That is what happens when a home is filled with love, instead of war stories and constant competition, when children feel like they're listened to and that you care about what they have to say."

"Well, you may not have liked the way we did things, but you seem to have done all right for yourself, Governor," Grandpa Haydenshire huffed. "I'm sorry if Logan's too weak to hear the truth, but that's entirely your fault for always painting things up roses instead of giving them the cold hard facts. That girl doesn't know whether she's washing or hanging on the line. You can't just take in every stray cat one of those boys finds that's willing to lie down for him!" Grandpa Haydenshire shouted, and Garrett dropped the cast.

Everyone was absolutely stunned by the assessment. Logan let his eyes close for the length of one heartbeat.

"Get out of my home!" They heard Governor Haydenshire snarl as the front door swung open. Despite all the rude and boorish things Grandpa Haydenshire had said over the years, this was the first time the governor had ever thrown anyone out.

"Could you all just give us a minute?" Logan pled.

With sympathetic nods, everyone found somewhere else to be.

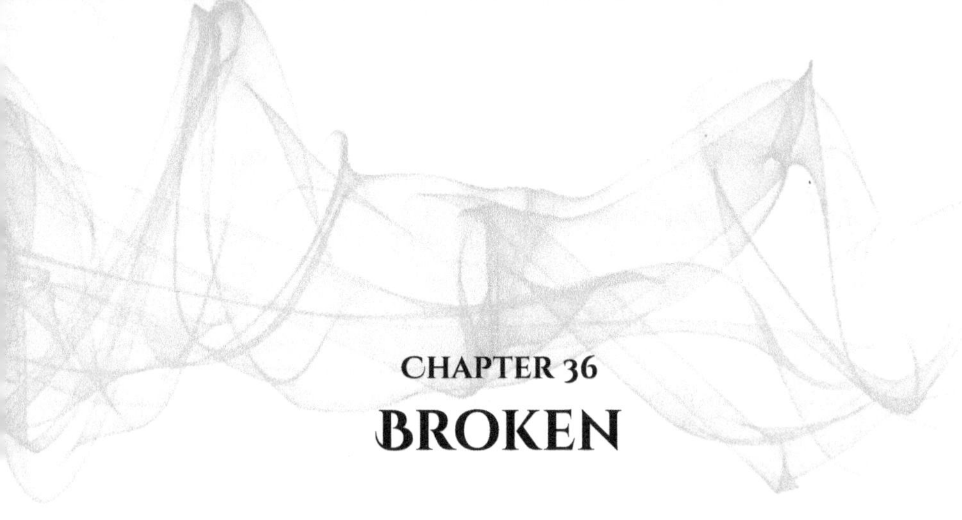

CHAPTER 36

BROKEN

Rainer scrubbed and rinsed dish after dish. He handed them to Emily to load into the dishwashers. No one spoke. Governor and Mrs. Haydenshire were whispering heatedly in the governor's office just off of the dining room.

Logan and Adeline had driven off in the Accord hours before, and though Rainer, Connor, Emily, and Garrett had all texted repeatedly, no one had heard from them.

Levi, Patrick, and Will all marched solemnly through the kitchen door. Everyone's heads lifted hopefully, but the morose expressions on their faces told them they hadn't located Logan and Adeline. The trip to the guesthouse and then to some of Logan and Adeline's favorite hangouts had turned up empty.

Rainer wasn't surprised. He knew they were in Logan's car somewhere talking, more than likely on Haydenshire property.

Tears sprang in Emily's eyes. Rainer dried his hands and pulled her to him. He kissed her forehead before he grabbed the next plate.

"I think we're gonna..." Will pointed out the door. Brooke had been asleep on the couch for a while. She seemed too tired to go on. "Text me when they get back."

Once the dishwashers were loaded, Rainer sank down on the

bench seat by the Haydenshires' kitchen window and pulled Emily on to his lap.

"Maybe we should go home. That's probably where they'll come," Emily urged.

Connor promised to let them know if Logan and Adeline showed up at the farmhouse.

Suddenly a shrill ring from Garrett's pocket had everyone hopeful.

"Haydenshire," he answered quickly. "Yeah." Garrett nodded as everyone waited with bated breath. "Tell them to wait right there. I'm on my way."

He grabbed his keys but then stopped just as abruptly. "Yeah… okay…no, I understand. Do you know where they were headed?" Garrett nodded again. "No, man, I appreciate you calling. I'll be in at the end of the week for a few hours." With that, he ended the call.

"They were at the station. Adeline wanted to see her mom," he explained. "Logan went with her, but he asked Fitzgerald not to call me 'til they left."

"Where are they now?" Emily demanded.

Garrett reached and tousled her hair affectionately. "I don't know. Logan wouldn't say."

Rainer's phone buzzed in his pocket. He read the text and then showed it to Emily.

> We're fine. I'll see you at work Monday.

Emily yanked the phone out of Rainer's hand.

> Where are you??

she texted frantically.

> Give Rainer back his phone, Em

was the reply.

~

Rainer drove the Hummer back to the guesthouse. Emily was nearly asleep when he parked.

"Come on, baby. Let's go to bed." He helped her out of the car. She let him lead her into the house. They changed clothes and crawled into their bed, a warm sanctuary from the hollow emptiness that filled them both. He wrapped her up in his protective embrace.

Not knowing where Logan was wasn't something Rainer ever remembered experiencing before.

"They're all right, right?" Emily begged.

Rainer clung to her. He wasn't certain what to say so he went with, "When you focus on Adeline or Logan, what do you feel, baby?" He reminded her of her own phenomenal powers.

She closed her eyes. Her Receiver's cast formed from her hand and filled the air around them. She concentrated. After several long minutes, she burst into tears.

Panic flooded Rainer's shield. "What did you feel?"

"They're not going to be okay," she sobbed.

Monday morning, Rainer left for work two hours early. He called Emily as soon as he parked the Mustang and walked into the Iodex office.

"He's here." His own breaths came easier as he stared at the back of Logan's head. He was seated at his desk. "I'll call you after practice."

He rushed to Logan. "Where the hell have you been? You scared us all to death." Fury filled the space that despair had vacated.

Logan raised his head. He looked horrible.

"What happened to you?" Rainer took in Logan's swollen red eyes and desolate stare.

Logan swallowed as Rainer grabbed the chair from his own desk and rolled it right in front of Logan.

"Uh..." Logan seemed too exhausted to formulate an answer. "Let's see here." He rubbed his eyes with the heels of his hands. "She wanted to see her mom. So, I took her, not that it got us anywhere, but I figured she had a right to ask her mother why she was doing this."

Thankful that no one else was in the office yet, Rainer placed a reassuring hand on Logan's shoulder to hold him up. He was on the verge of collapse.

"After that, we went to Great Falls to talk for a while."

Great Falls was a waterfall park near the Haydenshires' property. It was a common hangout for teenagers who wanted to park. Rainer had been there with Emily several times.

"Then." Logan shook his head in utter disbelief. "Last night, she kind of freaked and decided she was moving back into her mother's old apartment," he finally managed to force the words from his throat.

"What?!" Rainer was completely astonished. "But her stuff is at our house."

Logan shook his head. "We were there yesterday when you went back to Mom and Dad's. She packed all her stuff." He tried desperately to blink back more tears.

"Wait, why didn't you call me if she wanted to move? I would've helped you talk her out of it."

Logan's body gave a convulsive shudder. "She broke up with me."

"What? What do you mean she broke up with you? She's crazy about you. How did she get to work? What about all the stuff you've done for her?" Rainer was furious. Logan deserved a hell of a lot better than this.

"Yeah, that's why she broke up with me according to her anyway." His explanation was strangled by his emotion.

"Wait." Rainer drew a deep breath and forced himself to think. "Iodex showed up at the farmhouse Saturday night, but you said she freaked last night. What happened between Saturday night and Sunday?"

Logan studied Rainer for several long minutes.

"Tell me, please. We've been best friends since we were born. I want to help."

"She's a couple of days late, but I didn't know that until yesterday," Logan finally murmured. His voice was distant and weak. "So, between Grandpa calling her a stray cat, and my entire family being questioned about her, and her thinking she's pregnant, she decided that she's going to ruin my life. She just kept saying that she isn't good enough for me or my family, so she moved out and told me not to come back."

"But." Rainer shook his head. He couldn't decide which question to ask first. "But, if she's pregnant, don't you want to be there for that?"

"According to her, I don't deserve to be saddled with her and all of the problems she causes, so if she is then she'll either have an abortion or raise it herself and never tell anyone whose it is." He stated the utter absurdity of her decision. "It's her choice, I guess."

"Why did you let her move out?"

Logan shot him an infuriated glare. "I'm not going to make her live with me if she doesn't want to. I'm not a tyrant." He drew a deep, steadying breath and attempted to make the images a little clearer. "She's a healer, and you probably don't know this since Em's a Receiver, but healers have to be casted"—his voice crept toward embarrassment—"every single time, because her body heals itself so rapidly. She thinks she forgot a few weeks ago, and now she says it's all her fault. I repeatedly pointed out that she didn't get herself pregnant. All of Grandpa's shit about Brooke and Will drove her over the edge. She was supposed to start last Wednesday. She didn't realize she was late until yesterday. I guess she forgot about it or whatever."

"I'm so sorry." Rainer was desperate to find some way to fix this.

Logan clenched his jaw. His eyes shut tightly. "I slept in the parking lot of the apartment complex last night," he admitted.

"Logan..." It physically hurt him to watch his best friend fall apart.

"I'm not leaving her there alone. Not after what happened graduation night. I stayed until Brad picked her up for work," he choke

Rainer shook his head in horror. It was too much. He couldn't stand the image of Logan sitting in the car staring at the derelict apartment that had housed Adeline's mother's prostitution business.

She was the one who sold her body frequently for drugs. It was never Adeline. All Adeline had ever done was try to take care of her mother up until the night she was attacked.

"It's only a couple of days," Rainer urged. "She probably isn't pregnant. She's been under a shit-ton of stress with all Candy has dumped on her. That affects it, right?"

Logan nodded his agreement. "I know, but even if she is, that's fine too. I know we're young, but if she is then I'm in. I'd marry her tomorrow. If she wants to get rid of it, I'll be there for that too. I just want to be there."

"I know. Hey, why don't you go home and get some sleep? I'll okay it with your dad. He'll get Vindico to give you some time off." Rainer wasn't certain how long Logan was going to be able to hold it together if he didn't get some rest.

He shook his head defiantly. "I don't want to go home. I don't want to deal with Mom. Adeline doesn't want Mom and Dad to know she might be pregnant. I just don't want to do anything. Cal told me that because her mom never loved her she doesn't know how to be loved. She doesn't think she deserves it. I don't know how to fix that."

CHAPTER 37

CASUALTIES

By Thursday, Vindico was losing patience with Logan. Everyone was sympathetic, but Logan's insistence on sleeping in his Accord in the parking lot of the run-down apartment complex was rendering him useless. As Vindico was trying to finish training Rainer and Logan quickly, this posed quite a problem.

Governor Sapman had agreed that Marlisa's throw at the exhibition hadn't been an accident, and he'd informed the Sirens that Iodex would be on the field for the Angels vs. Sirens challenge that Saturday.

Vindico had used the opportunity to train Rainer and Logan in different urban terrains. They'd been out to the arena and had used everything from car batteries to the potential energy from fire extinguishers to fight. Logan had managed to drain a car battery but hadn't been able to do much with the energy.

Rainer was far more worried about the fact that he'd had to step in when Logan began purchasing multiple six-packs of beer to drink while he sat in that parking lot outside the apartment complex night after night.

"Rainer." Garrett gestured his head toward the coffee maker on the

233

opposite end of the Iodex offices. "Look at this." He thrust a stack of papers into Rainer's gut.

Rainer studied the forms. They were handwritten notes on some of the bank accounts owned by different members of the Interfeci.

Iodex had been watching the accounts ever since Mitchell O'Ryan Sr. had mentioned them to Vindico. He was waiting to drain the accounts as evidence until he saw where the money being deposited into them was coming from.

As Rainer studied the documents, he realized that Logan had been watching the accounts the day before and that his notes were not only illegible, the account numbers and transactions were incorrect.

Rainer had looked over the same accounts that morning, and three hundred and fifteen thousand dollars had been moved to an offshore bank account in Belarus, not Belgium.

"Dan's gonna shit if he sees this. Fix it and let me try to talk some sense into my little brother." He stalked to Logan's desk.

"Lo, let's go get something to eat," Garrett commanded, but before Logan could respond, a man in hospital scrubs was escorted into the Iodex wing by a security guard. He gestured his head toward Logan.

"Who is that?" Rainer quizzed.

"Brad," Logan stated without any tonality to his voice.

Vindico, who'd been standing at Tuttle's desk, heard Logan's explanation. His chiseled features rearranged quickly into an arrogant scowl. "Can I help you?"

Rainer appreciated his willingness to stand up for Logan.

But Brad kept his gaze locked on Logan. "Can I just talk to you, please? I'm trying to help you," he huffed as he took in all of the ominous scowls from Vindico's elite team.

To add to his menacing glare, Garrett summoned a vibrant green cast repeatedly. It looked almost like he was throwing a ball of energy in the air and catching it over and over again.

Rainer moved between Logan and Brad with a hate-filled glare.

"Please." Brad glanced around nervously.

"Fine, let's do this," Logan spat.

He shoved his chair back and threw his hands out. His invitation dared Brad to make a move. Disdain etched his entire body.

Brad's head shook slightly as he walked to Logan's desk. "You want to talk here?" He gestured around to all of the inquiring eyes.

"Why not?"

"If that's what you want." Brad furrowed his brow as Vindico narrowed his eyes and crossed his arms so that his already bulging biceps seemed to burst from the sleeves of his shirt.

Brad glanced nervously between Garrett and Rainer. He drew a steadying breath, hemmed, and then seemed to force himself to go on. "Look, I'm not interested in Adeline, so you can all lay off. I'm not stupid. I'm not going after an Iodex officer's girlfriend. I happen to like my face."

Vindico chuckled ominously. "Smart man."

"You've got to talk to her," Brad began his plea.

"Yeah, I hadn't thought of that. What a great idea." Logan rolled his eyes. "She won't talk to me."

"You have to do something," Brad demanded. "She's a disaster. If she makes one more mistake at work, they're gonna let her go. Georgetown prides itself on having the best medios in the world, and she was doing great, but this week…" He shook his head in disbelief.

He glanced around again and then edged closer to Logan's desk. "She's not, by the way. I thought maybe that's why she was so distracted. I did a test, and she isn't."

He stumbled over how to tell Logan that Adeline wasn't pregnant.

To Rainer's shock, Logan looked even more devastated. It seemed that some part of Logan had hoped she'd been pregnant. He must've felt like that would give him a fighting chance of getting her back, but now all hope was gone.

Vindico stepped in. "Hey, man, why don't you take the rest of the day off? Go talk to her."

Rainer suspected he was just as eager as Brad for Logan to either get back together with Adeline or to move on.

"No, not now. You can't come to the hospital. I've been doing all of her work for her to try to keep her job safe. If you show up and create a scene in the middle of her shift, they'll fire her today."

Logan looked sick as Rainer racked his brain to come up with some way to help him.

"All right," Logan nodded, "I'll try to talk to her tonight."
"Good." Brad seemed relieved.
"Let's go grab that lunch," Garrett urged again.
"Yeah, sure." Logan didn't sound enthused in any way.

CHAPTER 38

NEGOTIATIONS

LOGAN HAYDENSHIRE

Garrett slapped Logan on the back for the tenth time that week. Logan grimaced as he sank into the booth at Frye's. He wanted people to stop reassuring him, wanted people to stop telling him that things would work out, or that he would be okay.

He wanted his mother to stop baking him things and blinking back tears whenever she showed up at their house.

It wasn't okay, and it wouldn't be okay, ever. Nothing mattered anymore—not work, not Rainer, not his family, nothing.

He was hollow and weak. He'd slept in his car five nights in a row because he couldn't leave her there by herself, any more than he could've crawled all alone into the bed that used to belong to the two of them.

He was her Shield. That was all he was put here to do. He wanted to rage, wanted to war, wanted to destroy anything that set to harm her. But he couldn't fight the emotional trauma her mother had heaped on her in brutal doses. He didn't know how to fix this.

The pain was more than emotional. His entire body ached. His heart couldn't seem to find its steadying rhythm. He could hardly eat, and he didn't care. He welcomed the pain. At least it was something he could feel.

Garrett slid into the booth across from Logan and ordered them some burgers and fries along with Dr Peppers, in an effort to get Logan to eat something. Nothing tasted good anymore.

"Do you know what you're gonna say to her?"

"Probably nothing. Like I said, this won't be the first time I've tried to talk to her. She won't speak or even acknowledge my presence."

Garrett gave him a sorrowful look.

"I've texted her a million times. I've called. She has to know I'm sitting out in that fucking parking lot. She does nothing."

Garrett drew a deep breath. Logan braced himself. He clenched his jaw. This wasn't the first discussion various people had attempted to have with him about Adeline. He bit back the fervent desire to tell Garrett that if Rainer hadn't come up with anything to make him feel better, it wasn't likely anyone else would.

"Sounds like you're gonna have to make her talk to you even if you have to play dirty to get in her head, little bro." Garrett turned and thanked the waiter as he set down their plates.

"What's that supposed to mean?" Logan tried not to sound overly intrigued. Playing dirty wasn't his thing, but desperation had permeated his entire being.

"Well, not too dirty," Garrett redacted.

He must've sounded a little too interested. He didn't feel like eating, so he waited on his brother to continue. He didn't have the energy to prod him on.

"She feels guilty for all the stuff you've done and that Mom and Dad have done for her, right?"

"That's what she says, and that she feels like she has to be on her own because eventually I won't love her anymore." He shook his head. It pained him to think about Adeline telling him that. It was even worse to repeat it to someone else.

Garrett gave him a devastated expression. Logan appreciated the sentiment, but it didn't help him solve the problem.

"Okay, so maybe use a little guilt to get her to talk to you."

Fury sparked in his stomach. He glared at his older brother. "That's low."

"I know, but times are bad. Honestly, I wasn't going to tell you this, and it sounds like you have a lot longer than Adeline, but Dan's not gonna put up with you like this forever."

Logan swallowed hard. He tried to care. He dug deep but found himself simply unable. Work resided in the shallow depths, and pain was all that existed beneath. "I know."

"How about something huge or unexpected?"

Logan's brow knitted. "Like?"

Garrett sank his teeth into his burger and wiped his mouth before answering. "I don't know, a ring? I'll loan you the money."

"She won't even talk to me. Why on earth would she agree to marry me now?"

"I don't know. Girls like shit like that. Maybe a ring would make her feel more secure."

Logan considered that before forcing himself to eat a few fries. Garrett shook his head suddenly, with a slight chuckle.

"What?" Logan demanded.

"Nothing. It was an incredibly stupid thought."

"Tell me. I'd feel better if I wasn't the only idiot sitting at this table."

"You're not an idiot," Garrett soothed. "You're heartbroken. She crushed you, but this isn't over. It's not like she fell for Brad or some other guy. You're both crazy about each other. She's fucked-up, but who of us isn't on some level? You just gotta get her over herself."

Hope only led to more hurt so Logan only shrugged.

"For a second, I was gonna suggest talking to Mom because she has Grandma's old engagement ring, but like I said, really, really, stupid idea."

That, of all things, did make Logan chuckle. "Yeah, I will definitely not be giving her Gran's ring." He still couldn't fathom how his grandmother had put up with Grandpa for all of those years.

She'd died when Logan was four, so he hadn't known his grandmother that well, but he'd always hoped that heaven was a great reprieve from her life with Grandpa Haydenshire.

"No joke," Garrett offered apologetically. They ate in silence for several minutes.

Logan sorted through what he wished he could say to her. "What happens if she won't listen? What happens if she's lived in this kind of hell for so long, this is how she thinks life is supposed to be? What if misery is her normal? That's all she's ever really known. What if I can't get her back?" His horrific thoughts, the nightmares of his soul, unable to remain trapped in his fractured heart, suddenly took wing on his voice.

"May we?" Vindico interrupted Logan's hellish abyss.

"You mind, Lo?" Garrett looked thankful to see Vindico and Rainer. Logan wasn't thrilled that anyone but Garrett and Rainer had just heard his worst fears, but there was nothing he could do, so he slid over as Rainer climbed into the booth beside him.

"She's terrified, man," Rainer immediately provided, "and nothing kills love like fear."

"I know that," Logan huffed.

"Yeah, but you're going to have to help her see through all of that fear and back to you." Vindico grabbed a few fries off of Garrett's plate and threw them in his mouth.

"How?"

Rainer offered him a concerned smile. "The smartest guy I know told me that you have to make her understand that you're not only gonna keep her body safe, but that you're gonna keep her heart and her soul safe as well."

"Sam?"

Rainer nodded and continued. "Then he said that you have to talk over the fear. Make her hear you, and you gotta talk loud."

With a smile, Vindico nodded. "That sounds about right to me. But you're also going to have to let her know that you see her trauma and you're not afraid of it. That you want to be there to help her work through it."

"I'll try," Logan sighed. He was still too afraid to hope, but he swallowed down the fear and turned to Rainer. "Can I ask you a big favor?"

"Anything."

"Can I borrow kind of a lot of money? I'll pay you back." He turned back to Vindico the next moment, as his brain seemed to re-engage slightly. "And can I still have the afternoon off?"

Rainer handed Logan a signed blank check. "You aren't paying me back because I won't let you."

Vindico smirked. "You haven't really been there all week, so I don't see how it would make a difference. If whatever you're planning might make you able to be the phenomenal academy grad I just hired for the Elite team, then please do it."

"Sorry," Logan sighed.

After giving him a wry smile, Vindico shook his head. "Go get her back. Take it from me—letting someone you love this much slip through your fingers will be the biggest regret of your life."

CHAPTER 39

NONE SO BLIND...

Logan sat on the cold concrete floor of the apartment complex hallway. He glanced at his watch for the sixth time in ten minutes.

His heart would race momentarily but then it would return to its sluggish beat. The task was too much for it in its current condition.

He still didn't know what to say to her. All he wanted to do was hold her, be near her, feel her again, but that wasn't going to get her through the fear.

He had to talk, and she had to listen. His back ached from sitting and waiting. He leaned against the hard walls and haphazardly pulled at the cracked peeling paint while he waited.

Where is she? She should have been home by now. Logan stood and began pacing. He was unable to remain still. He heard a set of keys hit the concrete steps outside, and he turned.

She was there. She was carrying a basket of laundry, still wearing her scrubs, and hadn't seen him yet. Logan's heart finally achieved a sprint.

Her eyes were red and swollen. Her face was sunken, but she was still the most beautiful thing he'd ever seen. He stood there in that one endless moment and gazed at her. He prayed that some deity would give him the words he needed to make her understand how much he loved her.

"Adeline," he choked.

She gasped and dropped her keys again. He reached and retrieved them for her. "Can I help you with that?" He gestured to the laundry.

She shook her head combatively. "I told you not to come here."

After deciding that perhaps desperate times did call for desperate measures, he clenched his jaw for the length of one heartbeat and forced himself to speak. "Yeah, well, I gave you almost five years of my life, so I think I deserve one conversation," his voice edged toward fury.

"No." She was determined but clearly shocked by his demand.

"Yes," he insisted. "I'm not leaving, not until you've heard me out. I think you owe me that much. So, we can talk here, or in the apartment, or wherever the hell you want, but we're *gonna* talk."

Defeat settled in her eyes as she nodded. She refused to let him help her as she balanced the laundry basket and unlocked the door.

The apartment was basically the same as he remembered it from when her mother had lived there. There was virtually no furniture, only a bed in the one bedroom. Adeline had always slept on the couch. Logan noted the sleeping bag in the back corner of the living room.

"Has somebody else been staying here?" His heart felt like it might actually shatter into irreparable pieces of despair.

"No." Adeline shook her head. She set a stack of scrubs and panties on the small counter in the kitchenette.

As Logan studied the couch, he understood the reason for the sleeping bag. She certainly didn't want to sleep in what was once her mother's bed, and the stains on the couch must've made it equally as horrifying.

Though he fought them, the words slipped from his lips in an infuriated huff. "I don't guess I realized I was so awful to live with." He gestured around the disgusting apartment. A sob shook through her, and he instantly hated himself. "I'm sorry," he pled, but she shook her head.

He moved to her. He was desperate to hold her, to let her cry into his chest, to tell her that it would be all right, but she wasn't his to do that with anymore. The bitter truth settled in the pit of his stomach.

"Why are you here?" her voice shook violently.

Logan glanced back at the couch. He thought it might be nice if she could sit down to hear him out. He shuddered slightly at the thought of her sitting on that sofa and then began what he'd come there to say.

"I'm here because I love you. And, you know what else, if you'd broken up with me because you wanted somebody else or because another guy made you feel something I never could, then I'd walk away and let you have that because all in the world that I want is for you to be happy. I'd still be devastated, and heartbroken, and hell, just broken altogether, but I would. I would walk away and not come back if that's what you wanted. But that's not what you want, and I know it. I can feel it."

She started to object, but Logan shook his head.

"I know you're terrified of what might happen, and you've got yourself convinced that somehow you don't deserve me or that you're not good enough, but that's insane, and I'll tell you why. You make me a better person. You make me whole. You make my life worth living."

He willed her to understand what he was saying. "Without you, nothing even matters to me—not work, not my family, nothing! I'm gonna get fired because I'm a freaking disaster because I need you in my life. I don't even want to go on without you.

"And I know your mother told you your whole life that love hurts, but that's just one other thing she had so damn wrong. Love isn't what hurts. This, *this* that you're doing to us right now, this hurts more than anything I've ever experienced in my whole life, including my brother dying. I can't breathe. I can't think. Hell, I can't even summon because my entire existence hinges on you, so it's not you who won't make it without me. It's me who won't make it without you." The tears he was simply too tired to fight any longer fell rapidly down his face.

"And you know what else? It's not just that I'm so fucking in love with everything that you are. I really love who I am when I'm with you. I love us, more than anything else in the world. So please, I am begging you, don't do this to me. Know how much you mean to me.

Know that I won't survive without you. You're so much stronger than I am, and it's me who needs you, not the other way around. I'm the one who isn't good enough. I'm the one who doesn't deserve you." He gazed deeply into the depths of her tear-filled, onyx eyes.

She stared at him, both of them crying for one endless second.

"I'm not pregnant," she finally sobbed. He couldn't stop himself from pulling her to him. As soon as he embraced her, he was whole.

"I know, but that doesn't change one single thing I just said to you. And I'm sorry about what happened. I should've remembered to ask you every single time you gave me the extraordinary honor of being with you like that, and I didn't. I will never forgive myself for the hell that put you through. But just listen to me for another minute, and then, I guess if you want, I'll leave." He tried desperately to blink back the downpour of tears.

"I don't want you to leave. Please, please, don't leave me again," she begged.

Logan's body was finally able to draw a deep breath after six long days. The long-forgotten air seemed to drown his arid lungs.

"I don't want to ever leave you again." He willed her to understand. "Leaving you here Sunday, just to walk to my car, was the hardest thing I've ever done. But I need you to understand something." He swallowed and refused to let go of her. He pulled her into him tighter.

"If you had been having my baby, then it wouldn't have been just you who was pregnant. *We* would have been having a baby. *We* would have gotten carried away and forgotten the cast. *We* would get married and have a family together." He leaned back and cradled her face in his hands. "Because, baby, when you asked me to sleep with you, to give you that, and"—he forced himself to go on—"to share those moments with you, I would never have done that without that kind of commitment to you. I would've been right there with you, because I don't just have sex with you because it feels so damn good. I do it because I love you, and I want to be with you the way no one else has ever been. And if you don't want to have a kid right now, then *we* would be going to have an abortion. You are not alone in this world, Adeline. Do you hear me?

"When we're together like that, it is everything to me. And if one day we create a child that way when the time is right, then it will only be a good thing, because I just don't see how anything unwanted could come out of you and me being together. If I hadn't known when you and I decided to have a physical relationship that if it should somehow lead to a baby, I was ready for that, and we could make it work, I wouldn't have agreed to make love with you. I'm not walking away if the going gets tough, and you know what else? Nothing, not one single thing, could ever be as hard as trying to live without you. If you're beside me, then we can get through anything, but I can't do one damn thing without you."

She wrapped her arms around him and sobbed. She let him hold her. The feeling was exquisite. Just to be in the midst of her made him whole.

"I just feel like I don't have anything good for you. You're so much better off without me and all of my problems. Look at what happened to your family because of me!"

"No, baby." He shook his head and clung to her. "Everybody has shit going on they'd rather not have to deal with, but that's life. I want to spend my life with you. No matter what it brings, no matter what complicates it or makes it more difficult than it should be. If I get to hold on to you, then all of the other stuff is worth it. If I get to crawl into bed beside you at the end of whatever the day has been, then there isn't anything better than that. Life's gonna keep dishing up shit we may not like, but the only way I know how to get through it all is to hold on to you and never let you go again."

"I'm so scared." She finally punctured the tightly woven cap on her guarded emotions. She lost it all. She sobbed convulsively. Tears soaked his shirt as he held her tightly. "I may have to go to prison."

"I know you're scared. I am right here. And I know your mother creates nothing but chaos. I assume that's because that's all she knows, but I will not allow her to dump her trauma on you anymore. You are not responsible for her bullshit."

She finally fell apart, but it was all right. He knew, in that moment, as she clung to him with such ferocity her nails dug into his arms, it was going to be all right, because she was going to let him help her put them back together.

He squeezed her to him again. "I love you so much, and this is a hell of a place to do this, but I love you and I want you, and I will want you every single day for the rest of my life. I want to be with you in the good times and in the bad. I want to be the soft place for you to fall when the world is too much, sweetheart. I want that more than I want to draw my next breath. So…" He pulled away from her just long enough to get down on one knee in the kitchenette of her mother's one-whore drug den. He shuddered at the thought as he produced the ring box from his pocket. Her eyes goggled as she gasped.

"Will you please, please, let me be that, Adeline? Will you please marry me?" He popped open the box as she covered her face with her hands and cried harder. "Please, baby, I'm begging here. I can't do this without you, just please."

She nodded, and a timid smile broke through her anguished tears. He put the ring on her finger, stood, and pulled her to him just as doubt cast her face again.

"Logan, there are so many other women who would be so much better for you. What if I end up in prison, or what if there's something really wrong with me? Your family is one of the ruling families, and I don't even have a last name."

He held her tightly. His shield spilled out over them, the first he'd been able to cast in a week.

"I will not allow you to go to prison, and nothing is wrong with you. You don't need a last name or a stupid crest. This Realm is fucked-up with that nonsense. You are brilliant, and sweet, and kind, and good, and gentle, and beautiful…and perfect."

"No, I'm not. I still haven't started, and I'm not pregnant. There might be something really wrong with me. You don't want that."

Pain and terror shot through his veins as he cradled her to him.

"I want you just the way you are, and if there is something wrong then I want to be there for that too. No matter what, *you* are who I want. You're who I wanted six years ago when I saw you walk into sub-freshman orientation. You are who I want right now, and you will be who I'll want forever."

He shoved both of his hands up the back of her scrubs shirt and grasped her back tightly. If she couldn't feel it in his shield around her, then he would push his rhythms into her. "Feel me now. I'm not lying to you. I'm not making this up. The anguish you feel from me is from the past six days, and the love and adoration that's from right now."

"But what if there's something wrong and I can't have kids?" She shook in her terror, but he remained steadfast.

"I have seven brothers and a sister." He kissed her forehead. "We can have lots of nieces and nephews. I just want you."

"What if I have to go to jail? What if my mom keeps telling them I did all of that stuff?"

"I don't care what your mother says. You are not going to jail, but even if you did, I would come visit you every single day, and I would wait forever for you."

She seemed lost in a sea of confusion and desperation. She wanted so badly to believe what he was saying, but she couldn't quite allow herself that.

"What if I wanted to find my father?" She studied him intently. Shock washed through him. Adeline had never discussed finding her father in any capacity.

"Then I would pull every single string my family has access to in order to help you do that. You know, the one I'm begging you to become a part of."

Her chin trembled again as she nodded. "I'm only saying yes because I love you so much, and I can't stand being without you anymore. The past few days have been the worst of my entire life, and you know what my life was like before you."

"I don't care why you said yes. I just care that you did. Now, will you please come back home?"

"Yes." She shuddered. With a hesitant grin, she wrapped her arms around his neck as he lifted her up in his embrace.

"And you'll never leave again no matter what?" Logan demanded.

"Never," she vowed.

He nodded and let the words echo against his mending heart and wash through him. They soothed his aching shield.

"Can I help you pack?"

She smiled again. The sight lit Logan's whole world.

"Thank you," she whispered.

A few minutes later, they had her relatively few possessions packed, and they headed out the door.

He stopped suddenly and grasped her shoulder. "If you want to take a look back, do it now, because you aren't coming back here ever."

He had a few things he was going to insist upon before they left. She studied him as he continued. "And you just said you'd marry me, so that means all of me, Logan Haydenshire, the governor's son, so all of the money, and all the press, and all of the good and the bad that might go with that, okay?"

He was momentarily terrified she'd change her mind, but she nodded her acceptance.

"Then tomorrow we're going to see Will, and we're adding your name to my checking account. I'm going to get you a car, and you're going to let me buy you things that you need or want," he gave his final decree.

"Only if my paychecks go there as well," she made a demand of her own. "And I don't want to look back. I don't want any part of this ever, ever again. I don't care what you say. I don't deserve you, but I don't ever want to live without you again. So, I'll do anything you ask if you just promise that you'll never leave me again."

Logan's brow furrowed. "Baby, I never left you in the first place." He wondered if somehow he'd misread her. "You knew I was out in the parking lot every night, right?"

Confusion warped her rhythms. "What?!"

"I never left you. I won't ever leave you. You didn't know I was out there?"

She shook her head. "I told you to go. I thought you did."

"I'm never going anywhere. Ever."

Tears welled in her eyes, and he set her suitcase down. He pulled her to him and wrapped her up in his arms.

"Ever," he vowed again.

"I thought..." She thought she'd done an effective job of pushing him away because she couldn't allow herself to be loved. She'd tried to create the only reality she'd ever understood.

Logan shook his head. "I am never leaving you."

CHAPTER 40
MAKE ME WHOLE

Logan drove her home. He held her hand in his and told her repeatedly how much he loved her and how much he'd missed her. He pulled into the garage and opened her door for her. He clung to her hand as he lifted her suitcase from the trunk and led her inside.

Rainer and Emily met them at the door.

"I take it that went well?" Rainer grinned at him.

"Yeah." Logan held up her hand in his own. The diamond ring sparkled with hope and renewed faith.

Emily squealed and threw her arms around Adeline. "Okay, you can marry him, but if you ever break his heart like that again, I will hunt you down and strangle you."

"Yeah and I'll help her," Rainer agreed.

Adeline didn't seem to mind the threats. "That only seems fair, I guess." She reached back and took Logan's hand again.

"Hey, would you all mind...?" Logan gestured his head out the door.

"Already packed." Rainer pointed to a few duffle bags on the counter.

"Thanks, for everything."

"You're my best friend. It was my pleasure." With that, he grabbed their bags and led Emily to the Hummer.

"Do you feel all right, baby?" Logan guided Adeline to the sofa. He was still thinking about her concern over her lack of period.

She smiled at him. "I feel overwhelmed and so thankful to be here, and just…I don't know. I feel like I'm dreaming, and I'm terrified to wake up."

"Well, I've been living a nightmare for the past week, so a dream sounds like a really good thing to me." Logan cradled her on his chest. It was right where she belonged, and everyone else could just turn and walk away.

"I'm so sorry. I just…" She shook her head. She was on the verge of tears again. "Are you sure you want to marry me?" Disbelief echoed in her plea.

"I've never been more certain of anything, ever." He kissed the top of her head and rubbed his hands up and down her back. "Brad told me he did a pregnancy test. Do you need to see him again or another medio?" He wasn't certain what was going to happen, but he knew he'd be there no matter what.

Regret colored her features again. "Brad thinks it's because I was so stressed out over the drug testing and then breaking up with you. I haven't really been eating much," she admitted hesitantly.

Logan's eyes closed, and he bit his lips to keep from scolding her.

"So, he and Medio Candever, she's Brooke's medio, both thought I would start in a few days, once I calmed down, but Medio Candever said she'd be happy to do an exam next week if I still hadn't. There are several other medios in that practice who could see me if I can't get in with her."

"Okay." Logan gave her a reassuring smile. "If you need to have that done, I want to come with you, but nothing hurts or anything? There's no reason to think anything other than stress might be wrong?"

She shook her head then tucked it under his chin. The motion made everything in his world right again.

"I love you so much, and I think Brad and Medio Candever are probably right, but I will be there no matter what, even if there is something else causing all of this."

"I know you will." Her voice carried her astonishment. "I can't believe how lucky I am. I can't believe you slept in the parking lot. I can't believe anyone could love me that much."

He shook his head. "I can't believe you thought I'd leave you there. I'm your Shield."

She wrapped her arms around him tighter. "I know, but I told you to leave me there."

He reveled in the energy he could feel coming through her hands. He was desperate to feel more.

"None of us is more stubborn than Emily, but the Haydenshire boys are still pretty damn stubborn."

"Yeah, and I'm the stupidest girl in the world for asking you to leave and the luckiest because you didn't."

He sat back and eased her away from his chest momentarily. He brushed an errant hair behind her ear and gazed at her with tender adoration.

"You're not stupid. You're one of the smartest people I've ever met." His vow made her blush. The fever in her cheeks had his newly resurfaced libido pushing into overdrive. "You were scared, and I get that."

She gave a slight nod and then let her eyes close. She was reveling in his touch. Logan's heart sped and his breaths quickened. "But I will keep you safe, all of you. I don't ever want you to be afraid again. I will never let anything happen to you, sweetheart."

"I love you," she choked. "I love you more than anything else in the entire world, and I want to marry you and have a family with you, and I just want to be everything you've ever wanted, but I'm still scared I can't ever be good enough for you. I'm going to disappoint you."

"Baby, listen to me. You are already everything I've ever wanted, just exactly the way you are right now. You don't have to do or be anything other than who you are. The only way you could ever disappoint me is if you walk away again."

She shook her head combatively. "I can't." She shuddered. "I'm not strong enough to do that again. I need you too badly."

Another round of tears leaked from her eyes, and he rocked her back and forth. He soothed her and cradled her in his tender embrace. She added more tears to his already-ruined shirt.

"I promise it's okay. I'm right here." He wiped away her tears. "I will always be right here, right beside you."

"Your grandfather hates me," shook out between her stuttered breaths. This, of all things, made Logan laugh as he continued to wipe away her tears.

"My grandfather hates everyone. I'd say he's the world's biggest bigot, but that isn't quite true. He hates everyone equally, so I'm not sure what that is other than a sad way to go through life.

"And I don't give a damn what my grandfather or anyone else thinks. As far as I'm concerned, as long as you're right here beside me then nothing could be better, and Grandpa Haydenshire can fuck a pine tree sideways without lube for all I care."

She leaned up and grinned at him. Hope and timid hunger played in her tear-swollen eyes.

Logan reveled in the moment. He drank in her hesitation. He wanted to wipe away the pain and the doubt still swirling in her eyes.

Swallowing down an overwhelming amount of need, he guided her mouth to his. He forced himself to start slow. He brushed her lips with his own, but she wanted more.

With a heady groan of relief and expectation, he devoured her mouth. He slipped his tongue between her lips and intertwined it with hers in a slow rhythmic dance. Her lips swelled under his kiss. She shivered deliciously, and his world became whole once again.

"I want to take you to bed, baby," he whispered.

Her timid moan drove him wild.

"We don't have to do anything you don't want, but I need to hold you against me. I want to feel you. I want to wrap you up in my shield until you know and you feel how much I love you and that I will always keep you safe."

His name whispered from her lips as she clung to him. His heart hammered just to feel her wrap her body around his.

"Come here to me." He lifted her into his arms. He'd worked hard building the house and training with Vindico. He might as well show off the developing ripples, so he cradled her body to him. As he carried her to their room, he felt it again. His heart mended as he held her against him.

"I haven't slept here since you moved out." Sorrow permeated her rhythms as he brushed a kiss across her forehead. "And I don't ever want to sleep in this bed without you."

"I swear I'll never leave again. I'm so sorry." Her tears returned. He continued to cradle her as he pulled the sheets back and then laid her in the serenity of their bed. He joined her and kissed her again.

"Don't cry, sweetheart. You're here now, and that's all that matters."

Her hungry mouth beckoned his again. She moaned as she turned and clung to him.

He moved until her body was covered by his. He'd had more than a few beers over the past several nights. He'd been trying desperately to drown the grief and heartache in alcohol, but it hadn't worked.

When Rainer had called him on it, he'd stopped. As he lay there, feeling her pull him closer, knowing what she was about to allow him, he understood he'd wanted to get drunk on her. He'd needed to drown the tedium of the cruel world in the mix of their releases. There was nothing else that would fill him like being with her.

Slowly, he edged her shirt up over her head. She trembled as he pulled it off and then popped the clasp of her bra.

"I'm gonna take your clothes off, baby. I want to see you. I want to feel you, but then I'm gonna set the cast, okay?"

She gave a tentative nod and bit her lip, but then she let her eyes close in relief. She seemed to give her body over to him.

"Please," she begged, and he pulsed fiercely. His body tensed in starved desire.

Her eyes flashed back open as she felt him throb against her. She panted. Her body trembled as she moaned in expectation.

"That's what you do to me, baby." He wanted her to know the power she held over him. "You make me ache, and you're the only one who can make it better."

A desperate moan echoed from her as she writhed under him. She needed him to take it all away, if only for a little while. She needed him to stand between her and the world, and that was all he'd ever wanted to do.

Every problem, every pain either of them harbored in the depths of their hearts, could wait outside their door. He was going to make her do nothing but exist in the two of them together.

He pulled off his shirt. He wanted to feel her tender skin against him as he pulled off the pants and white cotton underwear she was wearing.

She clearly wasn't thinking she might be back in bed with him when she'd gotten ready for work that morning, but the juxtaposition between the innocence of the undergarment and the hungry look in her eye drove him wild.

She dragged her hands down his chest, groping and pulling his pecs in heated desire.

"Tell me what you want."

She reached and wrapped her hand around his length.

A low, guttural growl spilled from his chest.

"Please, I wanted to feel you against me for so long. I cried myself to sleep every night. I just needed you so bad, and I knew I pushed you away. I knew you deserved better, but when I'm with you, when I feel how much you love me, I know everything's going to be okay."

"Then feel me, baby." He let his hand trace over her lower lips. Timid heat and wet need clung to the jet-black curls. His gentle caress of their swollen need made her shudder deliciously. "Because I sure as hell am gonna take you."

His promises drove her wild. He could see it in her eyes. He could feel it as her energy spiked in hard, jagged waves he wanted desperately to soothe.

"You are so beautiful." He allowed himself a moment to drink in the imagery of her. His hands tracked up and down her body. He let his fingertips glide from her face to her neck. Then he cupped her breasts. Simply unable to wait any longer, he massaged her and felt her nipples pebble timidly in his hands.

A thundering moan echoed from his lips as they began to throb. Her body's reactions to him drove him wild.

He continued to explore her. He tenderly teased her navel, making her tense until he moved farther and spread her legs. He wanted to see her. His fingers glided over her lips, swollen full and ripe.

She writhed and bucked from the caress. The flavors of her and of sex filled his lungs. He slipped his fingers inside her carefully. He made certain he wasn't going to hurt her. She gasped and panted as she bucked her hips. She clenched. She wanted more.

He pushed deeper. The feeling of her tightening around his hand as her body prepared her for him had his heart thundering and his cock begging desperately to replace his fingers. A trail of ownership leaked from his head across her thigh. She moaned her adamant approval.

She was bound tight. The stress of the week they'd had, and of her life, had taken its toll. She needed him to set her free.

"The cast," she urged in a heated whisper. He clenched his jaw and willed patience into her. He moved until he was right beside her ear.

"Just relax for me, baby. Just let me make you feel better. Let me have this, and then I'll set the cast. I promise, sweetheart, I won't let you down again."

He continued to work her over. He caressed all of the places that made her energy spike rapidly. She couldn't seem to let it go, and frustration set in her eyes. He continued to soothe her with his voice.

"I'm right here. I'll always be right here. I'll do this all night if that's what you need. I'm not going to stop until I've made you feel it, until you know how much I love you."

Logan decided upping the ante might be helpful. He kept up his rhythmic strokes and then began to kiss his way across her collarbone.

He drowned her right nipple in the fiery heat of his mouth. He swirled and licked as she cried out for him. He knew what she liked. He began to suck fervently.

Back and forth, he pulled them deep as her eyes flew open, and she bucked under his hand. Her breath became frantic. She continued to writhe. She was almost there.

He begrudgingly released her breasts, but his tongue thirsted for something else. He continued his path down her stomach. Her abdomen clenched in heady anticipation.

With a deft move, he swirled his tongue around her clit and then began to suck as he pounded his fingers deeper with each rapid stroke.

She came undone. She screamed out for him and was unable to keep her body still. Her energy spiraled in waves all around him.

He concentrated and let the waves flood through him. The sizzle of her desire and her release permeated his rhythms. It pulsed inside the heat they were creating. Watching her give everything to him nearly drove him over. He eased his strokes until he was barely touching her as her breath calmed.

"I need you. Please, please," she whimpered. His heart thundered. She very rarely asked for anything at all, and for her to plead for him was more than he could ever have wished for.

"I'm gonna set the cast, baby," he summoned instantly. Her energy was swirling all around him. It dripped down his fingers. She'd already let him have her, so a moment later he closed her womb and moved over her.

She was still bound so tight he reminded himself to move slowly, though he longed to pound into her. He wanted to own her, to make certain she knew she was his.

He eased her apart tenderly with his hands as she begged, and then he prodded and pushed into her. The feeling was exquisite perfection. A deep groan echoed from low in his chest as he slipped into the tight, fevered space. He shuddered as he felt her body pulse and tremble around his length.

"Nothing could ever feel as good as you do." He thrust gently until he felt her give way under his insistent persuasion.

He permeated her fully. He filled her with all of him. He buried himself to his hilt as she writhed and moaned. She called for him.

"Yes, take me. Please." Her body contorted under his. She needed him. She needed to know he wanted all of her just the way she was, and that's exactly what he planned on showing her.

"You are all mine, baby. And you're gonna take all of me," he urged in a heated growl as he began to pound into her. He formed her around his length. "I'm gonna give you everything you need," he continued to soothe her as he covered her body. His shield pushed from his pores. It blocked her from the rest of the world. All that mattered was the way her body moved in time with his.

Her rhythms pulsed in desperate, frantic arcs as she let the love he gave so willingly enter and fill her. It reassured and restored her as she began to give way again.

She was on the edge. The climax began to consume her, and with another pounding, unrelenting thrust, she spiraled over. His name groaned from her, and he filled her with more than his energy. A shuddered curse exploded from his mouth as he spilled himself deep inside of her.

She quaked and convulsed as he held her. He refused to allow any space to exist between them. She reveled in the ecstasy of them together. She clung to him as fear seeped in where her release had vacated.

"Please, please don't let go of me. Please, just hold me."

He withdrew as carefully as he was able. He kept her wrapped in his protective embrace. "I will never let go of you. Not for the rest of our lives. You're mine, baby. That's my ring you're wearing, and I'm in this for life. You and me, that's it."

She nodded but was still clinging to him.

He wrapped his arms and his energy around her until she calmed. "Go to sleep, sweetheart. I'm right here. I will always be right here."

"Thank you. Thank you for coming to get me tonight. Thank you for taking me back. Thank you for making me listen to you. I'm so sorry for everything I've put you through."

"Baby, if that's what it took for you to realize what you mean to me and for you to agree to marry me, then it was worth it." He was unable to believe his own vow.

He released her just long enough to wipe away her tears before he wrapped her back up in his arms. She looked so small and frail in his long, muscled arms. He wanted to take care of her and of everything she might ever need.

Her eyes were still red and swollen. He could feel her energy falter in her exhaustion. She hadn't slept any better than he had.

"Let's get some sleep. I know you're exhausted."

She yawned with a slight chuckle at the confirmation. "I can't sleep without you."

"You never have to. Never again." With that, she relaxed as he held her close. He soothed her with his body as she fell into a deep sleep.

~

Logan awoke in a panic. The bed was empty. He threw back the covers frantically. He was terrified it had all been a dream. He tried to steady his breath and slow his racing heart. A moment later, she emerged from the bathroom.

"What's wrong, baby? Are you sick?" He yawned deeply and tried to guide her back into bed with him.

She smiled sweetly. "Hang on just a second." She began digging in her suitcase for something. Still trying to calm himself, he moved to her.

"It's three in the morning, baby. What are we doing?"

"I just had to set the cast. I'm sorry I woke you."

Logan was still confused as he glanced back at the clock. He noted that it was 3:18, but if she wanted to have sex at three in the morning, he was definitely game.

He still didn't understand why she was going through her clothes. Clothes were highly unnecessary if she wanted him again.

Suddenly, she cringed and placed her hand on her abdomen. Her entire body tensed, and Logan understood. She hadn't been closing her womb. She'd set the cast that Gifted women were able to set to make their bodies dispense with everything they didn't need in a day or two instead of a week.

"Oh baby, I'm sorry, but that's good, right?" He recalled the medio's thinking that stress had made her late.

"I think so." She looked relieved as he studied her. She pulled a pair of panties out of the suitcase and returned to the bathroom. After shaking himself in an effort to fully awaken, he went to the kitchen, grabbed some painkillers, and made her some tea. He returned just as she exited the bathroom.

"Thank you." She looked truly touched.

"Of course." He guided her back to the bed and handed her the tea.

She cringed momentarily and then swallowed down the pain medication. He braced her, ran a heat cast through his hands, and began rubbing her back.

"My cramps are really bad for some reason."

"I think maybe we scared it off with everything we did that night at the hotel, and then…" He drew a deep breath and tried to think of words to describe the past week. "I think this week took its toll. Your body is reacting to everything. That's normal."

She snuggled down beside him and sighed contentedly.

"Yeah, I think you're right. I know Brad kept me from getting fired this week, and my period, I just think I can't really make it without you. Nothing works right. You know?"

"Yeah, well, you aren't the only one, sweetheart. I can't tell you one damn thing Dan tried to teach me this week. I was a disaster."

"I'm so sorry," she started again, but he placed his finger over her lips.

"Stop. It's over, and you made me the happiest guy around when you said you'd marry me. So, let's just not think about it anymore, okay?"

She angled her face and kissed his jaw. He smiled unabashedly.

"When do we get to tell your parents?"

"We'll call them now if you want."

"Logan." She giggled.

He chuckled and cradled her closer. As he realized how long it had been since he'd cracked a joke or teased anyone, he was astonished at how quickly her being there had righted his world.

"I can't believe you didn't even tell your mom you were going to ask me." She yawned and snuggled into his embrace. His heart beat disjointedly for a moment.

"Only Rainer," he admitted. "I couldn't tell Mom. I wasn't sure you'd say yes." He hoped he wasn't going to upset her again.

"Does she still like me?" Adeline sounded terrified. Logan squeezed her tighter.

"Of course," he scoffed. "She loves you more than me. You know

that. I'm pretty sure she now hates Grandpa, but that's not really a
new development either."

He reveled in her giggle. It was the sweetest sound in the world.
He'd known from the moment he'd told some stupid joke at the lunch
table at the academy, and she'd giggled at him. That sweet melody had
him smiling for days after that.

He'd missed just being with her for so long, listening to her tell
him about her day, and hearing her laugh at his lame jokes. He didn't
want to go back to sleep. He wanted to stay up all night and talk
to her.

"Do you want to go back to sleep, baby?" He wanted to hold her
again if she was tired. To his delight, she shook her head.

"I missed you so much. Can we talk for a little while?"

A broad grin etched his features as he nodded and cuddled her
closer. "I was hoping you'd say that."

They stayed up for hours talking and reconnecting until they were
too exhausted to go on, and then they fell asleep wrapped up in one
another.

CHAPTER 41

ANY LENGTHS

RAINER LAWSON

After glancing at his watch again, Rainer grimaced. He refused to meet any of the pointed glares he was being thrown by Vindico and all of the task force.

He tried desperately to think of something to distract the team from Logan's tardiness. He racked his brain. Vindico had spent the last ten minutes pacing and looking highly irritated.

He finally spat, "All right, Lawson, where the hell is he? Why didn't he come in with you this morning?"

Rainer shifted rigidly in his seat. He was hoping to buy Logan a little more time. "Em brought me to work this morning."

Garrett furrowed his brow. "Why?"

He was going to have to spill the news. There was no way out.

Rainer willed Logan to come in at that moment. "Uh," he drew a deep breath. "He and Adeline got back together last night."

"Great. Maybe he can actually accomplish something now, but why is he so late?" Vindico demanded.

Rainer glanced at the door. He prayed it would open. "He proposed, ring and everything, so I'm sure he'll be here soon."

Everyone began laughing.

"I figured that would work." Garrett gave a hearty chuckle.

"Fine. Why don't we get started, and you can fill him in the next time Miss Parker's feet are on the floor." Vindico rolled his eyes, but he was laughing much to Rainer's relief.

He was definitely going to throttle Logan. He clenched his jaw as everyone began sniggering a few minutes later when Logan flew through the door, a full hour late.

"So nice of you to join us, Officer Haydenshire."

"I'm sorry. We overslept." His face turned the exact shade of Emily's hair. Rainer shook his head and rolled his eyes.

"The Haydenshire men do have great staying power," Garrett made everyone guffaw as Vindico rolled his eyes.

"Thanks for that, but now I'd actually like to share the work I've been doing while you've all been screwing around…literally."

A hesitant knock sounded at the door and Vindico smiled.

"Right on time. I like that," he goaded Logan again as he opened the door.

A security guard escorted in a brunette woman Rainer recognized, but he couldn't place from where. Garrett's eyes goggled as he furrowed his brow. He glared at Vindico.

"This is Bridgette Meyers. She's a waitress and dancer at The Tantra. She's agreed to do a little reconnaissance work for us to help us bring down Wretchkinsides."

Vindico looked extremely pleased by the news he was sharing. "Bridgette's dad and uncle are guards at Felsink, so she's known about the Realm for some time."

Bridgette nodded and eyed the men in front of her closely.

"Now, Haydenshire, it might be nice if you did something this week to actually earn the paycheck I'm signing for you." He shook his head to fend off Logan's apology.

"I'd like you and Lawson to go back to the safe house. Let's keep eyes on it this morning, and then you can meet us at Angels Arena. We're going to go over our positions and details for tomorrow's match. I want detailed descriptions and pictures of anyone coming in or out of that house. There's been a lot of traffic in and out of Riga and Moscow. They have to be going somewhere. As for the challenge tomorrow, I feel very strongly that the Sirens will be playing by their own set of rules."

Rainer's stomach churned.

"Now, go do something that doesn't make me want to beat my head against this desk."

"Yes, sir," they all responded.

"So, you'll call me later?" Bridgette drawled suddenly. She gave Vindico a grin.

"Uh, yeah, okay." Disgust momentarily perforated Vindico's tone and his shield.

"Bye," she waved, and turned to leave.

Garrett shook his head in abject disbelief as he followed everyone out of the office.

"Miss Meyers," he called to Bridgette as she made her way back out of the Iodex area. "Are you certain you want to do this?"

She looked pleased he'd called her back. She nodded and flashed Garrett a smile.

"Yeah, I mean, all of his guys are such jerks. They treat all of us like meat, and I could really use the extra money. So, why not?" Something in the shift of her eyes made Rainer wonder what exactly was going on in her mind.

Concern etched Garrett's chiseled features. "You understand that if Wretchkinsides finds out, he'll kill you," he stated without even so much as a blink.

"Dan said he'll keep me safe. You all have magical powers or whatever." She sounded deeply annoyed by that.

"Yeah," Garrett nodded, "but so does Nic. We won't be there when you're at work. We were all made when we arrested those guys last week. You'll be on your own. I think you should reconsider."

She rolled her eyes. "I need the money. I'll be fine." With a half wave, she exited the office.

"I doubt that."

"We'd better get going." Logan felt bad for being late after the week he'd had. Rainer was strapping on his Glock when Vindico made another appearance.

"Man, are you shitting me with that?" Garrett leapt. He threw his hand toward the exit doors. Fury lit in his eyes. "You're not only gonna have some Non-Gifted dancer spy for us, but you're gonna date her just to keep the information coming?"

"That's what she wants. I need someone who has more access to Nic's little shits than I do. What's your problem, Garrett? Why do you give a damn what I do?"

"That's probably the sickest form of prostitution I've ever heard of. Only you would agree with something like this. At least if you just screwed her, she wouldn't get herself killed. What happened to you? This would make Amelia sick."

"Why don't you go fuck yourself and stay the hell out of my life?" Vindico's office door slammed in Garrett's face.

Logan and Rainer stood frozen in shock.

"Go on," Garrett commanded them.

They both managed to nod as they headed out to the cars. Rainer shook himself as he tried to reconcile his boss using a stripper to get closer to Wretchkinsides. He cranked the Expedition.

"I take it you had a nice night then?" He tapped his watch. He was still irked that Logan had painted him into a corner with Vindico and the team.

Logan shot Rainer a goading grin. "Perfect, actually."

Rainer shook his head. He was thrilled to have his best friend back. "That's all I need to know."

"And yourself?"

"Great, and I actually made it to work on time."

"We really did oversleep."

Rainer laughed. "Sure you did."

Logan rolled his eyes, and Rainer could tell there was something he'd decided not to share, but he didn't need to know the details. He just needed his best friend to be himself again.

"Is Emily nervous about tomorrow?" Logan changed the subject.

"Seeing as how the last time she was on the field with that little bitch, she ended up with three broken ribs, I'd say she's rightfully concerned."

"No joke. If we'd been out there, we could've stopped that cast from hitting her, though. So, at least this time someone will be watching her."

CHAPTER 42

ANGELS VS. SIRENS

The next morning, everyone was up and getting ready. Rainer stopped every few minutes to embrace Emily and promise her that he'd be right there and wouldn't let anything happen to her.

Rainer and Logan were to be in full gear for the game, so Rainer wasn't able to wear one of the Angels T-shirts. Instead, he donned his black BDU pants and a black T-shirt with the Senate Crest on the pocket. "Elite Iodex" was written across the back, in yellow lettering that glowed in the dark.

He strapped on his pistol and waited for Emily to pull on her Angels uniform. He made certain he had the chain to wear her ring under his shirt and her grape-flavored ring pop in his pocket.

"Let's just get this over with," Emily sighed.

The arena was crawling with people when they arrived. Adeline took a seat in the box with Governor and Mrs. Haydenshire. Rainer walked Emily to the locker room. He stopped her just inside the hallway out of view of anyone else.

"I'll be right there the entire time. I will not let her hurt you again." Rainer slipped the duplicated ring onto her finger as he dropped the other over the chain and fastened it around his neck. He handed her the ring pop and kissed her forehead.

"Good luck, baby, but you won't need it."

She unwrapped the sucker and slid it onto her finger before licking it. They laughed together and shared another quick kiss before Rainer left to join Logan and the other members of Iodex on the field.

"Governor Sapman is attending the Neutrons and Bombers challenge in New York today, so the other officials are checking all of the joule meters and the course." Vindico gestured to the course, which hadn't been engaged yet but looked rather difficult, as far as Rainer could tell.

"I want you all stationed along both sides of the fields. You'll each have one Angel and one Siren to watch. Make certain nothing happens that isn't supposed to." He began assigning Angels and Sirens to each Elite officer.

"Lawson, since I know where your eyes will be anyway, I'll just be nice and let you have Miss Emily Haydenshire and Miss Rowena Harrison from the Sirens. She's an Enforcer, though, so keep a close eye on her as well."

"Yes, sir." Rainer scanned the field. He tried to learn as much as he could before the teams were released. It appeared to be a defensive course but would be tricky and would take quite a bit of energy to run. Two large drums of carbon were stationed on each side of the field.

Vindico began explaining the course as the gaming officials had explained it to him.

"Okay, so carbon from the tank and hydrogen from the air have to be converted to gas, then pumped through the engine. They can use the diode of hydrogen on the wall if they want, but it's a thirty-second time penalty if they use it."

"Then they have to harness and gather the heat from the engine and convert it to electromagnetic radiation to charge the solar panel, enough to start the electrical fire there." He pointed to black boxes made to light if provided enough heat. They were on the field near the solar panels.

"Another player will have to summon the heat from the fire and convert it to elastic energy to shape the rubber tubing until it's in position and correctly formed to launch the projectile carrying their iode into the safe zone. If the iode crashes outside of the safe zone, it's a five-minute penalty, until their iode can be restored. If they choose to use the diode of elastic energy there and there,"—he pointed to two diodes fixed on the stadium walls—"it's a three-minute penalty."

"Watch them close. This course requires quite a bit of heat transformation. It would be very easy to let some slip *accidentally*,"—he used finger quotes as he rolled his eyes—"and then use it to hurt someone. I want all of the Angels to still look like angels when this is over."

Rainer's shield spun in jarring spikes as he willed his heart to stop hammering in his chest.

"Take your positions. The teams are heading out in just a minute."

Everyone positioned themselves methodically around the field, but the teams remained in their locker rooms past the starting time. A Summation official raced to Vindico. They talked for several long minutes, with Vindico shaking his head morosely. With a final nod, he jogged to Rainer and Logan. Garrett moved in as well.

"The Sirens filed a complaint that there were too many Iodex officers who might have Emily's best interest at heart on the field. The attending Realm governors have to vote to see if you're all allowed to stay, but my dad and Governor Haydenshire are two of the three here, so I don't think it'll be a problem."

"And…"—he glanced around the field—"one of the Sirens had a meter that had been fixed to read at a constant three after the game play began, so Jessica Sanchez is being banned from the arena for the day, and the Sirens will start with a two-minute penalty. The teams don't know that yet," he warned as he moved back into position.

"Let's do this right, though, so no one calls foul. Allow me to restate the rules per the Gaming Governor," Vindico said loud enough for most of the stands to hear him.

"Obviously, you are not allowed to help any player from any team in any way. You may not give anyone energy in any format. You may only use defensive or protective maneuvers if the need should arise. You may not talk to any player during game play."

After sharing a quick glance with Garrett, Vindico waited for the challenge to begin. Rainer assumed he'd forgiven Garrett's intrusion from the day before.

A Summation official summoned and magnified his voice. "Welcome, everyone, to Angels Arena for our first Summation challenge of the season," he boomed to the roaring crowds.

It was then that Rainer saw Dominic Wretchkinsides slither into the opposing team's box above him. He swallowed down the bile that flooded his throat.

"I would first like to welcome the visiting team today, the Springfield Sirens." The crowd applauded as the team members' names were called and they rushed onto the field. They each waved to the crowds.

"And now we'd like to welcome the Angels of Arlington, Virginia, and thank them for hosting us here today."

Rainer whistled loudly as Emily's name was called, and she waved to the crowds. She turned to Rainer giving him a big grin and then stuck out her now purple tongue.

"Unfortunately," the official's voice broke up their displays of affection. "We've had a member of the Sirens who has been caught with an altered meter. Therefore, the Sirens will begin the challenge with a two-minute penalty."

Emily glanced at Rainer, but he gave her a soothing smile and a reassuring wink.

"So, without further ado…" The official hit a button to create the energy field aegis that protected the players from any energy from the fans. "Captains, ready!"

Rainer watched as Chloe and Marlisa took their positions. Uma Shann joined Chloe near the starting line. She was their Duco Predilect, and she would help determine and calculate the fastest way to get the iode into the safe zone.

"Summon!" the official shouted, and they were off.

Marlisa scowled as she paced and waited for the clock to tick to two minutes. In less than forty seconds, Chloe and Uma were back and explained their plan to the rest of the Angels.

Before the one-minute mark, Tenesha was on the field. She summoned and harnessed the molecules in the carbon and combined them with hydrogen from the air around her, to convert them into gasoline.

By the time she'd finished, the Sirens were on the field, and her joule meter was out. Marrieta, the Angels' Valeduto Predilect, stepped forward to refill her joule meter, but Chloe shook her head.

Chloe and Sasha returned to the field and poured the gas into the engine. The pistons began turning, but each of them had lost two bars of energy before they had the engine going quickly.

The Sirens Occamist was struggling with the carbon, and Marlisa was screaming and cursing at her. She seemed to melt under the pressure. The Occamist turned and screeched, "This isn't what that guy told your dad we would have to do!"

"Whoa!" Vindico, Portwood, and Rainer all cried foul at once as the referees halted game play.

When the Angels were allowed back on the field, they kept working while the gaming officials quizzed Marlisa and the Occamist on what exactly they'd found out before the challenge.

In the end, the Sirens' only Occamist was thrown from the game as well, and the Sirens were docked five full minutes for cheating.

By this point Emily and Fionna were on the field, gathering the heat from the fire that Sasha had set and shielded with the solar panel.

Once Fionna had gathered enough heat, she began shaping the rubber tubing as Emily kept a constant stream of additional heat flowing to her.

Emily's joule meter was dropping rapidly. It took quite a bit of time, but Fionna seemed to know exactly how the tubing needed to be shaped to get the Angels' iode into the safe zone without it bursting on the field. Before they were finished, the Sirens were allowed back in the challenge.

Marlisa had stepped in to convert the carbon to gasoline but was having a great deal of trouble with it. She finally managed the conversion just as Fionna and Emily were about to launch their iode.

Fury contorted Marlisa's face as she turned, shattered the oxygen from the diode on the wall, and summoned it along with heat to cast a fire.

Panic seized Rainer as he threw a shield cast over Fionna and Emily. Vindico had seen the same thing and cast as well.

Rainer had never set a stronger shield. The ring vibrated against his chest.

Vindico's double-banded shield pulsed rhythmically. It shaped itself around Fionna of its own accord. The look of abject confusion on Dan's face made Rainer wonder what his boss was feeling.

Marlisa was thrown from the game for the personal foul.

As soon as Vindico and Rainer released their casts, Fionna pulled the tubing, and the Angels' iode landed in the middle of the safe zone. The crowd went wild.

Emily raced to Rainer. Her joule meter was flashing on its last bar as he lifted her up and spun her in his embrace.

"We should've used the elastic energy diode. It took us too long," Emily fussed as he walked to the locker rooms.

Chuckling, he kissed the top of her head. "You won by, like, eight and a half minutes, baby, and if Chloe had decided to use the elastic energy, it might not have been enough to shape the tubing. So, you would have the penalty, and you and Fionna would still have had to form it. I think you were amazing!"

He was very accustomed to her critiquing her own work when no one else would.

Fionna and Sasha joined them at the entrance to the locker rooms. A moment later, Chloe and Garrett arrived as well.

"Okay, so you are all coming to the after-party tonight, right?" Chloe urged.

"Definitely." Emily looked thrilled. Fionna was grinning, but her mind seemed to be somewhere else entirely.

"Fi," Chloe huffed. "As exciting as I'm sure that must've been for you, that bitch tried to burn you two with an oxygen gas fire, so either ask him to the party or move on. You've had a thing for him forever. Just fuck him and get him out of your system."

Fionna shot Chloe a look that said for her to shut it. "I don't want to do that."

Rainer tried to determine what part of the challenge had Fionna so giddy. Chloe's exasperation did nothing to wipe the somewhat goofy grin off of Fionna's face.

Rainer recalled Vindico's shield had been thrown from very near her. It seemed to have responded only to her as if no one else on the entire field mattered to his shield. She would have felt the full force of his Double-Predilected rhythms.

A smirk formed on Emily's features and then she followed the other girls into the locker room.

Garrett put his arm around Rainer's shoulders. "You, my friend, are a very, very lucky guy."

Rainer certainly wouldn't argue that point. "In what respect?"

Garrett gave him his impish grin. "When the Angels win, they go wild! I mean *wild* wild!"

Rainer studied Garrett speculatively and shook his head. "Do I even want to know what you're talking about?"

"Just trust me. You need to bring your A game tonight because when they win, they're a whole lot more hellcat than angel."

Garrett looked thoroughly delighted with his evening plans. Before Rainer could reply to that, the girls emerged from the locker room and waited as the Sirens were escorted out by the Angels' security guards.

"So, are we gonna induct Katie and my little sister tonight?" Garrett grabbed Emily and put her in a full headlock as she tried to wriggle away from him.

"What does that even mean?" Emily spat as Garrett finally released her. She smoothed her rumpled hair.

"Of course, it's tradition." Chloe grinned at Garrett as he hoisted her bag to his shoulder to carry it for her.

Rainer knew that Garrett Haydenshire was never more gallant than when he was trying to get some girl into his bed.

"We'll see you tonight," was Garrett's response as he led Chloe to the arena exits.

"What does inducting me mean?" Emily quizzed Rainer this time.

"I have no idea." He was suddenly nervous about the Angels' after-party.

CHAPTER 43
WALK THE DOCK

The Haydenshires were hosting a luncheon for all of the Angels and their dates after the challenge. Emily was excited to get to her parents' house.

"I finally talked Connor into asking Katie to the after-party tonight." She sounded thrilled.

"Didn't they go out a few times at school?" He watched Emily pull a brush through her hair and reapply her makeup.

"Yeah, once, but then she started going out with Jay Flannigan, and that didn't end well. They broke up a couple of months ago. Connor didn't seem all that interested then."

Rainer didn't point out that Connor didn't seem that interested now either. "Didn't end well, how?" Rainer leaned against the bathroom counter.

"He cheated on her with Samantha Peterson, actually. Remember at the spring formal?"

Rainer shook his head. He had no recollection of the incident.

"You remember. Katie was in the bathroom crying for a really long time."

"I'm sorry Jay is a jerk, but I wasn't in the girls' restroom so I must've missed all of that."

Emily giggled. "Yes, but I told you about it."

"Yeah, but all I was thinking about was you in that tight purple dress, and I was busy calculating how I could get my hand up it without getting caught."

Emily beamed at him though she was shaking her head.

"Hey, I remembered the dress." He was rather impressed with himself actually.

Emily wrapped her arms around his neck. "I wore the purple bandage dress to the fall formal. I wore the green one with the white bow here,"—she pointed to her chest—"to the spring formal."

"Damn, that's right," Rainer admitted. "Okay then, I'm just gonna go with, I'm a dude, and I have no idea what you all do in the bathroom at dances except that sometimes you stay in there for a really long time."

Emily was still laughing as she began throwing lip gloss and her wallet into a different purse.

"I take it you liked the purple dress better than the green one?"

"No." He shook his head. "But you kept telling me I couldn't untie the bow on the green one."

A little while later, Rainer was sitting among a crowd of Angels along with the entire Haydenshire family. Chloe and Fionna were recounting just a few of the stunts Will and Garrett had pulled when they were all at the academy together.

Governor and Mrs. Haydenshire were shaking their heads as Brooke laughed at Will's permanent blush.

"If our little one gets into trouble at school, I'm going to have them call you," Brooke goaded Will.

"That would serve him right. When you do that, if you'd just let me know, I'd like to write the event down," the governor teased.

"Come on, Dad, you didn't get called all that often," Will scoffed.

Governor Haydenshire rolled his eyes. "Son, I have ten children. Your mother and I are on the favorites list of the school secretary's personal cell phone. I will say," Governor Haydenshire allowed as he took another bite of his sandwich, "we got called twice as often for Garrett as we did for you."

Another round of laughter lit the table as Garrett pretended to bow.

"What about Emily?" Chloe urged.

Connor laughed. "Oh, Em's a perfect angel, just ask Dad." He paused. "Or Rainer," he threw in with a hearty laugh as he rolled his eyes at his little sister.

Rainer winked at Emily. She was blushing but was unable to argue with her brother's assessment of the fact that she very rarely got into trouble whether she'd done anything wrong or not.

Governor Haydenshire hemmed before he nodded his defeat. "I probably did let her get away with murder."

"The real problem was," Garrett informed everyone, "Em would do something, and we'd all just be waiting for her to get grounded, or yelled at, or something, but then Rainer would tell Mom and Dad he did whatever it was, so Em wouldn't get in trouble. It was infuriating."

Every Angel at the table swooned as Governor and Mrs. Haydenshire nodded their agreement.

"We knew what he was doing," Mrs. Haydenshire admitted. "But I thought it was so sweet that in the end neither of them would get into trouble."

"Yeah, well, that was our plan all along," Rainer joked as everyone continued to chuckle.

Soon everyone was helping Mrs. Haydenshire clean up, then either heading home to get ready for the party or going out with one of the Haydenshire boys to explore the farm. As Connor led Katie out the back door, Rainer noted the very uncomfortable look on his face.

"Gonna walk the dock?" Rainer chided.

"Nah." Connor shook his head as Katie exited onto the back porch.

When Governor Haydenshire had decided to tear down the original dock and move it farther out over the lake, he'd drawn up the plans and shown all of the boys what they'd be working on that particular summer.

Will and Garrett came up with plans of their own. They'd presented them to the governor for approval. He was so impressed with his sons' initiative that he allowed them to build the new dock the way they'd drawn it.

He'd never figured out that Will and Garrett had concocted the plans to make certain the new dock was built farther south, several dozen feet closer to the overhanging hickory trees, so it couldn't be seen from the back windows. This blocked the view of Mrs. Haydenshire who seemed to always be in the kitchen.

That way Will and Garrett could bring girls out to the dock, and with a little bit of sweet talk and a whole lot of luck, they could generally feel a girl up without their parents being the wiser.

Rainer and all of the Haydenshire boys had referred to taking a girl out to try and get second base as walking the dock from then on.

Emily and Adeline giggled as they helped Mrs. Haydenshire with the dishes. When everything was cleaned up, Mrs. Haydenshire declared herself in need of sitting down. This caused Logan and Emily to panic since that was something she usually declared when she was expecting.

Rainer chuckled as Emily whimpered into his chest. "She might just really be tired."

She lifted her head and gave him a luscious grin. "I miss walking the dock."

"Uh, baby, we did a whole lot more than walk the dock last night." He leaned back to make certain no one else was in earshot. He was thoroughly shocked to discover that, despite the sheer number of people on the farm, there was no one in the kitchen or living room.

"I know, but remember when we used to sneak around all over the farm so we could make out? That was fun. I miss that."

Several thoughts flitted through Rainer's mind. It had been fun, and he missed those days as well.

He considered the sheer amount of stress Emily had been under the past week. Logan, Adeline, the Sirens, Samantha, the ring, and Wretchkinsides had wreaked havoc. He also knew that growing up was tough, and that Emily had traded one year of her childhood, one more carefree year in school, to be with him.

"Come on." He tugged her toward the back door.

A broad grin lit her face as she furrowed her brow. "Where are we going?"

"Have I ever taken you anywhere you didn't want to go, Miss Haydenshire?" She shook her head and was still sporting a broad, delicious grin. "Then trust me."

She took his hand and followed him out the back door. Images from their childhood filled his mind. Rainer recalled his adolescence spent growing up in the same house with the love of his life.

He took in the vast fields surrounding the farmhouse. His shoulders began to ease. The stresses of his current life washed away momentarily as he slipped into a younger version of himself.

Emily seemed to travel in time with him as they sank into the idyllic setting of their childhoods. Everything good, everything that had made him who he was, had taken place on this farm.

He'd lived at home with his father until he was fourteen, of course. But his dad had traveled extensively to other Gifted Realms around the world, and Rainer spent most of his time with the Haydenshires, even before they'd taken custody of him away from his uncle.

They passed the spot near the swing set where Emily had dared him to kiss her. He could still recall the way her cheek felt against his lips. He could still hear Connor and Logan pretending to gag.

He led Emily toward the loft as he let another memory play out in his mind. They'd been sitting up in Emily's loft, right after a late summer storm, just before school started back. He remembered his heart pounding frantically as he kissed her and tried to determine how to ask if he could do more.

She knew something was making him nervous. She could feel it. She'd given him that sassy grin and laid her head on his shoulder. "What's wrong?"

"Nothing." His voice had shaken slightly. He'd put his arm around her but was unable to focus on anything but her chest.

"I know what you want to do." She'd giggled when a deep blush had colored his face.

"No, you don't," he'd argued, though he knew she had his number.

"Yes, I do."

They continued walking, and he helped her up the ladder to her loft as he continued his reminiscing.

"It's okay with me if you want to."

His heart had hammered out an SOS as he'd worked up the courage to look at her again.

"What's okay with you?"

"This." She'd leaned in to kiss him again and grabbed his hands. She'd placed them right where he'd wanted them.

A little while later, he was still thoroughly shocked as he'd quizzed, "How did you know that's what I was going to ask you?"

She'd giggled again and cuddled up to him. "Because you've been staring at them for two weeks now."

With a few blinks, Rainer came back to the present. They sat down on the quilts in her loft. She laid her head in his lap, and he ran his fingers through her hair.

"Remember when we decided to French kiss?" Emily laughed hysterically.

He joined in her laughter as that memory spun into his mind. They'd been out on the dock catching frogs and had heard Cal teasing Patrick about licking spit with his new girlfriend.

Rainer and Emily had been in sixth and seventh grade, and Emily had demanded to know more.

"Get Rainer to show you how it's done, Em. I'm not telling you," Cal had informed her.

"We improved over time."

"It didn't help that I thought my entire tongue was supposed to be in your mouth." Emily shook her head.

Still caught up in his memories, Rainer recalled Garrett and Governor Haydenshire teaching him and Logan to drive a stick, and Rainer and Sam rebuilding his Mustang from the chassis up. Garrett had driven him and Logan to pick up the Mustang when it was finally finished.

Sam had quizzed Rainer on the inner workings of a car, and he'd had to pass before Sam would let him give him the money for the Mustang.

He recalled the first time he'd been allowed to take Emily for a drive all alone. He let his mind travel to the beach house and the dock at Buoy's. The warm, humid air filled his mind.

"Touch me, Rainer." He could still hear the urgency her voice held that night. It still drove him wild.

He recalled them out on the wooden deck of her parents' beach house, and how incredibly stupid he was to have fingered her there when her parents or any of her brothers could've woken up and found them at any moment. He hemmed between calling himself stupid or just admitting he'd been horny as hell.

Rainer shook himself from his reverie but decided he wanted to leave his worries and his problems at the gate to the farm, at least for the rest of the day. He moved until he was lying down and pulled Emily close.

"Can I walk the dock, baby?"

"I don't know." She beamed. "My dad might get mad if he catches us." She played her part well.

"We won't get caught," he assured her with a cocky smirk.

He lavished her mouth with his lips and slipped his hand to her backside. He gripped her and massaged heatedly. She arched her back and pushed her sexy ass into his hands.

He tried to keep the thought that he was doing nothing more than walking the dock firmly planted in his mind as he kept one hand kneading her ass, and he slipped the other under her shirt.

A moment later, he decided that maybe he'd dive off the dock instead of just walking it. He popped the front closure of the bra she was wearing. He wanted to feel her breasts in his hands with nothing blocking them from his skin.

She moaned as he groped just as he had the first time she'd allowed it. Just touching them through her shirt and her bra hadn't been enough. He'd wanted more, and she'd been willing.

"I felt so guilty after the first time we did this," he admitted in a heated pant just before he moved back in for another kiss.

She pulled away after several minutes. "Why?" She trailed her hands up his shirt, pulled at his pecs, and traced his nipples. He answered while kissing her.

"I felt like...I'd...pushed you...to let me take off...your bra." He devoured her mouth again as he gave his explanation.

"I wanted you to."

"Yeah, maybe." He caressed her face tenderly in his hands. "I never really gave you a chance to tell me no, though," he chastised himself. The guilty memory washed over him just as strongly as the memory of groping her for the first time.

"If I'd said to stop, you would have."

He felt a little better since that was certainly true. "I know, but I always tried to remember that you could feel how badly I wanted to do things and that you sometimes gave in because of that."

She shook her head. "You never pushed anything on me, and you never would. Remember the first time we went parking?" Her cheeks colored slightly as she bit her lip.

"I remember you were furious with me." He knew precisely why she looked so embarrassed. It was the day they'd graduated from the prep-school portion of Venton and began in the college program.

Emily had worked extremely hard and only had two additional classes until she'd be considered a full-fledged college freshman. She'd wanted to celebrate, and he'd driven her out to Great Falls Park. He recalled feeling extraordinarily guilty since they'd told her parents they were going to a movie and for pizza.

"You turned me down," Emily huffed, though she looked relieved as she stated the reason for their fight.

"I didn't turn you down," he argued, just as they had for the next several days after the incident had occurred.

He'd had her shirt unbuttoned and her jeans unzipped with his hand in her panties when what he was about to do had grounded him suddenly. He couldn't do it. That was where his sentiment *not in my car* had come from.

She was too special. She was the one he wanted to be with forever, and he knew it even at eighteen.

What they were about to do was too important. He wasn't going to take her virginity over the gearshift in his car. He'd re-buttoned her shirt and jeans and had driven her home.

She'd been furious. Rejection had shaken her deeply though he'd tried to tell her why he'd stopped.

She'd refused to speak to him for a week, except for the few times she'd shouted at him, but he'd steadily insisted and constantly reminded her why he'd refused.

"You were right," she admitted in a fervent whisper.

"I'm sorry, what was that?" he feigned shock.

She rolled her eyes. "You were right. I should've listened, and I'm sorry I got so mad at you." Her cheeks glowed a deep crimson in her apology.

Rainer shook his head. He wished he could return to his eighteen-year-old self and promise that someday Emily would admit she'd been wrong.

"I was a disaster. I couldn't figure out how to get you to understand, and you were so mad."

"I'm really sorry. I am glad we waited."

He brushed a sweet kiss across her cheek. "Me too."

"So," he was still caressing her face and enjoying just feeling her lie beside him. "Do you want to hang out up here or do you want to go get ready for the Angels' party?"

Part of him wished she'd say she wanted to hang out in the loft, but he knew that wouldn't be her answer. The sun was setting low in the sky, and the party was supposed to begin at eight.

"It'll be fun." She picked up on his hesitation. "You have to be an Angel or be invited by an Angel to get in, so no press or anything, just a fun party. We *did* win."

"You didn't just win. You won spectacularly." He broadened her grin.

He wanted her to celebrate her win. He wanted to take her to the party and let her blow off a little steam, but he hesitated to leave their refuge. It had been soothing to check all of the baggage at the gate for a little while.

If it was as private as Emily and Chloe had both insisted it would be, maybe they really could relax and have a little fun.

He'd be with her constantly, and he'd switched the rings back after the challenge. Rainer and three of her older brothers, two of whom were law enforcement trained, would be there. She would be safe, he reminded himself. He needed to chill and let her have some fun.

"Okay," Connor called as he entered the barn, "if either of you are naked, just say 'Rainer has a tiny cock,' and I'll leave."

Rainer sat up with a dramatic eye roll.

Emily leaned over the loft. "Uh, trust me, he's Gifted in more than just his protective casts." Rainer blushed violently as Connor gagged. "And…I've seen yours, so if I were you, I'd keep my mouth shut. I could tell Katie you're a nice guy and all, but you're half the guy Rainer is."

"Okay," Rainer huffed. "That'll be enough of that."

Connor rolled his eyes. He didn't seem concerned with his size in any way at all. "Dad wants to talk to you, Em. He's out on the dock."

"Why does he want to talk to me?"

"I imagine you're going to get the 'remember who you are and that you're my baby girl' speech." Connor chuckled.

"You want me to come with you?" Rainer offered.

He wished Governor Haydenshire would lay off. Emily had been stressed enough lately. He didn't think the "remember you're my daughter, a governor of the Realm" speech was necessary at the moment.

"No, I'll hurry him along. Then we can go get ready." She brushed a quick kiss across Rainer's jaw before she headed down to the lake.

He turned to Connor. "How was the dock?"

He wasn't really interested but felt like turning the tables on Connor after his rather lewd jab earlier.

"Didn't try very hard. She did invite me to the party with her tonight. I wish I cared."

Rainer wondered where that had come from. "If you don't want to come…" He couldn't think of anything else to say.

Connor just shook his head and took off toward the farmhouse.

CHAPTER 44

SWALLOW YOUR FATE

Rainer pulled on a button-down shirt he knew Emily liked and a pair of jeans. He was repeating the mantra, *Just have fun tonight. Whatever she wants to do, let her blow off a little steam. She deserves it,* in his mind as he sprayed on her favorite cologne.

He joined Logan on the couch. They watched TV as they waited for the girls to get ready. Rainer studied Logan as he casted and changed the channel incessantly. Something had him on edge.

"Are you okay?"

"Yeah. Adeline's just freaking about work last week, and everything that happened. She's really stressed about her mom. I just want her to have fun tonight, you know? She needs to just let it all go for a while. She's a disaster," he lowered his voice to make certain neither Emily nor Adeline could hear him. "She has another meeting with Stariff on Monday, so she had to ask off for a little while, which kind of had her panicked because she screwed some stuff up last week."

Emily emerged, wearing a black silk shirt that was cut on an angle so that if she moved just right it showed off her midriff. Under that, she was wearing a black and silver miniskirt that was shorter than any Rainer had ever seen her in. It showed off quite a bit of her legs.

"Wow!" He whistled and watched a flirtatious grin spread across her beautiful face.

Logan rolled his eyes and then teased, "Now, is that something that Emily Haydenshire, daughter of a Realm governor, should be seen wearing?" He mimicked their father almost to perfection.

"Yeah, I'm pretty sure it is." Emily laughed.

Adeline appeared. She was wearing a short black dress that was so tight it clung to her barely existent curves and had Logan's eyes popping out of his head. They took a slow journey down her long legs, which were bare from her midthigh all the way to her high heels.

Rainer elbowed him. "Don't drool on it, man. Then she'll have to get it dry-cleaned."

Emily and Adeline giggled, but Logan seemed unable to take his eyes off of her.

They all piled into the Hummer, and Rainer offered, "Hey, you all have fun tonight. I'll drive."

"Are you sure? I don't mind," Logan offered.

"No, I'm good. I'll have a beer or two, but nothing right before we head out." He hoped that would relieve Logan of any guilt.

Rainer headed back toward Arlington to the Angels personal bar, Anglington's. It was a Gifted club located in a warehouse, just like Angels Arena. You had to summon to be admitted, and most of the drinks were formulated with certain energy enhancements, sometimes making them more potent and sometimes less so. They also served unenhanced beer, wine, and mixed drinks.

Rainer drove the back roads and listened to Adeline apologize again about everyone being questioned on her behalf the weekend before at the Haydenshires'. She shared her concerns over her mother and the charges against her.

"Why don't we just try to forget about all of that just for tonight, sweetheart? Let's just relax and have a good time," Logan urged her.

Rainer and Emily shared a concerned glance over Adeline's plight.

"Garrett said it was around here somewhere." Rainer glanced around a cluster of industrial-looking buildings along a desolate street. He turned a corner and the car began to vibrate.

"Uh, I'm thinking it's that one." Emily pointed to a relatively small warehouse building with blaring music thrumming into the darkened alleyway.

He pulled into the parking lot. Garrett's Highlander and Fionna's bright yellow MR2 were parked nearby.

"Looks like the place." He turned off the Hummer and casted it as soon as everyone was out.

Emily summoned, then reached in her purse and flashed her Angels pass. The large bouncer nodded them in. He handed Rainer, Adeline, and Logan wristbands, which allowed them to be in the Angels' party for the evening.

"See, I told you there won't be anyone here who's not supposed to be," Emily reassured.

Rainer offered her his arm. She was elated. She was an Angel, and she was partying with the team. Rainer led her toward the flashing purple and green lights and the blaring music.

"Emily!" shouted from all of the Angels as soon as they saw her.

Emily was pulled from Rainer's arms and absorbed into the crowd of her teammates. They were all dancing as a single group.

"You just missed Stephanie," he heard Chloe call over the music. Stephanie Hendrix had played for the Angels for five years. She'd gotten married the year before and had announced she was expecting just following her honeymoon, which had effectively ended her Summation career.

Being under the field aegis, the energy that protected the players from any outside energy interference during a challenge, was dangerous for the developing baby and the mother. It interfered with the mother's ability to supply the Gifted energy needed to help the developing fetus form. If any woman became pregnant, they typically quit immediately. Some tried to return after they delivered but most moved on to other careers. Stephanie had been a very strong Receiver, and Emily had taken her place on the team.

Rainer glanced around the club. Arlington Angels memorabilia hung on every available wall. Above the vast bar were close-up photographs of different Angels logos that had been tattooed in various places on the Angels themselves.

There were lots of halos, wings, and lightning bolts tied up in the double As on arms, necks, ankles, and feet, but most of them appeared to be on the center of the girls' lower backs.

Rainer started to study the photos but then looked away quickly. Some of them were on what appeared to be their hipbones or very close to things he didn't have any desire to see of anyone but Emily.

The pictures were posed in such a way that it was difficult to tell where the tattoo was located but not impossible.

"Is Emily gonna get inked?" Logan was taking in the photos as well.

Rainer considered before shrugging. "Your dad would croak, but I think they all have them."

Logan laughed as he nodded. "When she decides to get it done, I want to be there when Dad sees it."

"If she does decide that she wants to, I can heal it for her so it's not red afterwards and it won't hurt her," Adeline offered. She was thoroughly enjoying everything she'd been learning at the hospital.

"If she wants one, I won't tell the Haydenshires you offered that," Rainer teased her as Logan reveled in her laugh.

Emily hadn't emerged from the mass of her friends, so Rainer continued to study the club. If all of the people in the club who were wearing the wristbands had been invited personally by one of the Angels, then the Angels knew hundreds of people.

"There you are!" Connor called as he and Garrett made their way to the table Logan had found for all of them. Garrett waved at a waiter, who was carrying a tray of drinks to their table and began handing them around. The rather large drinks were the color of a deep raspberry and smelled strongly of hard liquor.

"What's this?" Rainer set his drink on the table without sipping any.

"It's the Angels signature mixed drink. They call it Angel Essence," Garrett explained as Rainer nodded uncomfortably. "It's bourbon, vodka, tequila, and rum with cherry juice, and a cherry on the bottom. It's altered, so it doesn't hit you full force for a while. That way you can make it home with no problem. You just feel a little buzzed while you're here. It's supposed to loosen you up a little."

Rainer knew it was a testament to just how much "Essence"

Garrett had consumed that he added with a smirk, "You know, you have to suck hard to get to the cherry."

Logan gave him a disgusted look as Adeline's eyes goggled. "And exactly how much essence have you had?"

Garrett rolled his eyes at Logan. "Do you mean from a cup?"

"Geez, could you please stop being a prick?" Logan gestured to Adeline seated right beside him.

"My apologies, Miss Adeline."

Emily reappeared with Katie. They were each carrying a glass of the Angels signature drink.

"Come on, Adeline." Emily brushed a kiss across Rainer's cheek as she pulled Adeline up from her seat and dragged her back into the crowd of women who were all dancing together.

Rainer waved down the waiter and ordered a beer. He pushed the Angel Essence to the center of the table.

"Come on, Rainer," Garrett scoffed. "I taught you to drink. You'll be fine." Though it was true Will and Garrett had been sneaking booze to their younger siblings and Rainer since they'd been old enough to purchase it, which made Emily right around thirteen when she'd had her first sip of beer, Rainer knew better than to drink something that strong and then to drive, so he shook his head.

"I'm not drinking that and then putting Emily in a car I'm driving." He was growing irritated with Garrett's pushy attitude.

"Oh, great." Logan stared at the ladies on the dance floor.

"What's wrong?" Rainer turned to see what Logan was viewing. Adeline, Emily, Katie, and Fionna were standing in a group, laughing and dancing. They were all drinking one of the cups of the cherry-flavored liquor.

"Nothing. I want her to loosen up and have fun. She of all people deserves that, but Adeline holds her liquor about as well as a sieve."

Rainer couldn't recall Adeline drinking anything at any of the dozens of parties they'd attended at the academy. She usually clung to Logan or sat in a corner and read.

"You said you wanted her to relax and have fun," Rainer reminded him.

"I do, but I don't want her to be sick."

"I'm sure she won't drink more than one."

Logan nodded his agreement, but he didn't look entirely certain Rainer was correct.

"So, is this place open all the time or just for the season parties?" Rainer quizzed Garrett. The bar was heavily bedecked with Angels memorabilia to only be open twice a year.

Garrett shook his head. "It's open every night, all year. They just let the Angels use it when they want it for their private parties."

Emily and Adeline reappeared. They tugged on Logan and Rainer's hands.

"Come dance with us."

Rainer stood and tried not to chuckle as he watched Emily's eyes begin to spin slightly.

He led her back to the dance floor and spun her into him as they started to dance. "Are you okay, baby?"

"I'm fine. That drink is kind of strong, but I just feel a little buzzed. It came on fast, but then it stopped."

"Yeah, it's enhanced," Rainer explained. Emily did appear to be recovering quickly.

He smiled and then began moving to the beat of the music. It turned into more of a grind-fest, but Rainer didn't mind as he reveled in Emily thrusting her hips into his.

She spun and began grinding her backside over him as he held her waist. He leaned in until he could speak directly in her ear and his cock was nestled against her backside.

"If you want to go home, baby, I'll take that skirt off and we can do this all night."

She gave him a luscious grin and waggled her eyebrows at him.

Garrett and Chloe were hanging all over each other very nearby.

"Are you ready to be inducted?" Garrett called to Emily a few minutes later.

"I still don't know what that means," she shouted over the music.

Chloe and Garrett laughed as Garrett began making his way toward the bar.

"Adeline, I'm not sure you should have another. They're really strong," Rainer heard Logan urge.

"I'm fine, really. I feel good," Adeline assured him.

Rainer studied her. He had to admit she didn't look as tense as she normally did, and she appeared to be having fun.

He briefly considered getting Emily to encourage Adeline to give the drink to Logan, but Rainer halted as the lights on the dance floor fell and a drumroll echoed from the cover band. A spotlight fell on the bar.

Suddenly, Garrett was standing on the bar and summoning to magnify his voice. "I think it's time to celebrate today's victory!" he slurred slightly. Everyone cheered. "And, we have some new girls this season." He raised his drink in acknowledgment.

Rainer had a very bad feeling as he watched the ladies all applaud while Katie and Emily glanced around nervously. He wrapped his arms around Emily as she clung to him.

"Okay, ladies,"—Garrett waggled his eyebrows as Chloe came to stand beside Emily—"pick your guzzler!"

Chloe laughed and started toward the bar. Her eyes were locked on Garrett, who was beckoning her with one finger and was giving her an extremely lascivious look.

Emily turned to Fionna. "What's a guzzler?"

Fionna smiled at her. "Rainer will be your guzzler." She laughed as a dozen men pushed their way toward her. They were all trying desperately to be the first to volunteer for her.

The bartender was furiously wiping down the bar and filling twelve shot glasses with the essence mixture. He arranged several spray cans of whipped cream, a bowl of cherries, and another bowl of limes.

Logan and Adeline moved to stand beside Rainer.

"I think the captain should go first, don't you?" Garrett bellowed to the crowd. Most everyone hooted and whistled.

Garrett jumped down from the bar and pulled Chloe to him. "Music…" At his command, the band began to drum out a song with heavy throbbing beats and rather lurid lyrics. As the floor began to vibrate from the music, Rainer turned to see what Garrett was going to do next. While he was distracted, a guy Rainer didn't know approached Emily.

"Hey, sweet thing, is he your guzzler?"

Rainer spun back. Fury burned through his eyes. The guy took in Rainer's glare and stature. Rainer was in vastly better shape, due to Vindico's workouts. The guy stammered out an apology and moved away.

Emily patted Rainer's arm and then asked again, "What is a guzzler?"

Connor and Katie had made their way over by this point and Connor laughed. "I take it that in this case,"—he gestured toward Garrett and Chloe—"Garrett is the guzzler."

Emily furrowed her brow, and everyone watched.

Garrett began dancing with Chloe. He backed her to the bar and looked at her like he'd gladly take a bite if he could.

Chloe threw her head back in laughter as Garrett dropped to his knees in front of her after he'd thrust his hips into hers to the beat of the music.

After shooting a hungry grin to the crowd, he raised his eyebrows and began to lick from Chloe's knee until his tongue disappeared under the hem of her skirt. Logan and Rainer's mouths fell open as Emily's eyes bugged. The crowd began to chant Garrett's name.

He stood and leaned Chloe back over the bar. He grabbed and shook one of the cans of whipped cream then flipped Chloe's shirt up to just below her bra line.

Rainer and Logan's mouths were still hanging open in astonishment. They saw the top half of the Angels logo on Chloe's lower abdomen. The bottom half was covered by her skirt.

Garrett took the can and traced Chloe's stomach around her navel. A second later, a GH appeared written in whipped cream. Her navel was centered in the G of his initials.

He made quite a show of picking up half of a lime. Garrett ceremoniously squeezed the lime inside the whipped cream, then he scooped a cherry off of the bowl on the bar.

Chloe laughed again as she raised her head, and Garrett dropped the cherry into her mouth. She waggled her eyebrows and looked excited as she closed the cherry in her mouth.

Garrett grabbed one of the shot glasses and arched Chloe's back deeply over the bar. He let the liquor dribble down her stomach into the whipped cream and her navel.

He spun around and held up the empty glass. The crowd cheered. He turned back and began at the Angels logo on her hip. He lapped at the mixture he'd created and sucked the drink out of her navel. Then he licked his way up her and caught her face in his hands. He kissed her until he'd removed the cherry from her mouth.

He pulled it from his teeth, held it up with a broad grin, and then dropped it back into his mouth, chewing and swallowing. All around them the team and adoring fans were cheering Garrett on.

Rainer looked at Emily. He was reeling from what he'd just seen.

"He wants me to do that to you, his sister, here, in a bar full of people?"

Emily gave him a panicked look, but she didn't seem to have anything to say. Rainer spun to Logan and asked again, "He wants me to do that to your sister?"

Logan looked shocked and then handed Rainer a full-sized glass of Angel Essence. "That might help."

Rainer took a long swig as Emily downed another as well.

To Logan's astonishment, someone had handed Adeline yet another drink.

"Ad, I really think you've had enough."

Adeline shook her head and laughed. "Loosen up." She stumbled slightly. Logan caught and steadied her. "Did you want to drink it off me?"

Rainer and Logan shared an extremely concerned glance. They'd never ever heard Adeline tell anyone to loosen up.

Rainer couldn't worry about Adeline just then as other Angel players and their guzzlers were lining up to perform the belly shots.

"Are you ready?" Garrett urged. His hands were still roving all over Chloe.

Rainer was about to inform Garrett that there wasn't enough liquor in the entire commonwealth of Virginia to make him lay Emily out on a bar and pull her shirt up while a crowd cheered him on. He stopped short as he took in Emily's pleading gaze.

With a slight grimace she whispered, "Please, Rainer. Please just do it. The whole team is doing it. I can't be the only one who doesn't."

Rainer's heart hammered. He thought about what her father would say if he ever saw what was about to happen.

"Em, you do not want me to do that." He stated what he knew was the absolute truth.

"I know, but I have to. I'm an Angel."

Rainer swallowed the rest of the essence Logan had provided him in one sip, while he watched as both of the Angels' Shields, including Katie, were being used as shot glasses at the bar. He noted that Connor was not guzzling for Katie, but he couldn't ponder that at the moment.

Chloe looked astonished that there was any objection. "You have to do it," she ordered. "It's bad luck not to."

Garrett laughed. "Yeah, you know I made that up just to get you to do it when you first made captain."

Chloe rolled her eyes but continued, "It's tradition. Everyone does it for the first win of the season. It's only us here. No one will ever know."

Rainer sought Logan. He was hoping for a voice of reason, but Logan shrugged. He gave Rainer an apologetic expression then went back to trying to get Adeline to have some coffee.

Challenge lit in Garrett's eyes as he jumped back on the bar.

"Okay, everyone, we have a new Receiver on the team this year." Emily looked horrified. "She also happens to be my little sister." He nodded to Emily as the crowd began to cheer.

"I think we're gonna let the extremely famous Rainer Lawson..." More cheers echoed from the crowd. Rainer felt faint. "Who also happens to be her fiancé"—the crowd hooted, but then quieted down and waited to hear what was coming next—"induct her into the tradition. What do you think?"

Frenzied shouts came from all around, and after drawing a deep breath, Emily pulled Rainer toward the bar.

He gathered courage as he followed her. He tried to drown out the crowd thrumming his name in a fevered chant.

Garrett jumped back off the bar and whispered, "Make it look good, man."

Emily appeared lost between desperation and terror. "Just do it, and then you can kill him later."

Garrett began conducting the chanters cheering Rainer on.

"I may take you up on that." He tried to remember everything he'd seen Garrett do as he backed Emily toward the bar.

The band played louder. Hypnotic drumbeats and guitar peals echoed through the chanting crowd. He forced the masses of people watching them out of his mind and gave Emily one last pleading look.

She uttered through her teeth, "Just make it look good. Pretend it's just us."

Rainer narrowed his eyes at her. He drew a deep breath and kissed her. He let everyone see him lick her lips and dip his tongue in her mouth as his hands traveled under her skirt. He began massaging her upper thighs heatedly.

The crowd went wild. With a shrug, he decided it wasn't so bad. He willed away his embarrassment and picked up a cherry out of the bowl. He turned to the crowd and held it up. He raised his eyebrows with a cocky grin.

Emily raised her head and bit her lip. She giggled nervously for a second before he dropped it into her mouth. She held it between her teeth before she opened her mouth so it fell back toward her throat. She stuck her tongue out, showing how deep she'd dropped it.

Rainer let the whiskey he'd consumed work its own magic as he pulled one of the cans of whipped cream off the bar and shook it.

He lifted Emily's shirt, but not nearly as high as Garrett had lifted Chloe's. In an effort to cover as much of her as he could, Rainer placed his hand on her waist, and with a slight shrug, drew a heart around Emily's navel. The crowd swooned.

Emily beamed at the heart and nodded her head encouragingly. Rainer laughed and loosened up a little more. The bartender handed him the shot.

Emily threw her head back so her back was arched over the bar, and Rainer raised his eyebrows appreciatively, which was met with more whistling and loud whoops from the onlookers.

He tipped the glass over her, and Rainer briefly thought of what the Haydenshires would say if they saw this. He pushed that thought out of his head as he let the drink fall onto Emily's stomach and collect in her navel.

He refused to look back at the crowd, lest he lose his nerve. He kept one hand on her waist and licked up her and sucked the Essence out of her belly button.

When he finished the drink, he licked the whipped cream heart off of her stomach and dove in for the cherry. He emerged a moment later and flashed the cherry between his teeth before he began to chew.

He pulled her off of the bar, and they bowed to the now-applauding throngs of people who were descending on them. They made their way to a table as Dana's husband, Paran, began pouring liquor into her navel.

"That wasn't so bad, was it?" Emily's face still flushed.

"It's not that I don't enjoy licking things off of you. I just would rather do it in the privacy of our own bedroom."

"At least we don't have to do it again until next season."

Rainer closed his eyes and nodded his defeat.

Garrett and Chloe made their way over. "Very nice, Lawson."

"Did you forget that she's your little sister?"

Emily and Chloe giggled, as Garrett considered that. "Well, yeah, but a tradition's a tradition."

Rainer rolled his eyes. He still couldn't quite believe what he'd just shared with three hundred or so people.

Emily laid her head on his shoulder, and he wrapped his arm around her. She seemed to want to hide in him. It was a feeling he understood all too well. Before he could become consumed with worry over her, he heard Logan demand that Adeline stop drinking.

"Okay, we need to go home," Logan demanded as he moved back to their table.

Rainer glanced around the bar to take in his reaction time and his vision. The liquor hadn't really taken effect yet, but he still didn't want to drive after the large drink and then the shot out of Emily's navel.

"Let me have a Dr Pepper or something first." He knew the

caffeine and the enhanced soda would counter some of the effects of the alcohol, whenever they may decide to hit.

He ordered a Dr Pepper and watched the bartender work the fountain. He wanted to make certain that was all that he put in the cup.

After downing it quickly, Rainer headed back to the table as Adeline began trying to wind herself around Logan in a way she never would've done in public if she'd been sober.

Logan shot him a desperate look as he tried to fend off Adeline without hurting her feelings.

"Are you ready?" Rainer quizzed Emily.

"Definitely," Emily agreed as Adeline grabbed at Logan's crotch.

Logan jerked her hand away. "We have to leave now."

Rainer led Emily out of the bar. Logan dragged Adeline out behind them. She stumbled most of the way to the car.

Adeline, as it turned out, was a loud, lascivious drunk who repeatedly told Logan what she wanted him to do to her and what she wanted to do to him when they got home.

At one point on the journey, she laid out in the back seat, but Logan was sober enough to hoist her back up and threaten Rainer's life if he ever said anything about it.

Emily was well on her way to being smashed as well and found everything Adeline said hilarious, as the sheer number of Angel Essences she'd consumed began to take effect.

Logan was almost asleep when Rainer pulled the Hummer into the garage and wondered how he was going to get them all to bed.

CHAPTER 45

SHOT IN THE DARK

"Logan, can you get her inside, or do you need help?" Rainer's inquiry made Emily laugh harder.

"I'm fine," Logan assured just before he stepped out of the Hummer and then fell forward into the Mustang. Rainer cursed under his breath. He grabbed Logan's shoulders and guided him inside. He deposited him onto the couch and returned to help Adeline.

Emily managed her way in just as Rainer was trying to get Logan to help him take Adeline to bed. Instead, Logan pulled Adeline onto the couch, and they began a sloppy make-out session.

As Logan ran his hands up the short hem of Adeline's dress, Rainer grimaced. He suddenly had a horrible thought about all that had happened to Logan and Adeline the week before.

"Em!" he panicked.

"Yeah?" She seemed to be able to hold it together at least for the moment.

"You have to cast her. She's drunk. She won't shield you out."

Emily considered. "I don't feel good. I think I had too much. I don't know if I can do it right."

"Baby, I cannot do that to her. I just can't." His head began to pound. He wasn't certain if it was from the alcohol or from all that had happened in this seemingly endless night. "Logan would freak."

He shuddered as he tried to envision telling Logan that he'd harnessed his fiancée's erotic energies and performed the cast to close her womb.

"Okay." Emily seemed to steady herself.

"Just cast her. I'll take you to bed. I'll take care of you. I swear. I know you don't feel well, but I cannot do that." He pointed to Adeline, who Logan now had underneath him on the couch.

Emily summoned. Rainer watched her closely. It took everything she had in her. She paled as she performed the task.

Rainer put his hands on her to hold her steady. She drew a measured breath as she moved to Adeline. Rainer shoved Logan to the side rather forcefully.

"Get off of her, and go to bed!"

Logan stumbled toward his and Adeline's room. The liquor seemed to be taking full effect. Emily managed to harness Adeline's energy. She placed her hand on her abdomen and sealed her off.

Emily tinged green as she sank against the back of the sofa.

"Just a second, sweetheart. Just sit right there and let me get her to bed."

Emily began rubbing her eyes and forehead. She watched as Rainer lifted Adeline, then half carried and half guided her into the bed with Logan. He certainly wasn't removing her dress for her. She was going to have to sleep that way.

"Come on." He eased Emily off the couch. She leaned against him, and he didn't think she could take the twenty or so steps from the couch to their bedroom, so he lifted her up and carried her in his arms.

"I'm so sorry. I didn't realize it would be so strong. I think I only had two or three." Her head swayed as he walked.

"It's fine. I didn't know you'd had that many. Just try to get some sleep. I'll put some water beside you." He clenched his jaw shut to bite back the comment that she was going to feel like hell in the morning.

After she'd had some water, he helped her undress and pulled one of his Ioses T-shirts over her head as she fell back on her pillows.

"Go to sleep, baby."

She was out before he'd made it to the door. With an exhausted sigh, he shook his head and moved to the kitchen.

He grabbed more large glasses and made everyone water, but as he carried two of them toward Logan and Adeline's room, he was absolutely certain he didn't want to knock or enter.

"Nice, Logan." He knew that if Logan hadn't had vastly too much, he never would've done what he was doing, loudly, right then.

He left the cups on the coffee table and returned to the kitchen, grabbed the painkillers, and placed them on Emily's table, along with some antacids.

He slung his clothes into the hamper and took a long shower. He wanted to wash away the smoky smell and the sticky sweat that was all over him. It was one of the reasons he hated going to bars.

A little while later, he edged into bed beside Emily. He tried not to disturb her. He felt dizzy as the one drink he'd had started to take effect.

Rainer awoke in the middle of the night hearing Emily in the bathroom. He rushed to her. His head pounded with every step he managed.

He reached and held her hair away from her face as she vomited up pure alcohol. When she'd thrown up most of what she'd consumed throughout the evening, he handed her a cold washcloth and spread toothpaste on her toothbrush for her.

He glanced in the mirror as she apologized profusely. He was a little green himself. Moving his head at all was excruciatingly painful, so he just helped her back to bed and assured her that he thought they'd all had too much.

"I'm so sorry," she groaned as he covered her up. "I guess I had more than I thought. I really didn't feel drunk at the bar."

"I know. Me either, but my head is killing me."

She tried to pat his chest, but the motion seemed to be too much for her. Her face paled as her cheeks flushed a deep scarlet. She asked for another cold rag.

Rainer willed himself to be able to walk back to the bathroom. He re-wet the washcloth, chill-casted it, and handed it to her.

He managed to point her to the antacids as he placed the rag on her forehead. She chewed one and let her eyes close.

Moving hesitantly to his side of the bed, he let his head, which now felt like it must've weighed several hundred pounds, fall onto his pillow.

"I swear I will never have another Angel Essence ever again," she whimpered out her solemn vow.

CHAPTER 46

RESPONSIBILITIES

Emily was sick again around five, and Rainer's head throbbed so badly he could hardly see.

He tried to reason how he could feel so horrible after only one drink and one shot. He groaned as he fell back into bed after settling Emily. To his knowledge, he'd never had enhanced liquor before, and he was quite certain he never wanted to again.

The next time he awoke, he rubbed his eyes and did feel a little better. His head lifted from his pillow. He inhaled deeply…bacon. His mouth watered. Suddenly he was starving, and he didn't think he'd ever smelled anything better as he dragged himself to the kitchen.

Emily was still pale, but she did look more herself after having gotten all of the alcohol out of her system throughout the night. It seemed to have been a decent remedy.

"I'm so sorry. I can't believe I got sick, and I got everyone sick. And you had to take care of me." She set a plate down in front of him that was full to bursting with scrambled eggs, bacon, fried potatoes, and ham biscuits. She added a large mug of black coffee, which Rainer swallowed in just a few sips.

"Thanks, baby." He began inhaling the breakfast. Garrett's recipe for a hangover was an extreme amount of protein, fat, and caffeine, followed by copious amounts of water.

"You're welcome. I made everyone food. I feel terrible. This is all my fault."

Rainer devoured everything on his plate and took three painkillers, though the recommended dosage was two. A half hour later, he began to feel human again.

Emily ate with him. She cleaned her plate as well. Color began to return to her face and her eyes cleared. She'd made two additional plates, and left them casted on the counter to stay warm.

Logan emerged from his room. He looked both horrified and sick. After blinking several times, he leaned against the door he'd closed. He seemed confused.

"Are you okay?" Rainer handed him the painkillers and the water he'd made him the evening before.

"I need to talk to you," Logan demanded hatefully. He held his head in his hand. Talking appeared to make him dizzy. Rainer didn't have the energy to be snide, so he just sighed. He knew what was coming.

"Fine. Why don't you eat first?" He gestured to the food Emily had prepared. Logan eased to the table as Emily set down a plate identical to the ones she and Rainer had eaten. The more Logan ate, the angrier he seemed to become.

"Is Adeline okay?" Emily glanced at Rainer and tried to discern what was wrong with her brother.

"I honestly can't tell if she's just asleep or if she's passed out. But trust me, we won't be going to any more Angels' parties."

Tears began to swim in Emily's eyes and fury lit in Rainer's. "Hey, she sure as hell didn't tell Adeline to get shit-faced drunk last night. You want to be mad? Be mad at yourself. You should've stopped her."

"I'm really sorry, Logan. I had no idea everyone would get sick." Emily went on with her apology.

Logan swallowed down several sips of the coffee and his own bitter regret. He turned to Emily. "Can I talk to Rainer, alone please?" It was much more a demand than a request.

"Why?" Rainer knew she'd gladly take responsibility for everything that had happened, but attacking him would have her swinging in a matter of moments.

"It's fine, Em," Rainer soothed. "Why don't you go back to bed? I'll be in there in a sec."

Emily studied Logan speculatively as she fixed herself another cup of coffee and walked carefully back to their room.

"Don't forget we're all supposed to be at Benji and Sydney's wedding this afternoon," she reminded them just before she closed the bedroom door.

Logan turned on Rainer. He glared spitefully. "You wanna tell me how the hell my fiancée ended up in our bed, buck naked?"

Rainer's shield started to resonate with his anger. He shook his head in disbelief and refused to allow his shield to fully develop around him. When an Ioses Predilect felt attacked, their shield would fight for them. It took a while for them to learn to harness it themselves.

"Sure," he spat. "After I helped both of you to bed, you fucked her rather loudly. So, I would assume, if she doesn't have any clothes on now, it's because after you stripped her and banged her last night, you failed to redress her."

Anger continued to pulse through Rainer's veins. He was unable to believe Logan thought he would take Adeline's clothes off under any circumstances.

Disbelief rocked through Logan. He paled dramatically. "You didn't help her…?"

"Are you freaking kidding me? I would never do that."

Logan leaned back in his chair and rubbed his eyes with the heels of his hands.

"And, I had Emily cast her last night, so you're welcome for that too."

"Oh, holy fuck." In his stupor, it seemed Logan hadn't even gotten to that yet. "I am such an asshole. How could I have let her get so drunk? How could I have done that after I just swore to her I'd never let her down again?"

"Logan?" called a very weak voice from their room.

He leapt up and offered Rainer a pitiful look. "I'm sorry. I know you wouldn't do that. I just don't know what the hell we had last night. I've never been so hungover."

"You've never been so drunk."

"I know, and I'm sorry. Thank you for everything you did. I can't believe I was such an ass."

Rainer agreed though he was still hurt over the accusations. The sound of Adeline vomiting had Logan sprinting.

Rainer slammed the coffee carafe back into the maker after he poured himself another mug. He stomped the path Emily had made to their room.

"What was that all about?" Emily was lying in their bed, propped up on pillows, and sipping coffee.

"Logan's freaking out over everything he did last night." Rainer eased into bed with her. He sipped slowly from his own mug.

"Yeah." Emily gave Rainer a sorrowful look. Logan certainly wasn't the only one who regretted the evening before. "Would you mind holding me?" Guilt etched her face and fractured his heart.

"Baby," he soothed. She grinned. He wrapped his arms around her carefully. Neither of them felt much like moving, so he tried to position them so they were both comfortable.

"I'm really so sorry," she whispered.

Turning slightly, he tenderly kissed her forehead. She buried her face deeper in his chest.

"I take it you didn't like the after-party quite as much as you thought you would?"

She didn't have to tell him. He already knew the answer. That was one of the many wonderful things about being in a relationship with someone for as long as they'd been. He knew her well enough to know what she was thinking at least some of the time.

She nodded into his chest. She wouldn't reveal her face, but he felt tears begin to trickle down his chest.

"Em, it's over, and you don't have to go to the Angels' parties if you don't want to." She finally lifted her head and wiped away her tears.

"I know, but now everyone's sick and it's all my fault, and…I think I do have to go. The Angels are known for partying and everything." Her confession drowned out as guilt took up residence inside of her.

"You didn't make us all drink, and none of us knew how strong that was going to be. The Angels are known for being a fierce all-women's Summation team, but that doesn't mean you have to party like the rest of them if you don't want to."

"Yeah, I guess I have to figure out what parts I want to have in being an Arlington Angel."

She fell silent, and Rainer let his eyes close. They could figure everything out later, he decided as his body relaxed around hers. He just desperately wanted to sleep.

Several hours later, Emily gasped. Rainer's body shuddered. He tried to ease her upright. He thought she was going to be sick again.

"We're supposed to be at Benji and Sydney's wedding in two hours! I had no idea how late it was."

After settling back onto the pillows, Rainer scoffed, "Who cares? Let's skip it." If he didn't have to put on a suit and sit through a stuffy wedding of two people he didn't even like in the first place, it might've made the evening before and the ensuing hangover worth it.

"We can't."

He pulled Emily back onto his chest. He was certain she was being overly anxious about Logan's spoken RSVP to a wedding they'd only known about for just over a week.

"Sure we can." He eased her onto her side so he could wrap his arms all the way around her and let her hide in him. "Let's just stay in bed all day. I'll hold you. We can sleep, or watch TV—just hang out. Then, later, if we get to feeling a little better, I'll make sure you have a hell of a lot more fun than if we went to a shotgun wedding."

"That sounds perfect, but we have to go."

Rainer shook his head. He was pleased he could make the motion without feeling like he was going to keel over. "Why?"

Emily brushed her hand over his cheek and then tucked back into his embrace. "Because Mom and Dad are going, and it's gonna be a big Senate wedding."

Rainer tried to think of any other way out of going. "Okay," he finally stumbled upon something, "how about we volunteer to keep the twins? At least we could just hang out. I just don't want to be with anyone but you." He tried not to whine but failed miserably.

"We can't. Will and Brooke are keeping the twins. Dad was all 'you're my daughter and you know how your mother and I expect you and your brothers to act as a representation of our family, and I know the Angels have a reputation of doing things that you know I wouldn't approve of.'" Emily mocked her father's responsibility speech.

Once again, Rainer found himself trying to push the belly shot out of his head.

"We can't just decide not to go to a wedding we said we'd be at because we're hungover."

Rainer sighed. He knew she was right. He glanced at the clock.

"All right, but can we sleep a little more, then get ready, and please don't tell me we have to stay for the whole ridiculous thing."

Emily giggled again as she slid her body upward in the bed until her breasts were right at his face.

"Yum!" Rainer found himself suddenly feeling better.

"Here, I'll set the alarm for an hour, and I'll let you sleep here."

Rainer proceeded to slide his hands under the T-shirt she was wearing and began groping her.

"Deal," he agreed.

CHAPTER 47

STICKS AND STONES

A few hours later, Rainer was standing in the Sheltons' back yard. He poured Emily another cup of punch. Mr. Shelton didn't look any more thrilled at the reception than he had at the wedding.

Benji had been steering clear of Sydney's parents but did guide Sydney over to Rainer. They talked, and he even ran his hand over Sydney's nonexistent bump. He looked quite proud, for the moment anyway.

Per Emily's request, Rainer agreed to stop glaring at him whenever he walked by.

Emily was in a conversation with her mother and Serena. They were smiling and laughing, so Rainer stayed back. He didn't want to interrupt.

"Hey, Rainer," Samantha Peterson pounced. She sidled up to him while he was fixing a plate of finger foods for Emily. Rainer didn't try to hide his distinct eye roll.

"Oh, hey Samantha." He turned his back on her. Emily was scowling viciously.

"So, are you still living at the Haydenshires'?" She edged closer. He had the distinct feeling he was being circled like prey for the kill.

"No, Em and I moved in together." He narrowed his eyes at her, and bile rose in his throat as he thought about the quotes she'd provided the tabloids.

Samantha scowled but then cooed, "You know, you've been with Emily for, like, ever. Don't you ever wonder what it might be like with someone else?"

Vile repulsion washed over Rainer. "No, I don't." He waved his hand toward Emily, who appeared by his side instantly. She was set to detonate. Her vicious scowl could've singed Samantha's haughty sneer. "When you have everything you could ever imagine and then some, you just consider yourself a really lucky guy."

Samantha rolled her eyes and huffed, "Well, if you ever change your mind..."

"Not a chance in hell."

"I cannot believe her," Emily spat as Samantha sauntered away.

"She's a bitch, Em. Just forget about her." Rainer decided he didn't even feel guilty that Samantha had heard his assessment. Her face contorted in rage as she jerked Sydney from Benji's grip and they began whispering heatedly.

"Rainer!" He heard his name approximately a half second before Fergus Martin stumbled into his back.

"Hi, Fergus." Emily looked shocked.

"Hey, Ferg," Rainer joined the greetings. His brow furrowed. Fergus had a girl on his arm, one who didn't appear to mind being there.

"Tilly, hi. I haven't seen you in so long." Emily smiled kindly.

"I was in the classes abroad program last year, and when you decided to combine your sub-freshman and pre-freshman years, I didn't really get to see you all that often anymore, I guess."

"Yeah, I kind of had a mission." Emily laughed at her own dogged determination.

Rainer kissed her temple. He certainly didn't mind being her mission.

"I'm so excited to finally be a senior this year. I'm so ready to graduate," Tilly announced.

Several thoughts occurred to Rainer in that moment. If Fergus and Tilly were dating, and she was only a senior, then Fergus was either going to have to break up with her before school started back or decline his contract to become a Venton mentor.

"When did you two start dating?" Emily asked. Rainer could feel her Receiver's radar ease from her pores. She was trying to determine the depth of Fergus and Tilly's admiration.

Fergus never missed an opportunity to brag. "Tilly saw me in the library, and, I mean, who could resist?"

Tilly giggled delightedly as Rainer fought not to roll his eyes.

"He's so sweet, and he's always talking about Rainer and Logan. Is Logan here?"

"Oh, uh, no. His fiancée has a little stomach flu, so he stayed home to look after her," Emily eased out her lie.

"Uh, Ferg," Rainer gestured his head to the right. Fergus leaned and kissed the side of Tilly's head in a copycat movement that matched Rainer's.

They stepped a few feet away from the girls.

"How exactly are you planning on this working? You can't be a mentor at Venton and be dating a student."

"She's a senior. We're only a year apart. I'm crazy about her," Fergus stumbled over his excuses.

"Even if your mom is an academy governess, I really don't think a mentor dating a student is going to go over well."

"I'll think of something."

Rainer shrugged. He'd love to know how Fergus planned to get out of his latest debacle.

Samantha edged closer to Emily and Tilly. She was laughing ostentatiously with Rita McClendon, another of Sydney's bridesmaids.

Emily was still trying to ward off her headache and was eating the food Rainer had provided her.

As she took a discreet bite of a cucumber sandwich, Samantha attacked. "I don't know how she expects to fit into a wedding gown if she keeps eating like that."

Infuriated energy sizzled in Rainer's shield. He moved back to Emily in two quick steps.

"You know, Tilly,"—Emily was on the warpath—"it is just so

pathetic that she wants to call up the tabloids and fake a relationship with my fiancé because she's too much of a bitch to get her own guy."

"Emily Anne," Mrs. Haydenshire sighed. "Please be nice, even to Samantha Peterson." She'd made certain no one but Emily and Rainer had heard her.

Before either of them could respond, Samantha was joined by her mother, Yvette.

"Well, Lillian," Mrs. Peterson drawled nastily, "so rare I see you and Stephen not completely covered in children."

The Petersons were one of the Gifted families who always had a snide comment about the size of the Haydenshires' family.

Mrs. Haydenshire smiled and gave a fake chuckle. "Yes, well, we do get out occasionally, Yvette." Her tone was syrupy sweet. Her glare was deadly.

Rainer and Emily exchanged a grin.

Yvette Peterson seemed to have just noticed Emily and Rainer's existence. She narrowed her eyes in on Rainer.

"Well, Rainer, Samantha tells me that Emily has you caught up in her web, the Lawson ring and all." She grasped Emily's hand to see the ring. Rainer watched as Emily jerked her hand out of Mrs. Peterson's.

He forced a chuckle and put his arm around Emily. "I wouldn't call it a web, Mrs. Peterson. Emily made me the luckiest guy in the Realm when she agreed to marry me. I can't wait to get her down the aisle." He gestured back to the makeshift aisle running down the center of the Sheltons' overly manicured lawn.

Mrs. Peterson gave a very fake laugh and then took an appraising look at Mrs. Haydenshire and then up and down Emily.

"Yes, well, I suppose if you're looking to expand the Lawson empire, it would appear that birthing hips run in the family, so that should be helpful." She patted Rainer on the chest and adjusted his tie before she slithered away.

Rainer's mouth fell open as Emily lunged toward Mrs. Peterson, but Mrs. Haydenshire caught her before she could wrap her hands around either Samantha or her mother.

Mrs. Haydenshire shook her head and drew a steadying breath. "I swear, if that woman has one more face lift, her ears are going to meet at the back of her head. I'm surprised she can still blink."

She effectively broke Rainer and Emily from their fury as they cracked up.

Once they quieted, Mrs. Haydenshire gave them a knowing gaze. "Since Adeline is a Valeduto Predilect and they are so rarely sick, why don't you two tell me the real reason Logan and Adeline aren't here, not the reason you gave your father."

Emily and Rainer shared an uncomfortable glance, but neither of them spoke.

Mrs. Haydenshire sighed. "How bad are they?" Adeline had been violently ill since she'd awoken. Rainer couldn't count the number of times he'd heard Logan cleaning up after her. When she'd finally emerged to apologize to Rainer and Emily, her eyes were bloodshot, her face sallow and dark, and she was having trouble keeping anything down.

Emily and Rainer had informed Governor Haydenshire that Adeline had a stomach virus and that Logan had stayed home to care for her.

Governor Haydenshire seemed distracted as he'd informed Emily and Rainer that he thought perhaps Mrs. Haydenshire might be coming down with the same virus.

Logan wasn't throwing up but was thoroughly disgusted with himself for allowing Adeline to consume so much alcohol, and for what he'd agreed to do when they'd gotten home. Together they were quite a pair and certainly not up for a wedding.

"Logan's okay." Emily bit her lip. She didn't want to rat out her big brother.

Mrs. Haydenshire's eyes closed momentarily. "Do I need to go home?" She sounded disappointed but resolute.

"I don't think so," Emily hesitated.

Rainer's phone chirped at that moment. He pulled it from his pocket and read the text. He turned to Mrs. Haydenshire.

"Actually, I think that might not be a bad idea." He tried not to panic. Mrs. Haydenshire held out her hand. Rainer prayed Logan wouldn't feel like he'd betrayed him as he handed her the phone.

With a slight headshake, she headed toward Governor Haydenshire. He was having a discussion with Jack Stariff and Governor Willow.

"Dear," Mrs. Haydenshire interrupted.

"There's my beautiful bride." Governor Haydenshire's entire face lit as he put his arm around his wife. The love between them was palpable to those around them.

Yvette Peterson rolled her eyes as Governor Haydenshire kissed Mrs. Haydenshire's cheek. She smiled up at him and nodded a greeting to the men he was with.

"I'm still not feeling all that well. I think I'm going to head home with Emily and Rainer, but you stay as long as you'd like."

Governor Haydenshire begged the pardon of Governor Willow and Mr. Stariff. He guided Mrs. Haydenshire away from prying ears.

"I'll take you home, sweetheart. I certainly don't need to stay. I think maybe it's time you see a medio." The Governor looked gravely concerned.

"Oh no, I'll be fine. You stay. The kids are anxious to leave anyway." Mrs. Haydenshire glanced at the Petersons.

Governor Haydenshire huffed, "Can't blame them." Then all of the wisdom of raising ten children with the woman he was gazing at seemed to fall on the governor suddenly. "This wouldn't have anything to do with why Logan and Adeline aren't here, would it?"

Mrs. Haydenshire brushed a kiss across his jaw. "She's never done anything wrong in her entire life. It was bound to come out at some point. It sounds like she learned her lesson, but I need to keep her out of the hospital, as that would be a problem for both her upcoming trial and her career."

Governor Haydenshire shot extremely disappointed looks at both Rainer and Emily. Then, with a defeated nod, he kissed Mrs. Haydenshire's cheek.

"Let me know if I can do anything to help."

CHAPTER 48

MOM

Rainer drove Mrs. Haydenshire to the guesthouse as quickly as he was able. She was out of the car as soon as he put it in park.

Logan met them in the garage. "Mom!" He threw his arms around his mother and clung to her fiercely. "Thank goodness."

Emily and Rainer followed Mrs. Haydenshire into the house. Logan had called in reinforcements. Levi, Garrett, Patrick, and Connor were standing in the living room. They were staring down at Adeline on the couch.

She was as white as a ghost and kept shaking and convulsing under the vast number of heat-casted quilts Logan had tucked around her.

"I'm...so...sorry," Adeline managed as Mrs. Haydenshire moved to her.

"Sweet girl, we all have our breaking points. Let's just not let alcohol be our coping mechanism next time, okay?"

"Garrett," her voice turned commanding, "go to the house and get the red nausea medicine from the cupboard. Hurry."

"Yes, ma'am." Garrett rushed out the door.

"Emily." Emily appeared beside her instantly. "You and Levi go boil several cups of white rice. Double the water in multiple pots. Run up to the house for some if you don't have any. Hurry and go with Garrett."

"We have some." Emily flew to the kitchen. Levi followed after her.

"Use just a bit of salt," Mrs. Haydenshire called.

"Rainer, you and Logan make several cold washcloths, and keep them coming."

Rainer and Logan wet washcloths, and Patrick helped them cast them to stay cool.

"Thank you," Mrs. Haydenshire sighed as Rainer handed her the first stack of cloths. "Go help Emily hurry that rice along, and then have them boil some chicken broth. Quick now." She turned to Patrick and Connor. "Go into town..." She turned to look down at Adeline as she pressed the washcloths over her face and chest. "What's your favorite kind of Jell-O, sweetheart?" Adeline was gasping for breath and drenched in sweat. She didn't seem able to answer.

"She likes that strawberry kind you make," Logan supplied.

"Go into town and get several Jell-O and applesauce cups, some plain white bread for toast, and bananas. Come straight back." Patrick grabbed his keys from the kitchen table, and they rushed out the door.

Garrett returned carrying Keaton and the medicine.

"They were getting to be too much for Brooke." He gestured to Keaton. Mrs. Haydenshire smiled but continued to give Adeline a sponge bath. She was trying to cool her off without exposing her to most of Logan's brothers and Rainer.

Keaton demanded that Emily hold him, so she hoisted him to her hip while stirring the rice.

"Logan, measure out four tablespoons of that." Mrs. Haydenshire pointed to the medication in Garrett's hand. Logan performed the task quickly and brought the ruby syrup to his mother.

She summoned instantly, and everyone watched as the red liquid turned a brilliant, glowing crimson. The sheer power of her Double-Predilection lit inside the medication.

"All right, Logan, hold her up while she takes this."

"Yes, ma'am, thank you." Relief eased his entire body.

"Here, baby," Logan braced Adeline and held her upright.

"Ready?" Mrs. Haydenshire asked. With a slight nod, Adeline leaned forward as best she could. Mrs. Haydenshire spooned the medicine into her mouth and made certain she swallowed it completely. "Okay, now, lay her back and go get clean sheets and pillowcases. These are soaking wet."

"Yes, ma'am." Logan raced to the linen closet in the hallway.

"Lift her up carefully." Mrs. Haydenshire relaxed slightly as Adeline's condition began to improve. "Let me change these. Then lay her back down."

Logan smiled adoringly at Adeline. He cradled her into his arms as she laid her head against his chest. She tucked her face into his neck.

Mrs. Haydenshire gave them both sorrowful looks as she made quick work of making up the sofa.

"The rice is ready, Mom." Emily bounced Keaton on her hip.

"Good girl." Mrs. Haydenshire gestured back to the freshly made sofa, and Logan returned Adeline to the pillows. A little of her color was beginning to return.

"Drain the rice and put it in a bowl for her to eat tomorrow. Then bring me a bowl of the warm water it cooked in."

Emily handed Keaton to Rainer. He grinned at him and began entertaining him so Emily could work. Emily prepared a soup bowl of the rice water and set it on a plate with a napkin and a spoon.

"Here, Mom, I'll do it," Logan offered.

"Yes, dear, you will." Mrs. Haydenshire directed Logan to where she'd been sitting on the couch beside Adeline.

Logan carefully fed Adeline the water under his mother's close watch. After an hour or so, Adeline was able to relax enough to fall asleep. Logan set the now-empty soup bowl on the coffee table and sighed in relief. He covered her up, tenderly brushing a kiss across her cheek.

"Thank you," he shuddered as he hugged his mother to him.

"You're welcome." Mrs. Haydenshire's tone held disappointment and fatigue. "Now," she continued, "you can wake her up in two hours and give her another bowl, and you can do that every two hours all night long, Logan."

"Yes, ma'am, I will. I'm so sorry." Logan sounded like he was ten years old again.

"Good," Mrs. Haydenshire's face reflected her deep disappointment. "Rainer, Emily," she called them into the living room. Rainer hoisted Keaton onto his shoulders as he moved quickly to Mrs. Haydenshire. She turned to Logan. "Why didn't you come get me last night?"

Logan grimaced. "Because I was drunk too."

Nodding, Mrs. Haydenshire turned to Emily and Rainer. "And you two were as well?"

Rainer and Emily nodded dejectedly.

"And who drove home?" Her supreme disappointment rocked Rainer to the core.

"The liquor was enhanced," he admitted. "It didn't hit all at once, so I was fine until after we got home."

Patrick had returned with the Jell-O, bread, and applesauce then he left with Levi to get dinner for everyone else.

When they returned with several buckets of fried chicken and all of the fixings, they were joined by Will and Brooke.

Governor Haydenshire arrived last and everyone ate in silence. They were afraid of disturbing Adeline.

Two hours later, Logan gently woke her. She'd consumed enough water and calories to be able to carry on a slight conversation. Using all of the energy she could muster, she apologized profusely to Logan and the Haydenshires.

"Shh, baby, it's okay," Logan soothed. "It was my fault." The words seemed to taste very bitter as they left his mouth.

"Yes, it was." His father gave him a disappointed glare. "And you can think about all of the ways that you failed to take care of the woman you've pledged to marry next weekend when you help me redo Levi and Cal's old room for the twins.

"Perhaps peeling wallpaper, hanging beadboard, and polishing the hardwoods will help you remember how I taught you to take care of women in general, not to mention the one who is wearing your ring and has your heart." Fury rang in every word that exited the governor's mouth.

"Yes, sir."

"Governor Haydenshire, I'll help too," Rainer pledged.

"Me too, Dad." Emily nodded.

"I had a feeling you would." The governor shook his head at all of them. "Now, this is the last I'd like to hear about your evening last night."

CHAPTER 49

THAT ISN'T YOU

More than ready to leave his endless weekend behind him, Rainer kissed Emily awake the next morning. "Hey, there. Are you feeling better?"

After giving a slight moan, she wiggled closer to him under the covers. "Shh, I'm sleeping."

"We have to get up. You have to go to practice, and I have to go to work."

She tucked herself closer still. He held her tight and kissed the top of her head.

"Baby," he yawned, "we have to get going." He traced his finger down her side and threatened to tickle her awake.

"Stop!" She sat up, and Rainer laughed.

"If you get ready quick, we could grab some breakfast out before I take you to the arena."

"Waffle House?"

"Egg-white omelet and hash browns," he supplied her order for her. She crawled out of bed and pulled off the T-shirt she'd slept in. "Or you could come back to bed and let me play for a little while. Then we could just eat cereal." He waggled his eyebrows at her.

"Get up, Mr. Lawson. I want an omelet."

"But I want you."

Emily grinned and shook her hips for him. "You will have to wait."

Rainer stood and stretched. He slid to her side. "I don't want to wait." He reached around with both hands and grabbed her ass.

She swatted his hands away. "I'll make it worth your while." With that, she traipsed to the bathroom and shut the door.

A little while later, Rainer settled in Vindico's office with Logan. They waited for everyone, including Vindico, to arrive for the Monday morning meeting.

Rainer couldn't recall a time he'd been at work and Vindico hadn't. Bridgette, the dancer from The Tantra, and the argument Vindico and Garrett had gotten into Friday flitted through his mind.

Garrett had been called back to the Non-Gifted precinct for the day to assist with a drug bust in Reston.

Portwood and Ericcson entered, along with Tuttle. John Ramier, the Elite Iodex Technology Specialist, was absent as well. Rainer wondered if his wife had gone into labor.

They began discussing the challenge Saturday and what Wretchkinsides's next move might be, since he'd apparently had quite a bit of money on the Sirens beating the Angels.

Several minutes later, Vindico finally appeared. His arms were full, and an infuriated scowl shadowed his face. His seething glare landed on Rainer.

Rainer glanced nervously at Logan and then at Portwood and Ericcson, trying to figure out what he'd done.

"Everyone out!" Vindico shouted. "You two, stay put."

Rainer's heart raced as he racked his brain. He was still trying to determine what he'd done to elicit such fury.

Tuttle shot them a worried glance before he exited.

Vindico slammed the door shut behind Tuttle and spun to face Rainer and Logan.

"Did you have a nice weekend, Lawson?" Burning gall echoed around the question.

"Uh..." Rainer had no idea what the correct answer might be.

Suddenly, Vindico threw the contents of his arms onto his desk. Several of the day's newspapers, magazines, numerous thumb drives, and framed photographs spilled out over the desk.

Rainer was certain his breakfast was going to make a rapid reappearance.

"Just got back from Anglington's Bar. Your future father-in-law and I had to demand that these,"—he pointed to the framed photographs—"were taken off the walls before they opened for business today," he roared.

All of the blood in Rainer's body drained rapidly to his feet.

He glanced at the covers of three Gifted newspapers. They were all shots of him leaning Emily out over the bar at Anglington's.

The magazines had multiple shots of him reaching his hands greedily up Emily's skirt, licking her lips, and then throwing extremely cocky grins back to the crowd. There was a full-page shot of him emerging with the cherry and then taking a bow.

Rainer let his head fall into his hands and willed it to be some kind of horrible dream, but when he opened his eyes again they were all still there, staring back at him.

As he held up the thumb drive, Vindico seemed too furious to talk for a brief moment. "This is what Ramier and I spent all night trying to force off the Internet, the entire thing, from your pulling her shirt up until you sucked that cherry out of her mouth and bowed to your adoring fans. I have never been so disgusted in my life. It seems dozens of your admirers were more than happy to sell the shots and videos they took with their phones for a pretty penny to any news outlet that flashed cash."

Vindico leaned inches from Rainer's horrified expression and menaced, "You listen to me, and you listen good. I'm sorry that you have to deal with your fame that follows you around everywhere whether you wanted it or not, but you're an Iodex officer now, and Wretchkinsides will use everything he can find to make sure that we don't bring him down. Did you for one fucking moment stop to think about what your uncle could do with this? You know, the one who's trying to take half of your daddy's hard-earned money? This,"—he held up the picture of Rainer feeling up Emily's skirt—"is unacceptable!" Vindico bared his teeth furiously.

"And you," he lunged at Logan. "Do you happen to recall me sitting at your family's kitchen table telling you that being out somewhere, anywhere, that Candy Parker's lawyers could use to prove that your precious fiancée is nothing more than a drugged-up, irresponsible teenager could end up sending her to jail?"

Terror filled Logan's weak nod.

"Yeah, well, there are several shots of the two of you cheering him on! She doesn't look sober in any of them."

He threw his hand back and hit Rainer hard on the back of the head. Rainer clenched his jaw and refused to act like it hurt, but his head began to throb.

"Now," Vindico continued to shout, "if you think you could keep your hands out of your fiancée's skirt, I'd like you to actually get some work done today. After you take a trip down to the governor's office to beg his forgiveness for bending his only daughter backwards over a bar while you used her as a shot glass, you can come back and we'll decide what you two will be doing for the next week. By the way, your uncle's lawyer was very pleased with all of the press you got this weekend. Seems it did, in fact, play right into his case that you're an irresponsible moron, so he bumped the trial up. Now, it's early next week.

"So, why don't you go have a chat with your future father-in-law? I'm certain he can't wait to see you. After a long day of whatever the hell I decide to make you two do, you can go home and inform Miss Haydenshire that I don't give a damn if she single-handedly wins the Angels the Summation cup this season, this,"—he held up a shot of Rainer bowing to the crowd—"will never happen again! Leave!"

Logan and Rainer stood to go.

Vindico gathered the papers, the framed pictures, and the thumb drives and shoved them hard into Rainer's stomach.

"Here!" he snarled. "Souvenirs of your stunningly idiotic behavior."

Rainer stumbled out of Vindico's office. He couldn't breathe. Logan attempted to shield him with his body from the nervous glances of the Elite team, the other officers, and aides on the Iodex wing.

They'd all heard everything Vindico had shouted. Rainer leaned over and placed his hands on his desk. He tried to steady himself. He couldn't see. He couldn't believe this was happening.

It felt like a horrendous nightmare that refused to release him from its clutches. As Rainer sank down onto his chair, reality crashed around him like a tidal wave that threatened to overtake him.

He shoved the papers and photos into an empty drawer of his desk, and willed himself to breathe and for his heart to beat steadily.

"Do you want me to come with you to talk to Dad?" Logan offered. Rainer shook his head and stood again. He searched inside himself until he finally located his voice.

"No, I did this. Not you." He sounded like he'd just been rescued from a deluge. His muscles began to spasm as he considered what Governor Haydenshire had seen photographic evidence of.

"He knows we were all drinking. Maybe it won't be as bad as you think." They shared an endless glance, the unspoken confirmation that Logan was lying.

He began his death march toward Governor Haydenshire's office. Thoughts of Emily's body spread out on a bar for all the Realm to see, of his tongue dancing in her mouth, and of him, Rainer Lawson, sucking liquor off of her in a crowded bar, had him turning abruptly and falling into the men's room.

He moved to the sink and held on to the cold marble counter for support. He couldn't look in the mirror. His disgust with himself was too strong.

He turned on the faucet and splashed cold water on his face as he thought about what Governor Haydenshire must be thinking and of what he was going to say. The fact that he'd most certainly disappointed the only man who had ever really stepped in and been there for him made him violently ill. The fact that he let peer pressure lose half of his parents' estate crushed him.

He grabbed several paper towels from the dispenser on the wall and mopped his face. His heart still beat erratically.

You did it, so now you can face the music. He forced himself to put one foot in front of the other and make his way to the governors' wing of the Senate.

Governor Carrington was standing in the hallway as Rainer edged open the door between the Iodex offices and the governors' wing.

He gave Rainer a sorrowful gaze and placed his hand on his shoulder to brace him. "Rainer," he shook his head in consolation.

Rainer couldn't speak. He just offered the Crown Governor a terrified, desperate expression.

"Sometimes, when we're just twenty-one years old, and we have the weight of the world on our shoulders, we're just young enough to know we can and barely old enough to know we shouldn't. And the worst part of being in that horrible position is that we're just stupid enough to do it anyway. Don't let this define you, son. That guy in the papers this morning, that isn't you. I know that, and you know that, so now you just have to work a little harder to show the Realm that." His low, soothing intonation made Rainer momentarily feel like his world might not be ending.

"I'm so sorry," he managed to choke out. He was unable to take his eyes off of Governor Haydenshire's closed office door.

Governor Carrington patted Rainer's back consolingly. "I know you are. And, for what it's worth, as furious as he is, he knows you are too."

He gestured his head to Governor Haydenshire's door. "Go on," Governor Carrington edged Rainer forward. "Won't get any easier standing out here talking to me. I'm sure you know this, but your dad used to say, you can't solve a problem standing on the sidelines wishing it away. You have to put yourself in the game." Rainer nodded. His stomach twisted in sharp jarring knots. "You're gonna have to play hard, Rainer. Earn back his trust and his respect. Unfortunately, it won't be easy, but it's also not impossible."

With a single nod, Rainer swallowed down the terror that rose quickly into his throat as he took the last few steps toward the door.

BABY GIRL

His heart stuttered again as he forced himself to knock on the door.

"Come in!" Governor Haydenshire bellowed furiously. Rainer couldn't recall a time he'd ever sounded angrier.

His hands were drenched in sweat, and he had to wipe them on his pants before he could get the knob to turn. He opened the door painfully slowly and took a half step into the large, opulent office.

Jack Stariff was standing at Governor Haydenshire's desk. He shot Rainer a baleful glare. "I guess you're gonna make me earn my paycheck." He shook his head and exited the office.

Rainer tried to choke out an apology but found his throat so dry he was unable to make audible sound.

The governor stood behind his desk but said nothing for several long, hellish moments. Rainer would've preferred he'd screamed at him or cussed him out, though he knew Governor Haydenshire would never do that, not that he didn't deserve it.

The furious, reflective, disappointed grief that etched the governor's entire being cut Rainer to the quick.

"Sit down, Rainer," Governor Haydenshire demanded in a pained whisper.

"Sir, I am so, so sorry," he choked, but there were no words that could erase the damage those pictures had done.

He stared at the ground and willed his brain to come up with something, anything that would make the governor respect him again. He came up short every time the picture of him taking a bow with a cherry in his mouth settled in the mass of whirling desperation in his head.

"You've put me in a very difficult place," the governor informed him. His voice was low and injured. He began to pace behind his desk.

"I've always thought of you as one of my own, as my very own son. I celebrated your accomplishments with you, and I hurt when you hurt over the loss of your parents, over the hell the press has put you through over the years. Even when you and Emily were at odds, I hurt for both of you.

"I tried to help you work through the difficult life you've been handed. But now I not only get to live the shock and disappointment of one of my sons behaving in such a manner, but I also get to live the fury that comes with the knowledge that it was my little girl you laid out over a bar for all the world to see. She is my daughter, Rainer. Do you understand that?" His low furious tone finally broke into shouting.

Rainer let his eyes close in shame.

"Oh, I don't think so. You and Emily did this. You can open your eyes and face it, because the entire Realm is holding photographic evidence of it even as we speak. I understand that you're twenty-one years old, with more money than you know what to do with and that you think you've got this world all figured out, but let me be the first to tell you that you don't.

"I have never been more disappointed and disgusted with you than I am at this moment." The pain ingrained in the governor's quiet voice was a thousand times worse than Vindico screaming at him.

"Governor Haydenshire, I'm so…" Rainer begged, but the look the governor shot him made him stop speaking.

"What would possess you to do something like that? Don't you think that Emily deserves a little more respect than to be displayed on a bar while you lick something off of her stomach and then run your hands up her skirt?"

Fever flooded through him followed immediately by his blood running ice cold. His brain offered him nothing but drivel like Emily asked me to do it, or it was all Garrett's idea.

He knew that telling Governor Haydenshire that his little girl had asked him to do that would not help the situation at all. He would never sell Emily out like that, but he thought he should at least try to explain why he'd done it.

He swallowed down the rock-like enclosure in his throat and willed his heart to stop hammering quite so loudly. "I don't know, sir. Garrett had all of the Angels doing it and," he trailed off. He sounded reckless, irresponsible, and stupid blaming Garrett when he'd known perfectly well it was a lurid and tasteless thing to do.

Shame washed over him with threatening force. He let his head fall back in his hands. The pain on Governor Haydenshire's face threatened to overwhelm him.

"She is my baby girl," he growled low and furious. "I held her mother's hand when she gave birth to her. I changed her diapers and held her in my lap. I rocked her to sleep before you ever thought about it."

Governor Haydenshire glared hatefully as he continued. "I protected her from all of her big brothers. I was there when she dared you to kiss her at seven years old, and I thought right then, as I saw the look in both of your eyes, that it was done for. You were sold, soulmates from childhood, and I was thankful. If my baby was going to fall for anyone, I wanted it to be you. Right now, I'm thinking I was a fool.

"I was there when you left. I held her while she sobbed when you'd hurt her more trying to protect her than anyone has ever hurt her in her life. And I paid for the plane ticket for her to go and get you back, because I knew she wanted that more than anything else in the world. I knew what you were planning when you took her off to my beach house, to take away her innocence and her childhood. I let her go because I knew you loved her, and that she loved you more than anything else.

"I was sick, but I let her go because I thought you would take care of her." He edged closer to Rainer and narrowed his eyes. "And I agreed to let you put your ring on her finger, and that I'd give her away to someone I thought would always care for her, but this,"—he held up the picture of Rainer with his hands up Emily's skirt—"this isn't what I had in mind."

Rainer met the governor's devastated glare to see tears fill his eyes. He had never hated himself more than he had in that endless moment of terror.

"Quite frankly, you need to remember that it's my home you're living in, and that you've lived in since you were fourteen years old. And that it's my daughter you're crawling into bed with every night, despite the fact that you aren't married. I happen to think that my wife and I deserve a little more respect and a lot more consideration than what you've shown."

Rainer nodded his agreement.

"Lillian doesn't know about this," Governor Haydenshire concluded morosely. "She was sick this morning, and you and I both know she's not coming down with something."

Rainer tried to process that information but couldn't make sense of it at the moment. "I do not want her upset right now so, if you wouldn't mind, I'd prefer to not discuss this in front of her."

"Sir, I'm just so sorry," Rainer tried again, but Governor Haydenshire shook his head defiantly.

"I don't want to see you right now. And I don't want to hear how sorry you are."

With that, he moved to the door in his office and opened it. He gestured for Rainer to make a quick exit.

CHAPTER 51
NEVER AS GOOD

It was several minutes before Rainer understood that he was physically shaking. He could do nothing more than put one foot in front of the other and relive the hell he'd put Governor Haydenshire through.

All of the times growing up when Rainer had done something wrong and been summarily punished, either by his own father or by the Haydenshires, was nothing compared to the horrific disappointment that resonated in every word the governor stated as he'd let Rainer know exactly what he'd thought about their activities Saturday night.

Rainer trudged to his desk. His heart beat frantically. His blood ran hot and then cold at varied times. He fell into his desk chair, and everyone stared at him. Logan stood and moved to him.

"Lawson, Haydenshire, now," Vindico demanded from his office.

Not certain how much more he could physically withstand, he traveled wearily back into his boss's office.

"I've decided they could use a few more rock-slingers out at Coriolis, so why don't you two volunteer your services until lunch. Then, I suppose you can eat, since the law says I have to allow you lunch, but after that, come back here, and we're going to have team sparring practice until I decide you can go home."

Rainer and Logan nodded and made their way back out of the office, having never uttered a word.

"Here," Vindico threw Logan the keys to one of the Expeditions as they exited.

Coriolis prison was covered with topsoil and rock. It kept the uranium at bay, so that Gifted officers and family members could visit Coriolis without feeling the full effects of the prison until they were actually under the ground.

Rock-slingers shoveled rock on a daily basis, to make certain the uranium stayed where it was needed to keep the prisoners from being able to summon.

Typically, a Gifted person became a rock-slinger if they were unable to obtain employment anywhere else, as it was excruciating work.

It wasn't as horrible as actually going into the prison, but the uranium exposure would leave a Gifted person weakened and often sick.

To keep the effects from being too devastating, shifts were only a few hours long, but to shovel rock over Coriolis and then come back and spar with Vindico would be hell.

"Come on." Logan guided Rainer out to the cars. Rainer had no desire to drive. He had no desire to do anything at all, except figure out a way to earn back Governor Haydenshire's respect.

"What did Dad say?" Logan cranked the car and gave him a sorrowful expression. He refused to answer.

"As bad as you getting caught coming out of her bedroom?"

"Way worse."

"Maybe I can help. If you just tell me, then I'll entertain you with all of the ways I've ruined Adeline's life. Then we can discuss how clearly she was actually better off without me."

"Uh," Rainer drew a steadying breath. His voice sounded distant and frightened. "He said he'd never been more disappointed or disgusted with me. And that it was his little girl I had leaned over a bar for all the Realm to see. He said that he thought I would take care of her, which I obviously didn't." Rainer decided he deserved to hear it all again.

"Rainer, man, that's just..." Logan searched for a word.

"The truth," Rainer supplied.

"Did you tell him Em asked you to?" Logan seemed to feel a great injustice had been done. Rainer looked at him like he'd lost his mind.

A full minute later, Logan nodded his understanding that Governor Haydenshire knowing that Emily had asked Rainer to do that would have been the nails in the coffin.

"Your dad thinks your mom's pregnant again," he recalled that part of the lecture as it came back to him suddenly.

The car swerved as Logan gasped, "What?!"

Rainer found it odd that he couldn't seem to locate an emotion to associate with the next Haydenshire child. He could only feel his own deep regret and remorse.

"He told you that?"

"Yeah, in an, 'I don't want Lillian to be upset right now so don't tell her about you being a moron' kind of way."

"Ah geez! Don't they ever get tired of being looked down on all the time because of all of us?"

Although Rainer knew the statement was exaggerated, it was clearly something that concerned Logan. He turned the car past the entrance gates to Arlington National Cemetery, and a deep, desperate desire suddenly overwhelmed Rainer.

"Logan, please stop here. Just for a minute, please."

Logan nodded. Without question he pulled into one of the parallel spots beside the cemetery.

"Do you want me to come with you?"

Rainer knew that whatever he wanted, that's what Logan would do. Even if they never went to Coriolis and were fired for it, he would stand right beside Rainer.

Certain that he'd never deserve a friend like Logan Haydenshire, he still wanted to be alone. He tried to give Logan a reassuring smile but wasn't able. "I'll just be a minute."

"Take as long as you need, man." With that, Rainer threw open the door and took off in a heated sprint toward the Tomb of the Unknown Soldier.

He rushed over the hallowed ground. He ran faster until he was no longer certain his feet were hitting the ground as he moved behind the largest of the monuments and then headed west.

He hated that he knew how to find the spot so readily. He halted and walked. A funeral was taking place and respect was clearly something he needed to work on.

His throat closed and tears threatened to burn his eyes. He nodded his head as he passed Cal Haydenshire's cross grave marker.

Keeping his head bowed, he moved to the monument at the end of one of the endless rows of crosses and fell to the ground. He summoned and watched as his father's name, birth, and death dates appeared in the marble.

His parents had been buried in Arlington because of the sheer number of Non-Gifted lives they'd saved in their quest to make certain that the Gifted didn't abuse the Non-Gifted with their powers.

Rainer moved slightly and turned his cupped hand outward. He watched his mother's name appear. He sat there staring at the letters and numbers, lost for several minutes.

He wasn't certain why he'd needed to come so badly, not certain what to say, or how this was going to fix anything at all. He just sat staring at the marble headstone, the granite representation of all he'd lost and all he'd given up, of what had made him who he was, the devastation that had defined his entire life.

He knew his father would've been just as disappointed and horrified at what he'd done to Emily as Governor Haydenshire was. He felt sick.

"I'm sorry." He blinked back tears. "I just don't know how I screwed up so badly. I just…" Rainer wiped away the hot tears that flowed down his face. "I'll never be as good as you!" He shouted the thought that had haunted him since he'd watched his father's casket be lowered into the ground so many years ago. He pled to the pitiless granite and the merciless air around him.

"I don't think that's true, man."

Rainer spun around. He gasped as his heart flew. Logan had followed him. "And I don't think he ever expected you to be perfect." He sank to the ground beside Rainer. "I mean, at least Em's not going to end up in jail because of a belly shot."

Logan turned back to the monument and bowed his head. "S'up, Governor Lawson?" A slight smile formed on Rainer's face. "He's a good guy, sir. Try not to be too hard on him. He was only doing what Emily asked him to, and you were married—you know women will always get you into trouble," he vowed to the ether.

Rainer found it very odd to be sitting in front of his parents' graves, with all that had happened, laughing. After another few minutes, Logan stood and offered Rainer his hand.

"Come on. Let's try and clean up the mess we've made."

Rainer accepted Logan's help up.

"Bye, Dad," he choked and let his hands run along the cold granite. "I will fix this. I swear to you."

He turned to follow Logan back to the car with renewed fire burning inside of him.

CHAPTER 52

DIG DEEP

Rainer threw himself into digging his shovel into the gravel and hurling the rocks into the pits surrounding Coriolis prison. The physical exertion soothed him. The monotony somehow offered a healing salve as he wiped away the sweat that poured down his brow and onto the shirt he was ruining.

Some of the other rock-slingers had loaned them gloves, and they worked solidly right up until the sun stood directly over their heads.

"We better go." Logan stumbled slightly as the uranium depleted them.

Rainer walked several feet away to where the men were standing that they'd borrowed the gloves from. He handed them back and smiled. "Thanks a lot."

The men bid Logan and Rainer farewell and, with a wry laugh, told them to come back anytime.

Neither of them had much of an appetite, but Logan pulled through a drive-thru anyway. They'd both decided that the Non-Gifted world didn't deserve to have to smell them in their current condition.

"You have to eat," Logan commanded. "We have to go back and have the crap beaten out of us by Vindico."

Rainer ate his cheeseburger without any real enthusiasm. He

couldn't really taste it as his entire being was still focused on how to fix all of the many problems he'd caused, in a relatively short period of time.

"Do you really think Adeline's gonna end up in jail because of some stupid party?" Logan finally managed to verbalize the terror in his heart.

"No." Rainer shook his head. It was the truth, from his opinion anyway.

"I was going to ask Vindico if I could go with Adeline to her meeting with Stariff this afternoon. I don't guess I'll be doing that."

"I'm sorry. If it hadn't been me and Em, no one would've been taking pictures."

Logan shook his head. He wasn't letting Rainer take the blame because that was who he was. "I should never have taken her there. I knew better, and I did it anyway."

"Yeah, well, there's a lot of that going around."

"It didn't look nearly as bad in person as it did in the papers."

Rainer wasn't going to let Logan downplay what he'd done. "I did things to your sister, on a bar, in front of hundreds of people, I've never even done in the privacy of our bedroom. It looked just as bad when I was doing it as it does in those photos. We just aren't drunk now, and trust me, daylight tends to show all of your idiotic decisions with great clarity."

They spent the afternoon being crushed by Vindico. Rainer finally drew on deep resolve that he wasn't even aware he had. He clenched his jaw furiously and fought back. He began catching Vindico's hits and throwing them back. He let the fury, and the anger, and the hurt drive him. He met Vindico blow for blow.

"Good, Lawson." Vindico sharpened his focus. He drove harder, but Rainer didn't relent. His fists lit with ferocity.

"That's it, Lawson. Dig deep," Vindico ordered. "You want something in this life, or you want to fix something, you have to fight for it."

And Rainer understood. Vindico wasn't just training him on how to take down criminals. He was training him for life.

Five o'clock drew near, and Vindico called, "Tuttle, would you please drive to Angels Arena and pick up Miss Haydenshire? Bring her back here. Lawson isn't finished working."

Tuttle headed to the parking deck, and Rainer fought a shudder at the thought of Emily in a car with Ryan Tuttle, the horniest guy Rainer had ever met.

He's an Iodex officer. He'd never do anything to Emily, Rainer thought repeatedly as he shoved hard and let his fury project from him.

Finally, he threw out a shield cast that knocked Vindico to the ground. Disbelief shattered through Rainer. He glanced at Logan, whose mouth was hanging open in shock.

Portwood turned and offered Vindico a hand. He was chuckling. "Been a long time since one of us threw you."

"'Bout time one of you did." Vindico tried hard to hide his pleased expression.

CHAPTER 53
ME AND YOU

Several minutes later, Vindico released the team. Rainer and Logan decided to go home in their workout clothes. The clothes they'd come to work in were somehow more disgusting from digging all morning than the ones they'd worn to sweat in all afternoon.

He made his way back to his desk as Tuttle was escorting Emily in. Her eyes were bloodshot. She looked sick as she met Rainer's gaze.

It was the first time he'd ever seen her and not had the urge to go to her, to touch her, or inhale her scent. It felt odd to be angry with her, but he couldn't curb his fury.

She moved to him instead. "I'm so sorry."

"She cried all the way here, and, if it makes you feel any better," Tuttle offered, "I've been a guzzler several times. You know, you just get caught up in the moment. You don't really think about it. It'll blow over. You'll see."

Vengeance pulsed through Rainer as he asked before considering, "And do you remember any of the women's names you guzzled for?"

"Uh…" Tuttle looked confused. "I don't know. It was a long time ago. I was completely smashed."

Rainer assumed that would be the answer. Tuttle offered him another slap on the shoulder before he returned to his desk.

Emily had never been left crying without Rainer trying to comfort her. "I'm just so sorry."

He couldn't let her stand there crying, so he put his arms around her. Vindico came out of his office at that moment.

He rolled his eyes. "Geez, Lawson, is there anything you won't do in public?" He moved to a room off of the office area that was usually used for questioning. He flung the door open and gestured inside.

Rainer led Emily into the room and shut the door.

"I don't understand." Emily sank into one of the chairs. "Why is it such a big deal? Everyone else did it. No one else is all over every newspaper in the Realm."

"Because it was me…and because it was you." Rainer's voice was ragged and angry. "But you know what, Em? It is a big deal." He swallowed down raw emotion. He squinted and began to pace, lest he explode. "It's a huge deal, actually. That,"—he let the picture of him running his hands up the front of her skirt flash back through his mind—"that isn't a game, or something you do because you've made a Summation team and you've won your first challenge. At least it's not to me. I love you. I love you too much to have let you talk me into doing this. What you and I do, what we have, means more to me than anything in the world. You're not some random girl that I bang because it feels good at the moment. And to have put you on display, pimped you out for the Angels," he choked as he realized that's exactly what he'd done. "It makes me physically ill. Your dad won't even look at me. I have never been so thoroughly disgusted with myself."

Emily stared at him for several long minutes before she began to sob in earnest. She gasped for breath. He knelt down in front of her. He wasn't finished.

"And you know what? This isn't you, either. I do not believe for one moment that you really wanted me to do that to you in front of a bar full of people," his voice broke as he tried to steel himself against tears of his own as he watched her cry.

"We're not Garrett and Chloe, and I don't want to be. I want to be with you and only you. I want to marry you, and have a family, and be able to hold my head up when I come into the office. I want to be able to look your father in the eye because I know I have always done right by you. I want you to know how much I value everything we have. I want you to understand that I don't take anything we've ever done for granted. What you've allowed me, the amazing way it feels when I hold you, and to know that I am the only person who gets to have that with you is so much more important than any challenge or any party.

"I am the only person who gets to touch you the way I get to touch you or see all of you. That is something I could never have asked for, and I sure as hell don't deserve. But what I did to you Saturday night cheapens everything I've ever shared with you and everything I took from you all those weeks ago. Right now I hate myself for doing this to you."

She shook her head. "No! It's entirely, one hundred percent my fault. You didn't want to do it. I asked you to."

"Yeah, I know," he whispered. "But I'm supposed to protect you, even if it is from yourself." His father's words from so many years before thundered in his mind.

She stood suddenly and wiped the tears off her face.

"I am so sorry, and you're right, I didn't want to do it. It felt wrong. If you want me to quit the team, I will."

Rainer pulled her to him and shook his head. "I don't want you to quit, unless you want to, but I do need to know that we're not going to get involved in any other antics at the hands of Garrett, or Chloe Sawyer, or the Arlington Angels."

She nodded and took his hand. She headed toward the door. He followed her out and tried to think of some way for them to exit without an audience.

"We're going to talk to Dad," she determined. Her fingers fixed her long auburn hair behind her right ear as conviction etched her soft curves.

"Em, no. He said he didn't want to talk to me."

She nodded, but he saw the resolve form in her eyes.

"I'm not going to let you shoulder this by yourself. This was my fault, and I'm taking responsibility. You're not covering for me this time. I love you too much, and I won't let you take the fall for something I did all on my own."

As she made her way quickly toward the door, Rainer tried to reason with her. "Em, please listen to me. Your dad does not want to hear that his baby girl asked me to lay her out on a bar and lick alcohol off of her. Just let him be furious with me, please."

CHAPTER 54

NOT THIS TIME

"I'm going whether you come with me or not." She marched toward her father's office.

Rainer knew, with every fiber of his being, this wasn't going to go well, but he also wasn't going to let her go by herself.

Still pleading with her, he pushed open the door to the governors' wing of the Pentagon.

"Emily, please, please listen to me. Think about what was in those pictures. Your dad does not want to hear that you asked me to do that to you."

She shook her head defiantly and quickened her pace. Rainer caught her hand just before she reached the door and spun her around. "Em, don't do this. Just let him hate me."

Before he could continue, Logan opened Governor Haydenshire's office door. Emily scooted by her brother, but Rainer was stunned by his appearance.

"What are you doing here?" he asked as Adeline stuck her head around the door.

"Rainer, you didn't do this by yourself, and we're not letting you take the fall for all of us."

Suddenly, he heard Garrett's voice. "Dad, this wasn't Rainer's fault. I practically shoved him up there. I told him to make it look good!"

Rainer tried to reason how Logan and Adeline believed they had anything to do with this, but he followed Emily into the office.

Governor Haydenshire didn't look any better than he had that morning, and the glare he gave Rainer made his stomach clench uncomfortably.

"It wasn't Rainer's fault," was Emily's opening line to her father.

"Yes, it was," Rainer argued.

"Stop now!" Emily demanded in a tone Rainer had never heard her use on him before. Drawing a deep breath and fixing her gaze at a spot on the wall just above her father's head, her voice quivered. "I'm so sorry, but Rainer didn't want to do it. I asked him to because all of the other Angels were doing it. Garrett said it was the induction and what the Angels do after the first win of the season."

Garrett nodded his head adamantly.

"I just went along with it. And I'm so, so sorry that you had to see those pictures. I know that must've been awful, but you can't blame Rainer."

Rainer began to protest again, but Logan shook his head and took up where Emily left off. "Garrett jumped up on the bar and announced to the whole crowd that Rainer was going to induct her. Rainer was the only one of us who acted at all like how you raised us. He asked me for my help, and all I did was hand him another drink. This wasn't his fault."

Adeline began before Rainer could start. "Governor Haydenshire, I'm so sorry, sir, but Logan was distracted because I'd had entirely too much to drink. You saw me Sunday, and he was trying to take care of me. Otherwise, I know he would've helped Rainer dissuade Garrett."

The governor was rubbing his temples, and Rainer knew he was trying to convince himself not to yell.

Emily began to cry again, and Rainer reached out and took her hand. He stepped toward her to hold her when Governor Haydenshire screeched, "Do not touch her!"

Rainer jerked his hand back like he'd received an electric shock. Everyone stared in stunned silence.

"Daddy," Emily finally reprimanded, "I just told you it was me, not him. Why don't you believe me?"

"Because I keep telling all of you," Rainer cut across the governor's answer. "It is my fault. Look at this." Rainer held up the picture from the governor's desk of him sliding his hands up Emily's skirt.

"I did this, and I should have told Garrett no. And," he took an anguished pause, "I should have told you no." He gave Emily a sorrowful glance before turning back to Governor Haydenshire.

Emily shook her head combatively. "I got drunk Saturday, and I was sick most of the night and Rainer took care of me. He always takes care of me. Please don't treat him like this. He doesn't deserve your anger. I do."

Rainer seriously doubted him holding Emily's hair back while she vomited out the sheer amount of alcohol she'd consumed in his presence was going to do much against the images that had most certainly etched themselves indelibly onto the surface of the governor's mind, so he said nothing.

The silence grew more and more uncomfortable, and Emily finally huffed.

"What can I do, Dad? How can I make you see that it wasn't Rainer?" Governor Haydenshire raised his head and looked at Emily with raw pain on every line of his face.

Rainer had to look away. It was too fresh, too desperate, almost obscene.

In answer to Emily's question, the governor shot Rainer a mirthless glance before he turned back to his daughter. "You can give that ring back, quit the Angels, go back to school, and move back home until you can act like the daughter your mother and I raised, instead of like a brazen..." He didn't finish, but the sentiment was quite clear.

Rainer felt like he'd just been sucker punched. His stomach muscles clenched like he'd actually been hit.

"I'm sorry that I did this, but I'm not doing any of those things. I'm an adult, and I will take responsibility for doing this," she held up the pictures. "But I'm not going to run back home when I screw up, because that isn't what you taught me. I have to face my problems and deal with them, not run away from them just because that might be easier."

It couldn't have been more clear that Emily's decree was not what Governor Haydenshire wanted to hear, but he let his head fall forward in a half nod.

After steeling himself and drawing up to his full height, Rainer addressed the governor. "Sir, I cannot tell you how sorry I am that I did this, and it was entirely my fault and is my responsibility to bear. But please, please believe me when I tell you that even you don't hate me as much as I hate myself right now."

Governor Haydenshire started to challenge that statement, but with a shudder he murmured, "Please leave, all of you. I have never doubted my ability to be a good parent and raise good, honest, hard-working children as much as I do looking at all of you right now. Just get out."

Everyone filed out in a somber, silent march.

"Rainer, man, I cannot tell you how sorry I am. I had no idea." Garrett looked devastated.

Rainer drew a deep breath. "You didn't force me to do it. I should've refused, just like I said."

He took Emily's hand. The motion seemed to soothe her as she clung to his arm.

"The fact that people took pictures doesn't make what I did any better or any worse. It was a tasteless and crude thing to do, at least in public."

Garrett bristled slightly. "Yeah, you're probably right." Guilt etched his expression.

"He is right," Emily's tone echoed her deep sadness.

CHAPTER 55
FOR EVERY ACTION

Emily disappeared into their room as soon as they arrived home. Rainer tried to get her to eat, but she refused. She'd been lying in their bed crying intermittently despite Rainer's attempts to soothe her.

"Em, baby, come on." He sat beside her, and she fell into his lap with tears streaking down her face.

"This is all my fault. How could I have been so stupid? Everyone got sick, and now my dad hates you and me, and I probably lost you half of your estate. I just don't know how everything could've gone so horribly wrong."

Rainer knew she felt terrible about everything that had happened, but he suspected seeing how utterly devastated her father was by their actions had been what had finally taken her over the edge.

He lay back on the bed and held her tightly to his chest while she cried. When the tears had subsided slightly, he tried to make her feel better.

"We'll come up with some way to show your parents how sorry we are for all of this. I will fix this, if it's the last thing I do."

Jack Stariff had called to explain to Emily and Rainer how they needed to dress and behave for the next week for the trial against Stan.

Rainer had apologized profusely, which Jack had accepted, though he'd made certain he knew how in one evening, he'd changed an open and shut case to one that could go either way now.

Not certain that his body could contain the sheer amount of guilt he felt over what he'd done to Emily and the Haydenshires, Rainer forced himself to really consider the fact that he may have just lost half of his father's estate.

Still feeling sick, he decided to turn in early, but Logan knocked on his and Emily's door just as Rainer had pulled off his shirt.

"Hey, I'm sorry. I didn't mean to interrupt anything."

Rainer shook his head. "You didn't."

"I was just wondering if you'd go grab something to eat with me. Maybe a beer, but just one."

Logan's face was drawn and sullen. Terror swirled in his eyes, so, with a nod, Rainer pulled his shirt back on.

"Yeah, sure." He turned to Emily. "Will you be okay?" He thought he should really stay with her, but she nodded sweetly.

"I'm fine. You go." Her eyes were still bloodshot and swollen, but her concern over Logan was evident through the pink that had cast the whites of her eyes.

"Adeline says she'll sit with you, if it's all right," Logan offered.

"Of course it is." She sat up in the bed and pulled her knees to her chest.

Rainer kissed the top of her head. "I'll be right back."

Emily swallowed back another onslaught of tears. Rainer grabbed his keys and wallet as Adeline scooted into the room. She gave Emily a sorrowful look.

Emily patted a spot on the bed beside her, and Adeline smiled as she crawled under the covers with her. Rainer hoped Adeline could get Emily's mind off of everything.

He drove to Lesco's and wondered which part of their horrific day had Logan so visibly shaken.

They pulled into the parking lot, and Rainer exited the car to find several photographers and reporters, who had been following them in the hopes of getting Rainer to comment on the belly shot.

He clenched his jaw shut and ignored them. They both stared adamantly at the ground and refused to look up for the cameras. They tucked into a booth in the very back of the pub out of sight of the photographers.

Les made his way over to take their orders. "Somebody die or something?"

Rainer leaned back in the booth and forced a smile. "Just a really bad day."

Les gestured to one of his waitresses and told her to bring them two beers. "One good thing about a bad day," he offered as Logan and Rainer turned to gaze into his wise eyes and his crinkled grin, "they have an end. Tomorrow you get a chance to make the next one better. Every time the sun comes up is another chance." He gestured out the large windows of the restaurant.

Rainer took in the star-strewn sky and the rolling Virginia landscape lit by the moon. He knew his problems weren't going to disappear with the sunrise. He took a sip of his beer and longed for a moment when his torture would subside, even a little.

"How about some cheeseburgers with all the fixings?" Les offered. "Very few things in this world that can't be fixed with a really good burger, some fries, and a beer."

Neither Logan nor Rainer really cared what they ate. They were both just looking for a little solace.

"That'd be great, Les. Thank you," Logan offered humbly.

As they ate, they sipped their beers slowly. They made them last throughout the entire meal.

"So," Logan sighed, "this is kind of a disaster."

Rainer was too exhausted to filter his sarcasm. "You think?"

"I owe you an apology." Logan lost all sense of teasing.

"Logan..." He was tired of other people trying to take responsibility for his mistakes.

"No, I'm serious." He shook his head. "Believe me. Me handing you that drink when you asked for help definitely makes it onto the top ten list of my biggest regrets. Unfortunately, at this point, it's not even near the top."

Sighing, Rainer decided to allow that.

"I can't believe what I did to her. I can't believe Em had to cast her. She should hate me. I swore to her the night I convinced her to marry me I'd never let her down again. I'm sick over this," Logan poured his soul out onto the table in Lesco's pub, and Rainer's heart ached for his best friend.

"I know just how you feel."

"Yeah, well, believe me, the only difference here is that no one was photographing my many indiscretions that night. I can't believe I just let her keep drinking that shit, and now, she's in a ton of photos. What if she gets sent to jail because I'm such a freaking idiot?"

His pain seemed to steal his appetite. He threw down the burger, wiped his hands on a napkin, and then rubbed them over his face. He clenched his muscles as if bracing for battle.

Logan stared into Rainer's eyes for a long, drawn minute before dealing what he clearly felt was the lowest of all the blows. He shook his head in abject disbelief. "I don't even remember it. I don't even remember having sex with the woman I told, not one week ago, that I would always take care of her and that I would never let her down again."

"I know, but it was you and Adeline. It's not like it was your first time. I know you better than anybody, and I know that you might not remember it, but you wouldn't do anything she wouldn't have wanted you to do. It's not in you." Rainer willed Logan to believe what he was saying. "You're her Shield."

Logan didn't look so certain. "Yeah, maybe. But she deserves to be treated a whole lot better than that, don't you think?"

This particular anguish Rainer knew only too well. He also knew what it cost Logan to admit everything he'd just shared.

"Yeah, well, I stuck my hands up your sister's skirt in front of hundreds of people I don't know as they cheered me on. And now there are pictures of her stomach laid out on a bar with my tongue all over her, so…" Stating it out loud did nothing to help his conscience.

"The thing is," Logan's voice rose slightly, "she's not even mad. I mean, she should be mad at me, but she just keeps apologizing for drinking so much. I was right there. I should have stopped her." He was visibly disgusted with himself.

After eating in silence for a few minutes, Rainer sighed. "Yeah, well, I'm really good with us all avoiding partying after Em's challenges for a long while."

CHAPTER 56
ADULTS

When they returned home, Rainer noted that his and Emily's bedroom door was still closed. He hoped he wasn't interrupting anything as he knocked.

"Come in." Emily sounded more herself. They pushed the door open and found the girls on the bed with bridal magazines surrounding them.

Rainer raised his eyebrows. "Do we need to sleep on the couch?"

Emily laughed, but raw pain was still evident in her eyes. She shook her head. The girls stood and threw their arms around each other.

"I promise I'll do a really good job," Adeline vowed.

"And you promise you'll still love me even if I drag you to every bridal salon along the Eastern seaboard every weekend, and even if I go all bridezilla on you, and you'll help me get ready, and not let all of my stupid brothers do anything too horrible?"

Rainer's brow furrowed.

They watched as Adeline began bouncing up and down. "Yes, yes, yes."

"Okay." Emily beamed at her.

A few minutes later, Logan was dragging Adeline to bed while stating that he needed the day to be over.

"I take it Adeline is now a bridesmaid?" Rainer smiled at Emily, but she shook her head.

"Adeline is my maid of honor."

"Wow, that was awfully nice of you." She and Adeline had really only been friends since Adeline started dating Logan, but as Rainer thought about it, with Emily's aggressive class schedule, graduating a year early, and the sheer amount of time he took up in her life, Adeline was probably her closest girlfriend.

"She's one of my favorite people, and I decided that although I would thoroughly enjoy watching Samantha Peterson's face as I marry you right under her nose, vengeance isn't what I'm going for with our wedding. So, I decided against *her* as my maid of honor."

Thrilled that her mood had improved, Rainer laughed. He pulled off his clothes and slid into bed with Emily.

That's my little girl you're sliding into bed with every night, even though you're not married. Governor Haydenshire's words seared through his mind.

"Em?"

She studied him. Her soothing Receiver's cast began to work its way through his skin. She could feel his trepidation. Rainer shuddered from the heavenly sensation of her energy flooding his body.

"I want to get married soon, okay? And I know it takes a while to plan everything or whatever, but I don't want to wait. I want you to be my wife, and I want to be your husband."

Emily nodded. "Yeah, me too."

They shared a long gaze. Rainer knew she understood his deep desire. She shared his need to bind them together legally and spiritually as much as they were bound in their hearts and minds.

"Are you sure you still want to marry me?" she choked.

Rainer leaned away from her so he could look into her eyes. "Em?" He brushed her hair away from her face. It was still damp from her tears. "How could you ever think I wouldn't want to marry you?"

"I don't know. This is all my fault. I ruined your reputation and your family's name. I got you in trouble with Dad and Vindico. I might've even lost half of your inheritance, and I just can't tell you how sorry I am." Her breath shuddered as her tears returned.

"I don't think all is lost, baby. I know you're sorry, and I hate that we got caught up in all of that. We both knew better, but I swear to you I will fix this. I will make it so your dad will look me in the eye again. I promise you."

"Let's fix it together."

As she strengthened her hold, she flooded her energy through him, and he knew that was how it needed to be from now until the end of time. If anything went wrong, they needed to fix it together. It was the only way their world had ever worked.

He hugged her to him and let his energy surround her as well. He wrapped her up in his protective shield. He cossetted her in his guarding energies, and shut down the restless worries of her mind.

He felt it. He felt the desire that had been so oddly gone from him for most of the day. It returned suddenly. It coursed through his veins as he let his energy envelop her.

It was different, but when he concentrated, he could feel hers as well. The driving need he felt when he was with her, the desire for release and to be with her, they were all there, but somehow they were different.

He thought back over the past few days and then the past few weeks. He'd been careless, stupid, and cocky. He hadn't taken care of her. He'd taken care of his needs and of her wishes, but it had ultimately been selfish on both of their parts.

Fingering her under a table at a restaurant in New York was stupid and reckless. He forced his mind to tally the sum of his mistakes. He'd let his arrogant desires drive him. He'd wanted to do it right under the nose of the press. He'd wanted to make her feel it. He'd wanted to add that to his repertoire. He could make her come when she'd been terrified in a restaurant full of people.

He lambasted himself. She'd wanted so badly to be a part of everything the Angels did. She was terrified of being left out. So, she'd let her brother and Chloe Sawyer talk her into doing something she'd never willingly have done, and he'd allowed it.

He finally forced himself to admit the whole truth. He hadn't put up too much of a fight because he didn't mind people seeing him claim her and seeing what he could do to her.

He'd taken the most precious gift he'd ever been given and flaunted it as a cheap, tawdry show for people he didn't give a damn about.

Bitter regret seized him as he held Emily tightly. He clung to the only thing in his world that felt right as he allowed her to soothe him, but the desire was still there.

He wanted to be with her, but not for release or because it felt so damn good. He wanted to join their energies. He desperately needed to make her one with him, because he'd gotten so lost in it all. He'd let them be swept away in the heartless world around them, and he wanted her to be able to drown the hurt and the regret in him.

He wanted to take it all away. He needed to show her he'd always be a rock for her to cling to, and that he would never sell them out again.

He would be steadfast. He would never do another thing that would make her father doubt his love for Emily or make her feel like she was drifting out to sea. He would be her anchor from now until the end of time.

He raised his head and brushed sweet, hesitant kisses on her lips. If she would allow him, he wanted desperately to show her how much she meant to him and that their physical relationship was for the two of them alone. No one else would ever get even a small part of it ever again.

"You are everything to me." He kissed her again. This one was a ragged, desperate kiss that came from his soul more than his lips. "And I'm so sorry for the way I've been for the past few weeks. I cannot believe I sold you out Saturday night. I swear to you, if you'll give me a chance, I'll prove to you that I'll never ever do that again."

"I know, and you didn't." She kissed him again. "I got all caught up in what everyone thought about me. I wanted so badly for the world to acknowledge that I'm a real Arlington Angel. I felt like I failed when I couldn't finish that relay when I got hurt. I went to that party with something to prove, and it was so, so stupid."

Rainer knew that as well. "I think we both decided that we were all grown up and didn't have to play by any rules anymore."

Emily nodded. "And we were really just acting like stupid kids."

He couldn't have agreed more. "I just need you to know what we do when we're alone together with nothing between us, when I'm inside of you, baby, there is nothing in the world that means more to me than that. And I don't ever want anyone else to have any part of that. I think the photographers are always going to be there, and the whole freaking Realm seems to want a part of us, so we're gonna have to work that much harder to make absolutely certain that no one gets to make a claim on us. The cameras can take pictures of us holding hands to their hearts' content but nothing else."

Relief flooded through her rhythms as she nodded.

"This,"—he gestured to her body beside his own—"is just for us." He watched as solace and love colored her features.

"Thank you," her voice caught as she shuddered. "You are the most amazing man in the world, and I could never ever love anyone more."

"Will you let me show you, baby? I'll stop if you want. You just say the word, but I want to be with you. I want to feel you surround me, and I want you to feel me inside of you. I want to be with you. I want everything else to go away except for you and me."

"Please," she whispered in the darkness. "Just you and me. I don't want to think anymore. I just want to feel you. I want you to take it all away, please. I want to show you that I know how important it is. I won't mess it up again."

He didn't have enough strength to try to make her wait or to argue with her reasoning. She wanted him to take away the pain he'd caused, and there was nothing he wanted more than that.

He edged the T-shirt she was wearing off of her. Desperate desire to have her skin next to his surged through him.

He wanted to show her, to reassure her, to settle every fear, to silence every regret that lay coiled in the recesses of her mind. He wanted to drown every qualm in the energy he surrounded her with. She fumbled with his boxers, but he caught her hands.

"Let me take care of you." Though he'd said this to her before, the vow had never resonated in his soul quite the way it did as he pulled off the sweatpants she was wearing. He let his hands trace up her legs, and she shook.

"Close your eyes, baby. Just let me make it all go away." His voice was low and reverent in his deep desire to make up for all he'd done.

She obeyed, and he pulsed against her. A soft, tender moan escaped her. "I'm gonna set the cast." He would take care of her always in every possible way she could ever need him to.

He would not only be a devoted and caring husband, he would do everything in his power to guard her, to be her Shield, and he would be a consummate lover. He vowed to himself that he would be everything for her. It would be his life's mission.

He summoned and breathed in her scent, reveled in her touch, in the way her skin felt as he traced her abdomen, and she let him in. She allowed him to close her off. And that was something he'd never take for granted again either.

As soon as he made certain she was settled after he set the cast, he slowly revealed her all for himself. He slid her panties down her thighs. She was swollen and wet. The tender heat made him ache.

He longed to be inside her, but he wasn't playing fast and loose with her, or with them, ever again. As he slipped the lacy underwear off of her feet, he traced his hands back up to her fevered, swollen lips. She held his gaze. Her eyes beseeched him as a whispered moan escaped her.

"I want to touch you, baby. I want you to feel me. I want you to feel how much I love you. Feel what this means to me."

"Please," she began to writhe under his gentle caress. He traced over the soft red curls, wet from need. Her breath stuttered in heated anticipation. He concentrated on her energy as it flooded into him through his hands.

He'd calmed her worries, and she allowed him to allay the pain and soothe her. He slipped his fingers inside her. Her rhythms began to join with him. He leaned in and kissed her deeply, passionately as he massaged her. With a soft touch, he traced up over her clit with his thumb and then moved away. He let it build. He had quite a bit to make up for, and he wanted to take it all.

If it took him all night long, he wanted to give her relief from the pain and grief the harrowing pictures had caused. He forced them out of his mind and concentrated on nothing but her. Her body trembled and rolled for him.

"Does that feel good, baby?" He needed her to tell him.

"It feels so good," she whimpered and began to swell around him. Her muscles cinched. She pulled his hand deeper. Her body begged for more.

Longing took a strong hold of Rainer. He wanted to feel her around him. He needed to feel her pulse tightly, but he forced himself to wait.

Frustration set in her eyes. He concentrated, but she couldn't let it go. Worry and doubt still plagued her, and they hindered her release.

He moved over her and kissed her breasts. She shuddered and arched her back. Her nipples stood in stiff peaks, drawn into tight mounds as he laved his tongue over them.

Her breath quickened as a heady, "Yes," panted from her mouth.

He pulled one deep into his mouth. He sucked as she began to give way. He reveled in the knowledge. He held the things he'd learned from being with her, the things no one else would ever know, in the deepest wells of his heart. He dragged his teeth over the sensitive skin, and she cried out for him. She begged for the release that her body kept from her.

"Relax, baby," he urged. "I'm going to give you everything you need. I won't stop until you're ready."

Her breath quickened again as her eyes closed, and he felt her concentrate on what he was doing to her.

"I want you to come for me, baby." Her body began to give her over to him. "Just let it go and let me have it. I will always take care of you. Give it up for me. I've got you." She whimpered and gasped as it flooded around his hand.

He groaned in the ecstasy of them together.

"Please," she pled. Her first release drove her second as she bucked and writhed for him.

"You ready for me, baby?" He wasn't certain how much longer he could wait to feel her body move in time with his.

"Please, now," she begged.

"Spread your legs for me, sweetheart." Her energy spiked hard as he uttered the phrase. He knew it drove her wild. He could always feel her body quiver and her energy flood around him whenever he whispered it in her ear just before he made her his own.

This time was different. He was able to keep his knowledge of her tucked deep in the safety of his shield, but he was learning as well.

She wanted him to make her feel safe. He could feel that from her. He was able to focus on more than just trying not to go before she did.

Though he'd always wanted to take care of her, and had been worried about never hurting her, he'd grown up more in the past two days than he had in the past two years. He was stronger now in his knowledge, in his patience, in his body, and his mind.

He allowed himself a moment to concentrate so he could give her everything she needed. He pushed out his shield cast until it surrounded her in his protective energy. She moaned as he met her every need. She inhaled him in every panted breath.

He pushed into her slowly and reveled in her heat as he took her inch by inch. He let her feel him as he pierced through the heart of her and made them one.

"Yes!" Her muscles clenched tightly around him. She pulled him in deeper. He continued to thrust until he filled the tight space completely.

"Tell me what you want, baby." He was able to keep the shield cast over her easily, and he could tell she wanted something.

"I want more," she pled. "I want more of you." He'd never heard anything sweeter in his entire life, and he met her needs again. He transitioned until he was taking her hard, forcing her open to his hilt, as she cried out for him.

He flooded all of the love in his body into her as he surrounded her with his protection.

"That's amazing," she gasped.

He wouldn't allow himself any adulation. This was how it should have been all along. Before that moment, he'd only ever made love to her like he was a horny teenager. He knew he still had a great deal to learn, but at that moment he felt it as he made love to her like a man.

She wanted more, wanted him to take away anything that had ever hurt either of them. She wanted more pressure, wanted his friction… she wanted to feel the release only he could give her.

He plunged her depths and kept his shield flooded with his calming energies. They surrounded her as he cossetted her in his guard.

He took his time. He reveled in the way she felt inside and out. He caught her hands and held them to the bed over her head. She wanted him to take control and he did.

"Take it, baby. I don't want you to feel anything but me. You're all mine," he commanded, strong and in tune with her needs and desires.

She felt safe. Her energy spiked rapidly and her temperature rose.

"That's it." He pounded into her, giving her the friction and the pressure her body begged for.

"You ready, baby?" He felt her swell as her breath washed from her and her body flushed. She was fevered and pitched for release. "I want you to come with me," he commanded, and she lost it all. She spiraled from the highest peaks. Her release was so much more this time than it had ever been.

He buried himself deeply inside her and exploded. He filled her with everything inside of him. A deep, guttural groan echoed from his lungs and from his soul.

He held her to him, kissing her as she calmed. He let her body ease as the powerful orgasm cascaded over her in convulsive waves.

When it released her and she stilled, he withdrew. He kept her body tucked closely to him. He tried not to be impressed with himself, that he was able to keep his shield over her even after his thorough release.

"I've never felt anything so amazing." She clung to him. He felt her tears return, and he panicked.

"Baby, what, what's wrong?"

"Nothing. I've just never felt so loved. It was incredible." The tears fell softly from her eyes, but she was smiling.

Confusion rocked through him as tears were certainly not what he was hoping for.

"I do love you more than anything in the world. Even with everything I got wrong and that we screwed up, as long as I have you, then that's all that really matters to me." He let his words soothe both of their souls.

"You'll always have me. Forever."

"Then that's all I need."

They never redressed. Rainer begged her to let him feel her all night. He wanted to continue to revel in her soothing energy.

He brushed a sweet, tender kiss across her cheek and held her as she drifted off to sleep.

CHAPTER 57

...AND WHAT'S TAKEN AWAY

Rainer blinked confusedly as he sat up. He heard it again, but he couldn't understand what it was. Emily sat up and rubbed her eyes. It was pitch-black outside. He glanced at the clock —2:45 in the morning. Finally understanding, he picked his cell phone up off of the bedside table.

"Hello?"

"Lawson, get out here! Full gear," Vindico ordered.

"What? What's wrong?" Rainer's heart hammered.

"They've taken Serena. We've got to find her. I'm not sure what they're planning."

"I'm on my way." He leapt from the bed and began throwing on his combat uniform. He heard Logan's cell phone shrill in the next room.

"What's wrong?" Emily panicked.

"It's okay, baby. Just, uh, get dressed for me. I'm taking you to your parents." He buckled his belt and grabbed his gun and shoulder holster.

"Why?" She began pulling on panties and a bra.

"Wretchkinsides's men took Serena." He concentrated on what needed to happen. He focused on everything he'd been training for.

"What? Oh my god!"

Rainer's heart ached for what the Crown Governor must be going through.

In less than five minutes, everyone was in the Mustang, and Rainer was flying to the farmhouse. Logan and Rainer were quiet in their concentration as they steeled themselves to do what needed to be done.

Adeline and Emily shared terrified expressions but said nothing.

Rainer raced Emily into her parents' home. Governor Haydenshire met them in the kitchen.

"I wanted them to stay here." Rainer refused to let the events of his day keep him from doing his job. "I need to know she's safe, so I can concentrate on getting Serena back."

"That sounds like a good decision. Something a man would do. I'll be right here with them. Tell Dan and Regis to call me if they need anything."

Though it certainly wasn't a compliment or even an accolade, Rainer hoped he was beginning to show Emily's father that he would learn from his mistakes.

With a nod, he embraced Emily, though her father grimaced. He kissed her tenderly and then with more intensity until he broke away.

"I'll be back," he vowed as Logan made the same promise to Adeline, and they raced to the car.

Summoning, Logan harnessed all of the energy in the engine and pulled from the surrounding resources as Rainer drove and cooled the engine.

They arrived at the Pentagon in less than fifteen minutes. Throngs of police and other law enforcement officers stood in the Iodex offices.

Garrett was pacing, and Vindico stared at the call-tracer device the Crown Governor's cell phone was plugged into.

Everyone stood ready to answer the inevitable ransom call. The Crown Governor looked anguished as he sat quietly in the corner. He met no one's concerned gaze. Rainer's heart raced as he took in the pulsing nervous energy that surrounded him.

"Lawson, Haydenshire, I want you on impulse," Vindico ordered. They moved to the tracker.

"I want you three to amplify," he instructed Tuttle, Ramier, and

Garrett. Then he turned and bellowed to the large crowd, "I want every law enforcement officer here who has a car to spread out through all of DC and Arlington. Drive until you get my broadcast. He wants something this time. If I'm right, we're gonna get her back, but I'd like that done sooner than later."

With that, most of the men and women in the office dispersed quickly. Rainer's heart pounded in his ears. He swallowed down the terror of what might be happening to Serena.

"Come on, dammit, call!" Vindico growled. He stared at the tracker and then glanced at the clock on the wall with a grimace.

Time dragged on. Every minute seemed to last hours. Rainer and Logan stood reticent over the machine. A little after four, the phone rang. The noise sent chills down Rainer's spine. He concentrated and refused to let his hand shake.

"Ready?" Vindico queried. Logan and Rainer nodded. Tension crackled through the air as Vindico casted the phone. They summoned instantly, Rainer and Logan locked onto the electrical energy in the tracker. They made it work faster and run harder as Portwood kept it from overheating.

"Talk," Vindico demanded. As soon as the disguised voice began speaking, Tuttle, Ramier, and Garrett locked onto Rainer and Logan's energy streams. Other Iodex officers joined in. They broadcasted the signal from the tracer farther and farther out into the night.

The map lit with several red dots, and they began to pulse and trace.

"Bring five million dollars in unmarked bills to the rear parking lot of the Victory Theater on Lincoln and McKinley. The Crown Governor should come alone, or we'll kill her."

Vindico didn't speak. He tried to give everyone more time to lock on to and broadcast the signal farther. The triangulation on the map grew tighter.

With a nod from Garrett, Vindico replied, "The Crown Governor won't be coming. I will, and before anyone does anything, I need to know Serena is still alive."

"Regis," came a small, frightened female voice. Rainer swallowed down his fury and his fear.

"Serena, it's Dan Vindico. He's right here with me. We're going to get you out. Are you hurt?" Vindico's voice was somehow soothing and demanding at the same time.

"Yes," she whispered.

"We got it," Garrett mouthed.

"Serena, do you know where they've taken you?" Vindico showed no sign that they'd located her. The modified male voice came back on.

"Goodbye, Vindico. Be at the theater by five o'clock, or we'll kill her and walk away." The voice laughed derisively.

"That's not good enough. I want a photo," Vindico ordered. "Send it to the same line you phoned, or I'm not bringing you anything." The line went dead.

Vindico spun. He took in the map and motioned all of the officers closer. He whispered, clearly trying to keep the governor from hearing.

"This is Wretchkinsides's favorite game. We need to move. He's planning on shooting her, but not killing her. He has a much bigger plan in mind, but it's his men who are running this, not him. They're all bloodthirsty, fucking morons who might end up letting her bleed out. That's why he chose the theater on Lincoln and McKinley."

Rainer didn't understand how Vindico knew that but continued to listen intently.

"He's got her at the Townsend," Garrett announced. He'd worked out the GPS coordinates on the map.

"Let's go," Vindico called. "You three take one car." He threw Garrett the keys to an Expedition and then instructed Portwood to drive another with Tuttle, Ramier, and Ericcson. "I'll bring the governor." His body tensed for the inevitable battle.

Before they left, he picked up the encrypted radio and informed all of the officers in the area to meet him at the Townsend Hotel on Jackson. Rainer sprinted to the Expedition and climbed in just as Garrett began backing out.

"How did he know his guys might shoot her but not kill her? And why does he keep saying they aren't going to kill her?" Logan asked his brother.

"Summon," Garrett demanded. Rainer and Logan both harnessed the engine in the SUV. Logan forced it to move faster while Rainer kept it cool.

"Both Lincoln and McKinley were shot, but neither was killed by the bullet. They both died later. This is part of Wretchkinsides's sick game. He always does this. Everything means something," Garrett spat disgustedly.

"How do we know which room she's in?" Rainer kept his focus on cooling the engine.

"It'll be some other meaning. Dan always figures them out before I do," Garrett assured him.

They joined throngs of other law enforcement vehicles in the relatively empty parking lot of the Townsend Hotel. Everyone emerged to listen to Vindico. "Shields up. He's got men everywhere. They know we're here. Have your weapons drawn and ready to fire."

True to his word, Rainer hit the ground with everyone around him as a shot rang from the hotel.

"Do not fire," Vindico shouted from the ground. "You might hit Serena," he censured as officers near where the shot had come from took aim. "Listen up!" Vindico stood again but remained in his shield cast. "Elite Iodex is going in. Everyone in full shields, and I want six teams doing nothing but making certain I get every Iodex officer and Serena out alive. Do you understand?"

"Sir!" rang from everyone around Vindico.

"I want officers on every floor after we've cleared it. Keep any wondering guests in their rooms. Tell them we'll let them know when it's safe to leave." The Gifted police who were assisting nodded their understanding.

Everywhere Rainer looked glowed green from the sheer number of shields cast around him. Another bullet pierced the air near Vindico, but his shield ricocheted it back to a nearby car.

As they entered the lobby, all hell rained down. Rainer kept himself shielded as he dodged bullets and took down men on his right and his left.

He spun as a bullet headed straight toward Logan. They both

reflected it and watched in horror as it rebounded and pierced the heart of one of Wretchkinsides's men.

He crumpled to the ground in a pool of his own blood. Shots and casts resonated in the air. The decaying sheetrock of the old hotel puffed as it was hit with cast after cast. The air filled with the acrid dust and mixed with the stench of blood.

Forcing himself to breathe after what felt like hours, Rainer looked around the lobby of the Townsend Hotel. Blood stained the carpets. There was an officer down being healed by a medio medevac team who had pulled in just after law enforcement.

Rainer stayed on Vindico's flank as he'd been ordered to do. Vindico stalked to the vast concierge desk that ran along the back wall. He kept his gaze sweeping right and left to make certain no one else was coming toward him or firing.

Rainer noted the swimming pool. "Vindico." He pointed as he choked out his boss's name. Vindico jerked his head toward Rainer.

There was a body floating facedown in the pool. Vindico clenched his jaw for a split second before ordering two officers to go investigate.

Rainer swallowed down vomit as he edged closer to the concierge desk.

A long string of curse words escaped Vindico's mouth as he stepped over two hotel employees who appeared to have drowned in their own blood.

Vindico leaned over and rolled them onto their backs. He looked hopeful for a moment, but then shook his head. They couldn't be saved.

He removed a hotel master keycard from one of the men on the floor. He wiped blood off of it on his bulletproof chest protector and slipped the keycard into his pocket. Vindico and Ramier began studying one of the hotel computers.

"Pull up the guest name list," Vindico ordered.

Ramier was the technical specialist on the task force, and he was extremely talented. It took him only a moment to summon and lock on to the computer's energy before he could access it without the password.

A minute later, Vindico looked grave. His entire demeanor changed as he studied the computer screen. After all that they'd just watched and seen, how could a room number make him look like that?

He pointed to the screen and Ramier nodded. He offered Vindico a sorrowful look.

"317," Vindico rasped to the team and their protectors. Logan and Rainer shared a quizzical glance. Neither was certain how he'd known that.

Rainer glanced at the screen before falling back into line. The room was registered to a Gerald Lindley. That certainly wasn't one of Wretchkinsides's aliases, nor any of his top guys' names.

They stayed behind Vindico and moved like the well-oiled machine they'd been trained to be as they headed up the stairs.

A grouping of officers stayed in the lobby. They were arresting the men who hadn't been killed.

With every step, the thought that he'd just killed a man pulsed through Rainer's mind. They made another turn to continue their seemingly endless climb.

Everyone led with his pistol, ready to shoot if there was movement or on Vindico's command.

They stood just outside the door to enter on the third floor. Two men were seated on couches, watching TV in the snack area. Vindico rolled his eyes. He shot a fierce cast over the men, draining them of the ability to fight. After cuffing them, he took their weapons, then led the team down the hall.

Rainer tried to remember to blink as he read the number 317 on the perfectly mundane, tan hotel room door. He tried not to think about what a hellscape it might be on the other side.

Everyone watched as Vindico used the master keycard he'd taken from the concierge's desk. The Townsend was old and hadn't upgraded their keycard entries in at least twenty years. A magnetic pulse would release the newer versions with ease, but the older readers weren't as standardized, and they didn't have time to try different pulses.

He eased the card through the lock as quietly as he was able. He summoned to hold the lock open.

"On my go," he whispered.

Rainer's pulse pounded in his head. His muscles spasmed as he panted. Terror and vengeance coursed through him in equal measure.

One of the subordinate officers kicked open the door, and Vindico threw a shield, but Rainer saw no one, save Serena, who was bound and gagged in a chair.

Suddenly a single shot rang out. The sliding glass doors in the back of the room were open, and Rainer caught a glimpse of two men.

Vindico flung his hand to the right and redirected the bullet. He sent it spiraling back the way it had come. A harrowed, guttural groan came from one of the men as he doubled over and then fell forward over the railing. The second man leapt. They heard one echoed splash from the pool. The far more repulsive sound was the hollow crunch of concrete and bone that came after the splash.

The hysterical scream from below confirmed that one of the men hadn't made it to the water. Violent rage lit through Vindico.

"Gallic..." hissed through his teeth. "Get her. Carry her down. Governor Carrington is waiting. Take her to the medevac ambulance. I have something to take care of," Vindico growled as he spun and sprinted back out of the room.

Everyone moved. They spun to make certain no one else was hiding in the bathroom or closet.

Garrett paced carefully to Serena. "Just try to relax for me, okay?" he soothed in a kinder tone than Rainer had ever heard him use. He tenderly eased the duct tape from her mouth and the chains that held her in the chair. She began to sob as he lifted her easily into his arms.

Her wrists were broken badly. Her hands hung at odd angles. Rainer's anger boiled inside of him.

"Shh, shh, I've got you," Garrett soothed.

"Regis," she pled. Garrett swallowed hard and gave her a reassuring nod. "He's downstairs. I'm going to take you to him right now."

She was bloody and bruised. Her right eye was swollen shut, and her scalp held dried blood in the roots of her hair. Rainer shuddered as he kept his shield over her and Garrett.

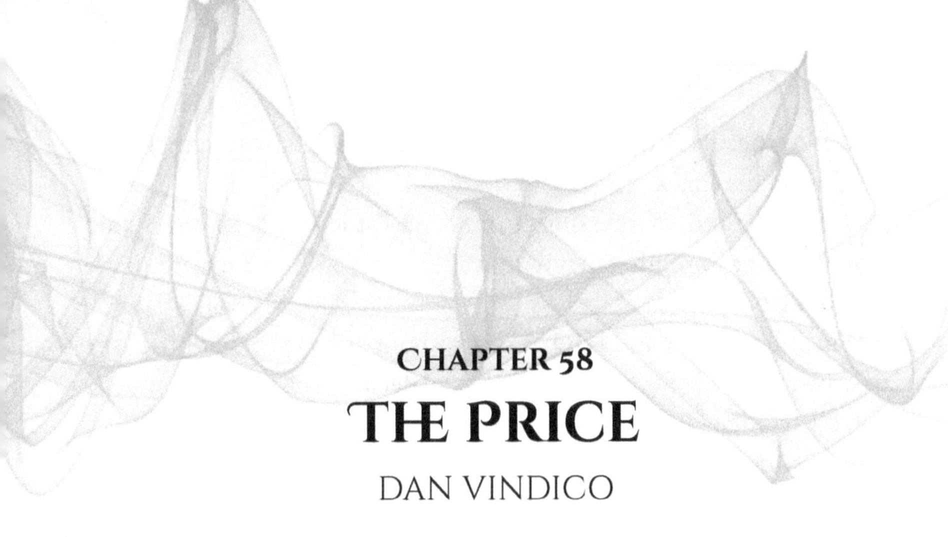

CHAPTER 58

THE PRICE

DAN VINDICO

"You mother-fucking asshole!" Dan threw Gallic's soaking wet body onto the black pavement on the street behind the Townsend hotel. "Did you really think I wouldn't catch you?" Gallic's chest visibly seized, and an involuntary groan choked from him as Dan's boot shattered several of his ribs.

"Let's hear it. What'd he pay you to turn? What did he offer you that would make you take her and hurt her when you were supposed to be keeping her safe? New car, new house in the Riviera? It had to be something good."

Dan slapped cuffs onto his wrists and sank his knee into Gallic's back over the ribs he'd just shattered.

"I asked you a question. Now answer me."

Gallic coughed up pool water and blood.

"He said if I didn't take her, Cascavel would. He had pictures, and he said he'd match the ransom," Gallic managed.

"Oh, right. So, you took her to keep her away from Cascavel. How noble of you. Pictures of what?"

"Of me and…"

"Of you and what? You and some other guy's wife?" Vindico demanded furiously, but Gallic shook his head.

"Pictures of what?"

373

Gallic's head tried to shake against the pebbled cement. Blood oozed from his cheek.

Dan was tired of messing around. He stood and jerked Gallic upright in one smooth, sinewy move. He shoved him forward, back toward the hotel.

"I'm still waiting, and I didn't get to shoot anyone in that little war zone you created. So, go ahead. If you decide to keep your mouth shut, I'll arrange for you to remain quiet forever."

"Just some stuff I was into. I don't know how he got them. I only took a few." Gallic's entire body shook as he tried to walk upright. He cringed as he fought not to cough.

"And what were we taking pictures of that would've looked so bad?" Dan's secondary Predilection homed in on Gallic. He swam through his fractured rhythms. Gallic wasn't married and he didn't have any children. Dan dug deeper until he landed on the malignant sickness that swam in Gallic's mind.

As he realized what evidence Wretchkinsides had, his body seized with frenzied rage. He fought with himself not to shoot Denton Gallic on the spot.

His hand twitched between his radio and his pistol as he weighed the options. He lifted his radio from his belt.

"I have Denton Gallic in cuffs. I need someone to get to the Crown Governor's mansion. Get me every computer in the guardhouse. Radio Coriolis. Tell them I'm bringing in a child molester and a kidnapper. He's to be kept in the back caves, and he's never coming back out."

CHAPTER 59

HIS PLAN

RAINER LAWSON

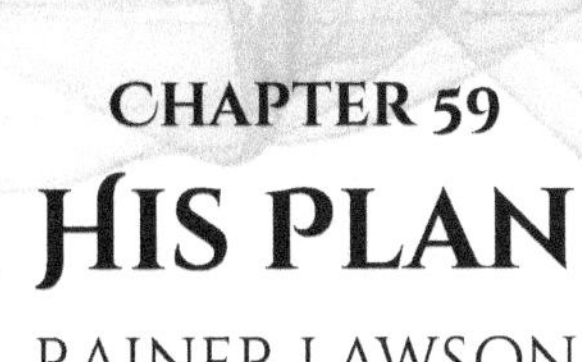

Vindico shoved Denton Gallic into a squad car. He had appeared in a storm of violent ire just as Garrett had laid Serena in Governor Carrington's arms. They all watched as the Crown Governor began to sob in earnest.

Rainer was still reeling from the radio call that the head of Serena's security team had actually been a child molester.

Seven medios were tending to all of Serena's injuries. They healed her as she lay in Governor Carrington's arms. He refused to put her onto the gurney.

All of the task force continued to glance around nervously and still had their weapons drawn. Rainer now fully understood all of his endurance training, the hours he'd spent summoning while sprinting on a treadmill or releasing multiple casts and holding them endlessly. His adrenaline waned and utter exhaustion set in.

"How did Vindico know he wasn't going to kill her?" Logan asked again. Rainer knew he'd heard the question before, but it seemed so long ago. It felt like it had been days, not hours since the papers had broken the story of his and Emily's belly shot.

Rainer felt dizzy. He placed his hand on the Expedition and leaned onto it for support. Vindico walked toward them.

"Good work, gentlemen." He seemed to have regained some of his composure. He looked more human and less like a furious animal that had been caged.

"And to answer your question, Haydenshire..." Vindico glanced around as the Crown Governor finally seated Serena on a gurney.

She was moving her wrists with ease now as the medios continued to clean her wounds.

"This is how Wretchkinsides works. If he'd wanted Serena dead and he'd gotten her here, he would've killed her. It would never have mattered how much money I showed up with. But he didn't want her dead. He wants Carrington to step down from office. And judging by the look on his face,"—Vindico gestured back toward the Crown Governor—"I'd say his plan just worked perfectly. He wants to control the Senate again, and he's well on his way."

Rainer's stomach seized as he contemplated Governor Carrington's resignation.

"Lawson, I'd venture a guess that this has probably been about the longest day of your entire life," Vindico's quip shook him from his distracted exhaustion.

He was unable to argue or even to speak coherently, so he nodded his agreement.

"Go home. Get some sleep. I don't want to see any of you until Wednesday morning, bright and early," he ordered the entire team.

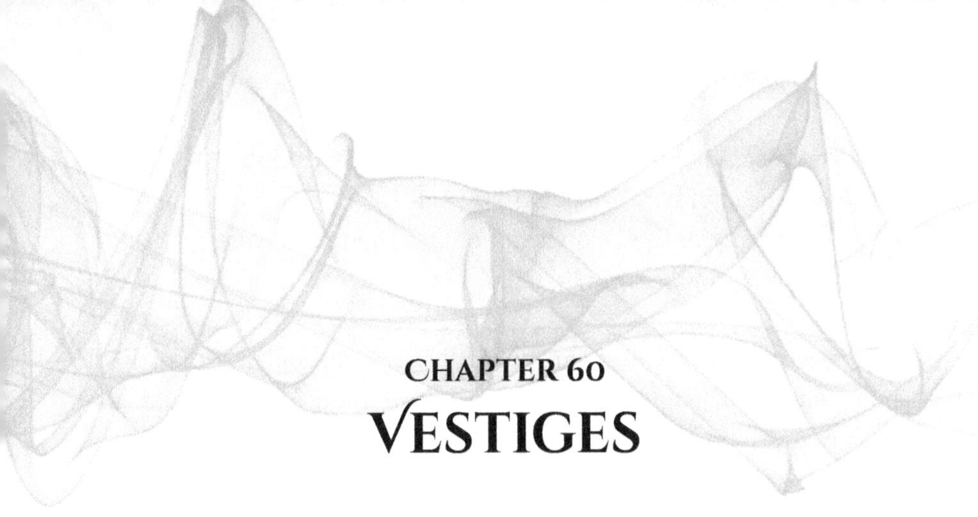

CHAPTER 60
VESTIGES

Rainer followed Logan and Garrett back to the Expedition. He watched the first vestiges of light appear over the DC skyline. He yawned deeply as he let the events of his night replay in harrowing detail in his mind. "How did Vindico know that was the room?"

Garrett had requested that Rainer and Logan talk to him, lest he fall asleep at the wheel. He looked morose.

"Wretchkinsides is a sick bastard," he huffed, though that much had already been proven time and time again. "Gerald is Amelia's father's name, and you know Lindley is Vindico's little sister. The one he's always trying to keep out of trouble."

Rainer did recall the stories about Lindley Vindico at school. They were rather legendary. She graduated a few years before Rainer and Logan started at Venton, but her reputation for being a wild child wasn't lost in the years between their graduations.

"So, basically," Garrett yawned deeply before continuing, "He's letting Dan know that anyone close to him is fair game."

"I can't imagine Vindico being related to somebody who did the stuff Lindley did." Logan was clearly recalling some of the stories.

"I don't know if Lindley really did half of the shit she claimed she did. I was a senior by the time she got there, but I think Patrick was just a year ahead of her. You could ask him."

"How did she not get expelled?" Rainer thought of one particular legend where Lindley Vindico had shown up to class completely naked.

"Everyone loves Governor Vindico so much, and they felt bad about what had happened with Amelia and Dan. And Dan and his other two sisters were such great students. He was head of Ioses." Garrett gestured to Rainer. "So the school governors just kept sweeping it under the rug. I was in a bunch of classes with Kara, and she's as straightlaced as Dan."

Garrett pulled the Expedition back onto the parking deck beside Rainer's Mustang. "Do you mind if I get a ride back to the farm? I'll get Chloe to pick me up from there."

"Sure."

"Shotgun!" Logan cried.

Garrett chuckled and smacked Logan on the back of the head.

"Will you ever grow up, or are you just working the 'I plan on staying eleven for as long as my fiancée will allow it' gig?"

Rainer laughed as he cranked the car.

Everyone was so relieved Serena had been rescued, relatively unscathed, that the joking seemed appropriate. Rainer couldn't join in, however. He was too exhausted. He listened to Garrett and Logan rag on each other for the entire ride home.

They climbed out of the Mustang, and for the first time in his entire life, Rainer was uncertain if he was wanted inside the Haydenshires' home.

Emily flew out the kitchen door and raced into Rainer's arms. He could tell she hadn't slept since he left. He embraced her and felt whole again. He clung to her and wondered if she could feel all that had changed since he'd left her with her father in the middle of the night.

"Is she all right?" Emily kept her hands on Rainer as terror choked her voice. He was unable to take his eyes off of her, so he simply nodded. He was afraid of the memories, of everything he'd seen and done in the past few hours. The man he'd killed flashed through his mind.

"Are you okay?" She laid her head on his shoulder and kissed his neck. After pausing to really consider the question, he shook his head.

He closed his eyes and breathed deep. He inhaled her heavenly scent. Her cast eased through his shield, and he drank her in. His voice shook, and he was thankful Logan and Garrett had gone back in the house.

"Will you come home with me, please?" he begged. "Your dad doesn't want me to touch you in front of him, and I don't want to let you go."

She lifted the back of the shirt he was wearing. She touched his back with her hands, and he felt her calm, soothing energies flood through him. He reveled in the healing she brought him. "Dad will be fine, and Mom made you breakfast. Come eat, and then we'll go home and sleep, okay? I'll stay with you all day. I'm not going anywhere."

Rainer wanted to stay right there beside his car. He could feel her wrap her energies around him. He didn't have anything left to give her. He was so thoroughly spent between the day he'd had and then the battle he'd fought in the dead of night. He had to sleep soon.

"Come on, sweetheart." Emily took his hand and guided him into the house.

"I really don't think your dad wants to see me."

"Okay," she allowed. "But Mom does."

"Rainer," Mrs. Haydenshire wrapped him up in her arms. "My sweet baby boy. What a day." She cupped his face in her tender hands just as she always had for as long as he could remember.

"Aren't you mad at me?" His voice faltered in his utter exhaustion, and he forgot that he wasn't supposed to talk about the belly shot in front of Mrs. Haydenshire.

To his relief, she seemed to know what he was referring to. She must've seen the papers as well. She grinned at him and shook her head.

"Because you're a twenty-one-year-old kid who the Realm and my own husband expect to walk on water, who got caught doing something my daughter asked you to do?" She was still patting his face, and he could feel her giving him soothing energies as well. "No, sweetheart, I'm not. And I'm working on him. Just give him a little time." She gestured toward Governor Haydenshire's office. The doors were closed, and she told Rainer he was on the phone with Governor Carrington.

Rainer studied her in utter shock. She smiled at him as she guided him to the table where she had prepared a tremendous breakfast for him, Logan, and Garrett.

"Would it make you feel better to know I was a little disappointed?" she teased.

Rainer nodded his admittance that it would. Mrs. Haydenshire laughed at him outright. "Okay, then I am disappointed, but not just with you. I feel equally disappointed in all of you. But right now, I want you to eat, and then I want you to sleep, and we can start making amends after that."

Feeling thankfulness flood through him like a healing lifeblood, Rainer stood and wrapped Mrs. Haydenshire back up in an embrace.

"Thank you," he whispered.

"Sweetheart, you should know by now that you're just like all the rest of them. You could never do anything that would make me not love you or not want you in my home."

Grateful adulation filled his soul as he let Mrs. Haydenshire's words mend his heart.

"Eat." She returned him to his seat. Rainer dug in. He actually tasted the food for the first time in over twenty-four hours. Emily held his hand as he inhaled eggs, bacon, and biscuits with honey, his favorite. She watched over him obsessively as he ate.

"I'm okay," he assured her between bites, but she knew him far too well. She shook her head, not buying his lie for even a moment.

As Mrs. Haydenshire was plying them with seconds, which no one was turning down, Governor Haydenshire emerged from his office. He looked stunned. His eyes fell on Rainer in a baleful glare.

"All right, enough." Mrs. Haydenshire shot a glare of her own right back at her husband. "I won't have this. We are a family, through good times and bad. We're going to be mad at one another or disappointed with one another throughout this life, but when we're together, at my kitchen table, then you can keep your feelings to yourselves."

Rainer was bewildered. He didn't know what to do. He certainly didn't want the Haydenshires fighting over something he'd done.

"And since I've decided to bring this up now," she dared anyone to dissuade her. "Stephen, I would like to point out that you've been aware of the Angels' induction." She popped Garrett on the head, thoroughly shocking him. "Since our own son, your flesh and blood, invented the depraved practice. I believe at one point he and our oldest son were written up in the Alexandria Gazette for inducting the entire team one year. Yes, that would be the night that Will threw up in my kitchen sink four times. I would also like to point out that several of our sons, at one point or another, have participated in the act and that you have not reacted this way until you saw our daughter up there doing it."

She raised her eyebrow, daring the governor to argue. "And I personally know Rainer Lawson just like I'd given birth to him myself." She turned to Rainer and gave him a sorrowful expression. "Not to take anything away from our dear Maggie and the effort it took her to get you here. God rest her sweet soul," she stated thoughtfully as Rainer nodded his understanding.

"But I also know my own daughter very, very well, and I would swear on this farm that it was not Rainer's idea to lay her up there. He wouldn't have done it if he hadn't been asked." She threw a knowing glare at Emily.

"I kept telling him that." Emily threw her hands out to her father. She looked relieved that at least her mother knew the truth.

"Stephen, honey, we've raised nine of them." She patted both of her hands on Rainer's shoulders. "And we have two more well on their way. I thought you knew by now, no matter how hard you try to get them to avoid it, sometimes there are just lessons that they have to learn the hard way."

Governor Haydenshire still looked dumbfounded, but Rainer wasn't certain if it was from his wife's diatribe or from his conversation with the Crown Governor.

"Now,"—Mrs. Haydenshire folded her arms across her chest

defiantly. She looked just like Emily, only blonde and thirty years older—"you looked like there was something you were about to tell all of us. So, after you apologize to Rainer, then I for one would love to know what Regis had to say about this awful night."

"I am not apologizing, Lillian," Governor Haydenshire huffed, but his eyes held Rainer's. "But I will do this. I will give you the opportunity to prove to me that you've learned something from all of this and that you will do a better job in the future of taking care of my baby girl. And,"—he took in the rest of the men at his kitchen table—"I completely agree with your mother that it is depraved, and if I ever hear of any of my children performing the induction again, there will be hell to pay. Trust me."

At that very unfortunate moment, as Governor Haydenshire rarely cursed, Keaton happened to toddle into the kitchen and then began repeating, "Hell to pay."

Emily bit her lips together as did Rainer and Adeline. Logan and Garrett cracked up. They were unable to hold in their laughter.

"Stephen," Mrs. Haydenshire sighed and lifted Keaton onto her hip.

Relief washed over Rainer in waves. That was all he wanted, just a chance to prove himself better than what he'd shown for the last few weeks. He hadn't realized until that moment how lost he'd felt when he believed the Haydenshires would hate him forever, and how much it meant just to be given a second chance.

"Actually, I'm going to have to ask all of you for quite a bit over the next couple of months," Governor Haydenshire considered as everyone fell silent to listen. "Regis has decided to step down from office and to make an honest woman of Serena." He smiled. "He plans to stay in office through next Friday. He wants to vote on your trial, Rainer, since I'll have to recuse myself since my son and daughter are either the official or the secondary beneficiaries of the money. They're having a small ceremony next Saturday to which we've all been invited. He's already phoned Nathan, and he and Tad will be coordinating the wedding. Regis has asked Arthur Vindico to step in as Interim until the election process is concluded."

Mrs. Haydenshire furrowed her brow. "I'm shocked he didn't ask you."

Governor Haydenshire swallowed hard. "He didn't ask me because he says he wants me to be able to focus solely on my campaign." He seemed to try out how the words would sound as he said them.

"You mean…?" Mrs. Haydenshire was visibly stunned. She was unable to finish the statement.

"Daddy, are you really?" Emily looked simultaneously thrilled and terrified.

"Running for Crown Governor," Governor Haydenshire concluded for both his wife and his daughter. "That is entirely up to your mother." He gazed at his wife. "He wants the process to start just after Labor Day. He wants us to have our family vacation first. But then it would mean a lot of travel and debates, and if we decide to do this, it would mean even more press. I just want to make certain you're up to all of that," he spoke to Mrs. Haydenshire like they were the only two people in the room, or in the world, at that moment. "And," he choked, "let's not forget that Dominic Wretchkinsides may have been set back tonight, but he ultimately got what he wanted. He wants Regis to step down, so he's also not going to want me replacing him. I have no idea what might come from that."

Rainer concentrated on his plate. He didn't want to intrude. He considered the annual family trip to the beach house and what he knew the Interfeci to be capable of in a harrowing juxtaposition.

The entire Haydenshire family had been going for an extended Labor Day weekend trip for as long as he could remember.

"Who would you be running against?" Mrs. Haydenshire asked, though everyone already knew the answer.

"Peterson's thrown his hat in the ring, of course, but Regis would be solely backing me."

To have the backing of the former Crown meant it was almost a shoo-in for the governorship.

"Well," Mrs. Haydenshire couldn't hide her immense pride as she beamed at her husband. "For the sake of the Realm, I think we're running for Crown Governor." Cheers filled the kitchen as she concluded, "Because I, for one, know that I cannot see Yvette Peterson on the cover of the morning papers on a daily basis while I have my coffee. A woman can only take so much."

"You're certain?" Governor Haydenshire quizzed with a wry grin over her reasoning.

Mrs. Haydenshire smiled at her husband and nodded. "I'm certain."

"Well, then, I am going to have to ask that all of my children"—he placed his hands on Rainer's shoulders and narrowed his eyes. Rainer was thrilled to be called one of the governor's own again—"refrain from doing anything depraved or uncouth that might end up in the papers at least until I've taken the oath."

They all nodded their adamant agreement.

"Hell to pay," Keaton added excitedly. Everyone laughed this time.

"Okay, well, we're going to need him to stop saying that before we put him in front of any cameras," Mrs. Haydenshire lamented.

A deep yawn overtook Rainer. He couldn't seem to stifle them anymore.

"I'm sorry." He didn't want anyone to think that he didn't care about the upcoming election or what was going on.

The governor sighed his defeat. "Emily Anne, you will only hear me say this once, at least before the wedding, but take him to bed."

Dan Vindico

Dan slammed his office door shut. His jaw clenched, and his head throbbed. Every time he gained a step it seemed to do nothing more than weight the ropes that bound him to his past.

Far too angry to sit, he paced until the tether chained to his temper finally snapped and he landed his fist in the side of one of the many metal filing cabinets that held his life's work.

Useless commendations and framed medals collapsed and tumbled to the carpet under the weight of his acrimony. The cold metal blistered his knuckles and bore the imprint of his rage.

The knock on the door did nothing to lessen his fury. He knew who it was, and he knew what he was going to say. He rolled his eyes, but then opened the door for his father.

"What?" Dan demanded.

Governor Vindico's already concerned expression morphed back to anguish. Dan was sick and fucking tired of his old man looking at him like that.

"Would you like to talk about it, or do you feel your office furniture deserves more of your abuse?" the governor inquired. There was no judgment in his tone, only distress.

"I'm fine."

"You've been telling me that for a decade now, and it still isn't true."

Dan's eyes closed and he forced air into his lungs. "What do you want, Dad?"

His father studied him for a long drawn minute. He eased into the office. "What happened tonight was not your fault, and Gallic was also not your fault. As I recall, you told Regis not to hire him." He hesitated but then said what he'd really come to say. "What happened to Amelia wasn't your fault either."

Dan leveled a hate-fueled glare at his father. "Are we done here?"

"Regis asked me to step in as interim, and uh…Stephen's going to run for Crown."

Another albatross on the chain around his proverbial neck. Dan nodded under the weight of it all. "Yeah, I figured he would."

"Can I ask you a question and you answer honestly this time?"

Dan lifted his eyebrows. "Guess that depends on what you ask."

Arthur rubbed his temples and seemed to consider. "I just, uh…I don't want to bury anyone else. What is the likelihood that Stephen will survive this campaign if Nic Wretchkinsides doesn't want him running?"

Dan shook his head. Rage and terror swirled into a rocklike enclosure in his throat. "Pretty sure you're asking the wrong question."

"Good god," Arthur choked. "It won't be Stephen. It'll be Lillian and the kids."

Dan stared his father down. "I'm still here, so it should be painfully obvious that Wretchkinsides doesn't kill men who stand in his way. He just makes them wish that he would."

ABOUT THE AUTHOR

J.E. Neal (aka Jillian) vastly prefers coffee to tea, guac to salsa, the beach over anywhere else, and the world inside her head over the one outside her front door. She also loves not having to choose.

Driven by the question 'what if,' J.E. Neal's world began to manifest. What if there were people with powers the rest of us couldn't see? What if the energy of our world could be summoned and used at their will? Characters with these amazing abilities took shape in her mind. She created—and continues to create —an endless number of stories full of delicious escape from our reality where emotions are visible, desire is palpable, and danger is universal.

Learn more about J.E. Neal at JillianNeal.com

ALSO BY J.E. NEAL

ENERGY OF MAGIC

Shield and Shattered Cages (Book 1)

Shield and Faltered Steps (Book 2)

Shield and Splintered Oaths (Book 3)

Shield and Humbled Crown (Book 4)

Shield and Vile Serpents (Book 5)

Shield and Coveted Splendor (Book 6)

Shield and Guarded Shadow (Book 7)

Shield and Worthy Sinner (Book 8)

Shield and Sacrificial Heirs (Book 9)